The PASSION

The Passion

DONNA BOYD

AVON BOOKS ◆ NEW YORK

This is a work of fiction. Names, characters, places,
and incidents either are the product of the author's
imagination or are used fictitiously. Any resemblance
to actual events, locales, organizations, or persons,
living or dead, is entirely coincidental and beyond
the intent of either the author or the publisher.

A V O N   B O O K S
A division of
The Hearst Corporation
1350 Avenue of the Americas
New York, New York 10019

Copyright © 1998 by Donna Boyd
Interior design by Kellan Peck
Visit our website at **http://www.AvonBooks.com**
ISBN: 0-380-97449-5

Library of Congress Cataloging in Publication Data:

Boyd, Donna.
    The passion / Donna Boyd. — 1st ed.
        p.   cm.
    I. Title.
PS3552.087757P37   1998   97-32291
813'.54—dc21   CIP

First Avon Books Printing: May 1998

FIRST EDITION

QPM   10   9   8   7   6   5   4   3   2   1

We want the same things Humans do: sex and power. The difference between us is that we are innately better at obtaining both. This is our greatest strength, and our greatest weakness.
—MARCUS QUELQUOIS, WEREWOLF, 1583

Why don't we hunt humans anymore?
It's too easy.
—A BARROOM JOKE, CIRCA 1990

Passion—1) a powerful emotion, such as love, joy, hatred, or anger;
2) an undergoing; to undergo [from the Latin *passus*]
—*THE AMERICAN HERITAGE DICTIONARY*, 1995

The
PASSION

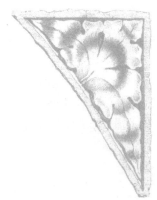

Prologue

THEY SAY IT ALL BEGAN WITH THE MASSACRE IN NEW YORK, SO THAT'S where I'll start my tale. But our story really begins much earlier, on the ice-slick rocks and in the fetid-smelling caves of early history, in the place where your memory takes you when you awake screaming in the night only half recalling what you once were. It's the story of the forest and the bubbling swamps, where death was brutal and life was savage and the evolutionary process must have warred with our own instincts, I think, when it came to survival.

There are those among us—among you, too, I observe—who glorify the wonders of the natural world with a kind of glassy-eyed fanaticism and urge a return to that purer, more innocent state. This testifies to nothing other than the fact that those who recommend the satisfactions of living in harmony with nature have never had to do it. Nature is evil. Nature is conflict, violence, betrayal; worms that crawl through the skin and breed in the gut; thorns that poison; snakes that fight in writhing, heaving masses until all lie dead from one another's poison.

From nature we learned to tear the flesh off the bone and suck out the blood—and to enjoy it. Do you want to return to that state? I do not.

But from this savage tangle of dark bestiality we have our common origin, you and I, sprung from but a single cell in the primordial ooze, sharing a common gnarled and malformed branch on the twisted tree of life. I am a historian and I know this to be fact, although there are those from both sides of that tree who would vehemently deny it. It is no wonder that we have, over the centuries, found each other to be so mutually fascinating. And that we have, each in our own fashion, struggled so valiantly to put that black forest, that windswept plain and ice-covered cave far, far behind us.

I have known Nature. I have known Civilization. Civilization is better.

And having understood that, you will now be better prepared to understand why I have undertaken this chronicle. I have faced severe opposition, of course. The odds are even that I may not live to complete the tale. Fortunately, I have always been of an adventuresome spirit and am frankly glad to discover, one more time, something worth fighting for.

The love of a good fight is, of course, one of the most obvious things we all have in common.

My detractors claim I am destroying an eons-old covenant of silence by writing this. Humans will read it, they cry, and then what will become of us all? What indeed, I can't help but wonder, do they imagine? Torch-carrying peasants storming the castle? Stakes driven through a hundred thousand hearts? Not that we haven't known such dark chapters in our united past, but the wild-eyed rantings of those conservatives bring to mind such absurdities one can't help but smile.

The liberals with their cool-eyed assessment of the situation frighten me much more. They warn of chaos to be unleashed, it's true, but they do so with a calculating amusement that makes one think they're almost looking forward to the day. Supremely confident in their superiority, they are not afraid. Maybe that shouldn't worry me. But it should worry you.

I am, of course, a follower of neither camp. As far as I'm concerned, a far more sacred covenant than that of silence has been broken already. So I put down this chronicle, perhaps taking my life in my hands, in the name of Civilization.

Are you reading this, human? I hope so. Because here is the truth.

I am werewolf. Quod Hominem, genus gerulfos. Warwoof, wehrwulf, waerul, varulv, garwall, garoul, warou, loup-garou. Lycanthrope. We have been known by many names over the centuries and none of them accurate, for we are neither wolf nor man but a breed apart. We have been with you since before the dawn of time.

Do you know me, human? You should. I shared a cab with you yesterday. You may have seen me lunching at Le Cirque 2000 last week and you've surely noted my name in the financial pages. And yes, it was I who smiled at your daughter across the smoky barroom and made her heart pound so loudly she could hardly think. And did I take her home when she sidled up to me and ran her not-so-innocent fingers down my thigh? You bet.

Oh, I know your world, human. I know it and I love it and I walk at ease within it. One might even say (and who wouldn't?) that I have mastered it. My race has centuries of cunning, skill and ambition invested in a mutually beneficial relationship with yours and it would disturb me to see all of that lost. Maybe what you are about to learn will prevent the inevitable. Maybe it will hasten it.

It is the custom among our kind to sing aloud the tales of our heroes and to write our secrets down. These pages contain many secrets, and the tales of heroes whose deeds may never be sung aloud. Let their words, then, speak for themselves. Heed them, remember them. And then decide.

PART ONE
New York, New York

The Present

৵১

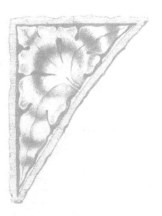

One

THE LIMOUSINE CAME OUT OF THE FOG LIKE A GHOST AND STOPPED AT
the curb before the big brownstone on Fifth Avenue. At three o'clock
in the morning even Fifth Avenue sleeps, and, wrapped as it was in
the cold November fog, the city seemed but a distant memory of itself.
Streetlights were muted, traffic sounds muffled, windows shuttered.
Steam vents released their ether onto sidewalks already carpeted with
clouds and disappeared. The night creatures retreated to the shadows
and were still. The silence was thick, flattening the landscape into a
one-dimensional representation of something that might once have
held substance. The night seemed suspended, hovering somehow between this world and the next, and the only thing that anchored it in
time was its smell.

Night mist and old exhaust, rubber tires, rotting food, human urine;
the used-up daytime scents of fine leather shoes and soft gloves, body
oils, Chanel perfume, damp wool, dead fur. The spray of a tomcat
who had recently passed this way, the offal of a small dog, the un-

washed clothing of a human castoff. The crisp bite of iron that was the gate sealing off the brownstone and its small square of lawn, the acrid smell of the fear of one who had recently passed through it. Pine needles. Rotting leaves. Damp stone. Blood. And death. Death lay behind those gates, and it was everywhere.

The driver smelled it as he got out of the car to open the door for his passengers, and he stiffened a little in shock before he could stop himself. But by the time he reached the rear door his features were once again composed into carefully neutral lines. He opened the door and stood straight and alert beside it.

The two men who emerged onto the smokey pavement would have attracted attention under any circumstances. Both were tall and lean and moved with a graceful economy that instinctively inspired admiration. The first man was the older of the two. He wore a woolen coat with caped shoulders, belted at the waist, and dark gloves. His hair was thick and white and fell to his shoulders. His face was craggy, his skin golden, his brows the same stark white as his hair. His eyes were a startling violet blue, a mesmeric blue, and had been known to render speechless for several minutes at a time anyone who happened to look directly into them.

The younger man was blond and lithe and wore his hair clasped at the nape with a band of leather. His features were stern and aristocratic, his eyes a deeper shade of the same blue as his companion's. He wore a long loose cashmere coat of Italian design and carried a pair of kid gloves in one hand. In more normal circumstances he exuded the kind of musky, vital sex appeal that was dark and dangerous and almost palpable on the tongue. Tonight, his eyes were cold and the danger was sharp enough to make the air around him crackle.

In the bright light of day, when the now-deserted avenue was awash with the pulse of humanity, the screech of traffic, the clatter of movement, these two could not have passed unnoticed. Eyebrows would be raised, sentences would be left unfinished, small backward steps would be taken to clear a path as they walked by. Heads would turn, gazes would follow, and for the space of a second, maybe more, thoughts would stutter and be forgotten. Later, someone might remark upon how tall they were, or how striking they looked, or how powerful they seemed. That was all.

In this dark dead hour of the morning no one was about to notice them. Yet the night seemed to hold its breath until they passed.

The older man stood before the iron gate, his face like stone, and gazed toward the silhouette of the brownstone, an etching in black against the night. The younger one paused and swept his eyes back and forth along the sidewalk. He joined the other man in two long strides and together they went through the gate.

For them, the stench was almost paralyzing.

At the bottom of the stone steps the younger one closed his hand upon his companion's arm. His muscles were hard, his heartbeat loud and heavy. His nostrils were flared, drinking in the scents, his pupils dark and dilated with the horror of the message his olfactory centers were receiving. He whispered through lips so stiff they barely moved, "It can't be."

Alexander Devoncroix's expression was unchanged. The lines on his face, the set of his mouth, even the fringe of his eyelashes might have been carved from granite. He started up the steps.

In a moment his son followed.

Their eyesight was evolved from a time when twilight hunters had the advantage, and oftentimes they saw better without artificial light than with it. The lights were on inside the house, however, turned down to a somber and respectful hue, and they illuminated a square on the porch briefly before the door closed behind the two men. But no lamplight was needed to reveal the details of what had happened here tonight.

A spray of blood glistened on the oak paneling of the foyer and darkened the pale blue Aubusson. It smelled cold, dark and clotted. They moved through the arch into the hallway, where another, paler blood smear on white silk wallpaper testified to a struggle. Sprays of blood on the ceiling. Bloody fingerprints on the glossy ivory woodwork around the doorway. The smell from the death chamber was dark and compelling and lured them on.

Once, in the fine high days of the Rockefellers and the Astors, the room had been a sunny parlor, with tall clerestory windows, ornately molded ceilings frescoed with pale clouds and cherubs, and two marble fireplaces. The ceilings were still frescoed and the fireplaces still marble, and the collection of carefully chosen and tastefully arranged antiques lent an air of subtle elegance and warmth that defied the decades. But these days the room was used as a reception area for the executive offices and laboratory facility of Research Concepts, a wholly owned subsidiary of the Devoncroix Corporation. Tonight it had been turned into a slaughterhouse.

Others had already arrived: trackers, analysts, the clean-up crew. They stood aside respectfully as the two high-ranking males entered, but the smell of their shock, outrage and simple astonishment intermingled with the violence and death-rot that filled the room until it was difficult to separate the savagery of the scene from the horror of its discovery.

A heavy bookcase had been overturned, spilling Camus and Tolstoy and Milton in a broken-spined jumble onto the floor. A puddle of blood on the big oak desk had turned black and congealed in mid-drip over one edge. Lamps were broken. Chairs overturned. There was a dark stain just above the wainscoting, accompanied by a starring of the plaster, where a body had been crushed against the wall.

The smell of the human was sick-sweet and nauseating. It was everywhere.

The three corpses, having reverted to their natural state in death, were crumpled on the floor in various stages of mutilation. The blond man knelt beside the nearest of these, a female, and touched the thick auburn fur gently. "Moria," he said quietly. Her neck had been snapped, her throat torn open, both forelegs broken and matted with blood. She had not gone easily.

Beneath the north-facing window was Tobias, a magnificent black wolf who in life had been one of the most brilliant biochemists of his time. His spine was twisted into an unnatural position against the wall, his entrails, pink and glistening, spilling out of a wound that split his rib cage. Rene, who was old and sometimes had trouble seeing, was nonetheless a gifted researcher who had been in charge of three of the most important development projects in the corporation. He had been the first to die, his skull shattered by a single blow.

The smell of the human was on their fur, in the carpet, lingering like a miasma in the air. Spatters of human blood were mixed with theirs.

The blond man dipped his fingers in the blood on Moria's muzzle and brought them to his nostrils, forcing himself to inhale, extracting every nuance of the hated scent from the serum. His head swam with images; revulsion shuddered through him. And he said hoarsely, "Human. How could a human have done this?"

He got to his feet and swung his eyes around the room, scanning for details he might have missed before. There was wildness in his gaze, fever in his eyes. The blood inside his veins was as cold as hate, but pulsed hot enough to burn his skin. He shouted, "No human could have done this!"

He was shaking, quivering with rage and pain. The others in the room could feel his heat and smell the acrid haze of his anguish; a responsive quiver of savagery leapt within them which they controlled only with great effort. His eyes moved from one to the other of them, the guards, the trackers, finally Alexander himself, seeking an answer or a challenge; but all remained silent, as was their place. Only in Alexander's eyes did he see compassion, but it was too little, far too late.

He strode past them, his face marble white and his breath roaring, and in the wake of him the air was electric. He pushed out of the room toward the back of the house, to the French door that opened onto the cold dark garden, strode through it with a powerful kick that snapped the lock and ruptured the hinges and sent glass spraying like a fine misty rain over carpet and patio; he burst onto the stone courtyard and into the night where he lifted his arms and threw back his head and released a cry, a scream, a howl of torment so intense that it seemed to chill the very marrow of the earth.

In the luxury high-rise two blocks down, lights came on and dogs barked, glassy-eyed with hysteria, at shadows on the wall. On Lexington, a man sleeping in a doorway sat up, his heart pounding in his throat, as the sound pierced the night. Across the East River a child whimpered in her sleep from a dream gone bad, and a wife awoke abruptly in her husband's arms, chilled to the soul. Alley cats crouched low, fur bristling, and rats that were bold enough to nibble at shoe leather in the subway tunnels fled for the safety of their dark holes. The night shuddered and writhed with the depth of his pain and when the sound died away the emptiness reverberated.

He dropped his arms and his head, and, alone in the shadows of the winter garden, he stood until the quaking subsided.

His name was Nicholas Antonov Devoncroix, and he was the head of an industrial and financial conglomerate so vast and so complex that no business in the world operated completely independent of it. Should the Devoncroix Corporation and its ancillaries suddenly cease to exist, so too would most of the world's major industries, banks and stock markets; technology would be set back half a century, research would grind to a halt, science and the arts would languish. He was the figurative and practical leader of over half a million of the brightest, most inventive minds ever to grace the planet; he alone was responsible for their moral, spiritual and physical well-being. He was a werewolf, and those were his people who had just been slaughtered. He felt the loss as keenly as he would have felt the amputation of one of his own limbs.

After a long time he lifted his head to acknowledge the presence behind him. From inside the darkened room the voice spoke softly, reflectively. " 'Killers all until we say/I vow I shall not kill today . . . I shall not kill today.' "

It was from a child's poem, a jumping-song that any wolfling with language skills could recite. Nicholas had often reflected that that, then, was the essential difference between humans and themselves: what they taught their children. But he was not thinking that now.

Nicholas turned slowly. A distant reflected light caught his face and gave it an otherworldly sheen. His eyes glittered like coals. He said lowly, "Wrong."

Alexander said nothing, nor did he allow any change of expression to register on his face.

"We have the blood scent. My trackers will find him by dawn." Nicholas's eyes narrowed. "But the pleasure of killing him will be mine."

Alexander commented neutrally, "It has been five centuries or more since one of us killed a human in anything other than self-defense."

"You don't call this self-defense?" Nicholas gestured brutally toward the slaughterhouse they had left behind them. "They were scientists, researchers, *humanitarians*, for the love of all that's holy! They were murdered without warning, without reason. And not just murdered but—" His voice hoarsened and one fist clenched as he ground out the word. "Savaged. Eviscerated. You would have me ignore this?"

Alexander asked reasonably, "And how will you explain the execution of this human to the authorities who come searching for his killer?"

"What's one dead human more or less to them?" Nicholas's voice reflected impatience and contempt. "Let them dare try to bring us to account. Are you suggesting the weakest of us couldn't handle a dozen or more blundering human policemen?"

Alexander nodded. "So you would kill the policemen. Then you would kill those who came looking for the policemen. Then you would kill to protect those who killed before, and then because some human annoyed you and finally for the sake of killing itself. Where will it stop?"

Nicholas scowled fiercely and made a dismissive gesture with his hand. "Your exercise in hyperbole is irrelevant. It would never come to that, and if it did, what does it matter? Haven't we been hiding our dead and keeping our secrets long enough? Haven't we turned a blind eye to human atrocities once too often? Maybe the Brothers of the Dark Moon are right. Maybe it's time to put the balance of power where it belongs."

"And all for the sins of one human."

Nicholas's eyes glittered. "One human who, one time, went one step too far. That's all it takes."

The elder's face remained shadowed, and his silence, this time, went on too long. His voice was carefully devoid of accusation or judgement when he spoke, but nonetheless seemed weighted down with both. "A moral code, once broken, can't be repaired. Think carefully before you plunge us all into war."

"*He* has started the war!" roared Nicholas. "It is done, can't you see that?"

"I think," said Alexander quietly, "you let your passions overcome your judgement."

Nicholas drew in a sharp breath and released it slowly. It was a moment before he spoke, although the beat of his heart was loud in the ears of the other werewolf. "You were a wise and compassionate ruler," he said stiffly. "I, perhaps, am neither. But I will do, as you have done, what the times demand."

He moved back into the room, footsteps crunching loudly on broken glass, and toward the door in long, controlled strides. As he passed him, Alexander said quietly, "It wasn't a human."

Nicholas spun on him, his shoulders square and his nostrils flared. The fire in his eyes leapt brightly for a moment with shock and disbelief, then was ice again. "You are insane, old man." His voice was barely above a growl. "The human scent is everywhere. Even you cannot have failed to read it. You're trying to distract me from what you know I must do—"

Alexander said harshly, "A human was here and three of our own are dead, so naturally it must have been the human who killed them? You are a fool and a pup, so certain in your notions you ignore the obvious." His voice took on a note of contempt as he challenged his son. "Try again, O mighty werewolf, and this time use your senses, not your prejudices. You will find you were wrong on two counts."

Nicholas stared at him, but already, as the rage and grief began to release their paralyzing hold on his senses, he could catch the scent of the truth. Humiliation, mixed with an equal amount of horror, seeped into the empty spaces left by departing certainty.

With his own pulses rushing like a sea in his ear, he moved out of the room and down the corridor, following the olfactory trail of blood and violence that was as clear as tracks in the snow. The last corpse was crumpled in the shadows against a wall, the shattered lamp he had dragged with him when he fell toppled on its side a few feet away. Nicholas approached hesitantly, then knelt beside the werewolf.

It was a male, unknown to him. His coat was rough and mottled, his muzzle sharp, his eyes, slitted open in death, yellow. He had a feral scent upon him that spoke of rough wild habitats and a diet of living things. It caused Nicholas to catch his breath, for he knew of no such creature in the pack. The blood of all three victims was on his fur, embedded in his nails, staining his teeth. He himself had died of injuries sustained in the battle; blood from a ruptured spleen bloated his belly and a snapped rib actually protruded through his flesh. He must have fought for some time knowing he was dying; the destruction of the others was that important to him. The only reason Nicholas had missed his scent before was because the stench of the human had distracted him. That, of course, was no excuse.

A werewolf, killing his own kind for no discernible reason. What kind of madness was this? How could such a thing be? Perhaps Nicholas could be forgiven the rashness of his assumption in blaming the human before even looking for another perpetrator, for this—this insanity, this senseless, mindless slaughter of innocent victims by another werewolf . . . it was unheard of. It was beyond imagining.

And yet it had, undeniably, happened. Nicholas's head swam with the impact of what he was seeing, and beginning to understand as the truth, even as a cold sickness filled his stomach for the magnitude of the error in judgement he had made. He demanded hoarsely, "Who is this creature? What can possibly be his purpose in doing such a thing?"

There was a significant pause. It occurred to Nicholas for the first time that his parent was as deeply affected by all of this as he was, if not more. But being the older—and, as recent events had just proved, stronger—werewolf, he showed none of his feelings. That was as it should be.

"I know him." Alexander's voice was low, and the surprise of the words caused Nicholas to look up at him quickly. Alexander's face was, as ever, implacable, though his eyes were dark with remembrance, or sorrow, or perhaps even horror. "He hails from a time long ago . . . a past I thought was buried. I don't know his name. But I remember him."

Then, with an effort, he seemed to force his attention back to the present. His gaze, and his voice, sharpened. "As for his purpose . . . perhaps it was nothing more than to manipulate you into blaming a human for his crimes. And he almost succeeded, didn't he?"

The coldness of horror crept through Nicholas's veins, turning his skin to ice and freezing his breath in his lungs for one long and painful moment. A moment ago he had been willing to turn as wild as this killer, to toss aside all he knew and all he valued for the satisfaction of bloodlust . . . and *he had been wrong.* One rash, mistaken assumption and he had been ready to declare war upon the human race; to cast aside centuries of breeding and civilization and careful restraint; to disgrace himself and destroy the pack; to let science, industry and art fall by the wayside—for the sake of a mistake. Because it was easier to believe centuries of prejudice than a moment's logic; because in the moment of deepest passion the savage always triumphs.

The shame of his failure reached deep into his soul.

Slowly Nicholas stood, careful this time to let none of his turmoil show in his eyes. "The human," he insisted evenly. "Why should a human be involved in such a thing? Who is he and what was he doing here?"

"Not a human, you fool," Alexander repeated harshly, and with more than a touch of impatience. "Find the pure blood scent. Tell me what you smell."

Nicholas looked around uncertainly, following the evidence of his nose to a splatter on the wall that held the strong scent of the human. He was acclaimed the most powerful werewolf in the pack, yet he had been wrong twice tonight already. He felt like a cub taking its lessons: angry to be so humiliated, yet humbled because the humiliation was just.

He dipped his fingers in the splatter of blood and brought them slowly to his nostrils. Human, yes. Human, yet . . . He stiffened, and brought his fingers closer.

He raised his eyes to Alexander. "Werewolf," he whispered.

Alexander's face was impassive.

"Is there another?" Nicholas demanded. The scent on his fingers, intermingled with human scent, was not that of the feral killer, or of Moria or Rene or Tobias. It was not like any werewolf scent he had ever known, so faint, in fact, as to almost not be werewolf at all . . . but it was. And he dared not leap to any more conclusions this night.

Alexander said, "No other."

In the pulse of silence Nicholas could hear the soft thrum of blood through his elder's veins, the expansion and contraction of lungs with steady, even breaths. He could hear the quiet rustling movements of the werewolves in the other room as they went about the business of attending to the dead; he could hear the painful, sickening sound of blood drying on wounds, muscle and sinew contracting as rigor mortis set in. And he could hear, although his lips never formed the words, his own unspoken question slamming into the stillness of the room.

Alexander's gaze was steady as he said, "It's no trick. You should have picked it up sooner. I did, the moment I walked into this building."

Nicholas demanded hoarsely, "How was it done? How could the creature produce such blood? Which is it, human or werewolf?"

Alexander replied quietly, "Both."

They walked down Fifth Avenue accompanied by the fog and the eerie echoing click of their own footsteps, muffled by the damp. A garbage truck clattered several blocks over, breathing out the sour stench of its cargo and the tired, flannel-wrapped sweat of its operators. In the distance a siren wailed, but it was not coming their way.

Nicholas had left the building without giving orders, without looking back. His operatives were good at their jobs; they would do what had to be done, but no more until he told them otherwise.

Nicholas said nothing for many blocks. He had spoken rashly before and had been shown the fool. He remained silent to acknowledge this fact to his elder, and he used the time to try to resolve the dozens, perhaps hundreds, of conflicting, half-formed thoughts that raced through his head.

At last he spoke. "Were they doing genetic research, then? Rene and the others—did they make this half werewolf?"

His voice was taut and the admonition of a human philosopher kept haunting the back of his mind: *When you look into an abyss, the abyss also looks into you.* He had looked into the abyss, and what looked back at him was the only thing that had ever frightened him in all his thirty-eight years on earth.

Alexander's tone was reflective. "That's a facile explanation, isn't it? And comforting, too. For what can be made by man—or werewolf—in a laboratory can also be unmade. Far easier, I think, than to allow that the monster might be an occurrence of nature—or that he might not be a monster at all."

Nicholas shoved his hands deeper into the silk-lined pockets of his coat. The fog tasted smokey and rich as it passed through his sinuses and down into his throat, like a barrel-aged wine, redolent of this brash human city with all its filth and foibles, majesty and charm. How odd that he should notice such a thing at a time like this. How much odder that he could still appreciate it.

He said, deliberately and with care, "A human-werewolf hybrid cannot occur in nature. They are two separate species. They cannot interbreed."

"Nonetheless," replied Alexander, "they have done so."

Nicholas breathed again, deeply, of the cold thick air. He kept his heartbeat calm. He listened to the sound of their footsteps, to the stealthy spring of a cat onto a nearby rooftop, to the sighs and murmurs and soft urgent movements of a man turning his lover in bed some four stories above. He listened, and was silent.

And when he had been quiet a sufficiently respectful time he said, flatly and unequivocally, "That is impossible."

He sensed the other man's smile in the dark; not so much amused as patient, perhaps a little sad. "And now you will tell me, noble Nicholas, that you've never shared the pleasures of the flesh with a human female."

Nicholas scowled, his shoulders tensing. "I hardly see the relevance—"

"Of course you have. They are incredible little temptresses and the forbidden plaything is always the most coveted."

"What you are suggesting," said Nicholas without hesitation, "is a deviancy beyond imagination. No werewolf could mate with a human in his natural state, much less conceive a child—it is *not a physical possibility*."

Now it was Alexander's time to be silent. Nicholas could see the hot puffs of his own breath superimposed on the fog, and he could hear the rush of it in his ears. He exerted control, and was calm.

"Why are you making these outrageous speculations?" Nicholas demanded lowly after a time. "What can possibly be the point?"

"I'm not speculating about anything," replied Alexander without a pause or even the slightest change of inflection. "I'm telling you that a natural hybrid exists. And I know who it is."

Nicholas felt the world stop. When it resumed again, nothing would ever be the way it once was, not the tick of a clock, the spin of a wheel, the orbital arc of a star. Not the life of man or werewolf or any creature that flew the skies or swam the waters or walked the soil of this planet earth.

When you look into an abyss . . .

They walked past shuttered buildings and silent brownstones, past traffic lights reflected in shiny asphalt. They crossed the street and took a footpath; they moved deeper and deeper into the pit of darkness that was Central Park.

Something breathed in a pool of black shadow to the east of the path they walked, a human with glittering eyes and the smell of vomit on his skin. He had a knife tucked inside his jacket, and the quickening of his pulse suggested he was sizing them up as prey. He shrank deeper into the shadows as they passed, though, and his hand slackened on the hilt of the knife. His pores had the smell of quick cold fear. Nicholas was vaguely disappointed by his cowardice.

He caught the scent of a group of his own kind, running in joyful play through the broad meadows near the lake, and his head tilted automatically toward them, soothed by their presence. It would have been an uncommon occurrence not to find werewolves abroad on a night such as this, enjoying the magnificent piece of wilderness they had carved out for themselves in the heart of the city, but Nicholas found their presence a reassuring surprise nonetheless, almost an omen. He longed to join them with a single-minded intensity that momentarily blotted out all else, to cast aside this cumbersome human form, to wipe his mind clear of moral choices and dark knowledge and weighty, weighty responsibility. To run through the night and drink in the fog and just *be*.

But the pleasurable, wind-borne remnants of his own kind soon faded into the background beneath the demand of closer, more disruptive sensations. Someone slept in the bushes, his teeth rotting and his liver diseased. Someone else rifled a trash bin half a mile or so down the path. Against the nocturnal rustlings and chatters of the zoo animals came another animal sound, muffled and desperate: a female helplessly struggling against the violence being perpetrated upon her by a male of her own species. She was weakening, and Nicholas wondered if she would die this night, brutalized and broken, her body tossed into the shrubs for the beetles and spiders.

"What pathetic, useless creatures they are," he muttered into the fog. "How did we ever let it get this far?"

The smile that touched Alexander's lips was dry and tired. "A question that will take more time than we have this night to answer."

The lights of the city grew dimmer still, swallowed by fog and the few stubbornly clinging leaves of maples and elms. They descended deeper into the night, into a silence so thick even their footsteps were swallowed, into a darkness only werewolf eyes could navigate. The human scents that lingered here were old and faint, tinged with confusion and unease. The wooded paths they travelled now were not carved by human feet or meant for human enjoyment, and those who wandered through seemed to sense as much, and did not linger long.

They moved through a maze of evergreens and tall shrubs, past the sound of slow-running water in a shallow stream. Nicholas tried to map the crisis in his head. A werewolf-human hybrid had somehow come into existence, if his own father was to be believed. It not only existed, but had been discovered by a wild werewolf unknown to him, the werewolf who had attacked the scientists at Research Concepts. Had he meant to kill the hybrid or liberate it? Had Rene and Moria and Tobias died in defense of the monster or in defense of their lives? What was the hybrid doing there in the first place, and what had become of it now? It had been injured, obviously, but there was no corpse, no smell of death in its blood. Was it staggering, wounded and dangerous, through the streets of New York even now? Or had it crawled off somewhere else to die?

And why, most important of all, did Nicholas feel that his own father knew the answers to all of these questions and more? Why wouldn't he tell them?

In the shadows a deeper, blacker shape loomed up before them. It seemed to leap out of nowhere and block the path, massive and majestic, fierce and powerful. It was a wolf in low crouch, its eyes narrowed and its teeth bared, carved of age-darkened marble and posed upon a granite column eight feet high. It had been guarding this private place for over a hundred years, and Nicholas never failed to feel a thrill of awe in its presence.

Alexander made his way over to the bench beneath the statue and sat down, with only a slight stiffness in the bend of his knees betraying his age. He was a hundred thirty years old, and could live in good health another twenty.

Nicholas sat beside him, feeling the cold of the stone through his coat and the stillness of the night in his bones. A snatch of something about the dark November of the soul floated up in his mind and he tried to remember what it was. The human poets were tormenting him tonight.

"Is it a test, then?" he demanded lowly, when he could stay silent no longer. He kept his shoulders square and his gaze centered forward into the night. "If so, I know I have already failed. I was wrong to blame the human and ignore the evidence. I've asked all the wrong questions. I've wasted time. This—creature you call a hybrid human is the key to it all and is even now slipping from our grasp. I should have gone after him myself. You're right, I let my passions overcome my judgement." And for the first time his voice faltered and thickened a fraction. "They were my people. They were my friends. And they shouldn't have died."

Alexander said, "This was one of the first places I visited when I came to the United States as a young man. The statue was here even then, marking this as our place. There used to be thousands of such acres of wilderness in every major population center of the world. Sad to say, as the century has grown, our places have become fewer and farther between. It would be easy to blame humans, but it's not their fault. It's our own."

"We weren't vigilant enough."

"Yes. We became more concerned with progress than survival." Then Alexander said, "Yes, it was a test, though not of my making. And you have disappointed me. I had thought, after all we've progressed this century, after all of my efforts and your mother's, you would have been less quick to call the human enemy. But it's instinct, isn't it? I wonder if we shall ever really overcome it."

Nicholas was silent. The intensity of his shame was like a cold vise pressing into his temples, for he could not ignore what his rash judgement might have cost them. He had been wrong. He should have known better and he had made a misjudgement, and it was one he would never forget. He had no excuse to offer, no apology to make. And three of his own were still dead.

Alexander said, "We have dominated this planet for thousands of years. There has never been a pack ruler who has not, at one point or another, faced a crisis that determined our destiny, even our survival. Your mother and I faced such a crisis at the end of the last century. And now, as we enter the millennium, human and werewolf, you will do the same. The choices you make will change the course of history. I counsel you only not to make them in ignorance."

"You gave me the power, *mon père*," Nicholas said stiffly. "You can take it away." It was the rote and proper reply for the young, ascending ruler to make to the standing ruler whenever their ambitions came into conflict. Nicholas meant it . . . and he did not. The thirst for vengeance was a dangerous thing, singular and obsessive, and it had the ability to blind him to everything that was important—even the ultimate welfare of the pack. Perhaps that was the most important lesson his elder had to teach him tonight.

Alexander replied, with perhaps a touch of irony, "I would not want your power at this moment, thank you. Nor would I want your choices."

Another silence. Humans scurried in the distance. Sirens. Garbage trucks.

Nicholas said very lowly, "*Why*? How did you come to know of the existence of this creature and why was it here?"

"Because," replied Alexander wearily, "I am responsible. I have always been responsible. It was I, you see, who first brought the human woman into the pack."

Five years earlier, in an inauguration ceremony that had drawn werewolves from all over the world to the Devoncroix compound in Alaska, Nicholas Devoncroix had been officially named heir designate to the pack leadership. Since he was the youngest offspring of the ruling family which had held its power uninterrupted for more than a millennium, the choice was no surprise, but the ceremony was essential. They were a people of ritual, of tradition and slow, certain change. They did not like surprises. Upheaval was vastly disturbing to them.

Nicholas tried not to think about what an upheaval of this magnitude would do to the pack.

Nicholas had been groomed from birth for his role in life. His primary education had been at an exclusive school in Switzerland which turned out more than its share of scientists, statesmen and prodigies in the arts—and which no human had ever attended—and he held graduate degrees from Princeton, Oxford and Cambridge universities. At twenty-three he had been president of one of the Devoncroix Corporation's most lucrative companies; at twenty-five he had perfected the satellite technology which was the basis of the entire communications and security system that blanketed the pack around the world. By age thirty he had been responsible for bringing into the collective coffers some thirty-two billion dollars' worth of new business.

From the compound in Alaska—a vast and secret, mostly underground complex which served both as company headquarters and as symbolic ancestral home to all the pack—Nicholas had travelled the circumference of the globe, from the rain forests of the Amazon to the mountains of central China, learning the business and the pack he was to rule. He had won at Wimbledon, broken the sound barrier in an experimental aircraft, climbed Kilimanjaro and Everest alone. He had negotiated delicate deals between humans of warring countries—all to the pack's benefit, of course—and settled dangerous disputes between competing clans within the pack. Although technically he would not assume control of the pack until the death of his father, in every other, practical way he *was* the pack. He was well loved, well respected. It was generally agreed without argument that Nicholas Devoncroix would continue the fine tradition of progressive, benevolent rulership his ancestors had established over a thousand years ago.

But now, sitting beneath the cold shadow of the stone wolf, Nicholas felt an emptiness grip his belly and he thought, *I have failed. Three of my own are dead at the hands of another werewolf. A monstrous hybrid human is at the heart of this disaster and I never even knew of its existence. The pack looked to me for protection, but I have failed. History will record that the beginning of the end was on this night, in this place . . . on my watch.* Perhaps the events had been set in motion long ago, but the consequences were his to deal with now. And he was not ready.

Alexander looked at him and read the bleakness in Nicholas's eyes before he could disguise it. Because it was a display of weakness for a leader to show self-doubt—even a leader who had not yet assumed power, and even to his father—Alexander politely pretended he did not see.

When he spoke, Alexander's voice was conversational, picking up the story as though it were a matter of mere passing interest. "I was living in Paris then, the only place, really, for a young, ambitious werewolf to be. Of course my home, my roots, were far from that carefree

24

metropolis, deep in the cold black heart of Siberia, but I'm afraid I had grown rather far from my origins.

"I used to spend a great deal of time in the company of humans, and was often criticized for it. But they were such amusing, delightful creatures, their philosophies so arcane, their pleasures so shallow . . . I adored the Winter Palace, and the intellectuals of Paris, the theaters of London and the grand ballrooms of Florence and Venice. There was a train, I recall, known as the Orient Express . . . but that is another story.

"Times were so much simpler then, too, the lines between myth and reality not quite so distinct. It was easier to believe the impossible, I think, for werewolves as well as humans, for the fences that keep our worlds separate from one another really were not built until well into this century. It was in many ways the most innocent age in all of history, when the savageries of the past were far enough behind to be little more than legends, yet before this time of instant communication and unlimited knowledge, which works so hard to destroy magic and make hope obsolete.

"It was just before the turn of the century, when the old leader Sancerre had died suddenly of a seizure of the brain, and left as his heir designee a young, unmated queen, inexperienced and ill-prepared. Needless to say, the pack was in disarray and ripe for a takeover, not that there was much to take over back then.

"Today we are involved in over a hundred different enterprises and industries, ranging from electronics to filmmaking. We have offices and representatives in every major city of every developed country on earth and we control most of the world's financial markets, technology and natural resources. But at the end of the last century, you must recall, for most of Europe the Industrial Revolution was just proving itself more than a passing trend. We hadn't yet grasped the potential of the future, and we were scattered, divided, each devoted in his own self-absorbed way to his own selfish indulgences and personal fortune. The young queen, of course, fell heir to the largest of these fortunes, and she was the constant target of schemes from ambitious young werewolves like myself—for both her power and her wealth. It was beginning to look as though she would spend the rest of her tenure as pack leader—however long that might be—doing nothing but defending herself. I felt rather sorry for her, actually."

Alexander must have sensed Nicholas's impatience, for he smiled, a very small smile, in the dark. "Shall I stop?" he inquired courteously.

Nicholas breathed deeply once, and again. He thought of human poets and philosophers, and the dangers that face those who chase monsters.

"I think," he answered slowly, after a long moment, "I have acted rashly once too often tonight. And if I do not hear what you have to say now, I may spend the rest of my life wrestling with questions to which I will never know the answers."

Alexander nodded, though whether the gesture symbolized approval or mere thoughtfulness was impossible to determine. "And if I do not have the answers you seek?"

Nicholas looked at him steadily in the dark, and gave the appropriate response. "Then I am not asking the right questions. The hybrid, Father. Who is it? Tell me."

Alexander turned his eyes straight ahead, gazing off into the darkness. His features were lost in the shadow of the wolf, and after a time he resumed his tale.

"It may surprise you," he said, "that this is a love story." And he smiled, softly, to himself. "Then again, in the greater scheme of things, it seems to me that all matters both werewolf and human eventually come down to that . . ."

PART TWO

Paris

1897

❧

[Humans] are savages at heart, just like we are. And that is the
one thing for which they can never be forgiven.
—FREDERICK PETROV, WEREWOLF 1648

Man is only great when he acts from the passions.
—BENJAMIN DISRAELI, A HUMAN 1844

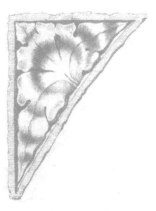 **TESSA**

Two

TESSA LEGUERRE HAD PLANNED THE MURDER OF ALEXANDER DEVON-croix for ten years. She knew she would never get a better chance than the one that presented itself the night of the October moon.

Six months earlier she had joined the household as a chambermaid, an accomplishment which had been far easier than it probably should have been, by appealing to the sympathies of the majordomo with her woeful tale of being orphaned (true) and penniless (untrue). She had even gone to the trouble of pulling off the top two buttons of her cotton shirtwaist to let a provocative few inches of skin show through before going into the interview, only to learn later that the subject of her wiles was immune to the charms of young girls, whether they be fully clothed or not. He did, however, find her English-accented French appealing, and mentioned it specifically when he gave her the position. It was that easy.

After that, she had only to avoid the sharp eyes of Madame Crolliere, the housekeeper, who carried around a riding crop and disciplined her girls with a sharp rap to the knuckles for a sloppy sheet corner or a damp washbasin, and to spend every spare moment learning all that was to be known about the house of Devoncroix.

Tessa had a quick and agile mind and a memory like a trap and in only a matter of days she had learned all the corridors and passageways of the twenty-three-room Paris town house, the cubbyholes and niches and hiding places, the closest staircases and the window embrasures which would hide a human form; which hinges needed oiling and which stair tread squeaked. She learned the quickest, quietest route from her attic sleeping quarters to the master's chamber; she learned how to make the journey without arousing her sleeping companions. She studied every detail of that inner sanctum, from the artwork on the walls to the carpet upon the floor, the crisp white shirts in the linen press and the rich woolens in the wardrobe, the perfumes and pomades in his dressing room, the leathers and the silks and the jewelled shirt studs. She could find each piece of furniture in the dark; she knew the broken latch on the window and the sticky hinge on the door. She had plotted every step of the night over and over again in her mind until performance was little more than an extension of imagination; a mistake or misjudgement would have been impossible.

She stole a knife from the kitchen, a fine six-inch blade of hammered steel with a solid ash handle. She had heard somewhere that ash was best for these things, and she intended to take no chances. She secreted the knife inside the ticking of her mattress, where it could be found only if one knew it was there. Lavalier, the chef, raised a furor over its disappearance and kept the downstairs staff cowering for days, until finally he fixed the blame on an underchef, who was promptly dismissed. The knife was replaced, though Lavalier continued to complain that the replacement never sliced as fine as the original, but for the most part that was the end of that.

Tessa had the plan, she had the knife, she had the means and she had the access. What she did not have, to her great frustration, was the victim.

The master of the house was away when she joined his staff, and he was to remain so until the first week of October or thereabouts.

Though patience was not one of her virtues, Tessa used the time to hone her intent, to settle herself more securely into her position, and to listen. She had waited ten years, after all. She was prepared to wait a few more months.

Tessa knew something of the households of the well-to-do—her own circumstances had been quite cosmopolitan until the death of her father had forced her mother to return to her native Cornwall, taking with her a reluctant and much-aggrieved Tessa—but she was impressed by the extravagance with which Alexander Devoncroix lived. Even the scullery girls were supplied with a change of clothing for every day of the week, and white pinafores that had to be bleached in the sun to be kept clean. He had a coal furnace in the cellar and burned wood in every grate, even in those whose rooms were unoccupied, because, it was said, he liked a cheery, warm house free of drafts.

The house itself was outfitted with every possible convenience. Gas lamps supplied lighting, from the servants' quarters to the enormous chandeliers in the entrance hall and all the way to the third-floor ballroom. There were toilet facilities, with pull-chains for disposal, attached to every bedchamber. Water was pumped into the lavatory with a turn of a handle, and heated by means of a complicated boiler system in the cellar. The marble bathing rooms were the most decadent—and fascinating—things Tessa had ever seen. There were laundry chutes in every bedchamber, so that guests had merely to open a drawer and deposit their soiled clothing, where it would slide directly down to the washroom and be immediately attended to by any one of five laundresses constantly on duty. Likewise, dumbwaiters, available with the pull of a tasseled cord, could deliver whatever a guest might desire to his quarters, where he had but to slide back a door and feast in hedonistic privacy.

The master's wine cellar was extensive, his hospitality renowned. Even when he was not in residence, no fewer than ten of the guest chambers were occupied. It was common knowledge among the staff that his guests were sometimes—the word was chosen carefully and always uttered delicately—peculiar. But no more so than was the master of the house himself.

Alexander Devoncroix commanded both adoration and fear, un-wavering loyalty and unspoken suspicion. He was, they said, a shock-ingly handsome young raconteur, a rake and a dissolute, a breaker of hearts and a charmer of virgins; an adventurer, a poet, a bon vivant. This was what they said aloud, with the indulgent pride a servant always feels for the qualities—be they vice or virtue—of an infamous employer, particularly if he is of a generous bent toward his underlings and most particularly if his own station in life is highly placed and enhances their own. All of this Tessa had no doubt was true. What was whispered about him, however, was even more intriguing—and, as Tessa had particular reason to know, even more true.

They called him a devil and a god, a sorcerer and an eater of chil-dren. They alluded to strange sounds and inexplicable happenings be-hind closed doors, in dark gardens and in the deep woods on moonless nights. Lewd things, bizarre things, unnatural things. Two would leave and only one would return. The footsteps of a man would begin and the tracks of an animal would end. The bedsheets would show traces of fur, though no dogs were kept in the house. And what of the odd structure of the house itself, with its many small hinged doors and latchless windows through which no grown man or woman could pass? They whispered the word "loup-garou." Shape-changer. Were-wolf.

That was why Tessa had come.

She first spied him—or at least a reasonable representation—in the gallery on the second floor of the house. There were magnificent paint-ings throughout the mansion, of course. The master was apparently fond of the Dutch masters; Rembrandt and Vermeer were among the most prominently displayed in the dining hall and study. Tessa, who knew only enough to marvel at their worth, took pleasure in simply wandering around the house, admiring the works of art.

Without a doubt the most striking of all the portraits was at the top of the second-floor landing, conspicuously arranged to catch the eye of everyone who traversed the staircase, entered the ballroom, or vis-ited the gallery. Tessa was not surprised to learn that the portrait was of the master of the house, for she had heard that these creatures were exceptionally vain. She had not guessed, however, that he had so much to be vain about.

The life-sized portrait featured a young man standing before the parklike expanse of grounds that was the east vista of the house. He was dressed in country attire: high boots, folded cravat, woolen jacket unbuttoned over his waistcoat. He leaned back with one elbow propped upon the wall, one leg slightly raised on a mounting block. He gazed at the onlooker with an arrogant, amused air, his aristocratic features managing to look at the same time both relaxed and alert, and his sharp blue eyes possessed of an oddly sardonic twinkle that was observable even through the impersonal medium of oil and canvas. His most remarkable feature was, of course, his hair: it possessed the color and satiny sheen of rich light mink, except for a swath about five inches wide that swept from the right temple back to the ends and which was the most remarkable shade of white gold. He wore his hair unfashionably long, loose about his shoulders like thick shiny satin, but this in itself did not surprise Tessa. She had heard that the hair of such creatures could not be cut. The painting looked improbable; Tessa was certain the artist had employed a certain license for the sake of romance. She was to learn, from servants' gossip and soon her own eyes, that the portrait did not do its subject justice.

The most unusual aspect of the painting, however, was not the human likeness, or even the skill of the artist. It was the secondary subject with which the master had chosen to pose. It was customary among aristocrats of both England and France to have their portraits painted in the company of a beloved pet—a lapdog, a mastiff, even a cat. Alexander Devoncroix had chosen to pose with his hand upon the head of a shaggy brown-and-white wolf. The eyes of the wolf were blue, like his own.

Tessa stared at that painting, feeling small and insignificant in its shadow, until she got the chills. She knew then for certain that she had done the right thing in coming here.

He returned, after what seemed an eternity of waiting, to a great fanfare and jingle of horses' harnesses in a shiny black carriage

trimmed with gold. Two buxomous, overdressed and overpainted females clung to his arms like cheap jewellery, which Tessa did not find
in the least surprising. What did surprise her—only a little, for she
had been prepared—was what a striking figure he made. He was even
taller and stronger than he appeared in the portrait, his sharp features
livelier, his sea blue eyes merrier. That champagne-colored hair with
its blaze of gold was even more arresting in person, and he displayed
it shamelessly as he walked hatless in the sun. His voice was warm
and mellifluous, which she had not expected, and his laugh loud, carefree and inviting, which also surprised her.

No one, however, could have prepared Tessa for the inexplicable
power, the almost mesmeric charm, of Alexander Devoncroix. He
moved like one of the Greek athletes of old, all power and grace and
fluidity of motion. Just watching him brought a clench of pleasure to
the throat. When he laughed, joy resonated in all within distance of
the sound; when he scowled—which he did very seldom—the sky
seemed to darken. In his presence the very atmosphere of the earth
was subtly charged with reverent expectancy, as though greatness
were an element unto itself and he, Alexander Devoncroix, was its
embodiment. Often Tessa had wondered how those within his household, knowing he was a monster, could let him live. Now she knew.

All the servants were lined up on that bright autumn day to welcome him home; they formed a double column deep into the great hall
and spilled out onto the steps. The most highly ranked were placed
first within his sight on the steps, and Tessa, who ranked well below
the parlor staff but somewhere above the scullery, was relegated to
the shadows of the interior hall, where she concentrated on rubbing
one foot against the other to keep her legs from falling asleep.

He consigned his two females to the care of his personal valet, who
had arrived with him, and began a leisurely stroll down the line, pausing to greet each and every member of his staff and taking time to
carry on long conversations with many concerning matters that had
transpired during his absence. Occasionally he would inquire about a
family member or the state of one's health. Some might have found

such a gracious display of concern for the personal affairs of one's underlings admirable, particularly in a bachelor, but Tessa, whose back hurt and whose toes tingled unbearably, found it annoying in the extreme. Until he came to her.

She had hoped he would pass her by, that he would be tired or bored by the time he got to the chambermaids and let her go with merely a nod. He did seem to pause less often as he came down the line to the lower ranks, and except for a flirtatious word or two with the prettiest of the girls, he did little more than call a name. But when he saw her an alert spark came into his eye and he said, "Ah, Poinceau, what have we here?"

The majordomo, who walked beside him, explained, "A new chambermaid, monsieur, passably good, but still in training."

Alexander Devoncroix reached out his hand, took her chin lightly in his fingers, and tilted her face so that it caught the light. He was smiling, in a gentle, amused way that seemed to be designed to put her at her ease. "*Enchanté*," he said.

He moved on, but she would feel the warm imprint of his fingers on her face, see that smile and feel the sweetness of his breath across her skin—*Enchanté*—for days afterward.

He was a monster, but he was beautiful. And for a glimpse of that kind of beauty, that essential charm, human beings will forgive a great deal.

From the day of his arrival the balls and banquets and musicales became constant, the house overflowing with guests. The young master loved to entertain, and when he was not entertaining he was being entertained elsewhere. One was likely to meet a wandering guest—or even the master himself—in the corridor at any hour of the day or night, and he rarely slept alone. It was a singularly licentious household, but Tessa had been warned about that. She had also been warned about the times a group of them would assemble out of doors and be gone all night, and the sounds that came from the parks and alleyways, the riverbanks and dark fields on those occasions would chill the blood. Tessa heard no such sounds, but it was true that more than once the master disappeared from his chamber, along with several of the guests, and was gone the night through, only to return unheard or unseen by any of the servants and be found sleeping in his bed with the bright morning sun.

And so it was that between one event and another, no clear opportunity presented itself for Tessa to conclude her business until this, the night of the October moon. The initial spate of parties and houseguests had faded as all of Paris entered a small respite to prepare for the advent of the holiday season, M. Devoncroix included. He had been to the theater, and afterward to a soiree at the home of the Marquis de Fortier; this Tessa knew because she made it a habit to look at his cards and because his personal secretary, Crouchet, thought she was amusing and could be teased into sharing information with her he probably ought not to have. Tessa waited, wakeful, until she heard the carriage pull up before the front door and, peeking out of her window, saw him enter the house alone. She knew then that this was to be the night.

She slipped the knife out of its hiding place and waited, clutching the weapon to her bosom, the eternity of an hour to make certain he was abed. Then, with a tread as soundless as hours of practice could make it, needing no light to guide the path that was etched in memory, she made her way down the stairs and through the corridor that led to the master's chamber.

There she paused with one hand on the latch and the other fiercely clenching the knife in a high position against her breast, her heart pounding with triumph and excitement and the certainty of the moment that had come at last—and also with dread of what she might find beyond that door. Would it be the monster, crouched in waiting with its glinting eyes trained upon her from the darkness? Or would it be the beautiful young man, peaceful in his sleep and never guessing it would be his last? Perhaps he wouldn't be asleep at all. Perhaps he had heard her outside the door and was prepared to spring upon her the minute she stepped through. Perhaps he wasn't even inside, and she would have it all to do again another night.

Then do it she would, she resolved, but she couldn't stand in dry-mouthed fear outside his door another moment. With a silent turn of the well-oiled latch, the door swung open and she stepped inside.

No monster awaited her.

He lay naked and sprawled atop the covers, his limbs silvered in the moonlight that spilled from the open window. One leg was bent slightly toward the other, his hands loose at his sides, his rich hair with its enchanting pale streak fanned out upon the pillow. His chest was firm and oddly devoid of hair, as was his entire body, even beneath his arms and that place low on his abdomen where all adults had hair. His sex was pink and half plumped upon one thigh. His face was turned to the side, his lips parted in deep and even breaths. Tessa could smell the wine as she approached; wine and musk and the sharp evergreen scent that seemed to be his signature. Odd, but she had never noticed the smell of a man before and called it pleasant. But then M. Devoncroix was no ordinary man. He was not, in fact, a man at all.

It was with this assurance—*he is not a man, he is not*—that Tessa gripped her courage and stepped even closer, clenching the knife as though it were a lifeline rather than an instrument of death. She stood over him. Still he did not arouse from his alcohol stupor to notice her. *So he is not*, she thought a trifle smugly, *perhaps as magical as one would think . . .*

But he looked magical, lying there atop the rumpled covers with his strong, lean calves and his smooth, open palms, like something an Italian artist might have sculpted. Magical, lovely, vulnerable. Look there, the way a strand of satin hair was drawn across his face and fluttered with each breath, and yes, was that not the pulse of a heartbeat visible in the strong vein of his throat? Alive, vital. Beautiful.

She remembered his smile, the gentle grasp of his fingers on her chin. He had soft hands, like an aristocrat, but strong, like a craftsman. His touch was nothing like she had expected it to be.

Tessa's heart felt bruised from the power with which it flung itself against her rib cage, and the knife was slippery in her hand. Not a man, she reminded herself fiercely. Not a man but a monster, a killer . . .

Tessa crossed herself awkwardly with her right hand, then closed both hands around the hilt of the knife. She could do this. She had spent her entire adult life preparing for this moment.

She fixed her eyes on the smooth swell of his breast muscle, the gentle rise and fall of each breath, the firm outline of ribs beneath, the satiny sheath of skin. She raised the knife, and saw the blade shake, pulse, throb in rhythm with her heart. A glint of moonlight on steel, the warmth, the almost living warmth, of hard pale ash wood beneath her fingers. She raised it high—*not a man*—and plunged it deep.

There. Splitting skin, crackling bone, tearing muscle. She felt the impact jar her shoulder muscles as her mark struck home—*yes! the heart, surely the heart!*—and she staggered backward, shocked by the force of it, as at almost the same moment his blue eyes flew open and his howl of rage and pain filled the room.

Oh, it was a thing of horror, that cry; it seemed to pierce the very fabric of the sky and, spiraling downward, suck in all the coldness of space, echoing all the agony of misspent souls, breaking upon the confines of the suddenly small chamber like shards of glass upon a marble floor. It chilled Tessa's blood. It stopped the beat of her heart. And when she saw his eyes, sharp clear blue in the moonlight, dilated with pain, blurred with confusion, her breath stopped, too. *Not a man, not a man* . . . She took one more step backward, and then she was against the wall.

He lunged naked from the bed into an upright position and, swaying a little on his feet, he grasped the handle of the knife that protruded from his chest and pulled it out with a howl of pain. Blood sprayed in an arc with the movement, spattering Tessa's hair and face and white nightdress. She didn't blink. She didn't breathe. She knew she was going to die.

He cursed at her and flung the bloody blade away. He tried to grab for her, missed, staggered. Half turning, as though to reach for the bellpull, he stumbled into a marble table and overturned it, sending pin-dishes, porcelains and candlesticks crashing down. He tried to catch himself against the curtains and brought them, billowing and blood-splattered, to the floor.

By this time there were distant sounds of alarm from belowstairs, as his first great roar of pain had been enough to wake the dead. He flung himself toward the door, a red wet fist pressed against the seeping wound in his chest and his face twisted with agony. He reached it, slamming home the bolt with the weight of all of his body just as a pounding began on the panel and the voice of his valet could be heard crying, "Monsieur! Monsieur, are you quite well?"

"Leave me!" he commanded hoarsely. His mouth was close to the door, but the effort required to shout those two words was visible. He pushed away from the door, leaving a bloody streak upon the pale silk that covered it, and his eyes, dark with rage and pain, found her again.

There was nothing beautiful about him now. His magnificent hair was tangled and damp with blood and sweat, his lips colorless, his fine features distorted. In his nakedness, smeared with blood and sheened with perspiration, he looked like a demon fresh-risen from hell. No vestiges of the Renaissance angel to which she had at first compared him remained, and she was glad—and she was terrified.

"You cursed human trollop!" he swore through teeth clenched with pain. "You should die for this, you treacherous female viper. I should slice up your liver and serve it to dogs. I should—"

He sucked in his breath against a spasm of pain. He pressed his fist tighter against the bleeding wound, squeezing his eyes closed, and caught himself against the wall as his knees began to buckle.

Die, die, please die. She knew she hadn't the courage to even whisper the words, though they sounded so loud in her head she was afraid at first she had shouted them. But she had not spoken aloud, and he did not die.

He lifted his head, eyes still tightly closed, and parted his lips as though to better get his breath. The hand that was splayed against the wall for support tightened, then lost its strength and Tessa thought, *Yes, die, please* ... But instead of him collapsing on the floor as she had expected the pain that twisted his face seemed to transform into an intense concentration, and then—yes, there was no mistake—to relax into one long, slow inhalation of quiet pleasure.

The anguish that tightened his muscles released its hold in a visible wave of laxity that smoothed first the corded tendons of his neck, then the bunched ligaments of shoulders, arms, abdomen, hips. Thighs lengthened, calves strengthened, knotted hands opened. His head was thrown back, his arms upraised as though to embrace a miracle. And a miracle was exactly what it was.

Tessa, sinking to her knees, saw it in the air first, smelled it, tasted it, felt it deep in the pit of her stomach, in her bones; no, in her soul. Afterward she would not be able to describe it, or even remember it in full. She knew only the feeling of ecstasy that swelled within her, the great and wondrous certainty that she was witnessing something beyond all human imagination.

Was she terrified? Yes, in the sense that all creatures are held in terrified awe of that which reminds them of their own insignificance. But no thread of horror penetrated her raptured paralysis, no finger of dread. This was magnificent, this was beautiful. She could not be afraid.

There was a tingling of light, a dancing of energy, a pure and powerful radiance that held him in its grip yet seemed to emanate from him; a swelling whirlwind of power that seemed to suck the very essence of life from air and light and to transform it into something greater than it had ever been before. There was an explosion of color and soundless delight, and what once was human was no longer.

The wolf came down on four paws, shook itself with a rippling of satiny pale mink-colored fur, and looked straight at Tessa. It was a magnificent creature, as large as a man if not larger, with a blaze of white gold arrowing from its temple. Its eyes were ice blue, and there was a bleeding wound near its sternum which stained the pale fur dark.

She could see its sides bellowing in and out with quick harsh breaths in the way of an animal in pain. It lowered its head and curled its lip over sharp canine teeth. It moved toward her, a low growl reverberating throughout the room. Tessa knew then to be afraid, but it was too late. He sprang at her.

The blow knocked her sideways and onto the floor so hard that she lost her breath, her lungs expanding and contracting uselessly for several endless, agonizing seconds while the room spun around her. When she regained her senses she was flat on her back on the floor, the heavy weight of his two forepaws pinning her down, his hot breath searing her face. Saliva dripped from his bared teeth onto her throat, and blood from his wound dampened the thin muslin that covered her breast. The rumble of his anger was her death knell as she looked up into the eyes of this wolf and saw hunger there.

His lips curled back, and with a great snarling, tearing sound he lunged at her throat. Tessa had no time to scream or to even think of doing so. She waited for the sharp teeth to sink into her flesh, for blood to spurt and breath to die, and then—nothing happened.

His eyes were an inch or less from her own. The hot juices of his mouth wet her throat, and perhaps there was pressure there, tooth or muzzle. But then she saw the most peculiar thing of all the incredible things she had seen this night. His muscles stiffened, and into his eyes there came a moment of what was clearly decision. The instinct of the beast waged war with the higher processes of denial, and reason won. She felt his muscles trembling with the effort of self-constraint, but he backed away from her.

He let her live.

He took another few steps backward, breathing hard, sides heaving. Then he collapsed upon the floor.

Tessa lay where he had left her, dragging in little gasps of air that sounded like sobs in the suddenly still room, shaking, wondering, trying to grow accustomed to the fact that she was alive when in fact she should have been dead.

As should he.

Panic struck her like a cold blade when she looked over at him. He was still, quiet; even the fur had lost its sheen. A seeping crimson stain matted his fur and spread upon the pale carpet beneath him. Her breath caught in her throat as she looked at him, and then faintly, indistinctly, she saw the rise and fall of his chest.

Tessa got her hands and knees beneath her and crawled to him. Desperately she tried to stanch the flow of blood with her hand. She stroked his thick coarse fur. It felt cool, and his breath was faint. When she gently lifted his head into her lap, he was limp and unresponsive. She bent low over him, rocking back and forth. "Don't die," she whispered. "Oh, God save us, please don't die."

That was when she knew she had been wrong. All along, she had been terribly wrong.

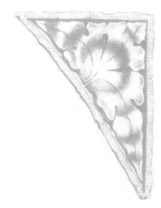

Three

TESSA LEFT THE ROOM ONLY BRIEFLY, FLYING DOWN THE STAIRS IN HER nightgown with just the moonlight and her memory to guide her steps. She reached the butler's pantry and tore through the shelves of supplies, filling her arms with soft towels, gauze bandages, camphor and laudanum. She snatched a kettle from the kitchen and, grabbing her skirts above her knees, ran up the stairs again, taking them two at a time.

An intruder had entered the room in her absence.

It was Gault, the master's valet. He wore a red tapestry dressing gown and no slippers, and his dark curly hair was loose over his shoulders. Until that moment Tessa had not realized that his hair was easily as long as the master's.

He had lifted the limp body of the wolf from the rug on which he lay bleeding and placed him on the bed, and he was bending over the prone figure when Tessa entered. She dumped her supplies on a table and rushed at him with nothing but the copper teakettle for a weapon.

"Get away from him!" she cried. "No one gave you permission to enter!"

He turned on her, dark eyes blazing. "Nor you, I'll wager! What have you done, you foolish girl?"

She hesitated a few feet from him, kettle upraised to strike, chest heaving with emotion and exertion. His eyes swept the room, from the bloody knife in the corner to the medicine on the table to her stained hands and nightgown, and the narrowing of his eyes told her he had no difficulty in discerning the truth. And the truth did not reflect well on her.

For just a moment, there was a tremor in her resolve. He straightened, steely anger darkening his face, and he took a step toward her. But she stood her ground, tightening her grip upon the teakettle, setting her jaw.

"He bolted the door against you," she reminded him. "He won't be happy to know you're here."

She saw a flicker of uncertainty cross his eyes. Clearly, he was accustomed to his master's eccentricities, particularly where those of the opposite sex were concerned, and he was not quite as sure of the appropriate response to this situation as he would like to be. He scowled. "I don't know what games you were playing, but it is to your very good fortune that his wound is minor. Obviously, it's not my place to decide your punishment."

She swallowed hard but maintained his gaze and the strength of her voice. "Nor is it your place to interfere. Leave now and I may not tell him you were here."

She thought for a moment that he might refuse. He glanced at the still, limp form of the huge wolf on the bed, and the sight of it was evidently nothing remarkable to him. Then he looked at her.

"He'll need blood broth," he advised matter-of-factly, "and plenty of it."

For a moment she wavered. "Blood—broth?"

"Fresh chicken or goat. Fortify it with sugar and brandy and warm it to drink. His wound must be cleaned . . ."

He moved toward the bed, but Tessa stopped him with a sharp "I can do that."

He gave her a look that was eloquent in its contempt and skepticism. "If I thought you could do any more harm, I'd tear your throat out with my own hands," he told her, in a voice just as flat and detached as the one he had used to advise her about the blood broth. "As it is, I will attend him in the morning. You are a very, very lucky little human."

It occurred to Tessa for the first time as he departed that Gault might be of the same remarkable species as his master. The possibility held no especial interest for her. After all she had experienced that night, nothing could startle her ever again.

She bolted the door after him, quickly added more coal to the stove, then put the kettle on to boil.

Armed with gauze and camphor, filled with trepidation, Tessa approached the wolf. His eyes were open to narrow slits, but glazed and unfocused. They showed no reaction as she came near, to her great relief. She knelt beside the bed, cautiously extending a hand to part the blood-stiff fur around the wound. It had stopped bleeding, for which she fervently thanked God. But then she stopped and stared. What once had been an ugly gash was now pink, puckered flesh, lacking only a needle's breadth from being knitted and whole. The wound was almost completely healed.

A sound issued from his throat, a growl or a moan, and he moved restlessly. Tessa quickly backed away. The pace of his breathing had increased, and it frightened her. "What?" she whispered frantically. "What can I do? What do you need?"

She wished she had not sent Gault away so summarily, and wondered if it was too late to call him back. He would know what to do. But the master had not wanted him here; he *had* bolted the door against him. Had she been wrong to respect his wishes?

His panting was shallow, quick, accompanied by a high, thin wheezing that filled the room. Tessa's stomach tightened with helpless despair; she raised her hands to her ears to block out the sound. And then she remembered.

Once again she flew down the stairs, threw open bolts, plunged into the night. She tore across the stableyard and into the chicken house, where she snatched two sleeping fowl from their roosts and wrung their necks before they had time to utter more than a squawk. She dispatched their heads on the chopping block with barely a grimace, and hung them up by their feet to drain into a bucket. She rushed back inside to grab two more.

She continued in this fashion until the bucket was filled; then she prepared the broth as directed, with strong brandy and plenty of dark sugar, all the time wondering if Gault could have been lying to her, or if she had misunderstood, or in fact had dreamed the entire unlikely episode from beginning to end.

She carried the steaming mixture upstairs, where he lay just as she had left him, dull eyes watching her guardedly, breathing short and rapid. She poured a little of the broth into a saucer and held it close to him. He lifted his head a little, then drank greedily.

Over and over she filled the saucer, bending and straightening until she could no longer feel the pain in her back and she thought her body would snap in two at the waist. When he dozed she fed the fire and stroked his fur and murmured softly to him, and when he woke she brought more broth.

It was just before dawn when exhaustion overcame her, and Tessa fell asleep in her chair.

When she awoke she was looking into the bright blue, very human eyes of Alexander Devoncroix. "Who the flaming hell are you?" he demanded, scowling.

Tessa leapt to her feet, overturning her chair, and stumbled a few steps backward. He was propped up on one elbow in bed, his lower extremities now more or less decently covered by the duvet, his smooth muscled chest displaying nothing but a slight pink shininess over the place where the knife wound had been. Tessa could not believe that she had slept through that incredible transmutation of forms, and then she wondered for one brief, disoriented moment whether she might have been asleep from the beginning and had only dreamed what she remembered . . .

"Well?" he demanded. "I asked you a question, girl."

"I—I . . ." She saw the bowl with the congealed remains of the blood broth; she saw the saucer from which he had drunk. She saw the bloody towels with which she had cleaned him, the knife, the broken porcelains. She gulped a breath, but the only words that she could find were a feeble and inane "You—you're speaking English!"

His scowl, if possible, grew even more fierce. "Of course I am. Aren't you?"

"I—yes, I—"

"Your name, damn it!"

She gulped again and with all the courage at her command she held her position; she did not turn and flee. She even managed to speak, and her voice did not sound nearly as hollow or as feeble as she felt inside. "My name is Tessa. I—you were injured and I—"

"And you're the one who tried to stick a knife in my ribs, and made a mess of it, too." He pushed himself upright in bed, dragging a blood-encrusted hand through his hair. He grimaced when he looked at his fingers, and his voice was impatient. "The next time you take it into your head to play the assassin, wench, be more sure of your aim." He stifled a groan and touched his fingers gingerly to his chest. "I feel as though my ribs have been kicked in by a horse."

He sat back against the pillows with an exaggerated wince, rubbing the healed scar. "Damnation, I need a bath, and I'm in no temper to deal with you now. I'm starved. Where's my valet? Don't just stand there gaping, girl, fetch him! And clean yourself—you're offensive to look at. Attend me in an hour. Now go, before I have *you* for breakfast! Gault!" he shouted, flinging himself forward.

Tessa ran to the door, fumbled with the bolt, threw it open. Gault was waiting there with an army of servants, each bearing a covered dish or a tray or a cart from which meats and breads steamed and simmered, filling the corridor with their succulent aromas. The valet smirked at her, giving the impression that he had been waiting outside the door for no other reason than to put her in bad graces with the master. And when she edged past him, her heart thundering in her chest and her eyes wide and wary, he suddenly lunged and bared his teeth at her, hissing. Tessa could not prevent the cry that escaped her as she fled, and she heard his laughter all the way to her attic room.

Doubtless no one would have stopped Tessa if she had left the house then. Certainly no one—no one human, that is—would have blamed her. In fact, that alternative never even occurred to Tessa. She had spent so much of her life simply planning the murder, waiting for it, hoping for it, etching out the details night after night in her mind, that there had been no room left over in her imagination for what would happen afterward. Whether he lived or died, Tessa had no place to go from here.

Not that she could have left him in any event. Not now. Not having seen what she had seen and knowing what she now knew, and with so many questions swirling unanswered in her head.

Mme. Crolliere approached Tessa as she vaulted up the back stairs, her countenance thunderous and her crop raised. "There you are, you wicked girl! You think you can steal from your bed and shirk your duties to conduct your nasty little liaisons—not in my household you cannot! *Alors!*"

She stopped suddenly when she noticed Tessa's bloodied garments, her disarranged hair and wild eyes. Mme. Crolliere's own eyes narrowed, and her nostrils flared noticeably as she took in the story in scent. "Ah, so it was you with the chickens!" she observed with a satisfied smirk. "I will inform Lavalier and let him deal with you. He's anxious to put someone's head on the block and no one will be sorry to know it's *you*. And if you think you can ingratiate yourself to the master, I will tell you now that he discards little nothings like you as easily as he tosses aside old linen. And I will not have it with *my* girls, I've told him—"

Staring at her, Tessa said dully, "You're one of them, aren't you?"

The housekeeper's eyes narrowed once again, although her sharp chin seemed to jerk a little with suppressed amusement. Her only response, however, was a disparaging sniff. "Clean yourself up, you filthy creature, before someone sees you. I'll not have it said that one of *my* girls stank up the house. Off with you!"

She raised the riding crop again threateningly, and Tessa fled to her attic room.

No one would have blamed her if she had run farther.

But she scrubbed the coal dust from her face and the blood from under her fingernails, dressed herself in a clean frock and pinafore, and tied back her hair. All of this she did by rote, without thinking of the reason for it, or what she intended to do when her toilette was finished. She stood before the mirror and inspected her appearance automatically, but the face that looked back at her was not one that she recognized.

The girl she knew had spent a lifetime plotting her vengeance, had seen her opportunity and taken it. But when she reviewed the events of the night, she was swept by a wave of horror and confusion so intense she had to sit down. What had she *done*? What madness had overcome her, that she should spend the night nursing back to health the very creature she had spent all her adult life plotting to destroy? He was evil, she knew that to be so; it *must* be so . . . And yet, in the grip of that miraculous transformation, he had not been evil. He had been a creature of light and magic, of power and beauty, and *she*, small and clumsy and earthbound, had been the evil one. When he had had her beneath his mighty paws with teeth poised to tear at her throat, and when he had backed away and let her live—then he had not been evil. She, who had plunged a knife into his chest while he slept, had been evil.

Yet how could all these years of knowing be wrong? How could the incredible miracle she had witnessed last night and the killer monster she had hated for the past ten years be one and the same? She had fallen under the spell of his transformation; that much was certain. There was no other reason to explain her irrational fear for his safety, her determination that he should not die. *Could* she have been wrong about him all this time? Or was she wrong about him now?

She could not leave this place without knowing the answer.

And so it was that, with a weakness in her knees and a tremor in her chest, Tessa retraced her steps to the massive carved doors of the master's chamber precisely one hour later. She stood for a moment, trying to breathe steadily, trying to gather her courage, and knocked.

His muffled shout bade her enter.

He was stretched out upon the divan in a sunny corner of the room, surrounded by stacked platters that held little more than scraps of bone and crusts of bread. A jug of new wine from his own vineyards—which were well known to be among the most prestigious in France—sat half empty at his elbow, and he refilled his glass with a flourish as she entered. How he could have consumed so much food in the short time Tessa had been gone was beyond her ability to comprehend, but it seemed to have had a beneficial effect—both on his well-being and on his disposition.

In the hour since she had left him, the blood had been scrubbed from the wallpaper—although when she looked closely she could detect the faintest of stains—the bed had been changed, the carpets had been swept. The draperies were drawn back and late-morning sun spilled through the tall windows, illuminating the gilded mirrors and deep-toned masterpieces, sparkling off the teardrop lamps and chandeliers. The transformation was amazing, but no more so than was the miraculous recovery of the werewolf she had tried to kill.

He wore gray flannel trousers topped by a silk dressing gown which was a rich blue color only a shade darker than his eyes. An ivory ascot was cavalierly wrapped around his neck and its folds tucked into the dressing gown. His lustrous hair was brushed back over his shoulders and tied loosely there; his color was good, his eyes bright and alert. Beside him stood Gault, attired in a peacock green jacket and trousers and a magenta shirt, his arms folded across his chest, his black eyes glinting wickedly.

Alexander beckoned her over with the hand that held the wineglass, an amused expression on his face.

"And so you have returned," he observed. "Gault and I had a wager. I won. Will you have some wine?"

Tessa stood with her shoulders straight and her hands folded properly before her, determined to make a good show of it no matter what her fate. She deliberately did not look at Gault.

Alexander had spoken to her in French, so she replied in kind. "Thank you, no," she said. "I'm glad you won your wager, though."

He glanced up at her with dry skepticism, sipping his wine. "I'm given to understand you ordered Gault out last night. That I would have liked to see."

"You bolted the door against him," she explained. "I thought you didn't want him here."

Alexander scowled and shot a glance at his manservant, whose expression did not change, and whose gaze, it seemed, remained fixed upon Tessa with a particularly malicious intensity. "And have it known that I was taken in my sleep by a human—and a mere pup of a girl at that? I should think not."

Then he shrugged, his brows knitting in annoyance. "Not that I deserve any better. It was my own fault."

Tessa had had no idea what to expect when she entered his room, but his rather banal conversation was not among the possibilities. She was so disoriented that for a moment she could do nothing but stare.

He didn't *look* like a monster. But then, he never had.

He gestured to her abruptly, the irritation in his expression deepening as he commanded, "Sit down. You're making my neck hurt."

Now he spoke in English, and it was the second time he had switched languages since he'd begun speaking. Apparently he chose his language as casually as another man might choose a handkerchief, according to his whim.

Tessa glanced around and, seeing that every surface in the near vicinity was covered with empty plates, bowls and cups, crossed the room to fetch a little straight-backed chair with a blue velvet seat. She arranged it a few feet in front of him and sat down, once again folding her hands in her lap.

He watched with interest but when she was seated spoke not to her but to his valet. "Well, now, Gault, what do you think? We have before us a murderous little female and a damn poor one at that, who not only refuses to express any remorse for her act but actually dares to show her face in my chamber again after such an unspeakable crime. What shall we do with her?"

"Skin her," responded Gault immediately. "Hang her by her heels and cure her over a hickory fire."

Tessa paled and could not stop her gaze from darting to Gault in a terrified manner, which she immediately regretted. The malicious satisfaction on his face was enough to make her quickly shift her gaze back to Alexander, who had followed the brief exchange with lazy amusement.

"I don't know, Gault," he said. "That seems a bit severe. Perhaps we'll simply chain her in the cellar and let the rats do their work."

"A waste," replied Gault.

Alexander addressed her unexpectedly. "You are not in the least afraid of me, are you?"

Her stomach was quaking and her hands were sweating. She lied. "No." And then, when she saw the sharpening of his gaze, she added quickly, honestly, "At least—I don't think you will skin me or chain me in the cellar."

"Why not?"

Tessa drew a steadying breath and tried as unobtrusively as possible to blot her wet palms on her pinafore. Her heartbeat was loud in her own ears, but gradually calmed its terrified rhythm. "My life was yours last night," she said, meeting his eyes, "and you chose not to take it."

His expression remained unmoved. "Perhaps by the light of day I've reconsidered."

"Skin her," advised Gault.

Alexander held out his glass for a refill, keeping his thoughtful, assessive gaze fixed upon Tessa. "I don't know," he said to Gault as the latter splashed red wine into his glass. "Perhaps I will keep her around."

"For what possible reason?" Gault gave a plausible demonstration of outrage, withdrawing the bottle.

"My own amusement," snapped Alexander. "Do I need another reason?"

Gault lowered his eyes.

Alexander sipped his wine, his expression reflective. "Perhaps I will keep her as a pet, and educate her."

Gault snorted. "A futile exercise. I doubt she's educable."

Alexander raised his eyebrows. "Is that a wager?"

Gault looked her over skeptically. His gaze made Tessa's skin crawl. "What will you teach her?"

Alexander raised his glass again. "Marksmanship, for one thing."

Gault grinned. On his face, mirth was an evil thing.

Tessa gradually began to understand that her attempt on the master's life had been more of a joke to them than a genuine threat. Perhaps she should have been reassured, but in truth she found their amusement more frightening than anything else they might have done. What manner of creatures were these, and how little about them did she, in fact, know?

Alexander sprang to his feet, causing her to start involuntarily. He circled her chair, looking down upon her from his great height, and it was with considerable self-restraint that Tessa refused to crane her neck upward like a child in order to follow his movements. Her heart was pounding and a clamminess in her stomach was making her ill.

"So, my dear," he demanded abruptly, "what do you think? Shall I educate you, or have you for lunch?"

Tessa swallowed hard and pressed her hands together tightly in her lap to steady her voice. But she did not look up at him. "Pardon, monsieur, but I do not think you will eat me for lunch. And I already have a quite adequate education. I can read and write in two languages, and do ciphers, and play the piano passably well, and—"

"But you know nothing of us," Alexander interrupted sharply. "You have no idea what it is you tried to destroy—for I assume your intent was to kill me, not merely irritate me."

Tessa whispered involuntarily, and so softly it was barely above a breath, "I do."

Alexander stopped circling and snapped at her: "What?"

"She said, 'I do,'" supplied Gault.

"I know what she said," returned Alexander irritably. "I want to know what she meant."

Tessa took a deep breath. "I meant that I do know what you are."

"Do you indeed?" Alexander dropped back onto the divan, his eyes narrowing with mild surprise. "Then my task should be much easier." He leaned against the pillows and swung one foot up onto the surface. "Yes, Gault, I think she will be worth the trouble. I will keep her."

Gault said, "You will be sorry."

"No doubt." He gestured toward the clutter of dishes and empty glasses. "You may leave us."

Gault began to clear away the dishes.

"So tell me, *chérie*," Alexander said to Tessa, "what are you thinking now? Are you sorry for your crime? Do you speculate upon your fate? What punishment do you think I should exact for your perfidy?"

At last, Tessa gathered up her courage to meet his eyes. "I am exceedingly sorry for my crime," she said fervently, and was somewhat surprised to realize she spoke the exact truth. This only confused her more.

He inclined his head slightly, as though in approval. "And why are you sorry?"

She swallowed hard. She had no ready answer for this. "I've never, um, used a knife in that manner before. I found it—unpleasant."

His eyes fairly danced with laughter. "Is that so? May I offer that it was no more enjoyable from my point of view, either." Abruptly he sobered, and his voice was barely more than a growl. "You should have thought of that before you stabbed me, wench."

"I thought you were a monster," she replied miserably.

Gault murmured, "There are those who would not argue that point even now."

Alexander shot him a threatening look, then returned his attention to Tessa. His tone was severe. "Very well, you are sorry. Should that exempt you from punishment?"

Tessa made herself raise her gaze to his once again. "If I thought you would kill me for your revenge, I would not have come back. But I knew you would be . . . displeased."

Alexander tossed a look filled with challenge and amusement at

Gault as he passed with a tray filled with dishes. "You see? I told you she was bright."

Gault replied, "There is a difference between intellect and cunning, monsieur. You will rue the day."

Alexander turned back to her, his expression sanguine. "Yes, my dear, I am displeased. And you're right again—I probably won't eat you or kill you for it. But surely you don't expect me to just forget the incident."

Tessa took a deep breath, faced him bravely, and said, "I expect to be dismissed, monsieur."

For a moment he did not react at all. Then he gave a half-stifled grunt of laughter and raised his glass for a sip. "Did you hear that, Gault? A servant tries to kill her employer and she expects to be dismissed. Yes, I would agree that's a reasonable expectation, wouldn't you?"

"And then we will skin her, n'est-ce pas?"

Alexander smiled, watching Tessa while he sipped his wine. "I'm thinking it over."

In a moment Gault finished stacking the dishes onto a cart and left the room. Alexander must have seen the tension drain from her shoulders and arms when Gault was gone, because it wasn't until then that he chose to speak.

"You seem unsurprised by what you've experienced," he observed.

Tessa's nerves were worn raw by Gault's gibes and Alexander's indifferent cruelty, and she still could not venture a guess as to what her eventual fate might be. Anxiety and frustration were her courage, and without intending to speak at all she retorted, "As do you, monsieur!"

He lifted an eyebrow. "Thank you. While I must admit being stabbed in the chest with a kitchen knife is not a common occurrence in my experience, I like to think I've taken it with some aplomb. You, on the other hand, cannot claim to witness every day such as you've seen these past hours."

Tessa's curiosity could not be contained another moment. "Why didn't you die?" she blurted out.

Again an eyebrow twitched expressively. "Do I detect a hint of bitterness in the question?"

"No, please, I only . . ." But when she saw the twinkle in his eyes she drew a breath, composed herself, straightened her shoulders and continued. "I only meant that your attitude has been . . . cavalier since you recovered. It was as though you knew you couldn't be harmed. Is it true, then? Are you—are such as you—invincible?"

"Well, if I were not, I would be a fool to tell the woman who just tried to kill me, wouldn't I?"

He regarded her thoughtfully for a moment, and under his gaze she felt vulnerable, naked, yet at the same time oddly empowered, as though the mere fact of his regard gave her importance. And then, abruptly, he said, "*Alors, chérie,* enough sparring. You intrigue me. I will answer your question if you will answer mine."

Tessa had no idea which question he referred to, but she nodded cautiously anyway.

He said, "I am not invincible. Your aim was bad, that's all. We have rapid recuperative powers, but that marvellous nonsense that mythology loves to bandy about—the silver bullet, the stake through the heart—it is, alas, mere romance. If I make light of the incident, it's only because my life was never in any real danger . . . unless, of course, you consider the very real possibility that I might have died of embarrassment. You bested me, and that's humiliating. And personally unforgivable, of course. Now, satisfy *my* curiosity. You said you knew what I was. What is it exactly that you know, and how did you come to know it?"

Tessa wet her lips, and for a moment—no more—debated the truth in her head. She decided upon a compromise, and gave her answer in part, cautiously. "I have heard tales of such creatures as yourself, and I've believed them in my heart. I was not surprised to know these tales were true. But to believe the stories, and to see with one's own eyes what I have seen . . ." She struggled with the words, pressing one clenched hand against her heart and summoning forth her best French. "Such a wonder makes surprise seem like a small thing indeed, and—

and the miracles of old but pale imitations of the marvel I've witnessed."

She stopped, her heart racing with remembered awe, and was afraid she had said too much. But his expression remained merely interested. "A partial truth, at any rate," he observed. And he must have seen the startled flash of guilt in her eyes, because he gave a negligent turn of his wrist and added, "You wonder how I know. I can hear the change in your heartbeat and smell the uneasiness on your skin. You may lie to me if you wish, but I'll always know it."

Then he demanded, "What causes you to believe now that I am not a monster? Why have you changed your mind?"

Tessa summoned all her courage and met his eyes boldly. "I have not said that I've changed my mind, monsieur. I want to believe, I wish I *could* believe, that you are not the monster I took you for. But—I must be cautious."

He looked startled for a moment and then let forth a shout of laughter. "You are the most peculiar girl!"

He circled her once again, glass in hand, examining her from head to foot. He resumed his seat at length, sipped his wine, and frowned. "What you have done is no minor thing and I don't want you to take it lightly. Never in my days have I been so offended, and by a perfect stranger to whom I've done no harm. I should probably be a great deal angrier with you, but I can't put aside wondering how the devil you did it—and, perhaps more to the point, why."

Tessa was afraid when that question was answered her interview would be over, as would her chance to understand this wondrous, terrifying creature. So instead of replying, she inquired earnestly, "Why didn't you kill me when you had the chance? You had the knife in your hand, yet you tossed it aside. And later, when you stood over me . . . the hunger to kill was in your eyes. I could see it."

The brief narrowing of his eyes reflected surprise at her perception, and then a kind of regret, a reliving of the moment. "Yes," he murmured, "it was."

He made a dismissive gesture with his wrist. "We do not kill humans. It goes against our deepest moral code—and besides, it's a waste of energy. We don't use weapons, either. We never learned to, we never needed to, and you'll find none in this house—except those, of course," he added with another fierce frown, "that you invent."

"Then am I the only—that is, the others in this household, Gault and the rest, are they all—like you?"

"There is no one," he replied with a disdainful arch of his brow, "like me."

And just as she was about to sink limp with relief, he laughed.

"Many of my servants are human," he told her; "the senior staff is not—Gault, Poinceau, Mme. Crolliere, Lavalier, and others. It would be impossible to find humans capable of performing their jobs with the efficiency I demand. Humans, while amusing, are not very bright and are oftentimes lazy."

He seemed to enjoy watching for her reaction to his words. Tessa was far too overwhelmed with all that had happened—was still happening—to know whether she gave him one or not.

Once again the words flew out of her mouth before she stopped to think about them. "But—your servants. How can they *not* know what you are?"

Only when it was spoken did she realize how foolish and irrelevant the question was. Yet, rather than mocking her, he seemed to consider the matter, as if it were a subject with which he had never concerned himself before. "Perhaps they do," he decided with a shrug. "What difference can it make? They are servants."

The careless autocracy of the statement rankled, and she returned, "Then you won't mind if I tell them. Perhaps I'll tell the newspapers, too, and the Comtesse de Crele, who was your guest the other night, and the Prime Minister of England and anyone else I please!"

A spark of interest caught his eyes, although his expression remained mild and barely amused. "Tell whomever you wish," he invited. "Of course, then I'll have to cut out your tongue. As for the Comtesse . . ." He sipped his wine, watching her. "She will be somewhat difficult to impress since she, you see, is one of us."

Tessa simply stared at him for a moment. The comment about cutting out her tongue was lost in the revelation about the Comtesse.

"I knew about you," she said softly, and mostly to herself. "But . . . others . . ." She looked at him in bewilderment, feeling humble.

His smile was small and condescending. "So you *do* have something to learn after all."

Tessa was breathless with the scope of it all.

"Of course," he said, "I shouldn't want you to think I am entirely representative of all my species. I am far superior to most, you understand . . ." The sparkle in his eyes was full of charm and Tessa melted into it, as had no doubt many others before her. "But, to be perfectly honest, I have also been called indolent and reckless and . . ." He shrugged as he finished off the wine in his glass. "Outrageous. For which you may be grateful, by the way. If I were not somewhat outrageous I would probably be a great deal less kindly disposed toward you now. My tolerance toward humans is one of the things for which I am most frequently criticized, you see."

Tessa said earnestly, "I'm glad."

He regarded his empty glass briefly, then swung his feet to the floor. "And now, my curious little kitten, if I have answered all your questions sufficiently . . ." He cast a questioning look at her, and she nodded hesitantly. He stood and crossed the room, retrieving another bottle of wine and a dish of confections from a silver tray on the bureau. "Perhaps you will be good enough to answer one of mine. Why in the devil did you come at me with a knife? What can I have ever done to deserve such treatment? I don't even know you."

Although his tone was mild and his expression was pleasant, Tessa sensed the confusion behind the question, a touch of what might even be considered hurt. It was the insult that concerned him more than the assault, the reason more than the result.

Tessa's shoulders tensed, and the words dried up in her throat. She had known the moment was coming, but she was not prepared to deal with it. She did not want to give him the answer he sought; she did not even want to think about it, for despite all else, this one thing had not changed.

Still, the truth was there and she had to say it. If for no other reason, she owed that to the man whose death she had sought to avenge; she owed it to herself.

She spoke in a clear steady tone, watching him carefully, trying to make herself understand now what she had never thought to question in all these years. "You killed my father."

"What?" Outrage sharpened his features and he snatched away the dish of candies he had been about to offer her, tossing it carelessly onto a marble-topped table. The dish shattered, and glass and chocolate showered like sparkling confetti across the floor. "That is a pernicious lie! I've never killed a human in my life! Not," he added, frowning with brief remembrance as he filled his glass, "that I haven't been tempted to dispatch a few."

He tasted the wine, seemed to find it satisfactory, and paused for a moment to let its flavor do its soothing work upon his temper. He crossed the room for another dish of candies, selected a marzipan, and appeared to enjoy that taste in a similar fashion.

In a moment, his good humor apparently restored, he returned to the sofa and arranged himself upon it, crossing one knee upon the other and stretching out an arm across the cushioned back. He regarded her with little more than casual interest now.

"Who was this father of yours that I am supposed to have killed?" he inquired.

Tessa pressed her fingers together in her lap. "His name," she said, "was Stephen LeGuerre."

His face went very still. His eyes appeared to darken with the slow dilation of his pupils as he looked at her. The wineglass, half raised to his lips, did not move.

"Stephen?" he said in a near whisper. "You're Stephen's daughter?"

He moved suddenly and with the swiftness of a panther, so that she couldn't have escaped him if she wished and she had no time to decide if she should try. He was bending over her, her face grasped tightly in his steely fingers, and with the pressure of his hands he pulled her to her feet. His eyes were urgent, scanning her every feature as though the only thing of importance in the world was that he should commit her face to memory—or find, perhaps, in his own memory a face that matched. His grip was strong and would surely leave red marks on her skin; his breath came quick and hot. The terror that went through her was not for her own personal safety—she was far beyond that—but an instinctive, primal reaction to being that near to a creature so magnificent, of being held in his grip, of being at his mercy. She could not catch her breath, and her chest ached with trying.

Finally those iron fingers relaxed; a softening came into his eyes. "Yes." The whispered word was like a caress as it floated across her skin. His gaze, moving over her, was gentle, almost wondering. "You are Stephen's daughter. I see it now."

He passed his hand lightly over her hair, memorizing by touch as he had by sight a moment ago, and danced his fingertips over the puffy marks his grip had made on her skin. His gaze was far away and his smile was filled with sorrow, rich with pleasure. "Stephen LeGuerre," he said softly, "was the first human I ever loved."

He retrieved his wineglass and stood for a long moment with his back to her, staring into it, silent and lost to her. He turned abruptly, his eyes alight with memory. "We were boyhood friends, did you know that? His father was a vintner on my uncle Gerrard's estate in Bordeaux, where I was sent to learn the trade. Stephen's father was a skilled man, with brown gnarled fingers that always reminded me of the vines he worked, and he was very bright, which was why Uncle Gerrard employed him . . . When Stephen grew older and completed university, he proved to be even brighter, and set to work exporting our wine to England and the United States. He made a good deal of money, I believe. Stephen and I, we were inseparable almost from the beginning. I was very serious in my youth, though you may not credit it now"—his eyes twinkled briefly with fond remembrance—"and he taught me to laugh. He reminded me not to be so pompous. He taught me all that I know about humans . . . about trust . . . about friendship."

With the last his smile faded slowly and the twinkle in his eye was driven away by shadows. He lowered his gaze once again to his wineglass, and Tessa's heart caught in her chest with a sudden ache—for the memories she could not share, for the father who had been taken from her too soon, for the surprising tenderness of this creature who mourned him as she did . . . and who was his murderer.

In a moment he looked at her again, though this time his smile seemed wry and forced. "So he told you of me, did he? His daughter. He spoke of you often, and his great affection for you gave me cause to doubt all the things we have been taught about the way humans regard their young. He mated with an Englishwoman, I recall that, but I think after a time the match proved to be less perfect than he had hoped . . . She did not like living in France, I think, and he did not like living with her."

His lips quirked a little with amusement, and then he seemed to recall himself. "I beg your pardon. I hope I haven't offended. Your mother—she is well?"

Such unexpected courtesy took Tessa aback, and she had no chance to dissemble. She thought briefly of her mother, a small dried-up woman who had seemed withered by the winds of life, constantly thirsting for what she could not have. Even as a child Tessa had wondered how such a humorless shell of a woman could ever have married a bright spirit like her father. Now, of course, she realized that her mother had once been a beautiful girl, and thought it was a shame her father had been unable to see the bitter soul behind those pretty eyes. She knew without asking—had always known—that her father would not have shared the secret of the loup-garou with his wife.

And she wondered what her mother would think if she could see her now.

"No, you're right," Tessa said. "She hated living in France and returned to Cornwall after—after we received word. I had just turned ten. For the rest of her life I heard nothing but how she despised you, and blamed you for taking my father from us. She was jealous, I think, of the time he spent with you, and always had been. She died last year a bitter woman, and I'm not sure she was ever happy. As soon as I could I came here, to France."

He nodded. "Then you are an orphan, and I am sorry." His eyes quickened with interest. "What did he tell you of me, your father?"

Tessa pressed her hands together tightly. It was difficult to speak of, even now. Especially now. "He used to set me on his knee in the nursery when I would awake crying in the dark and he would stroke my hair and whisper in my ear fantastical tales of his adventures with a man who could turn himself into a wolf at will. And oh, how glorious he made those adventures sound! The way the sun lit upon the spires and minarets of ancient lands—"

"Yes!" he cried excitedly. "We did that. We set off by train and by boat to see Egypt on his twenty-first year!"

"And how a bear once stalked him in the great North Woods, and how his friend Alexander savagely fought it off—"

"Ha!" exclaimed Alexander, laughing. "That is a lie! We both took off like scalded cats and didn't stop running until we'd seen the border of Germany."

"He told me," said Tessa, "how this creature, this marvelous creature who could take the form of wolf or man, could hear whispers behind closed doors half a province away, how he could tell by the smell where a man had been and with whom and what he had done, though it all might have occurred a week ago . . . how he could speak any language without a trace of an accent upon hearing it once, and memorize entire symphonies by merely glancing at the notes and quote the philosophers and perform complex mathematical and scientific operations in mere seconds. He told me you were strong, strong enough to lift a building off its foundation . . ."

Alexander grimaced. "An exaggeration. Pound for pound, we are no more than five times stronger than the average human male."

Tessa nodded. "And that you can see in the dark, and run as fast as a train, and . . ." Her brows knit faintly as the memory came back to her, a recollection she had willingly ignored all these years past. "That you were kind. That you were . . ." She struggled over the word. "Civilized." Tessa looked up at him. "He said you were the most civilized man he had ever met."

The straight line of Alexander's jaw was clearly visible, his expression set. His voice took on a slight huskiness when he demanded, "Is that all?"

Tessa shook her head. "He told me . . ." Her hand crept to her throat, touching the pain of memory that seemed to be lodged there, and her gaze lost focus as she looked back in time. "He used to hold me in his arms, and his eyes would grow bright, as though lit by an inner fire, and he would say to me, 'Tessa, never fear the unknown, the unbelievable, the miraculous. For these are God's ways of telling us there is hope . . .' He loved you, Alexander Devoncroix," she said thickly, looking up at him again. "And for this he died."

The agony in his eyes was something she had never seen before, incomparable in man or beast. He demanded hoarsely, "Who accuses me thus? Who told you this perfidy?"

"He went away with you!" she cried. "He was killed by a wolf, his body torn to shreds on the American plains! My mother told me this, but I knew the truth she did not—that *you* were the wolf! That you, the creature who could change his form at will, the friend my father treasured so—that you had betrayed him in the end and, in the form of a wolf, had killed him! You deceived my father into believing that you were civilized and for a time I believed it, too, but it was all a monstrous lie. You are evil. From the beginning of time we've known that; even the Church teaches us so. You are the spawn of the devil, snatching babies from their cradles and devouring them whole, slaughtering careless travellers on the highway in the dark of night, terrorizing the countryside—everyone has heard the stories!"

He regarded her with a mixture of outrage and amusement. "What utter nonsense!"

"Of course, most people regard these stories as mere fairy tales," she continued breathlessly, "but I knew differently. I *knew* what you were. And when I heard how my father died—my father, who trusted a monster!—what was I to believe except the obvious?"

Slowly, his eyes closed. The anguish on his face was exquisite, and it was a long, slow passage of time before he could bring it under control. "Tessa," he said at last, lowly, "I did not kill your father. I did my best to save him."

The sound of her own heart, pulsing strong in her ears, was all that filled the room. And then Alexander began to speak.

"It was the last of our great adventures," he said, his voice soft with remembrance. "We crossed the ocean, we saw the sights. High in the mountain passes of a place called Montana, America, we walked the wilderness, we talked our dreams, we stared long into the moon on nights so clear they practically melted on the tongue." He drew in a slow deep breath, tasting it, making Tessa taste it.

In a moment he resumed, his tone controlled, almost easy. "We saw wolves, more than once, and admired them. But wolves, as you no doubt know, are far too efficient a species to attack armed humans, such as Stephen, or loups-garous, such as I, who could have dispatched them in an instant. They left us well alone, as did we them.

"In fact," he continued flatly, and he took a drink from his glass, "it was a pack of wild dogs, left behind by Indians, or perhaps the remnants of some cattle drive or abandoned white settlement, that attacked our camp one twilight for the venison Stephen was dressing. I killed two of them, snapped their spines, and I bear the teeth marks of another on my flank. But I was too late to save Stephen."

The room was heavy with the simple finality of that statement; the air was thick with it. Time itself seemed to recoil in helpless horror over the futility of it, echoing backward into nothing.

And then, abruptly, there was a sound. Sharp, high, tinkling, the stem of his wineglass snapped between Alexander's fingers and the bowl shattered on the floor. Wine pooled like blood on the polished boards and spread to stain the fringes of the carpet.

Alexander's face contorted with sudden ferocity, and he flung the useless stem of the wineglass against the opposite wall. "I am strong!" he cried. "Man and beast, they bow to me! I and my kind have ruled the earth for thousands upon thousands of years—and yet I could not save Stephen. He died uselessly, foolishly, upon the forgotten plains of wild America, at the mercy of dogs, and *I could not save him!*"

Tears were streaming down Tessa's cheeks; sobs, silent and painful, racked her chest. Her grief was for Stephen, the father she had loved all her life but had begun to know only in these last minutes. She grieved for herself, the child she had been and the woman she was now, the years wasted in hatred and bitterness, the dreams denied her, the lies she had believed and the truths she had forgotten. But oddly, most poignantly, her tears were for Alexander, for the pain he showed so shamelessly, the vulnerability he did not try to hide.

In his eyes were sorrow and turmoil. In her heart was the same.

Hesitantly, trembling a little with tears and uncertainty, Tessa reached out a hand to him. Alexander took two steps toward her and sank to his knees, embracing her, burying his face in her skirts. His shoulders quaked. "Tessa," he whispered, "I am sorry. For both of us . . . I am sorry."

She had wanted to believe he was not a monster. So desperately had she wanted to believe the tales of her childhood, given to her by her father. Now . . . she could.

She lowered herself to his level, she wrapped her arms around him, and together they grieved.

And so it was that Tessa LeGuerre, aspiring murderess, and Alexander Devoncroix, loup-garou, came together in a bond that would change their lives, and forever affect the destiny of both their peoples.

Four

THE WORLD THAT OPENED UP FOR TESSA WAS BOTH INCREDIBLE AND IN-
evitable; astonishing and yet wholly natural. If she was aware of the
fact that she was among only the very rarest of humans who were
privileged to know this world, she did not dwell upon it. She was far
too busy absorbing and immersing herself in everything that world
had to offer.

"You are in my care now," Alexander told her. "Stephen would
have wanted it that way. But that does not mean you are allowed to
become a lazy girl. I said I would educate you and I will."

"What will I learn?" she asked him, for already she knew the futility
of pointing out the obvious—that she was sufficiently educated for her
station in life—when he had made up his mind.

"Everything."

He removed her from the attic dormitory and gave her a room of
her own on the second floor. He bought her books and pretty frocks,
and he referred to her as "his ward." His human friends thought she

was his mistress, which Tessa thought was very fashionable and to which she found no reason to object. What the other loups-garous thought she did not care to examine too closely.

She was endlessly fascinated with trying to discern which among his staff, houseguests and acquaintances were loup-garou, and one thing she learned very quickly was that each was as different from the other as was any group of Frenchmen or Englishmen, or any humans at all. This astonished her, as though such extraordinary creatures should immediately be identifiable by a halo of light or a displacement of air when they moved. Some, like Alexander, who was impressive in appearance and commanding in presence, were easily identifiable by their simple magnificence. In others, Tessa learned, that magnificence was a bit more subtle.

Crolliere, the dour-faced housekeeper, was stern and humorless—although Alexander insisted that none of his species was completely without humor, that being one of their most distinguishing characteristics and certainly demonstrative of their intellectual superiority. Poinceau was brilliant and efficient and a master of all that was correct. Gault was cruel and shrewd and nimble of mind and body. Lavalier, the chef, was eccentric and flamboyant but nonetheless a genius in his trade. And that, then, was the first thing Tessa learned to identify about them all: a certain genius, whether it be for their work or in other matters, a quickness, a facility and a subtle power over their environment that set them apart from all others. The second thing she learned they all had in common was an unmistakable—although often politely disguised—contempt for her.

These two characteristics in combination—their inarguable sense of mastery and their disdain for inferiors—made Tessa uneasy around them long before she understood the cause. She wondered how many humans in their everyday dealings with these creatures sensed the same and could not quite explain why they were uncomfortable in their presence. When she mentioned the same to Alexander he was amused by her observation, for he almost always regarded her insights with the same indulgent approval with which one might encourage a precocious child.

"*Très bien, chérie,* you have discovered our secret." He had fallen into the habit of speaking to her in a mixture of French and English, switching back and forth from one language to the other with a dizzying speed. He claimed he did it to sharpen her language skills and her auditory acuity, but Tessa thought he did it as merely another subtle reminder of his innate superiority.

His eyes twinkled as he framed his declaration in the air with his upraised hands. "Humans, *attention*: a guide to identifying *les loups-garous* on the street. They are smarter than you and they make your skin crawl. Apply yourself to something more useful, *petit chou*," he advised. "For example, of the three Greek philosophers to address the nature of social reform, which one was werewolf?"

Werewolves, she had discovered, were exceedingly fond of philosophy and had an endless store of quotations and debates always at the ready. Tessa's interest in the subject, however, was limited, and she replied irritably, "I don't know and I don't want to know, and I'm not going to help you win your silly bet with Gault. Perhaps among your kind it is fashionable to fill your head with useless information, but if you ask me, it's far more valuable to know how to roast a mutton than to name its genus and species!"

He frowned at her. "I did not ask you about mutton, I asked you about philosophers. And since you obviously don't know, I shall tell you the answer, and remember it well: all of them!"

She never knew when he was teasing, for his sense of humor was as bizarre as it was unpredictable. She informed him, with a superior arch of her brow which was an unconscious imitation of a characteristic expression of his, "What I meant regarding the mutton, monsieur, was that from my point of view it is much more useful to be able to recognize and understand the werewolf than to quote him."

He smiled at her kindly. "I know what you meant, *chérie*. And while it is possible that you may one day be able to recognize every werewolf you meet, you will, I assure you, never understand us."

Nonetheless, Tessa resolved to try. And while Alexander continued to press his own concept of a suitable education upon her, and she occasionally made a halfhearted attempt to cooperate, the only subject she was really interested in studying was the loup-garou. And on that topic she was insatiable.

Though Tessa's adjustment to her new circumstances was by no means effortless or uneventful, never once did she question the rightness of her being there, and soon she could not imagine any other life. While Alexander sometimes accused her of being quarrelsome and opinionated and often pretended to be out of temper with her, he never denied her anything and was in most ways an indulgent guardian and a tender friend. And Tessa, who occasionally still awoke in the morning wondering why she did not flee this unnatural place with all possible speed, had only to hear his voice in the hall or catch a glimpse of him in passing to remember why. Because of the werewolf who had wept in her arms for a lost friend; because of the creature who was too civilized to take his revenge upon one who had tried to murder him in his sleep. Because having seen what she had seen and knowing what she now knew, she had no life but this one, and no other place in the world she would ever belong except by his side.

And so over the weeks that followed, as Tessa set to work carving out a niche for herself in this strange new place, a subtle shift of power occurred in the Devoncroix household which its master neither approved nor discouraged. If he complained about the quality of the meat at dinner, it was Tessa who could be found lecturing the butcher before the chef could even get to him. If his collar was not stiff enough or a coat button was sewn on loosely, it was Tessa who took the matter up in no uncertain terms with the laundress. And when he began making vague plans for a midwinter ball, Tessa fell into place without hesitation and assigned herself responsibility for the arrangements from beginning to end.

Resentment simmered among the senior staff, for the success of a household was completely dependent upon its strict hierarchal system, and this was something Tessa was coming dangerously close to violating. No one dared challenge her directly, however, because it was clear she had become a favorite and they could smell Alexander's protection upon her. Eventually, however, the situation was brought to Alexander's attention and he was forced to speak to Tessa about it.

"In a well-run household—or society, for that matter—everyone has a place and functions within it," he told her sternly. "Duties are assigned according to status. You have no status, you have no duties, you therefore have no right to interfere with the functioning of those who do."

She listened politely and then said, "That's perfectly feudal."

He nodded. "Precisely. A system that has worked for us very well for tens of thousands of years."

"But which *we* abandoned centuries ago!"

"*Et voilà!* You see which is the superior species today."

"I hardly see how that can be so. This is 1897 and you are still living in the Middle Ages."

"The Middle Ages have much to commend them," Alexander returned, frowning darkly to hide his growing mirth. "There were fewer humans alive then."

Finally, however, Alexander admitted she did require purposeful employment, and chambermaid would not quite suit. As a matter of simple expediency, he named her his personal secretary and officially put her in charge of plans for his upcoming winter ball, promoting the werewolf who once held that position to a clerical station in one of his banks. Tessa was persuaded to deal with his staff in a more respectful manner, and his staff was persuaded to regard Tessa with more tolerance, and Alexander, to whom conflict of even the most minor sort was a dreadful inconvenience, was able to put the matter behind him.

Only Gault was less than pleased with the solution. "Humans," he grumbled darkly, "they're nothing but trouble, all of them. And you, my fine sir, are far too gullible to their wiles. They will be your downfall someday."

To which Alexander only laughed. "Allow me my foibles and poor amusements, if you will, old friend. Life is dull enough already. It would be beyond bearing if I were perfect, *n'est-ce pas?*"

Though he didn't always show it, Alexander was delighted with the new human in the house; it was difficult to be completely indifferent to one who regarded him with such rapt attention and displayed such undisguised fascination with every detail of his life. Tessa latched on to him like a shadow in bright sunlight, bombarding him with endless questions, watching his every movement with big, all-seeing eyes, studying and absorbing each syllable he uttered as if it were the very nectar of life itself. She was at times as vexatious as a small puppy, bounding eagerly from one subject to the next and always underfoot, but she was equally as difficult to harden one's heart against. And she was so very much like her father in so many ways. Alexander had not realized before how much he had missed his friend, and it was good to have a young human about again.

"I don't know what to call you," she remarked to him one morning as she helped him curry his horse. This was a job he was loath to turn over to the grooms, finding it pleasurable in itself, and Tessa had immediately thrown herself into the task with an enthusiasm to match his own.

"'Monsieur' will do nicely," he returned cheerfully, gliding the brush along the horse's flanks with long smooth strokes. "*Mon liege* even better."

"No, I mean . . . what is it that you call yourselves, you creatures of two forms?"

That made him laugh, as she so often did. He kissed his fingers to the air and declared, "Magnificent, that is what we call ourselves! Glorious, dazzling, splendid, *formidable* . . ."

But then, because her question was an earnest one and because he found her determination to learn as much about his species as possible endearing, he eventually explained, "Every human language has a word for what we are, but each word is capable of describing us only in part. Our own language is not spoken with the tongue and is understood only in wolf form—by scent and posture and sounds from the throat, and what we call ourselves is something no human can ever know. There is no word for it. So you see why we have no argument with whatever word you choose—'loup-garou,' 'werewolf'— they have no meaning to us, but seem to serve your purpose."

She then wanted to know which of his acquaintances were werewolf and which were not; and among those who were, which were coming to his ball, and how might she tell the difference? He threw up his hands in exasperation.

Over the next few days Tessa learned to distinguish some werewolves by the brilliance of their eyes, the fineness of their bone structure, and the length and luxuriousness of their hair, which Alexander confirmed grew so exceedingly fast as to make it almost impossible to keep barbered. She learned of the werewolf's great love of music and spectacle, and of the large numbers of them who made their fortunes in the arts. Occasionally Alexander would drop the name of a famous actor who was werewolf, or a diva of the opera or a violinist who caused great crowds to weep whenever he played. And although Tessa knew Alexander took pleasure in teasing her about such matters, on this she did not doubt him.

They loved to eat and were, even the least of them, grand gourmets, yet as a species they were exceptionally lean and energetic. Their sense of smell was so highly refined that special soaps were required by the laundresses to remove latent odors from clothing which humans would never detect but which werewolves found unbearably offensive. Their vision, though extraordinary by human standards, was their weakest point, and nearsightedness was often a problem—although, Tessa was given to understand, even the least accomplished werewolf could see better in the dark than could the average human in clear daylight.

Though Alexander—and, to a lesser extent, Poinceau, Crolliere and even Gault—teased her with suggestions, Tessa never gained a clear idea as to how many of their kind there were or where they might be found. And she discovered no easy or foolproof way to distinguish them in a crowd.

With each passing day Tessa put together bits and pieces of the truth about these strange creatures among whom she lived, but the complete picture continued to elude her. Still, it was weeks before she could ask the one question that had been grinding at her mind from the beginning.

Alexander had taken her walking along the Seine. It was a clear sunny day and just cold enough for Tessa to enjoy promenading in her new fur-trimmed coat and matching hat. As always, she loved being seen with Alexander, the beautiful man of such exceptional presence that he caused heads to turn, both male and female, wherever he went. She flattered herself to think he liked being seen with her as well, because he seemed to enjoy taking her about, whether in his open carriage or mounted on the sleek bay mare which contrasted so nicely with his favorite chestnut, or sometimes in his flashy, noisy motorcar. It had occurred to her that he liked taking her out for the same reason he liked driving the motorcar on the streets of Paris: because it created a stir.

They made a striking couple, the tall, long-haired werewolf and the small brunette human, and they attracted their fair share of attention from others who had chosen this fine day to stroll the promenade and to see and be seen. For a time she played her game of trying to identify which of those to whom Alexander bowed and raised his hat were werewolf and which were human, but he seemed determined to confound her.

"No, *chérie*, it is not the length of the hair or the structure of the cheekbones or whether one is taller than one's human counterpart. It is purely a matter of genetic superiority, which you cannot change and surely will never be able to detect. And don't put your brows together that way—it spoils the look of your face."

She scowled anyway, watching as he swept off his top hat and made a low bow to a pair of stylishly dressed ladies passing in an open carriage. "You are wrong, monsieur," she told him ungraciously. "I can very easily tell which of your acquaintances are werewolf and which are human by the depth of your bow. Those two, for example, are obviously of your own kind or you wouldn't be making such a spectacle of yourself."

"Ha." His eyes twinkled as he pulled his gaze away from the departing ladies, who put their heads together and hid their smiles behind pearl-buttoned hands. "Wrong again. That was the Marchioness de Tourideau and her sister the duchess, both quite charming and, sadly, human. But they do give excellent parties."

Tessa's frown only deepened with irritation. "Well, then, perhaps you will be good enough to tell me the secret. How may I know them?"

He grinned. "You have no need to know them, *chérie*. Be assured, they will always know *you*."

Tessa's expression became thoughtful. "Have you ever been in love with a human?"

He laughed. "What astonishing notions are floating about in that pretty head of yours today! Next time, we will buy you a bonnet with more ribbons; then you will not have to think so hard!"

Tessa stopped and, dropping his arm, turned to face him. The wind rising from the river ruffled her skirts and stretched its chill fingers over the spot where her calfskin boots ended and the silk stockings began. "Were you and my father lovers?" she inquired.

He grimaced a little as he glanced down at her. "*Chérie*, speak in English. Your accent is making my ears hurt."

She repeated the question in English. She knew he could sense her tension, could hear it in her voice, in the beat of her heart and even in the movement of her blood through her veins; it was a question that had vexed her too long in silence. But he made her wait another thoughtful, inscrutable minute before he answered, and then the answer was not at all what she might have wished.

He nodded across the way to a passing couple, lifting his hat to the lady. His gaze returned to Tessa's eyes, narrowed slightly against the reflected light of the late-afternoon sun but otherwise showing no change of expression whatsoever.

He commented mildly, "What a very peculiar question. I should think after living among us for these weeks you might have acquired some sophistication, but I'm beginning to fear that's a vain aspiration. I loved your father, yes. But that's not what you want to know, is it? You want to know whether we had sex together, and I don't think I will answer you. You're far too curious as it is."

She retorted, "You're always saying curiosity is a virtue."

"In a werewolf. In a human it is merely annoying."

"You won't make me less curious by refusing to answer my questions."

He looked at her for a moment, his expression unreadable. Then he murmured, in English, "Just so."

His features gentled as he explained. "*Chérie*, we do not make love with humans, not in the way you mean. Although there are certain pleasures we can share, those pleasures are no more meaningful to us than a good meal or a warm bath. Since there can never be a mating between the species, intercourse between us would be absurd and, frankly, a little repugnant. You can surely understand that."

Tessa did not understand, not completely, and her curiosity, far from being satisfied, was only intensified. She was both relieved and strangely disappointed. She said, "Do you find me repugnant, then?"

He laughed. "No, I find you impossible—and irresistible! Now stop with your incessant questions and prove yourself useful. Describe to me how the early works of Franz Schubert reflect the influence of Haydn and Mozart, and, given such influence, why he is referred to as the father of German lieder."

He took her fingers and again tucked them securely beneath his arm, resuming their stroll. Tessa felt the cold air redden her nose, the sun warm on her cheeks, the thrill of his presence tingling in her skin. And it was very difficult to be annoyed with him. "I'm tired of your silly lessons. Why do I have to know these things?"

"So you can converse intelligently with me, of course."

"Why are you the one who decides what is intelligent conversation and what is not?"

He chuckled. "The answer to that should be obvious."

"I don't understand why you care so much about human poets and artists and musicians. They have nothing to do with you."

"I don't care about them. But I insist that you do." He stopped then, and turned to her, gazing into her eyes earnestly. "Once, long ago, our kind roamed the hills and burrowed in caves, and our poor mean lives consisted of nothing but hunting and sleeping, fighting and dying. And then we discovered this." He tapped his forehead. "No claws can threaten it, no teeth can devour it, no humans can hunt it down with metal sticks or confine it with iron chains. Our intellect. It is our strong-est weapon. Without it, we would have lived forever in the forest. Because of it, we went on to build the pyramids and the great canals, to invent the telegraph and the internal combustion engine and to look with our telescopes to the skies. We have thought great thoughts and sung great songs and created works of art that will endure long after your kind has disappeared from the face of the earth. We have created *civilization,* and have dragged you poor humans, more or less unwill-ingly and in utter ignorance, along with us. This is what makes the werewolf, *chérie,* not what is in the face or the bearing or the elegant clothes. What makes a werewolf is on the inside, and that is something you can never see. And it is precisely because you don't understand this that we will forever look down upon your kind with such great pity."

She regarded him with wide dark eyes. "You built the *pyramids?*"

He gave a sound that was half laughter, half grunt of exasperation, and he rolled his eyes to the sky. "*Mon Dieu!* My pearls are indeed cast before swine!"

She pouted prettily for a moment, put out of countenance by the comparison. Then she said, "If that's the case, and if I shall never be as smart as a werewolf, I don't understand why I should waste my time on German musicians."

For a moment longer he looked frustrated, and then he gave a re-signed shake of his head and laughed softly. He tucked her hand once again into the crook of his arm. "There, you see? A case in point! Every time it begins to look as though there may be hope for your race, some impudent young girl declines to waste her time with *Austrian* com-posers. How shall you ever improve the lot of mankind if you do not learn to build upon what has gone before? Shall we do everything for you?"

"Well, I'm tired of it all and I have no ambition to improve on anything at all. I don't want any more lessons."

"You have no choice."

"I could leave."

"Where would you go?"

"Somewhere I don't have to talk about Greek philosophers or dead composers."

He chucked her under the chin with a gloved finger, his eyes twinkling. "You won't leave, *chérie*. You're enchanted with me."

Enchanted, she thought, and then she couldn't help smiling. Yes, that was what she was. Enchanted.

Those were good times, those bright cold days of innocence and discovery, as Tessa blossomed beneath his tutelage and he took pleasure in exploring truth, nature and his own personal history through her wide and hungry eyes. But all too soon those lazy hours of ease and splendor came to an end, and winter was upon them.

It began, as far as Tessa was concerned, with a heavy black-bordered envelope in the morning post, although when she looked back upon events she realized the disruption of the household had really begun the evening before, when Alexander, missing dinner, had shut himself in his chambers and requested to be left undisturbed. Gault, Mme. Crolliere, Poinceau—all of them, she now realized, had been conspicuously absent since at least that time, and the house seemed to have been engulfed in a funereal pall long before the black-bordered envelope arrived.

She understood the black bordering, of course. She did not understand the crest in the corner, engraved in gold, which was a circle with one crescent shaded, the whole pierced through with an arrow. But instinctively she knew the news was bad, its source powerful. Neglecting the rest of the post, she took the envelope to Alexander's chambers. His prompt response to her knock suggested he had been waiting for her.

He was up and dressed, the remains of his breakfast neatly stacked upon an uncovered tray near the window. He sat at his desk, writing letters. He had completed quite a stack of them already.

Her heart was pounding with trepidation as she presented him the envelope. He took it without rising, and without expression he opened it. He removed a card, upon which was written a single word. Tessa strained to read it. *Sancerre.*

Calmly, still having spoken not a word, Alexander returned the card
to its envelope. He had a strange look about him, a wildness in his
eyes, a sharpness in his profile, and yet there was a stillness overall,
an almost forced self-constraint.

Tessa whispered, "I—I don't..." She cleared her throat. She
strengthened her voice, though not by much. "I know you are grieving.
But I don't know for whom."

Without looking at her, he said, "Sancerre. He was our pack leader.
He was old, his death was not unexpected. It is nonetheless a painful
thing, and the rituals must be observed."

Questions burned in her chest—what was a pack leader? Who was
this Sancerre and what did his death mean to Alexander? What were
the rituals and how were they observed? It was, however, to her credit
that she spoke not a word of them, and even lowered her eyes so that
Alexander would not see the vulgar curiosity there.

She said simply, "What can I do?"

He smiled at her then, and lifted his hand to caress her cheek. The
approval in his eyes was worth all that the silence cost her, a hundred
thousand questions unanswered.

"Tessa," he said gently, "I knew I could rely upon you."

Then his manner became brisk, and he turned his attention back to
his desk. "Our people will be gathering from across Europe to attend
the ceremony. Those who are prohibited by distance will commemo-
rate in their own way in their own place. These are my personal letters
of condolence to the family, which must be sent with the next post."

"But..." Her eyes widened as she understood the implication. "You
knew. Before the card came."

"Of course we knew. We always know. He was our leader." His
expression grew serious. "Tessa, I leave my house in your care tonight.
You must dismiss the human servants. Send them to their families and
their homes. Tell them to bar their doors and stay within until morning's light. And you will do the same. Stay inside, mourn the passing
of an era in the quietness of your own heart. Do not go abroad this
night. Do you promise me?"

The urgency in his eyes compelled her, not that she would ever consider refusing a command of his for any reason. She nodded slowly, solemnly, and said, "I promise."

She never knew for precisely which reason he had exacted that promise, nor did she know what took place under that evening's moon. But the City of Light was dark that night, and from somewhere deep within the countryside in the blackest hours before dawn there arose a cry, a howling, an ululation of anguish that gathered force as it lengthened and possessed the power to chill the human soul.

Some, awakening in a cold sweat in the dead of night, attributed it to the wind. But Tessa knew differently. Huddled deep beneath her coverlet in the vast, still emptiness of Alexander Devoncroix's house, she squeezed her eyes tightly shut, and she knew.

It was days before the household returned to a semblance of normalcy. During that time Tessa put all her skills to use to maintain order with a skeleton staff and was pleased by the fact that, by the time the senior staff began drifting in one by one, the smooth flow of the household was such that they might never have been gone. Not that any of them noticed, of course, nor that they would have commented upon the fact if they had.

Everyone, including Alexander, was busy; busier than they had ever been. Tessa learned that, in addition to the vineyards and an estate in Lyons that he owned, Alexander Devoncroix also managed controlling interests in several banks, both in Paris and beyond. The demise of the leader Sancerre had apparently caused disharmony and uneasiness in every sector, and Alexander was kept continually managing one crisis after another. Until now she had known him as a bon vivant and a roisterer, concerned only with personal pleasures and lavish comforts. She found this new side of him—decisive, energetic, commanding—both astonishing and admirable.

At one point he stopped her in the hall just long enough to say, "I hope the invitations for the ball haven't gone out, *chérie*. It would be inappropriate at this time, I'm afraid."

"Of course. But—"

He was gone without a word as to when he would return, and certainly with no indication of interest in rescheduling the ball.

Tessa had looked forward to the ball and was disappointed, but so many things of interest were going on around her that she could scarcely keep up with them all, and had little chance to regret what she'd missed. It was almost a week, in fact, before she had an opportunity to discuss with Alexander what, exactly, had transpired.

Before the upheaval, it had become their custom to share morning chocolate and plans for the day. Tessa would bring him the early post and he would go through it with wry comments about each sender; she would pelter him with questions and he would answer them until he ran out of patience; then he would assign her little chores to keep her occupied when he could not.

On the day that matters had at last calmed enough for them to resume this morning ritual, there was almost a week's worth of unanswered cards, notes and letters to be sorted through. They met in the sunny little sitting room off his bedchamber, he in his dressing gown and she in a soft cranberry wool skirt and shirtwaist with a white collar and cuffs that she had had made up only that week. This was the first opportunity she had had to wear it, and she hoped he would notice. He did not disappoint her.

"Very becoming, *chérie*," he exclaimed and made her twirl around to show him the cut and the fall of the skirt. "The color brings a glow to your cheeks. I quite approve."

She wanted to tell him that the glow was more likely due to his compliments than to the color of the shirtwaist, but knew he would only laugh. She sat down across from him at the little table and poured chocolate from a silver pot. He turned his attention to the morning papers, scanning each in turn, as was his custom. He read incredibly fast, and could often quote text after having glanced at it for no more than the blink of an eye.

She gave him a moment, then inquired, "All is well abroad now? With the, um, pack?"

"Difficult to say," he murmured, turning pages. "These things are unpredictable, so much history involved. Damned nuisance from my point of view, of course."

She took a breath. "Will you tell—what was it that took place that night when you and the others went away?"

He folded the paper and met her eyes sternly. "Some things," he replied, "are not to be known by humans. Ever."

Nothing in his tone or manner left room to pursue that subject. Tessa didn't try.

In a moment she said, "But if you have no leader, what will happen now?"

"We have a leader," he replied absently, scanning another paper. "The little Devoncroix queen will take her place, for as long as she is able to hold it."

Tessa gasped excitedly. "But *you*'re a Devoncroix! Does that mean—?"

He shook his head. "No, no, there is no relationship. A long time ago there was a struggle for succession and the Devoncroix won. Those families who wished to ingratiate themselves to the new ruling class changed their names to indicate their loyalty. We are nothing if not practical." He folded the paper and glanced at the basket of sweets the cook had prepared. "Is that plum cake?"

She served him a cake and presented him with a stack of invitations. "I will answer them if you like," she volunteered. "Just sort them according to Yes or No."

"My dear, how did I get along without you?"

"Do you know the new queen?"

"Hmm. Only to dance with."

"What's her name?"

"Elise. Elise Devoncroix."

"I don't know that name."

"You would if you'd lived in France instead of England these past ten years. She's at all the best parties during the season, never misses an opening night at the Opéra. Of course, she is in seclusion now. But perhaps I'll introduce you this spring."

"Will there be a coronation?" demanded Tessa eagerly. "A grand ball, a promenade—"

He chuckled, still sorting cards. "It's rather more complicated than that. The line of descent passes through the youngest, you see—providing the youngest is qualified to rule, of course. So, much like human monarchies, we know who will be our next leader as a matter of tradition. But it doesn't become official until the naming ceremony, at which time the old leader virtually steps down and turns the scepter, as it were, over to his successor. This Sancerre did some years ago. However, without the protection of the old ruler, the new ruler is always vulnerable to challenge until she—or he—chooses a mate, at which time there will be a coronation. It's a grand affair, too, lasts for days."

"Are humans allowed to attend?"

"No, *chérie*."

She was disappointed, and it showed in her tone. "I don't know what you need a queen for anyway. What is there for a ruler to do?"

He looked up, thoughtful for a moment. "Why, that's an interesting question," he observed, and seemed surprised by it. "In times of old, when the pack was small and lived in the wild, it was very important to have strong leadership, of course. But in practical terms today—in human terms, if you will—I can't think of anything of particular merit that the pack leader does. Still . . ."—and he smiled—"like your human monarchies, it is very important for us to have one.

" 'Yes,' " he said, handing her the stack of cards in his right hand, "and 'No.' " He gave her the ones in his left.

Tessa passed the letters over to him, thumbing curiously through the "yes" stack of invitations he had returned to her. "Which of these will be at the homes of loups-garous? Will the new queen attend any of them? May I?"

He didn't reply, which was not so very unusual. Patiently, she started to repeat herself, but he held up a hand for silence.

His face was very still as his eyes moved over—no doubt for the second time—the single sheet of paper in his hand. When he finished, there was a slight knotting in the muscle at the back corner of his jaw, but no other change of expression. And his voice was mild as he murmured, "*Alors.* I can't say this is completely unexpected. But no more is it welcome."

He refolded the letter carefully, but not before Tessa had seen the bold black signature at its end. *Denis Antonov.*

"Who is he?" she inquired. "What—"

"My brother," replied Alexander. The slightest sardonic edge colored his tone as he added, "He has asked me for a visit."

"But your names—"

"A long story." He indicated dismissal with a wave of his hand and got to his feet. "My dear, I'm afraid all those lovely invitations will have to be regrets. Find Gault, if you please, and send him to me at once. And, oh—there's a case of cognac in my cellar of which my brother is particularly fond; Poinceau will know the one. He must make arrangements to ship it out at once. Now, quickly, quickly, there's no time to waste and a hundred things to do."

Alexander left the following afternoon, having arranged to depart from Gare de l'Est on a train that departed within the hour. No amount of pleading, pouting or threats from Tessa would persuade him to allow her to accompany him.

"But where are you going?" she cried. "How long will you be gone? What am I to do with myself in all that time? What if you need me? How will you—"

He quieted her with a finger placed firmly across her lips. "*Mais, chérie,* how can you be so selfish? To whom would I entrust my household if you were to come with me? No, no, you must stay here, and take charge. I'll not travel easy until I know it is so."

She regarded him skeptically, particularly when she saw the twinkle come into his eyes as he glanced at Gault. But before she could voice another protest he turned to Poinceau, who was in actual fact in complete charge of the household staff and before whose quiet commands all others—even, on occasion, Tessa—bowed. He said in smooth, quiet, melodious French, "My old friend, this young female is the daughter of a man I have held close to my heart since childhood. She is without a family now, and has no protection but my own. She is my ward. I commend her to your safekeeping until I return."

This last he said clearly, so that all the servants assembled in the hall might hear. Poinceau, who had been at best indifferent to Tessa's fate since her arrival, looked at her steadily, turned his gaze to the master, and nodded. The vow was made. Others—Mme. Crolliere, for example, who had longed to put the impertinent little human in her place for weeks now and, perhaps, envisioned the master's absence as a perfect opportunity to assert her opinions—chafed under the restraint, but there was no doubt that compliance would be given, and without question, simply because he had commanded it.

In this way, Tessa had observed, the loups-garous were far more sensible than humans.

Still, as he turned to go, she caught his arm. "How can you do this?" she begged. "How can you leave me here alone?"

He looked at her with a mixture of affection and exasperation. "*Chérie*, you are the most aggravating, exciting, complicated, confusing and enchanting young female I have ever met. If for no other reason, I beg you would allow me leave to collect my breath!"

At her involuntary dimple, he smiled. "There. That is better."

He took her chin in his hands, as he had done the very first time they met. "I will have returned before you've scarce had time to miss me. Meanwhile, apply yourself to your studies and make me proud."

And then, with hardly any warning whatsoever, he bent down and kissed her tenderly on the lips. "Beware, *chérie*," he said softly, smiling down at her. "It is said that the kiss of a werewolf can make you mad."

Tessa did not answer. She did not speak again as she watched the last of his luggage being loaded onto the carriage, as he swung himself inside with a last wave of his hand to the assemblage, as she watched his carriage drive away. She stood at the door with her fingertips pressed oh so lightly to the place where his lips had rested, and she tasted his kiss far into the night.

PART THREE

Siberia

Winter, 1897

❦

Civilization is our only accomplishment.
—ALDRICH BAYLOR-LYNCHON, WEREWOLF 1643

Man is to be found in reason, God in the passions.
—G. C. LICHTENBERG, A HUMAN 1765

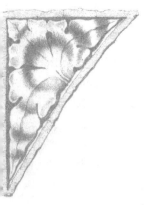

ALEXANDER

Five

I CAN PERHAPS BE FORGIVEN THE FACT THAT, ONCE OUT OF PARIS, I barely gave the human Tessa a backward thought. My mind was far too occupied with concerns about what lay ahead of me to dwell much upon what I had left behind—except perhaps, in brief regret: an eiderdown bed, opening night at the theater, the taste of chocolate on a crisp morning. There were moments, once I left Paris behind, when I wondered whether I might ever know any of those things again.

I travelled by rail in my private car across the misty fields and sooty cities of Europe, with only a handful of servants to assist me. There was my chef; a couple of boys to attend to the luggage; and Gault, who entertained me with card games, philosophy and his own brand of evil wit. I tried, as I was wont to do with most things in life, to make the journey as pleasant as possible, and I did my best to avoid dwelling upon what lay at its end. Gault did not ask foolish questions, which is why he was my most trusted personal servant. I knew very well why Denis had summoned me, and it was not something I wanted to discuss with anyone.

The politics of our race are a complex yet beautifully structured thing. In a time recalled now only in song, a vast pack roamed the ice-locked tundra of Siberia; many believe we are all descended from that original pack. What is known is that for many centuries—perhaps more than we can guess—the pack leadership was passed down through the family Antonov of Siberia. What life was like during those ancient times one shudders to speculate; suffice it to say that were-wolves had their Dark Ages, too, glimpses of which might be seen even now if one looks hard enough into the depths of human fairy tales. But we emerged into a renaissance of the spirit and a new understanding of the value of what we now call civilization; perhaps inevitably, the rebirth was not accomplished without conflict.

Some twelve hundred years ago, when the human population was greatly occupied with riding out in metal armor to conquer whatever was in its path, when the great cathedrals of Europe were mere piles of stones waiting to be shaped and polyphonic music was a concept only dimly grasped, there came the defining moment in werewolf history, one which is generally seen to represent a giant step forward into the abundance we now all enjoy. The Russian Antonovs, who had ruled through power and force for centuries uncounted, were overthrown by the French Devoncroix—who were then known as Devan, Devon, or Devox—through a combination of craftiness, cunning, and perseverance.

Unlike human jousts for power wherein thousands upon hundreds of thousands are maimed and killed in battle, werewolf contests are decided in a much more efficient and clear-cut manner. A leader who cannot defend himself certainly cannot be relied upon to protect the pack, so all that is required to assume power is to overthrow a single werewolf. By tradition, the challenge must be formal, the battle public, and death the outcome. The Devoncroix waited until a combination of fortune and timing favored him: the old and powerful leader broke his neck on an ice slick, leaving behind an adolescent heir who was easily defeated in the challenge. This display of wit and skill is something no werewolf can fail to admire, and the pack rallied behind the Devoncroix immediately.

It must be remembered that the Antonovs brought the pack through the most brutal periods in this earth's history and are, in fact, the only reason we all survived to take advantage of the more beneficent age ushered in by the leadership of the Devoncroix. Eventually the two lines intermarried, and many more simply adopted themselves into the Devoncroix family—which is why a full third of the pack bears the surname Devoncroix or a variation thereof—and the Antonovs were all but forgotten.

Certain of us have not forgotten, however. I am a direct descendant of the ruling Antonov who lost his throne to that long-ago Devoncroix, and my brother never allowed me to forget.

For twelve centuries the pack leadership remained unchallenged. Change for its own sake is not something we embrace, and no one had found serious cause to question the leadership of the Devoncroix in all this time. One could not fail to notice, however, certain similarities in the situation that arose with the last Antonov and the circumstances that presented themselves in 1897, with the death of Sancerre Devoncroix.

Though I was loath to do it, because I knew the vast, lonely and sometimes dangerous path that awaited me on the last leg of the trip, I left Gault and the others at the last rail stop, in St. Petersburg, from which place I would make my own way across the plains to Siberia. Because of our enhanced hearing, it is difficult to keep a secret from a werewolf, and there were certain things about Denis and his companions I did not want even Gault to know. It was therefore necessary that I meet my brother alone.

And so, after a day spent feasting my eyes upon the elegant, cosmopolitan sights and sounds of that most beautiful of cities, and gorging my belly on all its culinary delights—a practical necessity, considering what awaited me—I said a casual goodbye to my servants and struck off for the wilderness beneath a brilliant full moon.

Our ability to travel great distances in relatively short periods of time by changing from one form to another is, of course, one of the great advantages we hold over all other creatures on the globe. In human form we can take advantage of the technology which causes machines, rather than our bodies, to consume energy, which saves wear and tear on the latter. But in wolf form we can go where machines are unable and where humans dare not venture, where flying creatures nest and crawling ones burrow and where those who can't outrun us quickly become our fuel. We are virtually tireless in this form, and can run for days without stopping. There is a certain danger, in fact, in succumbing to the ecstasy that grips us while running for a long time without end; some of our couriers have been known to literally run themselves to death.

And yet there is nothing more empowering, more stirring or irresistible than the pull of a dark night and the open countryside; there is no anticipation in all the world more glorious than that which grips us at the beginning of a long journey unencumbered by human form.

I recall the beginning of that journey specifically. Once clear of the city lights, I shed my clothes and neatly folded them into a leather bag, which I stowed beneath a rock. All things being equal, I would return for them and assume my human form before returning to the city. Such are the minor nuisances of living in modern society; one must always remember where one leaves one's clothes.

There is no sensation in all the world like that of cold night air on naked skin after weeks of being confined in layer upon layer of human clothing. I reveled in it, stretched to embrace it, drank it in like rich dark wine. My dread, my anxiety, the burden of my human intellect dropped away and were swallowed up by the night. I threw back my head, I raised my arms, I let myself *be*.

And, ah, what words now can I find to describe this Change, this miracle, this wonder we call the Passion—for uncounted centuries our poets and chanteurs have tried to describe it, and words have failed them even as they do me now. Yet eternally we are compelled to try to capture the ephemeris, to memorialize the ethereal in a clumsy shell of words. It is almost as though we yearn, in some indefinable way, to share this, the most defining moment of our being, with humans.

As though in the telling we might impart the miracle and in the hearing they might receive it. A foolishness, I know, for why would we want such a thing? And impossible as well. Nonetheless, we continue to try.

The Passion, whether triggered by pain, high emotion, joyous will or the simple relaxation of our human form, is always a magnificent thing, an earth-stopping wonder that no outsider can fully comprehend. That is, of course, its essential magic—that it is now and will forever be a grand and glorious mystery.

The fire rises up from the belly, a swelling hunger, a rolling wave of intensity that sucks dancing sparks of energy from the air and sets in motion a whirlwind of power, pure and unvarnished. In this moment of transmutation, as we are caught up between one world and the next, universes dance on our fingertips, angels pause to bow to us; we are creatures of neither heaven nor earth yet masters of both. We are the savage and the god, the beast and the poem; we are the essence of all creation. The Passion, with all its many metaphors and philosophical implications, with the lessons and variations of a thousand lifetimes to tell, is quite simply the reason for our existence. It is why we are Nature's most perfect creation.

The hunger, the joy, the longing redoubles on itself until it becomes an explosion of pure emotion, a vortex of light and color that has the power to transcend the laws of matter and energy. In the blink of an eye, the clap of a thunderbolt, the space of a sharply indrawn breath, we grasp the power and claim it. We pass from one state to the other; we Become. We master.

I had heard it said, and I had no reason to question, that those rare humans who have been privileged to witness the Passion undergo a kind of rapture of their own, that its effect upon them is an enchantment which many found impossible to break. I could certainly understand how this could be, and looking back, I wondered if that might not have been the case with Tessa. I thought about her on that cold bright night as I shed my clothes and my human form and gave myself over to the ecstasy of being once more. I thought about her briefly, and let her go. And from that time until I reached my brother's house I gratefully thought about nothing at all.

It was not an easy journey, even in wolf form, which is why I did not make it very often. The frozen Siberian plain is every bit as unappealing as it has been portrayed, with winds that sweep down like tidal waves and stir up vast sheets of snow that can travel across the desert for mile after blinding mile. At times the entire plain seems to undulate with a life of its own: eddies of snow, whirlpools of snow, driving, biting, whispering, snickering, howling, roaring, thundering herds of snow. At other times, the worst times, the world is so devoid of life, day into night, night into day, one wonders whether one has not accidentally stepped off the edge of the earth and is now condemned to wander some endless unpopulated netherland for all uncounted eternity.

I brought down an elk early on, and once or twice stirred up a burrow of winter rabbits, but as I moved deeper into the wilderness and higher on the plain, game grew scarce, and I had to content myself with bark and what few frozen berries the birds had left and an occasional ground rodent. The great disadvantage of travelling in wolf form is the vast amounts of energy it uses and the corresponding number of calories required; had I not gorged myself for days beforehand, it is doubtful I could have survived on the meager findings of the land long enough to reach my destination.

I slept in caves or hollow logs during the coldest part of the night with my tail curled around my nose to warm the air I breathed, but I never stayed still for more than a few hours. The memory map in my head and the need for warmth kept me moving, not to mention the hunger that, toward the end, grew to be an all-compelling force. Yet despite the discomforts, and there were many, there was a primal pleasure in it so simple and so intense it precluded all other considerations. The taste of the wind, the bite of the cold, the delicate sound the snow crust makes as it snaps beneath the step and the way it seems to echo forever—life is never as real as it is then, so rich and textured one could almost slice it up in slabs and live upon its multilayered nourishments during the long, barren months of winter. At times like those, we know *what* we are and *why* we are more clearly than we shall ever know anything again, and the knowledge itself is delicious.

Open any book of illustrated Russian fairy tales and you will see a picture of how the Palace Antonov appeared to me that icy sunrise as I arrived, footsore and rangy and more than ready to abandon the pleasures of the wild. Snow draped its spires like frosting on a cake; the morning sun backlit its windows with a golden-rose glow. The glitter of ice upon stone made the entire structure sparkle as though it were fashioned of diamonds. Smoke billowed from a dozen fireplaces, bearing on the air the scents of roasting meats and busy servants and utter, peaceful civility. My brother's scouts would have been reporting my position for days, and all was in readiness for my arrival. Home had never looked so beautiful to me.

My childhood memories of this place were of a ramshackle old castle, drafty and dusty; of crumbling mortar and scarred tabletops; of labyrinthine rooms and endless nooks and crannies to explore. I had not, of course, grown up here, for we were very civilized werewolves by my father's time and kept our family home in Paris and a country estate in Provence. Aunts, uncles and cousins had strongholds in London, Amsterdam, Rome, and as far away as Montreal and San Francisco. But for family gatherings they had all come home to this, Palace Antonov, in all its crumbling splendor, to hunt its fields and drink from its streams and picnic on its ancient stones.

The family gatherings had, over the years, grown fewer and farther apart, and the old place had fallen deeper and deeper into neglect. Then Denis had come and restored the castle to every bit of its former glory and more; it was once again home to dozens of industrious, productive werewolves and headquarters for hundreds more. These werewolves were no relation to me and there were many things about them I did not even like, but they were Denis's family now; his pack. And this was still my home.

It had been three weeks since my brother's missive reached me, and I knew he was anxious to see me. But there are certain priorities, and not even for his sake could I defer my hunger, nor did he expect me to. I gorged myself on venison and blood broth fortified with hot milk, and I slept for a day and a half curled up by a fire that blazed without faltering. When I resumed my human form and the fine wool suit that had thoughtfully been laid out for me in my chamber, I joined my brother in the vast library downstairs.

Legend would have it that Denis was a savage, a crude barbarian who preferred violence to intellect, brute force to the subtle arts. Nothing could be further from the truth. Denis was an accomplished man, well educated and as refined as he cared to be. That he lived his life far from the reaches of what we knew as the civilized world was a matter of preference, not necessity; that his philosophy advocated a return to a simpler—some say a purer—life was a conviction that few would have had the courage to follow. He was in many ways a hero of his time; history, unfortunately, will never show him in that light.

Palace Antonov was, for all intents and purposes, my ancestral home, but it had fallen into disuse and disrepair until Denis took it upon himself to restore it. This was my first trip home in many years and I could not help but admire the polished stone floors and brilliantly hued carpets that covered them, the huge fireplaces that never went dark, the intricately carved moldings and sconces that decorated the walls. He might have rejected the civilized world in principle, but my brother was no fool; he was perfectly willing to take the best of what it had to offer and apply it to his own use.

Everywhere I passed there were industrious servants, polishing, scrubbing, repairing, providing. There were no humans at Palace Antonov. Like any good leader, Denis knew the value of work to do and a job well done, and he provided meaningful employment for werewolves far beyond the domain of the palace. He had applied the same ambition and determination with which he had restored our ancestral home to restoring the Siberian pack, and what once had been a scattered, half-barbaric assemblage of loners and misfits was now a force to be reckoned with. Just how great a force was not something I particularly wished to know, but was certain I would not leave this place without finding out.

Denis was waiting for me with arms outstretched when I entered the library, and we embraced strongly. My brother was a beautiful werewolf, standing six and a half feet tall with a mane of wild auburn hair and eyes the color of an Arctic sky. He had a deep, commanding voice and strong hands and shoulders broad enough to shame Atlas. He smelled of snow on fur and star-bright nights, of fierce raw energy and the strength of the hunt. Simply being near him made me proud, as though our blood relationship somehow gave me claim on the power that was uniquely his. It was good to be home.

"And so, *mon frère*, you have arrived at last! We were beginning to think you'd been eaten by a boar!" He spoke French because I was accustomed to it, but after a time we switched, almost without noticing it, to Russian, and then eventually to a combination of both.

He was wearing a long loose robe of soft heavy fabric, trimmed with the coarse fur of a bear around the neck and sleeve openings. It was the sort of garment one wore when one was used to changing form frequently and without inhibition. Because in times of old only the most well-fed—and therefore the most powerful—werewolves had the freedom to change at whim, it was also a traditional symbol of status. Although my fashion tastes are a bit more fastidious, the robe suited him in a way it would have done few other werewolves.

Two members of his pack, in wolf form, were stretched out before the hearth, one on either side of the fire. Although they appeared relaxed with their forelegs extended before them and their tails at ease, their eyes were alert and their ears pricked forward; I knew that they would move swifter than lightning should circumstances require. These were Denis's personal attendants, his bodyguards, if you will, and their presence in the room in no way implied that I was perceived as a threat. They were, once again, a symbol of status. Only our pack leader employed such attendants.

There were others in wolf form, wandering in and out of the room, roaming the corridors. Such a thing would never have been permissible in my household, of course, but I found the fact that it was so acceptable here strangely stimulating.

The contrast of all this subtle, simple savagery against the backdrop of leather-bound volumes, gilt-framed artwork and plush upholstered furniture was, needless to say, striking. Such was Denis's world, and I was for a moment sharply, intensely envious.

He had poured cognac and I could smell wild fowl roasting over a spit; it made me salivate. I drank the cognac down and remembered, with a sigh of pleasure, the advantages of assuming human form. Denis read my expression and laughed.

"You've grown soft, little brother," he said, blue eyes twinkling. "It happens to all in the company of humans—their offensive scent clogs up the senses, their incessant chatter deafens the ears. But a month or two with me will put you to rights again."

"Thank you, no," I responded, and stepped forward to warm my hands before the fire. Even now it was hard to get the chill of the journey out of my bones. "The only senses I worry about losing are the ones that allow me to enjoy a good cognac—and I notice you haven't precisely turned your back on that particular product of civilization, either."

He grinned and refilled my glass. "Ah, but no human hands created this nectar, or even sealed the bottles. The oils of their skin would have caused the fruit to spoil, which is why only we can make a drinkable brandy—or wine, for that matter."

As a matter of fact he was right about that, although I couldn't resist remarking that the cognac he so enjoyed was also a favorite of humans. Actually, I've often observed how interesting it is that human connoisseurs always prefer those rare and excellent vintages which they themselves have had no hand in creating. An example, I think, that even humans know perfection when they taste it.

Denis looked me over with a practiced eye and remarked, "You look fit. Although I could have made the trip in half the time."

I saw no need to point out that most of my journey had been spent on the luxury of human conveyances; it would only have precipitated an argument I was too content at the moment to conduct. I said, "Matters are unsettled in Paris just now. I had things to attend to before I left."

His gaze sharpened, and he nodded. "I'll want to hear the news, of course. But for now, sit down." He swept an arm toward a big, Moroccan leather chair which was drawn up at a comfortable distance before the fire. "Have some cheese, tell me what you think. It's rare I get to play the host to a peacock like you."

"I should think it's rare you get to play the host to anyone," I commented, slicing cheese from the wedge. "Who would ever find you here?"

Denis sat across from me, settling the folds of his robe around him, and stretched his bare, weathered feet toward the fire. No one in this household wore shoes. They all looked exceedingly comfortable.

Denis said, "Oh, we're not so remote as all that. A human sheepherder wandered in before the hard snow. We ate him for dinner."

I paused with a slice of cheese halfway to my mouth, and stared at him. I must have looked the perfect fool. Denis burst into uproarious laughter, and even the two sentries sat up, grinning.

I scowled and popped the cheese into my mouth. "How I've missed your lovely sense of humor, brother mine. What a shame I can't take you about and show you off at parties."

"I will certainly make a point of polishing my manners before that time. How do you like the cheese? The high-valley females put it up last spring."

"It's very fine," I told him, and allowed the glance I swept around the room to include all that I had seen since arriving. "Every time I visit I am more astonished at what you've accomplished, and continue to accomplish. This is all . . ." I made an all-encompassing gesture with the hand that held my glass. "Most impressive."

He sipped his own brandy, a comfortable twinkle coming into his eyes. "But not impressive enough to persuade you to abandon your cosmopolitan ways, eh?"

"*Jamais*," I assured him. "My life, though not quite as grand as yours, leaves little to be desired."

"Except the freedom of your nature," Denis pointed out, and there was no humor in his gaze now.

I did not answer, but neither did I drop my eyes. What I did, in fact, was help myself to another chunk of cheese and the coarse hearty bread that went with it.

In a moment Denis shrugged, then sipped his brandy with the slow, thoughtful luxury of a true connoisseur. "It's just as well, no doubt," he remarked. "It's never a good idea to keep our forces too concentrated, and your presence in Paris has always been a valuable one."

With an abrupt change of subject he could not help but notice, I said, "Do you still have your old cook, Isla? Hasn't he fallen into his own fire yet?"

There was a slight tightening of the corners of Denis's eyes, just enough to let me know he recognized my ploy. But he was gracious enough—or intent enough on the purpose for which he had brought me here—to permit me my evasions.

He smiled and replied, "If you can't smell the old renegade from here, I *am* worried about you."

We laughed, and the conversation fell to neutral subjects; to games we had played as youths and acquaintances we shared and harmless pack gossip. When supper was called, the bottle was half empty and I was feeling quite sentimental. By the time our plates held nothing but bones and two bottles of very excellent wine—from my own cellars, of course—were upturned on the table, I was restored, content and very glad I had come.

Denis led me from the table with an arm around my shoulders. "And so, my young brother, what is it that they do for entertainment in Paris these days? With no antelope to run and no humans to skin, you must have a dull time of it indeed."

I was beginning to find his jokes about humans a trifle tiresome, but since I knew he did it only to annoy me I refused to let him realize he was succeeding. "It is difficult," I admitted, "but somehow we make do with the theater, the opera, the grand symphony, the museums. Occasionally, when we are unable to bear the boredom, someone will host a fete for five or six hundred of the most accomplished people in Europe . . . Still, I was reduced to spending last season in Italy, if you can fathom it, with nothing to do but bask in the sun and feast on wine and fresh meat."

"Bah," he scoffed, scowling. "Human entertainments, human pleasures. Your mind will rot with its constant exposure to such pap, and before long you'll be telling me you actually enjoy it."

I was somewhat bothered by the fact that I could not tell, this time, whether he was joking.

We had reached the great hall. The flames of the tall wall sconces swayed in the draft created by the vastness of the room and cast wildly distorted shadows hither and yon—a giant wolf head here, a wavering human form there, a crouching beast of indeterminate shape surging up from yet another corner. It was impossible to heat or light the castle by modern means, or at least it was inefficient to try to do so, and one doubts Denis would have employed gaslights or coal heat if he had been able. The stark medieval atmosphere was appropriate to this place, and comforting, in a way, even to someone like me—for a short time anyway. It never does to wander too far away from one's past, for therein lies the danger of forgetting one's way home.

That, at least, was what my brother had always taught me.

Outside the tall window a squabble erupted over a fresh kill; there was snarling and snapping and the smell of wild goat's blood. The sight, the smell, the sound stirred the embers of fire in my blood and quickened my pulse, and I was drawn to the window as though polarized. The moonlight was bright and the scene surreally etched not a half-dozen steps from where I stood: two big males, one brown and one black, disputed ownership of the carcass, which was so fresh that steam still rose from its open throat. My nostrils flared to catch the scent through the glass, excitement tightening in my belly. I was sated, but I was suddenly and intensely hungry; my mouth filled with saliva and my stomach cramped with yearning.

And when the big black swooped in, teeth bared and voice raised, to drive off the brown, and when lithe, fierce bodies twisted in battle and savage cries split the night, my eyes went sharp and a growl started in my throat that was purely involuntary. I could taste the fur in my mouth, feel hard flesh yield to the snap of my teeth; my muscles strained to join the fray and my heart raced, fierce and free with anticipation of victory.

Denis stood close beside me, adding his own powerful perfume to the sensory orgy, his own heat to the fire in my loins. He murmured, "Ah, yes, little brother, tonight we feast." His fingers clasped the tight muscles at the back of my neck, and his hot breath tantalized my ear like the whisper of a lover. His fingers massaged my neck; the power of his heartbeat commanded my own. The ferocity that swelled within me was violently sexual, intensely savage, and, fueled by the close proximity of a werewolf as powerful as Denis, was the most thrilling, dangerous and almost uncontrollable sensation I had experienced in recent memory.

The two mighty creatures outside met in a final brutal clash of teeth and claws and victorious snarls; then a spray of pink snow frosted the windowpane, and the brown streaked away with a fur-covered haunch in his mouth. The black watched him go for a brief, barely interested instant, then sank his teeth into muscle and bone and tore open the chest cavity of the goat.

I turned from the windowpane, my breathing quick and my pulses roaring. A female was standing there with a robe in her hands. It was black, and hooded, and woven of a heavy wool to keep out the bite of the wind. Upon the left shoulder was an insignia which only the eyes of a werewolf, trained to look for it, would see—a half-moon, black on black.

The robe was mine. I had worn it on the occasion of my last visit here, and many times before.

The fever began to leave me.

Denis took the garment and held it out to me, smiling. "Come," he invited. "Let us go meet our brothers."

It is very difficult to control the rhythm of one's heartbeat, or the scent of fear-laced adrenaline, before a werewolf as powerful as Denis, especially in the state I was in just then. I thought I was prepared for this moment; I had been preparing for it since before I left Paris. Still, I knew I could not deceive my brother, not completely, and not for long.

He could sense the cooling of my blood, hear the slight change in the rhythm of my pulse which, although it did not slow, grew heavy with alarm. I lubricated my throat. I found my voice.

"Alas," I said, more smoothly than I had thought possible, "I'm afraid I would make poor sport tonight. I'm still footsore from the journey, and a little drunk. Another night, *n'est-ce pas*? We have many before us."

I saw the sharpening of his gaze, the flare of his nostrils as he smelled uneasiness on my skin. And yet, in a moment, he let it pass. "Of course," he said, and his tone was as unconvincing as mine had been. Werewolves, when they lie to each other, make pathetic spectacles. "I forget from whence you came. Sleep tonight, grow strong. You'll be back to what you once were in no time at all."

Instead of the robe, I took from him a lamp to light my way upstairs. This was an insult without apology, for only a poor werewolf indeed needs a lamp to find his way in the dark. But I accepted it in good grace and was glad that was all I had to deal with that night.

Six

THERE ARE THOSE WHO MIGHT SAY IT WOULD HAVE COST ME NOTHING TO run with them that night. There was a part of me, in fact, that yearned to do so, and I sat awake in the glow of the fire for a long time, listening to the sounds that drifted across the night-frozen miles and struggling to suppress my own passions. The pack run is one of the most exhilarating, liberating, and actually necessary elements of a werewolf's existence, and why had I come here if not to enjoy the freedom afforded by this place to indulge my instincts to the fullest?

But another instinct, from a much different source, was tugging at me that night. It was the small, still voice of reason, and it whispered to me to be careful. It was with a rare display of good sense that I listened to it.

As difficult as it is for us to keep secrets from one another in human form, it is virtually impossible to do so in wolf form. The language of posture and stance, of scent and gaze and rushing breath, has no vocabulary for falsehood. They would have sensed my uncertainty, known my vulnerability. There were certain secrets I was not quite ready to reveal.

This was no casual invitation issued by my brother. This was no ordinary run and the werewolves on this plain were no ordinary members of the pack. The run would be a declaration of commitment, the kill a triumph of teamwork. Afterward they would resume their human forms and don their black hooded robes, each bearing the crest of the dark half-moon. They would gather in a clearing protected from the wind and let words give shape to their intent, and the words they spoke would be words of war.

This I knew.

Stories abound of the Brothers of the Dark Moon. I suppose they have been with us in one form or another since the beginning of time. They have been variously called Human-Haters, Wolf Lovers, Moon Worshippers. Their goals and philosophies have varied across the ages, but for the most part they advocate the superiority of the werewolf species (a premise with which it is difficult to argue) and a return, by whatever methods are necessary, to a state that will permit the werewolf to claim his position of natural dominance on the planet. They have never, as far as I know, consumed human flesh or attempted to mate with a wolf, and I don't believe their religious leanings, if any, involve the moon at all. They have throughout our history been a covert group often scorned and occasionally feared, with pockets of disciples here and there in every part of the world.

At the end of the nineteenth century the group had come together in one place for the first time in centuries. The organization had its headquarters in the heart of Siberia, with my brother Denis as its head.

Denis had always had a talent for persuasion, for inspiring crowds, for taking grand ideas and making them manifest. He had also always been a rebel, even an anarchist, and in his early twenties he had already been preaching the doctrine of the Dark Brothers in every major city of Europe. Our family was humiliated and did everything in its power to disassociate itself from him. Sancerre, the pack leader, was alarmed enough to assign an entire detachment of guards to monitor Denis's movements. Denis wisely realized that few revolutions were

successful without the blood of martyrs to fuel them, and he was not
ready to offer up his own blood for that purpose yet.

He was still a young werewolf when he made his decision to reas-
sume our ancestral name and return to the plain from which we
hailed—and where, as far as Sancerre was concerned, he and his
followers could do little harm. I was young, too, ripe for adventure
and inspired by my brother's nobility and by what seemed to me a
desperately romantic lost cause when I joined him. In werewolves as
in humans there is a time when rebellion for rebellion's sake is as
inevitable as it is irresistible, and the philosophies of the Brotherhood
were designed to fire a young warrior's heart. I soon got over my
passion for anarchy—as soon as I returned to Paris that summer, as a
matter of fact, and met up with Stephen for a month-long voyage upon
the Mediterranean—but Denis did not. And he never was able to accept that the more the years separated us, the less we had in common.
Or perhaps it was that I simply never tried very hard to make him
see.

We were Antonovs, the Ancient Ones, the rightful heirs. The old
ways were the only ways, and they were the ways of the Brotherhood.
On what grounds could I possibly argue with that?

The Brotherhood of the Dark Moon was and always has been an
outlaw organization. The penalty for belonging was exile, which in
our culture is a punishment far worse than death. But that was not
why I wanted to separate myself from them. It was simply a matter
of what we each held to be true, and it was difficult for me to embrace
any philosophy that had at its center a declared hatred of humans.

I knew the time was coming when I must make this truth known,
finally, inarguably and without qualification, to my brother, the werewolf I most admired in the world and the only one whose approval I
had ever sought. Surely I could not be blamed for wanting to postpone
that inevitability for as long as possible.

I was able to postpone it, in fact, for two weeks. In this I had an
unexpected ally, which was the simple reality of Denis's loneliness.
There is an ancient adage that warns us against the dangers of growing

too attached to either of our forms, for, it says, "to neglect the body is to grow worms in the soul." It is all well and good, in other words, to indulge one's physical nature—to chase the moon, to roll in the grass, to snatch the meat steaming off the bone—but to forget the discipline of one's human form is to be but half a werewolf. Denis lived a life enviable to many: changing at whim, accountable to no one, in complete command of his own destiny. But with whom was he to play chess, or read poetry, or debate the ancient philosophies? The answer was, for the next fortnight at least, me.

Denis was avid for news from the world beyond and had peppered me with questions since my arrival: What was the last play I had seen? Had I been to Vienna last season and had the symphony orchestra performed Wagner? Who had danced the lead in this year's *Giselle*, and was it our own exquisite Marguerite de la Theophile? Strange pursuits, one might think, for a werewolf who had upon my arrival accused *me* of growing soft, but music, art, the theater—especially music—these are life's blood to a werewolf, protein for the soul. I almost pitied my brother that he should have to live so deprived.

I did not imagine there should be a more devious reason for his interest in life as it existed beyond his boundaries. I should have. But I did not.

I arose that day two weeks after my arrival to a morning too fine to ignore. I smelled a bounteous breakfast of hot milk and roasting rabbit, boiled and sugared grains seasoned with fat, goat kidneys and salted venison. But there were other, even more compelling scents on the air and they called to me from beyond the window—fresh snow and evergreen, a mountain stream rushing, the musk of a big cat, an elk munching branches. Werewolves at play. Ice in deep shadows and pale pink sunshine on snow. It was a morning to run.

I pushed open the door and walked naked onto a balcony covered with powdery new snow. The cold withered my testicles, numbed my toes, and the air bit into my lungs as I drew it in. Snow fog lay low over the tops of trees, some bare and some laden with long green needles drenched in white. The branches groaned and whispered to themselves; small creatures scurried and chattered as their claws scraped back layers of snow in search of breakfast. I could hear the rustle of a bird's wing two kilometers away, while the sun hung poised on the horizon, barely more than a promise, in a lemony haze. On such a morning was all creation born.

I followed the balcony toward the steps that led to the ground, smiling as I remembered how Denis and I, as reckless youths, used to try to leap from the balcony, change in midair, and land on the ground in wolf form. We had both broken legs more than once, and were fortunate to have done no more damage than that. Only the exuberance of a pup could excuse such a feat, or expect to survive it.

I stretched to embrace the dawn, throwing back my head with a cry of sheer pleasure, and leapt from the balcony. I landed on all fours in wolf form, my fall cushioned by the snow, and shouted my victory. I took off at a full run, filled with the glory of the day and the wonder, the marvel, the absolute miracle of myself.

The cold air stung my eyes and combed back my fur; it tasted like nectar on my tongue. Trees and roots and amorphous snow shapes swept by. I chased a rabbit and caught it in a flurry of blood and spraying snow, devouring it lustily. I broke the ice from a shallow brook and drank my fill. And then I smelled werewolf on the air.

My ears pricked for the sound of his heartbeat, and my hackles rose until I identified it. A hundred sensory impressions flooded me as I circled for his trail, found it, and followed. The heat of his blood, the sound of his breath, the scent left by his paws in the snow—familiar and good, a welcome invitation. And now he was joined by another, a female whom I didn't know; she excited me. In a moment I picked up their tracks and by that time she caught my scent and called a greeting. I announced myself and, hearing no objection, ran after her.

Denis was lying in ambush position behind a snow-covered fallen tree. I like to think that, had I not been so distracted by the female, I might have noticed him, but he had always been better at this game than I. He charged and knocked me off my feet before I ever caught his scent. We rolled, snow flying and excitement surging, and I got him by the neck. He threw me off. I ran. He caught me again and tumbled me to the ground. I kicked with my hind legs and clawed with my front and threw him off. I lunged and got him by the forearm. Snow and fur flew and the female paced and postured excitedly while we wrestled and snapped and snarled and turned each other on the ground. He let me get his throat, though not without a hard, muscle-straining fight. The female leapt into the fray, nipping me playfully on the shoulder. I gave chase, and so did Denis.

It had been years since I'd had so much fun.

We let her outrun us, which was only polite, then stretched our muscles in the full force of a male competitive run. We leapt streams and high deadfalls; we dodged fallen trees and plowed through undergrowth. Our breath trailed foggy streams behind us and our bodies steamed. It was marvellous.

We circled around to pick up the scent of the female again, which led us to the summerhouse—a thick-walled stone structure built around a hot spring. Denis stopped outside it and the air crackled as, with a subtle mastery I had always envied, he spun, shook himself and resumed his human form. "Come," he called to me, laughing as he tossed back his hair. "Let's swim."

I followed him inside and changed in the doorway, moving immediately across the stone floor to slide into the steaming water. Denis was already in the pool with the female, who was a lithe, golden-eyed brunette with firm upturned breasts and pale pink nipples. Their bodies were slick with water and steam as they caressed each other; she, with her back to Denis while he stroked her torso and her breasts, stretching her arms overhead to caress his neck and shoulders, turning a small pink tongue to lick droplets of water from his arm.

I took pleasure in watching them for a moment, those two strong and beautiful werewolves in their silent dance of lazy sensuality. Then I dropped down into the water until it reached my neck, drawing the moist, heated air deep into my lungs. I was still tingling and throbbing from the Change, senses heightened, muscles aching. The heavy warmth of the pool seeped into my pores and filled my blood with a rich sluggish heat. I stretched forward, parting the water like an otter, and took the female by the waist, teasing her breasts with my tongue. She laughed with pleasure and reached under the water, taking my penis, which was still full and firm from the power of the Change, in her hands. This was a marvellous sensation, to be stroked and caressed by lingering, skillful fingers while the eddies of steamy water swirled about me, to taste her soft salty flesh against my tongue.

"I smell no mate on you," I teased her, licking the water from the inside of her elbow.

"That's because I have none," she replied. Her eyes sparkled with pleasure when I parted her thighs with my hand, and stroked the delicate flesh between.

"Careful, Alana," Denis said, "he is a careless reprobate who will only break your heart. Besides . . ." His eyes glinted at me as he bent to kiss her shoulder. "I don't think he cares for our climate."

"It's beginning to grow on me," I murmured, and, when Denis left us to submerse himself in the water, I lifted her legs around my waist and pushed myself inside her. She linked her arms around my neck and I sank down deep into the water so that we both were covered by it, arms and chests and necks, heat outside and heat inside. I threw back my head and arched my back to feel even more of her. I caressed her buttocks and she massaged my chest with her palms. Slippery flesh against slippery flesh. It was exquisite. We stayed that way, kissing and caressing and stroking each other, until every nuance of sensation was extracted from the moment, until our bodies were so saturated with contentment that they separated naturally. In human form, the penis will remain engorged for only a short time after the Change, and then only if we will it. But during that time the sensation is intense.

Our tongues mated lazily, leaving the imprint of our tastes within each other's mouths, and I said, smiling into her eyes, "It was a genuine pleasure to meet you, Alana."

"You are very nicely formed," she returned to me, and ran her hands over my form one more time before leaving the pool.

I thanked her for the compliment and watched her bend to kiss Denis, then wrap herself in a cloak before hurrying from the building and back toward the main house. I released a sigh of utter contentment and lay back in the water, submersing myself from head to toe. I stayed under until I could hold my breath no longer and then rose with a great thunder and splash, gasping for breath and shaking out my hair. I left the water reluctantly and joined Denis upon the heated rocks that baked in the glow of a central pit of coals.

"You do," I admitted as I stretched out beside him on a warm slate slab, "have a passably fine life here."

He smiled lazily and cracked one eye to look at me. "Tell me, Alex. What thought have you given to a mate?"

"Not much at all."

"The selection must be choice in Paris."

"It is. That's my problem. The selection is so delicious it quite makes my head spin and I find I can't decide anything at all." I glanced at him. "What about you? You're older than I am, and your selection doesn't precisely seem to be impoverished, if I may say so."

He smiled again and closed his eyes. "True enough. But it's difficult, in a closed environment like this. I fear I may have to search abroad."

That piqued my curiosity for a moment, and I thought what an odd spectacle that would make, to see Denis out and about again among regular society, courting a mate. But the heat was seeping into my bones and it was hard to hold a thought. Denis was asleep, and in a moment so was I.

By the time he raised the subject again, I had completely forgotten it.

In the way of Siberian winters, the magnificent morning gave way to a ferocious storm by midafternoon. Still, I recall that as one of the most enjoyable days I had ever spent under my brother's roof. We played chess, we consumed an excellent supper of lamb stew and winter apples, and afterward we sat by the fire, listening to the wind howl outside our thick stone walls and sipping an exquisite Bordeaux. It was then that he put to me his final and—had I but known it—most important question, the one to which all others had been leading: "What do you know of the Devoncroix queen?"

I knew, in fact, quite a lot, but little I felt comfortable sharing with him. I kept my tone negligent and my posture at ease as I sipped my wine. "Elise? She's a strong werewolf, runs a tight household and a sturdy company. She's young and wants seasoning—and a proper mate—but I think she'll do."

Denis asked casually, "Any prospects in that area?"

"What? A mate?" I shook my head. "Not that I've heard. Of course, until now she hasn't been seriously considering qualifications, but I imagine she'll start narrowing the field this season."

"Can she defend her position until then?"

"She's a strong werewolf."

In truth, that was a concern. Any newly ascended werewolf, male or female, is vulnerable to being overthrown in that crucial period between the death of the old ruler and the taking of a mate. It had been centuries since an unmated werewolf had ascended the throne, and all of us were a little anxious over whether or not she could hold it.

Denis said, "Do you know her?"

"Of course. Only slightly. We know the same people, go to the same places. Of course."

"Do you dine with her?"

"Occasionally." I was becoming uneasy and couldn't say exactly why.

"Run with her?"

I scowled. "Great gods, no! Of course not! I told you, I barely know her."

Denis regarded me with eyes that were amused and speculative, the peculiar curve of a half smile on his lips. "Odd. I had heard differently."

My cheeks were heating, and that made me even more annoyed than I already was. "Then you heard wrong. What the bloody hell could you be expected to hear from this place anyway?"

"Oh, you'd be surprised. I heard, for instance, that you two cut quite a figure on the dance floor at Sancerre's grand ball some seasons back."

I scowled into my wine. "She was a pup and I was being kind."

He chuckled. "Come along, Alexander, no need to pose with me. You've been enchanted with the creature since your first Change, admit it."

I glared at him. "What is this all about?"

Denis did not answer immediately. Instead he rose to refill my glass, and his own. He resumed his seat and he regarded me gravely. "It is about," he said, "the future of the pack."

Denis leaned forward a little in his chair, the low fire of intensity burning dark in his eyes. "Look at us, Alex, look at the pack—or what passes for a pack—as we are today. What has this queen inherited? A scattered band of werewolves all dressed up in human clothes, going about their human pursuits, growing old and indolent on meat they don't have to kill, squabbling amongst each other but lacking the will for a real fight . . . each of them confined to their own petty concerns and circumscribed by their own petty boundaries for all of their miserable little lives. Where *is* this pack of hers? Where is the grandeur, the magnificence, the *power* of what we are? We are invisible, Alex, that's what we are, faded and impotent and lost amongst a planet teeming with parasites.

"Tell me this," he insisted, barely pausing to draw breath. "If she put out the call, this Devoncroix queen, would the pack rally? Would anyone hear her, would anyone come? *Would she know if they did not?* Who are we, that is all I ask! And why aren't we now all that we could be—all that once we were?"

He drew a breath; the power of his gaze held me. He said, "We must be reunited again, little brother. And it will take a strong leader to do it."

This must be understood about my brother: he was a compelling, even mesmeric, orator. The personal magnetism that radiated from him like an ether and could persuade large crowds to madness or valor was never more apparent than in his speech, for when he was passionate on a subject he would not rest until everyone around him shared that passion; this was his majesty.

I felt that majesty, and even though I knew his argument and its fallacies, I *wanted* to be persuaded by it. And in truth he was right. As the century drew to a close we had wandered far from our origins. The term "pack" was an anachronism, the pack leader a figurehead.

I said, "Are you suggesting, then, that the queen is not the leader to bring together the pack?"

He sat back and smiled. "Since it was the Devoncroix who allowed the pack to deteriorate to its present state, I should think not."

And this, then, was what I had feared, almost from the very beginning. Denis had decided it was time for the Antonovs to reclaim the pack. And he, as head of the family, would assert the mission of the Brotherhood.

Now that the moment was upon me, I felt calm, very much in control. My voice was steady, as was my gaze, and I said clearly, "Denis, if you attempt to overthrow the queen you may succeed, but you will not live to enjoy the taste of your victory. The pack is Devoncroix now; the Antonovs are despised in principle. Furthermore, you're an outlaw, a symbol of everything we've struggled to put behind us. If you assume power you will never be accepted, and you'll only succeed in destroying the pack you'd hoped to unite."

There was a flicker of something unpleasant in his eyes—perhaps he had not expected me to be quite so blunt—but it was gone in an instant, and replaced with an approving smile. "Precisely," he agreed, sipping his wine. "And that's only one of the reasons I would not consider overthrowing the queen by force. The other, of course, is that I might lose."

I simply stared at him.

He chuckled, and though it was a pleasant enough sound, there was contempt mixed with something oddly like disappointment in his eyes. "What a fool you must take me for, brother, if you think a traditional challenge is the best my imagination can do. Have you ever known me to be so lacking in subtlety?"

I was the fool, for allowing myself to be lulled into a sense of confidence by considering only the obvious, for thinking for one moment that anything Denis planned would be in any way crude or unrefined—or lacking in originality. The sharpening of my curiosity was acrid on the air, and my humility genuine as I said, "I apologize for misjudging you."

Denis's gaze was steady and perceptive. "We have grown apart over the years, you and I, if ever we were the same. I can hardly fail to notice that the convictions that drive my life's force are but a matter of passing amusement for you—and no, don't try to hide your eyes, I've seen it there already, years ago. Our differences in philosophy are not at issue here, because we have something much more important in common, and we always will have. We are Antonovs," he said, and he leaned forward a little, once again capturing the room with the fire in his eyes, the low urgent timbre of his voice. "The blood of kings runs through our veins. A millennium past we blazed the way through the wilderness. We fought off wild animals and savage humans; we fed the pack with the strength of our muscles and the cunning of our minds. We were the ones, Alexander; *we* brought the pack out of the dark night into this brash bright day, and whatever glories are now enjoyed exist only because we made them possible! Great gods, Alexander, can you not see that the pack has never needed us more than it does today?"

He lunged to his feet, crossing the room in two great strides to the decanter of wine, filling his glass. "We stand on the threshold of a new century," he said, "and who can tell what it might hold? How are we to survive it, much less conquer it, without a leader who will call the pack to unite?"

Everything within me was singing in tune to his passion; I could feel the heat in my cheeks and the glow in my eyes and I wanted to spring to my feet with upraised fist and cry, "Yes, *mon liege*, lead me into battle! Yours to command!" Such was his power. Such was the unarguable *rightness* of his logic.

Yet I knew my brother, I knew there was more. And it was for this reason, and with the utmost self-restraint, that I kept my own passions in check. "History has proved it a difficult matter to rally a people without a cause," I pointed out. "True, we've forgotten pack ties. We've even grown lazy, some of us, but are any of us suffering? Do our children lack for meat or shelter from the cold? Does any one of us want for anything he could not have if he is sufficiently motivated to obtain it? Perhaps," I argued—and in part because he expected me to—"the time for the old pack ways, even our very definition of what the pack is, has passed. We reap the fruits of a peace well earned because we *have* conquered. And without an enemy, it is difficult to raise an army."

Denis's eyes glittered in the long shadows cast by lamplight and wind-tossed firelight. "Well spoken, my young friend. Yet you ignore one important and quite obvious fact. The enemy is here, all around us, and it is the same enemy it has always been, the only enemy who can pose a threat to us today: Humankind."

Although I had half expected it, the sheer absurdity of his statement left me for a moment flabbergasted. "Humans? A threat to us?" I couldn't keep the incredulity and amusement from my tone. "Surely even you can't believe that—and if so, perhaps you'd best leave the wine aside for tonight. Maybe forever."

But Denis wasn't smiling. "Use your brain instead of your facile tongue and perhaps you won't be so quick to retort," he said. "Think about it and you will see that yes, for the first time in history, humans *can* threaten us. They have a device that allows them to hear across the miles, just as we can. They can keep their meat fresh without ice and heat their homes without wood and drink without going to the stream—all of these things we learned to do centuries ago. They've even learned how to keep themselves clean, or at least cleaner than is common, so they live longer and breed better, and more of their young survive to consume more of what is necessary for life on this earth. I shan't stand here and preach you a sermon. You have a mind to see the truth when it barks in your face. Humans are gaining advantages they never before dreamed of, and only more can await them in the new century. There has never been a more dangerous time to be alive, or a more important one."

His words were sobering, and I could not scoff them away, much as I would have liked to. That humans, despite all their poor accomplishments, could ever grow to seriously threaten our position of dominance was, of course, unthinkable, absurd in the extreme. But that they could give us considerable cause for worry . . . this was another matter. Denis was right, and there was a coldness in the pit of my stomach to admit as much. I, and all those like me who had blithely enjoyed our centuries-long summer in the sun without thought to the future, had been very short sighted indeed. Now, as we stood poised upon the brink of a grand new century, there were wages to be paid.

I sat at ease within an overstuffed chair a toasty distance from the fire, a half-drunk glass of wine in my hand. I noticed as though for the first time the remnants in the glass, lifted it to my lips, and drained it. Still, my voice was a trifle thick as I said, struggling for a mocking tone, "What do you propose we do, then? Declare war?"

Only the faintest trace of a superior smile graced Denis's lips as he crossed the room with the decanter, and filled my glass to the brim, suffocating the bouquet. I drank deeply.

He said, "That would be premature. Eventually, of course, the human parasite must be annihilated, for the sake of our species and every other on the globe. You know that; it doesn't bear discussion. However, the first order of business is to unite the pack toward a common destiny, and as I believe I have just demonstrated, there is only one werewolf equal to that task."

"Yourself."

He nodded.

I felt as though I were going around in circles. Perhaps it was the wine. "But if you overthrow the Devoncroix, you will succeed in nothing but fragmenting the pack into a dozen warring factions. We cannot survive so drastic a shift in power, not at this point in our history."

Denis nodded calmly. "Which is precisely why I intend to marry the queen."

The fire popped loudly. Outside a wind spirit screamed around the corners of the house, sending tendrils of cold drifting in through windowpanes and doors. Inside, the silence was so profound one almost could have scooped it up by the handful and used it to pack the cracks around the doors to keep out the wind. Even my heartbeat was still, and I barely breathed. I know this, because Denis watched me with the intensity of a predator at a rabbit hole, and should anything about my physiognomy have changed, he would have registered the fact immediately with a savage, satisfied gleam.

But I was very still.

I said at last, "How, precisely, do you intend to do that?"

It was a reasonable question. There have been very few political marriages in our history. The reason is simple. We are a people of great passion and deeply felt emotions. We love once, we love intensely, we love for all time. Although casual couplings such as the one I had shared with Alana are as common to us as dances are to humans, and although we happily engage in a variety of sexual pleasures with any number of partners throughout our lives, sex, for us, is an entirely separate thing from mating. While we can enjoy many sexual acts in human form, we can mate only in wolf form. We mate for life, for once we have chosen our mates through the act of sexual union which will result in the conception of the young, an instant empathic and telepathic bond is formed between male and female which joins them to one another, for better or worse, until death.

I've often thought that this might be a design flaw our Maker might now regret, for one can't help but notice it's not often repeated elsewhere in nature. Certainly we would be a more prolific species if there were no incentive to maintain the family unit; we would reproduce faster and bring more variety into the gene pool. But then one must wonder whether we might be as successful as we are—intellectually and physically—if we employed a less selective breeding method. If we, for example, were compelled as humans are to couple indiscriminately and produce offspring in such a random and careless fashion—and in numbers well beyond our ability to support—could we ever expect to rise in achievement much above the level of humans? It is a prospect that would make even the most liberal-minded among us recoil, and, all in all, I think I much prefer our method of maintaining the species—flawed though it may be.

At any rate, though they are not unheard of, marriages of convenience are extremely rare in our society, and what may begin as a social agreement never remains that way. There are no spousal abandonments, cruelties or murders among mated couples, either, and betrayal within a marriage is physically impossible. A male and female who realize that they will be mentally and emotionally bonded to the other for the entirety of their lives are likely to be reluctant to take such a step for reasons of anything other than the greatest affection.

It hardly bears stating that no one can be forced into a mating; both parties must come of their own free will. That is why Denis's plan was so outrageous, so daring and fraught with risk—and so unparalleled in its brilliance.

He answered my question in the only possible fashion. "Do you think I lack the necessary persuasion?"

And that was what was so truly terrifying. My brother, powerful, charismatic, commanding . . . could any female, once he had determined to woo her, resist his fatal charm? And the Devoncroix queen—how could she fail to see the advantages of the match, the uniting of Antonov and Devoncroix after centuries of divisiveness . . . for that reason alone she might consider him, and, once under his powerful sexual and intellectual spell, could she really be trusted to rely upon her own judgement?

Perhaps I underestimated her. But that was the course my thoughts took.

My gaze fell to the glass in my hand. I took a long sip. I said, flatly, what was only the truth. "She will not receive you at court. Her bodyguards won't let you near."

Denis just smiled. "Ah, but they will let *you* near. You, in fact, my most charming and cosmopolitan sibling, will be welcomed with open arms as a favorite at court. You will be urbane and witty and entertaining, sympathetic and supportive and reliable. You will make yourself indispensable in her trust. And then, when you bring your outcast but repentant brother into her grace, she cannot help but look upon him with favor." He lifted his glass to his lips; he drank. His eyes, and his voice, were as flat as a fast-frozen lake. "I will do the rest."

My throat was very dry, but I could not make myself drink. I just looked at him, this werewolf, my brother, the most powerful visionary I had ever known. Never had anyone been as right as he was; never had anyone been as wrong.

He was born to lead. He should have been leader, he would have been leader. But he was born several centuries too late.

I leaned forward, and placed my wineglass upon the small table adjacent to my chair. I got to my feet. I met Denis's eyes.

I said, "That is an elegant plan, stunning in its simplicity, powerful in its logic. I'm humbled to have been included in it." I meant every word. And it was no effort for me at all to add, "But I will not help you."

Denis showed no reaction at first. He waited, as though expecting more. When he saw I was finished, he inquired mildly, "Did I mistake you? Didn't I hear you say you barely knew the queen and danced with her just to be kind? Can it be you have not yet quite recovered from your puppish infatuation?"

I said firmly, "This isn't personal."

"I assure you, it is very personal to me. Why won't you help me?"

My heart was beginning to knot in my throat. I could smell the anger on Denis, like hot tar burning, and my own reactions from now on would be visceral and impossible to disguise. Fortunately, I was through with dissembling. I knew only the truth, and that was all I spoke.

"Because," I said, "it would be a betrayal of myself, my queen, and the pack. You would try to manipulate your mate to your own ends, Denis, and that is not only dangerous but despicable. You would come to her under false pretenses, and you would use me to do it. But most essential of all is the simple fact that you are wrong. You're wrong about humans, you're wrong about the pack, you're wrong about the queen. And you're wrong about me. I'm sorry."

His eyes flared. "You know I have no chance of success without you."

I said nothing. The silence pounded against my ears, and his.

"And so." His voice filled the room with ice. Even the fire shrank and sputtered before it. "This is my due from my brother."

It is a very difficult thing for one werewolf to meet the gaze of another, more dominant one. The effort of holding my brother's eyes, of not shrinking beneath the force of his fiery glare, made my head throb and sparks of pain dance in the air between us.

I said evenly, "This is your due from a loyal member of the pack, and your brother."

The look that came into his eyes was cold enough to freeze the blood in my veins, hot enough to combust paper. It was an unforgiving look, a killing look. And then it was gone.

He said softly, "No. I was not wrong about you."

And then, almost casually, he dropped his gaze to his glass. Immediately the throbbing in my head ceased, and I was briefly dizzy with relief.

He said, "I cannot pretend I'm not disappointed. But neither can I pretend I'm surprised." He looked at me then, and the grimace that strained his features might have been intended to be a smile. "You are a strong werewolf, Alexander. I underestimated you. But I can't fault you for that."

Then he lifted his arm, dropped it around my tight shoulders in an embrace. The joviality in his voice was forced, but the smile on his face came more naturally now. "So we'll talk again, you'll give me a chance to convince you. Shall we run tomorrow? The storm is dying down and the caribou will be out to feed."

I forced a smile of my own, and said I would like that very much. But I could smell the hatred in his pores, bubbling to the surface with a stench as sweet as burning flesh, and I knew I would be a fool to spend another night in my brother's house.

I have often thought how history might have been different had I made another choice that night. From the distance of years it is far too easy to look back, to assume more blame—or credit—than one is due for what might or might not have been. The simple fact is that at that time I made the only choice possible for me to make. I lost my brother and my friend, and I set off from that place with a lump of ice in my chest where my heart should have been.

It was not a propitious night for travel. Six inches of snow had already fallen over an icy crust and more was blowing thickly through the air. The wind roared and piled thick drifts against walls and riverbanks; sturdy branches snapped with the sound of cannons beneath the weight of ice and hard wind. The cold was indescribable. In human form my fingers and toes would have frozen in moments and snapped off at the roots. Even though I was in wolf form, the wind cut through to my skin and froze the breath in my lungs. It was a dangerous night to be about, in more ways than one.

I set off across the woods that surrounded the estate toward what we called the Great Wilderness Road. It is not actually a road at all but a mere footpath in most places, passable only by four-footed creatures. Still, it is the shortest route across the Siberian plain. My head was bowed low against the wind, my progress slow because of the ice that weighed down my coat and accumulated between my paw pads. Even today I can taste that cold, so fierce it seemed to scald the tongue with every breath and freeze the bones like twigs in a pond. I hope never to know its like again.

There was no way I could have foreseen what was coming. I was blinded by needles of driving snow and deafened by the howl of the wind; likewise the tangled, contrary bursts of gale winds tore scents hither and yon, disguising any possible interpretation of what they meant. I was virtually lost in a sensory void.

I emerged from the copse where a frozen stream marked the path I should take and there they were, a dozen pairs of eyes—no, more; twenty—glinting in the dark, forming a slow, silent circle around me. The smell of cold fur and dampness, of werewolf power, of purpose. The sound, like the roar of a distant ocean beneath the wind, of heartbeats pulsing with strong, sure intent.

I do not know whether they meant to kill or merely maim me. My brother was not given to idle posturing, so I knew that what they had in mind was more than a warning. I made the decision in an instant, one of those choices that come more from instinct than from logic and are usually regretted later—provided one lives long enough. I charged.

The element of surprise, in this instance, served me well. I took down the one on my left and broke through the ranks. I made it perhaps a dozen yards before the circle closed again, this time in earnest. I don't know how long I fought, ripping out fur and twisting bones. I was young and strong, but these were Siberian werewolves, bred by nature and trained by Denis to be the best in the world. I acquitted myself well, but I doubt I could have lasted more than five minutes with them.

I knew I was going to die and I knew the bringer of my death would be the big gray beast who had already torn a gash in my shoulder and had twice had me by the throat. I was weakening and knew I would not be able to break away again. With my last strength I got hold of his ear and tore. His howl of pain was mixed with a louder, fiercer shriek, and was quickly consumed by it. With my peripheral vision I saw the rest of the pack begin to scatter. The two of us broke apart only seconds before a huge tree, uprooted by the wind, crashed down upon our battlefield.

I had run perhaps half a mile before I realized his ear was still in my mouth. I spat out the bloody wad and trudged onward, head to the wind.

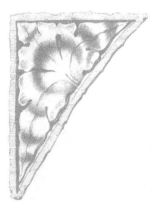

Seven

IT WAS SPRING WHEN I ARRIVED HOME, FOR THE JOURNEY WAS HARD AND I was forced to make much of it in wolf form. In truth, I did not hurry. Once out of Siberia, and thus away from the dangers of Denis's pack, I took a certain grim comfort in the solitude enforced by my natural state, in the rich solid flavor of the wind and the vastness of the Russian wilderness. I sharpened my hunting skills on the scarcity of winter game, I stared long into the face of a cold distant moon, I slept when I was tired and I ran when I felt the urge. It is necessary, from time to time, for a werewolf to simply surrender to his nature and *be*. In this way Denis lived a truer life than any of us would like to admit.

Gault travelled behind with the luggage and the rail car—this is why, after all, one has servants—while I completed the last hundred miles or so in wolf form. I stopped outside the city at the home of a cousin for sustenance and clothing and the use of a carriage to take me home. Gault had wired ahead of my arrival, so all was in readiness when I reached Paris, lean and hard with the rigors of my journey and aged with disillusionment.

The season in Paris was well under way, the streets awash in the pastel colors of blooming trees and ladies' frocks. The sights that had never before failed to stir my sense of joie de vivre left me cold that April day. Invitations and calling cards overflowed their silver trays, yet not the faintest trace of curiosity stirred me. The servants were lined up on the steps to greet me, and I walked past without seeing them.

I do not recall that I even saw Tessa that day, yet I must have done so, because she was the first to realize what I needed and to see that it was supplied.

I awoke to the scent of food—real food, meticulously prepared and delicately seasoned—and to the sudden intense knowledge that I was ravenous. I gorged myself on steaming meats in thick wine sauces; flaky pastries; rich, multitextured cassoulets. And for the first time since leaving my brother's house I began to remember what it was to be civilized.

When I looked up from my feast, almost insensate with over-indulgence, Tessa was there, smiling at me approvingly. "There, now," she said, "you're beginning to look more like yourself."

"Ah, chérie," I said, and opened my arms to her. She sank down beside me on the bed, stroking my hair, holding me as a mother would hold a child. I buried my face in her bosom and, drunk on the sweet, heady, wholly human scent that rose from her skin, tumbled helplessly into the deep sleep of exhaustion once again.

It was thus for three days. Whenever I awoke Tessa was there, and so was the great quantity of food she had ordered to be made ready: an entire roast mutton, a side of beef, the fatty parts of innumerable barnyard animals, not to mention the endless platters of grains and sweets that were necessary to restore my body's natural balance. It is a truism that Nature could not support us if we lived our lifetime in the wolf state; our nutritional needs are so enormous we would soon strip the planet bare. Add to these baseline requirements the additional energy expended by the difficulty of the journey and the healing of my physical wounds, and my caloric needs quickly exceeded all that was reasonable. Delivery carts came and went in a steady stream; I'm sure the vendors must have assumed I was giving a banquet. Only later did I realize that it was due in great part to Tessa's efficiency that this enormous undertaking had been achieved so flawlessly.

I suppose I should have been surprised that she was still there. I had left her precipitously, after all, and only on brief acquaintance, I had been gone a season and I had made little if any provision for her care in the meantime. But such was the extent of my self-confidence—indeed, my conceit where humans were concerned—that I would have been surprised had she not awaited my return, patiently and without complaint, even if it took years. I would have been happy to have put my entire household inside a glass to remain, suspended in motion, until I returned, and in some respects I suppose I imagined that was how it had been. I was the center of my universe. Now I was home. She was waiting. All was as it should be.

In between bouts of shameless gluttony I slept the sleep of the dead, and when finally I awoke, refreshed and restored and clearheaded enough to order a bath, Tessa was there as ever to take charge.

While I soaked in scented water and had my hair shampooed and my nails clipped by a winsome young werewolf by the name of Mercedes, Tessa ordered in an army of servants to clean and air the room. When I emerged an hour or so later, the linens had been changed, the feather mattress fluffed and aired, the winter draperies taken down and the summer ones installed, the rugs rolled up, the floor polished, and every window stood open to the cleansing April breeze. All of this represented quite an accomplishment, even for werewolves. I was both amused and amazed by the general good humor with which my staff tolerated Tessa. She was like a precocious puppy about whom everyone grumbled but secretly indulged, and for whom everyone reserved a bit of no-doubt misplaced pride.

I found her in my sitting room, where she had set up a tea tray and cakes. I prefer chocolate myself, but made allowances for the British side of her heritage. I stood at the doorway, my arms folded across my chest, one ankle crossed over the other, and regarded her with an indulgent smile that disguised utter contentment.

"And so, *chérie*," I said. "You seem not to have suffered much in my absence."

She turned from fussing with the tea table and swept me a deep curtsey, her eyes sparkling. She was wearing a fancy yellow dressing gown with many ruffles and lace flounces which dipped low over her bosom and showed a provocative few inches of petticoat at the hem. The shade was one of my favorites and it was most fetching on her. Her riot of dark curly hair was caught back with a clasp and brought high to tumble over her shoulders; her brown eyes danced impishly. She was, in a word, as restorative as sunshine to me, and just as necessary to life.

"And you, monsieur," she retorted. "How have you fared without me?"

"Not so very well, I fear." I crossed the room and took my place opposite her at the table, helping myself to a cake.

"It serves you right. You should have taken me with you."

I could have swept her off her feet just then and smothered her with kisses. I could have drunk of her until she was limp. I could have drowned myself in her scent, her supple silken skin, her lithe young muscles. It was so very good to be home.

I smiled at her. "Did you miss me, *chérie*?"

She paused with the teapot just above my cup and assured me fervently, "More than life."

I was more sure at that moment than I have perhaps ever been in my entire life of exactly what was so wrong about Denis and all those who followed him, and I was desperately glad I had had the courage to walk the other way.

I took a bite of the cake and sat back, reveling in the sweetness that melted on my tongue and in the sight of Tessa, the smell of her, the sound of her pulsing, sighing human heartbeat as she sat across from me, pouring tea into china cups. Diffuse rectangles of pale warm light from the open window crept across the gleaming floor, and that was how her presence acted on me: slowly creeping, filling me with light and warmth. I could only enjoy.

"You look enchanting," I said.

"Thank you," she replied. "I went shopping."

I was pleased. "So you haven't been entirely dull while I was away."

Her eyes went wide, those infinitely expressive, always fascinating big brown eyes, and she paused with the teapot over my cup. "How could anyone ever be dull in such a house?"

I chuckled and agreed. "You are indeed a fortunate young human. Has my staff been kind to you, then?"

She was thoughtful as she filled my cup. "Not kind," she decided, "but tolerant. And I have learned how to manage them."

Again she made me laugh. There she was, a human female not long past her twentieth year, left alone for the winter in a house filled with werewolves, and what had she done but "learn how to manage" them. How could Denis fail to adore these creatures? How could anyone remain unmoved by their charm?

Her expression was tender as she put down the pot. "I'm glad to see you laugh. I wasn't sure, from the way you looked when you arrived, that we would ever see it again."

I sobered, but briefly, and cast around for a distraction. "Are those sesame rolls?"

She used the silver tongs to place a roll on my plate. "Now tell me," she insisted. "Tell me about Russia, and all the things you did there. And about your brother, and why he didn't return with you. Are you close? Will he visit? What did you bring back? Or perhaps that is why Gault is delayed—to sort through all your treasures!"

How I had missed that endless chatter, those ceaseless questions. Her words swarmed around me like hummingbirds, bright and colorful, ensnaring me in their playful web. "I brought no treasures," I told her, "for you are spoiled already. And I will tell you all my adventures, but first I want to hear of yours. How did you fill your days? Have you been content? Have you learned anything in my absence?"

She laughed with pleasure at my imitation of her habit of rapid-fire questions, and a luscious color came to her cheeks. "Content, you say?" she returned in mock thoughtfulness. "Let me consider. I live in one of the grandest houses in Paris amidst luxury few in this world will ever taste, among creatures so fantastical that even if I wanted to tell my tale no one would believe me . . . I have, in this past year, born witness to secrets so profound they have never been guessed at in all the history of the world, and you ask if I am content?"

By now all frivolity had left her tone, and her eyes were shining with the simple wonder that came so easily to her. Her fingers clasped themselves together intently in her lap. "When I was a child," she said, "and I listened with a child's ears—half in awe and half in fear—to my father's tales of magical adventures, I never dreamed that I might one day be privileged to live among the mystical beasts, to know their secrets and share their trust, just as he did. When I hated you—all those years that I believed you to be a murderer and a vile monster— my heart was breaking because I had lost not only my father but some- thing that was, in a way, even more important . . . the gift he had given me, the stories he had told me, the will to believe that somehow, some- place, such creatures as he described did exist. Oh, I know I am ex- pressing myself badly, but can you understand? Being here, knowing you—now at last I know my father, I see what he valued in you, I know the friendship he felt for you, I share his delight. You have given me back my childhood," she finished simply, and with a small helpless gesture of her open hands, seemed to imply that words had, at last, failed her. "Could anyone ask for more?"

I was filled with joy to hear her say this, to see the light of conviction that radiated from her eyes and glowed in her face. This small human with her riot of dark curls and her freckled nose, with her big eyes and the smile that was so like her father's, this young female who barely a season ago had tried to kill me in my sleep, became for me in that moment the essence of all that was good and simple and right in the world. I desperately needed to hear her say that. I deeply needed to believe it.

I got to my feet and came around the small table to her. I took her face in both my hands, tilting it upward to mine, and I looked into her eyes. "*Chérie*," I said, "*je t'adore.*"

I felt the warm glow of pleasure against my fingers, heard the racing of her pulse and the soft explosions of breath in her lungs. Her eyes sparkled with mischief and delight, and a laugh of delight caught in her throat as she returned, *"Moi, aussi! Je t'adore, Monsieur le Loup-garou!"*

I laughed and caught her hands, pulling her to her feet. "Tessa, you are right! I was a fool to leave you behind and I will never do so again. I haven't laughed once since I've been away from you, I swear it. Now, come." I put my arm around her waist and led her to the sofa in the sunny corner of the room. "Come sit with me while I tell you my sorry tale. Let me hold you close and rest my chin upon your head so that I might have the courage to say what should never be spoken."

She sat first, pretty skirts spreading about her with the scent of clean cotton and human musk, lavender water and pale salt sweat. She drew me down beside her, her face gentle with concern and avid with interest. "Tell me," she said. "Tell me what happened to you there."

I settled her against me, there in the patch of sunshine by the open window, her head upon my shoulder, my arms around her waist. I inhaled the flavor of her, and bathed myself in the musical sounds of her body—the rush and swish of blood through vessels; the soft tympany of valves that opened and closed; the murmur of digestive fluids; the whisper of breath. It was the symphony of life, and it soothed me.

I said, at length, "My brother tried to have me killed."

And there, once said, the whole story came pouring out, sometimes harshly, sometimes dispassionately, sometimes in slow, painfully chosen words and sometimes in a rush of fury. I told her of the Brotherhood, and of their dark mission to subjugate or annihilate humans. I told her of Denis's brilliant but twisted plan to seize power by seducing our queen, and of the role he expected me to play in it. I told her of my cowardly escape in the night, and of the battle I had fought—and won only by the intervention of sheerest fortune—for my life. I think, until I said it, I was not entirely aware of how deeply the whole of the experience had affected me. And there, perhaps, is the only value that I can see of words.

There were times that I writhed with shame, because I knew that having now heard all that was the worst of our race, she would never look at me quite so starry-eyed as she had before. Yet who else could I tell the whole of it to except a human? Not even Gault could be trusted with the knowledge of my involvement with the Brotherhood, and to which werewolf could I expect to confess my deep uncertainties without making myself vulnerable to contempt? For a time I even forgot that it was a virtual stranger to whom I was confessing; being with Tessa was almost like having my old friend Stephen back.

"And so," I said at last, heavily. "You see we are not such noble creatures as you imagined. There is a dark side to our nature. And perhaps the darkest of it is that even now I am not certain I made the right decision."

Wafted in on a sun-warmed breeze came the scents of the city: chestnut blossoms and horse offal, burgundy wine and baking baguettes and the flavor of almonds, a woman's perfume, an animal dead in an alley, the river dark and dank. And the sounds: the shrill of a whistle, the jingle of a harness, the grind and grunt of mechanical things from factories far away, the guttural tone of a peasant's curses, music from a Victrola. I thought about trains that could convey humans across great distances, and telephones that could allow them to hear with an acuity which for centuries had been our exclusive domain.

And then I heard Tessa's heartbeat. Tessa's breath. All else was but dim and distant noise. She was my anchor, and I waited, foolish with anticipation and dread, for what she might think of me now.

She said, "Your queen. Is she so weak-minded as to let your brother persuade her against her principles? Or does she agree with him about the role of your race on this globe?"

"No," I said firmly, although I had not the first idea about Elise Devoncroix's personal convictions. I said only what I hoped to be so. "She doesn't agree with him. And she isn't weak-minded."

"Then," Tessa pointed out sensibly, "she would have destroyed him. So you have, in effect, saved your brother's life by turning him down. You made the right decision."

Et voilà. In the world of humans and young girls, even the most complex moral dilemmas can be reduced to a simple equation. It is thus because she declares it to be. My heart melted in my chest to know such a creature.

My throat was thick was gratitude and for a moment I couldn't speak. Mutely, I kissed her silky tumble of curls. And then I kissed the sweet soft bow of her upturned mouth, and then I pushed my fingers into her hair and I kissed her hard, I kissed her hungrily, I kissed her until the rush and swell of her blood was like a symphony in my ears and she was gasping for breath. And I loved it. I loved the heat of a young girl's sexual passion stirred to life for the first time, I loved the taste of her lips and the moist velvety flesh inside, I loved the flaming heat on her skin and the bright, dazed expectation in her eyes, and I loved that she looked to me, with excitement and trepidation, to have that expectation fulfilled.

And I loved the way she pretended a savoir faire she did not have. She looked at me for a long and steady time, though her heartbeat still roared and her muscles still trembled and breath still labored in her breast.

"Tell me," she queried at last, in a voice that struggled to maintain an even tone and to overcome her breathlessness, "about this—mating bond you referred to, between werewolves. What does it mean?"

That Tessa was an intellectually advanced female for her time was demonstrated by the fact that she would think to ask such a question, and I admired her for it. Though some might fault me for being so frank with a human about matters so close to our very essence, I could do nothing but answer her to the best of my ability. It was not an easy task to put so complex and important a matter into words a human could understand and I had to spend a moment organizing my thoughts.

"There are two times in our existence when a werewolf becomes joined with another, and the barrier between minds is dissolved and thoughts flow unimpeded from one to the other." I frowned with the effort of making myself clear, for language was a clumsy impediment. "At these times the two *become* one another. They live what the other has lived, they know what the other knows, they see what the other has seen—they know each thought, secret desire, grand ambition and low shame of the other—all in the space of moments, mere moments. But the bond that is formed by this knowing, this touching of the deepest, most intimate part of the soul, is something that never goes away, waking or sleeping, till death and beyond. The first occasion is when a male and female come together in the act of mating, as I've explained. The other is when one werewolf kills another."

I smiled faintly, exhausted by the effort required to put the concept into cohesive form for her—a concept that was so visceral, so deeply woven into the fabric of our nature, it was not only never discussed but rarely even considered. "So you see why we choose but one mate for our lifetimes, and why there are so few murders among us."

I could smell the excitement on her skin and see the wonder in her eyes, but was unsurprised. It was a marvellous thing to hear spoken, and even I was awed on such occasions by the miracle that we were.

But when she looked at me, cheeks flushed and eyes alight, I was surprised by the question. "This mating bond, this sharing of thoughts and secret knowledge—could it not be the same between a werewolf and a human?"

My startled silence was followed by a soft laugh, and I assured her, "No. It cannot."

She was quiet for a moment, her brow knit in studious occupation. And then her expression relaxed, and she lifted her arms and looped them about my neck. "I think," she announced, "that you may make love to me anyway."

My spirits danced. "Oh, no, you little temptress." I caught her hands and removed them from around my neck, kissing her folded fists. "For I am just devil enough to do it, and I would spoil you for human men."

"I don't care for human men," she told me.

Her eyes were bright and big and sparkling like a thousand stars on a breezy night. How I adored her. "How do you know? Have you ever lain with one?"

"I have not."

"There, you see? You speak in ignorance, *chérie*." I twisted one of her curls around my index finger and tugged it playfully.

She laughed in a sweet husky way, snatching the curl from my grasp. "See how you have neglected my education?"

"You must have a lover," I agreed. "I shall make finding you one a priority."

"I told you, I'm not interested in human males."

"Then I will find you a pretty female."

Her gaze was direct and earnest. "I want you to be my lover."

What a darling girl. What innocence and adoration in her face, what delightful expectation. My heart swelled with affection for her. It would have taken a stronger werewolf than I to resist such sweet allure.

"My dear, I cannot," I told her, and kissed her mouth gently, tenderly. "But I can show you such pleasure as I am able to give and I can teach you, perhaps, the wonders of carnal love that lie ahead."

I undid the top buttons of her dressing gown, and watched her cheeks grow hot and her pupils grow dark. Ah, this is always the best part, to see their blood rise, to feel them tremble, to hear their little hearts pound to bursting with the pleasure we can give. No, the best part is the taste of soft firm flesh against the tongue, pearly hard nipples swelling to ripeness, the gentle rising shape of the female breast as it fills the mouth. Vanilla and honey. That is a combination that always brings back the taste of Tessa to me, and to say there was no joy in it for me would be an untruth.

I pushed back the folds of her dressing gown and massaged her belly, sliding my fingers down to tangle in that thatch of fur where she was still as savage as her hirsute ancestors, and lower still to that center of pleasure between her loosening thighs. Her heat rose with the fast-hot rhythm of her heart, the quick little choking breaths, and her scent was exquisite. I suckled her breasts until she moaned out loud and I felt her small womb tighten for want of my fingers, which I pushed inside her gently until I felt the resistance and heard her small high cry of astonished sensation. As painlessly as possible I tore her maidenhead and eased the passage of her pleasure, stroking her, caressing her, licking and suckling her thrusting breasts and drinking in her tight little cries of ecstasy as though they were my own until she lay limp and damp across my knees, utterly spent.

I kissed the wet curls of hair that clung to her face, I teased open her eyes with my tongue. Carefully I withdrew my fingers from her, which were stained with her virgin's blood. I smiled. "There, you see. Your lover will thank me for this. It is a service I have performed for others before you, and have not yet had one complaint."

She looked at me with parted lips and unsteady breath, with eyes that were fevered and uncomprehending. I kissed her again and lifted her onto the divan, and I went to wash my hands.

I returned with a cloth wrung out in warm water, which I used to wash the dampness from her thighs. I loved the smell of her. Sex and blood. It was intoxicating.

When her ablutions were complete I drew the folds of her gown about her and swept her again into my lap, cuddling her in the sunshine. In all this time she had not made a sound or moved at all; her heart, slowly seeking its normal rhythm, and her breath, whispering and catching, were background music to my ears.

She laid her head against my shoulder and she said, "What will become of us now?"

It seemed to me a rather odd question, but Tessa was always surprising me with the originality of her thoughts. I answered, "Why— nothing, I suppose. We will go on as we have before, except . . ." And I kissed her forehead, trying to tease a smile from her. "I shall be jealous if you like your human lover more than you like me."

"Never, monsieur," she assured me ardently, and lifted her big dark eyes to me, filled with adoration.

I was amused and indulgent. What a great lot of importance these humans attach to sexual pleasure when the act, for them, can be nothing more than a fleeting ripple of sensation. We, the ultimate sensualists, know it for what it is and accord it a proper position in our lives which has nothing to do with love. But Tessa, deep in the throes of the sensate magic our kind inevitably, and too often unintentionally, work upon humans, had no choice but to answer to her nature. And it fell to me to be tolerant of it.

"Don't be deceived, *chérie*," I said lightly. "You will fall desperately in love with some handsome young human and forget all about me. You will bear him a dozen children and I—" I lifted a finger of admonishment when she opened her mouth to cry a protest. "Will find a mate among my own kind. These pleasures that we share will be nothing more than a fond memory for you."

Her eyes clouded. "But why can't I be your mate? Why can't we lie together like husband and wife? Why must there be others?"

"Understand this, *chérie*," I told her firmly. "Such a thing is impossible between werewolves and humans. It is a simple matter of physiology, and since you are such a bright and curious human, I will spare you no detail. At the point of arousal, whether sexual or emotional, the werewolf will inevitably resume his natural, bestial form. The only exception to this is when we have just changed forms, for it requires a period of recovery before we can change again. In human form we can't maintain copulation long enough to inseminate a female. Do you understand what I mean by that?"

At her shy, uncertain nod, I continued. "No human female could accept the penetration of a male in wolf form even if he desired to mate with her. No human male could penetrate a female in her natural form; it would be physically impossible. No doubt this is Nature's grand scheme to prevent cross-contamination between the species. Do you understand this, Tessa? Have I left in your quick, curious human mind any question unanswered?"

She whispered, eyes swimming, "*Je t'adore, Monsieur le Loup-garou.*"

I stroked her cheek with fingers that smelled still of her musk. "*Et je t'adore, Mademoiselle l'Humaine.*"

She caught my fingers and kissed them sweetly. "I will have no other lover," she whispered. "But you . . ." She lifted eyes to me that were dark and anxious. "What can I be to you?"

I smiled at her. "An impertinent little human who asks too many questions that are of no consequence, and who must never forget . . ." And now I let my expression soften. "That she is my dearest treasure and my truest friend." With that I kissed her closed hand again, and saw her melt beneath my touch.

She drew near to me, and kissed my throat. Such tenderness, such innocence, such sweetness to make the heart break. Being with her, curled together before an open window in the sunshine of a spring afternoon, was like emerging from a dark murky pool into crystal mountain waters; bathed in effervescence, I was renewed.

She tilted her head back, smiling softly, and she said, "I'm so very glad I found you, Alexander Devoncroix. Whatever else you think of me, please believe that."

Then she cast down her eyes, and in a quite different tone announced, "And because I am feeling so well disposed toward you at the moment, I think you may have your surprise after all."

I played her game. "What, *chérie*? You keep secrets from me in my own house? What are you hiding? Let me see."

Eyes sparkling, she leapt to her feet and withdrew from her pocket a gilded envelope. My heart stuttered a beat or two when I saw the crest and I was embarrassed, for I forgot, momentarily, that she could not hear the irregularity of my pulse or guess the reason for it. I snatched the envelope from her and tore it open with my thumbnail.

"It arrived a month ago," Tessa was chattering, straining to position herself to read over my shoulder. "I wanted to forward it to you, but Poinceau wouldn't give me the address . . . It's from her, isn't it? What does it say? Is there to be a coronation? May I go?"

The flowing gold script read simply, "Elise Devoncroix is pleased to offer her hospitality at Palais Devoncroix upon your return. Awaiting your leisure."

It was signed personally with her signature design: a cursive initial *E* crossed through by a looping, flowing *X*. My throat was a little dry as I returned the card to its envelope. My heart was racing.

"Well, *chérie*," I said in an admirably negligent tone, "we'd best start packing."

Eight

M̲Y̲ C̲OUNTRY̲ H̲OME̲ I̲N̲ L̲YONS̲ W̲AS̲ N̲OT̲ S̲O̲ G̲RAND̲ A̲S̲ T̲HE̲ H̲OUSE̲ I̲N̲
Paris, for life in the provinces was much more relaxed and there was
little need to try to impress. Moreover, lying as it did a mere twelve
kilometers from the Palais Devoncroix, the estate was not a place
where I ever presumed to do any formal entertaining. That right belonged exclusively to the royal family, and it would have been a foolish—and socially short-lived—werewolf indeed who tried to compete.
I kept a small staff in residence, of course, but it had been a year or
more since I had spent any appreciable amount of time there. Preparing for the move was no small undertaking.

First I dispatched a note to the Palais informing the new queen of
my intention to open my country house for the summer, and adding
that it would be my honor to call upon her when I arrived. This business of sending formal notes, cards and invitations was a custom bor-
rowed from humans but one we quite enjoyed, and we employed it
as much as possible to lend an air of ceremony to our undertakings.

In matters of urgency, of course, we would simply send a runner—always faster and more efficient than the human post—but for the most part we preferred to have these little niceties written down.

I sent Poinceau and Crolliere, with their respective staffs, ahead to open the house, and kept Gault, Lavalier the chef and, of course, Tessa with me to close up the Paris residence. This was not a situation which sat well with either Gault or Crolliere, the latter of whom still saw Tessa as one of her "girls" and who simply could not understand my attachment to her.

"You spoil that human shamelessly," Gault told me irritably. He was understandably put out—not because we were packing to leave again when he had only just arrived home, but because he was the last to know about it. "All the best werewolves in Paris are talking about you. The next I know, you'll have her sleeping on your pillow like a kitten. It's disgusting."

"The best werewolves in Paris find her as amusing as I do," I returned, "and if they did not, they wouldn't be worth my notice, now would they?"

I was at my desk, dashing off notes to acquaintances and business colleagues, and I had little patience with Gault's complaints. Besides, it was true. Tessa had been on my arm almost constantly in the past few weeks as I made the round of calls upon my acquaintances—both human and werewolf—to catch up on a winter's worth of gossip and to inform them of my plans for the coming season. She really was an insufferable little pest whom it was easier to indulge than to discipline, but I also enjoyed having her along. She still made a little game of trying to identify the werewolves among my friends, and when she thought we were alone she would whisper to me, "Ah, monsieur, but she is too beautiful—she must be loup-garou!" or, "He is very charming, isn't he? Too charming for a human, I think."

Werewolf ears, of course, delighted in her "secret" game, and soon came to deliberately invent diversions and misdirections for her to make it more interesting. Nonetheless, she was right in her guesses more often than not, particularly about the males. It has been my observation that humans almost always have an instinct for the werewolf of the opposite sex, no doubt because of that inexplicable attraction they feel for us.

"She is an annoyance and an embarrassment," Gault grumbled. "She should be roasted over an open fire and ground up to season my meat!" Of course, he said things that outrageous only when Tessa was present, and for a while he had succeeded in intimidating her. This time, however, I glanced up in time to see Tessa, who was just crossing the threshold with two new summer frocks to show me, pause to make a gruesome face at him, wrinkling up her nose and sticking out her tongue. I laughed until I couldn't hold the pen, not so much at Tessa's face as at the expression on Gault's.

In the midst of all the chaos and despite Gault's mutterings, we were a happy group that spring.

It took us three weeks to make ready for the move, not only because of the physical preparations to be made—couriers flew back and forth between Lyons and Paris with requests for new draperies and wall hangings, place settings and bed coverings, the usual miscellanea that never seem to survive more than a season or two—but because of the goodbyes to be said and the business matters to be concluded.

My two banks ran very well without me, thanks to the excellence of the werewolf staff I employed and the generosity with which I employed them—but also thanks to the fact that, as casual as my management style was, I never let them forget that I was the controlling presence and that nothing ever took place within those walls about which I did not know. Fortunes were involved, after all, both werewolf and human, and it was important that I make every member of my staff feel the responsibility as keenly as I did. For the most part this was a simple undertaking—I have never understood why humans make such a difficult matter out of managing a business (and in general doing it badly)—but occasionally a bit more personal attention was required. The death of Sancerre was one such occasion, and this departure from Paris, coming so soon after a winter in Siberia and, before that, six weeks in Italy, was another. I made my presence known, I put my people in place, I reassured them I was still in control.

In addition, those personal calls I made, those nights at the Opéra, those attendances at the ballet and the theater were more than a matter of courtesy. I had been away too long; I had to have news and I had to have it quickly and accurately. With Tessa, charming brat that she was, to distract and disarm my colleagues, I quickly learned, among other things, that a faction of the pack in the United States had panicked upon learning of Sancerre's death and closed several factories and shipyards, disrupting the economy of that country for months afterward; that six families personally known to me had delivered healthy spring infants and so had a dozen or so whom I did not know (I instructed Tessa to send gifts to all, as was the custom); that Micheline de Fortenoy had suffered a failure of the heart and was to be succeeded as head of her family by her nephew Philippe; that the artist Galgois had had a show in London and sold, as expected, the most mediocre of his canvases to humans for extraordinary amounts of money (the best of his work went, of course, to werewolf collectors); and that the young queen Elise had, in the time of my absence, driven off two challengers whom she did not consider worth her notice, and actually defeated one in battle. The bones of that unfortunate werewolf had long since been burned in a garbage heap and his name would never be spoken again.

I felt a surge of perfectly natural admiration and pride to know that our leader had acquitted herself so well.

Not only was it necessary for me to arm myself with knowledge—which is, as even humans know, the only tool of survival it is impossible to do without—but my appearances about town served another equally important purpose. I let it be known far and wide that, despite long and recent absences and whatever might have been speculated to the contrary, I was not only alive and well but thriving in the favor of the pack leader. I never failed to mention the invitation to the Palais which necessitated that I leave Paris—alas!—once again, and I usually expressed a hope, sometimes condescending, sometimes genuine, that I might see there as well whichever companion with whom I happened to be conversing. Tessa found it all very amusing and highly pretentious, but one could hardly expect her to understand. Among us, status is everything. To fail to protect that status is to leave oneself vulnerable to all manner of undesirable developments.

At any rate, after all these weeks of preparation, it took us barely a morning to make the trip to Lyons by train. Out of consideration for Gault, who had no love of mechanical conveyances and who had spent far too much time on them during the winter, I took Tessa as my only companion and gave him permission to precede us the night before in wolf form. Tessa was a delight, as excited as a child to be making the trip she had spent so long anticipating, and wholly refreshing in her rapt appreciation of the scenery. I think sometimes we werewolves forget what it must be like to know the world only through the poor shallow senses of humans—to see the green without being able to smell it, to observe the bird flight without being able to hear the thrum of its delicate wings upon the air—and it serves us well to see with their eyes occasionally, so that we might better appreciate what we are.

Gault met us at the station with a carriage and several wagons for the luggage. He and Tessa had their usual squabble, which resulted in his making a grand declaration that he refused to ride inside a closed carriage with a filthy-smelling human, and stalking off to endure a very uncomfortable trip over bumpy roads on one of the luggage wagons.

Tessa pouted over this a great deal, and insisted when we were in the carriage, "I do not smell bad!" She looked at me challengingly. "Do I?"

I tweaked her under the chin. "Not to someone who wants to have you for dinner, *chérie!*"

Such innocent days, such happy times.

I spent the next few days walking through my vineyards, talking with my vigneron, and approving the year's Beaujolais while I awaited word from Palais Devoncroix. The note came a week to the day after we had arrived, stating that the queen would be pleased to receive me on the morrow.

"At last!" declared Tessa, evincing a relieved impatience that reflected my own but to which I would never have admitted. "Such a great lot of trouble, so many gold-embossed cards going back and forth, for such a simple thing as a neighborly call. I doubt even the Queen of England makes so much fuss when entertaining the President of France!"

"Ah, but she is not a werewolf," I responded, and allowed her to snatch the card from me, dancing close to the window so that she might better study the elaborate, flowing script.

"It doesn't say what time," she observed, surprised. "Whether for tea or luncheon or any meal at all. How will I know what to wear?"

"You may wear whatever you please," I replied, and sat down to compose the note that would accompany the case of wine I would send to the Palais by way of response that afternoon. "Because you will not be going with me."

A deadly silence followed. I was occupied with a turn of phrase and barely noticed.

Then she said, "What do you mean, I won't be going? Of course I'm going! We've come all this way and waited all this time—of course I'm going!"

I waved a hand to silence her. "Tessa, stop buzzing about my ears. I'm trying to concentrate."

She came swiftly to my desk and sank down on her knees before it in a swirl of skirts and lavender perfume. "But you promised! Months and months ago you promised to introduce me, remember?"

"Yes, and I shall. But not at the Palais, and not tomorrow."

"Why not?"

Her pretty upturned face and the distress in her eyes gentled my exasperation with her. "Because, chérie, you were not invited. And because to bring a human into the presence of the queen without permission would be—" I searched for the word, in French or English, and settled for a close approximation. "Impertinent."

Her big eyes clouded with disappointment, perhaps even a misting of tears. "But—"

"No more arguments, please; we'll talk about it when I return. Now go and find Gault and send him to me. Go now, hurry."

In another moment she rose on heavy feet and left the room.

*   *   *

La fin de siècle. What an interesting time to be a werewolf. Much of the human population had begun to tire of royalty and rituals; pageantry and spectacle were variously considered either passé or ostentatious. Werewolves, on the other hand, have always known the value of a strict social hierarchy and never lose a chance to celebrate, as lavishly as possible, the traditions that govern it. For us, pageantry, spectacle and, yes, ostentation are always in fashion, and were never more so than at the turn of the century.

The Devoncroix estate was located just outside Lyons, a vast walled compound of some several thousand acres of lush parks, deep woods, streams, pools and gardens as well as virgin wilderness that supported species of wildlife known nowhere else in France. The average Frenchman would be astonished to learn just how enormous the complex was, but no more than he would be to know what resided within it. Here Mlle. Devoncroix lived precisely as she should have done, as her family had always done: like royalty.

To the humans who lived around them, the Devoncroix were considered mildly eccentric and far too wealthy for those eccentricities to matter. The Palais itself was an imposing structure which, like many of the châteaux of its kind, had been designed in a time when it might be called upon to feed and shelter large numbers—in this case, a good portion of the entire pack—for an unlimited time. Unlike other châteaux, however—human châteaux—Palais Devoncroix had never been allowed to fall into disrepair or disuse. It was still one of the most beautiful in the valley, employing the best of Gothic and Renaissance architecture, and constructed of immaculately cut blocks of pale pink stone imported from Italy and an abundance of glass. It spread gracefully across a knoll surrounded by a green park, its ornate majesty captured in a large reflecting pool at the bottom of the slope. Coming upon it for the first time always took the breath away.

The Palais was outfitted with marble hallways and Roman pools, running water and gas lamps. Wall coverings and draperies were changed every year, extravagant new furnishings ordered periodically from around the world. All of this, of course, kept a great many human craftsmen well employed, which in itself generated enough goodwill to dispel the occasional murmurings about the odd goings-on behind castle walls. The Devoncroix, like many of us, kept a few human servants and employed many hundreds of others in their various enterprises, but none of them lived inside the Palais. The three-hundred-eighty-member household was composed entirely of werewolves, for this was, after all, our last bastion.

We arrived in style, Gault and I, as was only proper, in my finest crested carriage (for, as one whose ancestors had wisely changed their name all those centuries ago, I was permitted to display on the right-hand door of my carriage and my rail car, but nowhere else, a five-by-five centimeter blue—not gold—crescent and arrow) of polished black with silver appointments drawn by a sleek team of black horses in silver harness. My driver was turned out in fine cobalt, my horses' tails plumed and dancing with high spirits. I could, of course, have taken my motorcar, or driven myself in an open barouche, and since we were neighbors and had known each other for years, neither would have been a particular breach of protocol. But I loved the spectacle: I loved the way the travelling farmers and vendors with their wagons full of merchandise pulled off the road and removed their hats—even if only to scratch their heads in puzzlement—when we passed. I loved the way the children ran out from their houses to gape, and the way the local gentry reigned their mounts and turned to stare. *La fin de siècle.* I would miss it when it was gone.

The approach to the palace was along a three-kilometer avenue lined with chestnuts and offering an occasional superb view of the still blue canal that encircled the palace proper and provided the water source for the entire complex. Now and then I caught the scent—though not a glimpse or a whisper—of the two guards in wolf form who flanked our carriage, some dozen meters into the trees on either side, and whose sole function was to escort us to the palace steps and to be ready to rip out our throats at the first sign of treachery.

As we rounded the curve that first brought the palace into view, Gault climbed down from the driver's seat and nimbly opened the door and swung inside the carriage to do a final inspection of my appearance. He was an impossible fusspot, but that was precisely what made him such a good personal servant.

He centered my stickpin and smoothed back the fall of my hair. I shrugged him away impatiently. He wrinkled his nose. "You smell like that human," he said.

In fact, I had been bothered by a distinct trace of Tessa all morning, and smelling her made me wonder whether I had treated her badly by leaving her behind. I decided to bring her a present upon my return, for she was foolishly delighted by small gifts, and put the matter out of my mind.

I said, "She helped me choose this jacket. I should have had it laundered."

"You certainly should have. You can't go into the presence of the queen smelling like a human."

"It appears I shall have to, doesn't it?"

Gault's face suddenly went quite still. He was staring at the space beneath the seat opposite, beneath which was stored a supply of folded lap blankets. "Unless," he said quite clearly, "we kill her first."

I saw then what his vantage point had allowed him to see sooner: the blankets gave a definite, startled twitch.

I listened for the heartbeat the pounding of the hooves had disguised from me before, the sigh of her breathing. I swooped down and hauled her out by ankle and wrist, eliciting several undignified howls of protest and pain in the process. How she had ever managed to wedge herself unnoticed into that small space I couldn't imagine; that she had been able to conceal her presence from me for so long humiliated and infuriated me.

"You impossible little human!" I flung her onto the opposite seat so hard that she bounced. "How dare you do this thing! Are you deranged?"

"I only wanted to see the palace!" she cried, rubbing her bruised wrist. "I would just have looked around and then gone home. You never would have known I was here!"

She had wrapped herself in one of my long coats, which explained how she had disguised her scent from me for so long, and the heavy muffling blankets had helped. But she must have been sweltering in that small closed place; her face was flushed and damp and there were dark stains under the arms of her pale yellow gown as she shrugged out of the coat and pushed it away. Her hair was mussed, the ribbons askew, her face and gown smudged with dust. I made a mental note to speak to the groom about slovenly housekeeping even as I railed at her. "Do you have any idea what you've done? Is it your intention to make me look the fool? Is *this* the way you repay my kindness?"

She managed to look both belligerent and hurt at the same time. "I told you, I only wanted to see what all the fuss was about. I wasn't even going to come near your queen, who as we both know is not a real queen at all but just a very wealthy loup-garou who has no power over me whatsoever—"

I saw Gault lunge for her and had to hold him back. "Throw her out the door," he advised in little more than a growl. "Let the guards eat her."

Her eyes went wide, as they often did in response to Gault's threats. I had no sympathy for her now, however, and replied with impatient pragmatism, "Don't be absurd. If we throw her out now we'll be accused of trying to sneak her in for the devil knows what nefarious purpose, and we'll be the ones shredded for fodder on the palace steps." I cast a hasty glance outside the window and came to a quick decision. "There's nothing but to make the best of it now. Don't say another word, Gault, and for the love of bloody hell, clean her up."

Gault glowered at me, but it was clear there was no other alternative except to brave it out. And though I cursed her through a thousand painful deaths in those last few seconds before the carriage pulled up into the grand courtyard of the Palais Devoncroix, the truth was I wasn't as concerned as I might have been about bringing Tessa into the presence of the queen. I had my reputation for outrageousness to fall back on, and the fact that Tessa was, for the most part, well behaved and presentable. Still, I couldn't think of a punishment severe enough for her when all of this was over.

Tessa gave a muffled screech as Gault suddenly lunged forward and swept her face with the flat of his tongue. He used his handkerchief to scrub the dust and perspiration from her skin while she sputtered and gasped, and then he jerked the ribbon from her hair—along, I could hear, with a considerable number of hairs themselves—and re-tied it in a more or less presentable fashion. She screeched again and tried to pummel him with her fists as he began to lick her neck and her hands and her exposed bosom.

"Stop it! Alexander, make him stop it! Look what he's—" That was as far as she got before Gault clapped his hand over her mouth and I instructed her shortly, "Hush. Better you smell like him than dust and sweat, and think if you will how unpleasant it must be for Gault."

I picked up my walking stick and uncrossed my ankles as the carriage drew to a stop. Gault, who was taking a good deal more pleasure in Tessa's distress than was probably called for, held his hand tight to her mouth and hissed malevolently in her ear. "Another screech out of you, my dear, and I will come while you are sleeping at night and pull your teeth out one by one. It is a common discipline for unruly cubs!"

He released her abruptly, and whether it was due to his threats or to my unwelcoming expression, she made not a sound. She spent the next few seconds before the carriage door was opened trying to wipe his saliva from her skin and rubbing at the red marks his fingers had left around her mouth.

I ignored the startled glance of the footman and offered my arm to Tessa as she descended from the carriage. Gault, having executed his duties by seeing me safely to my destination, went off to seek the company of those of his own status—and no doubt to remove the taste of human from his tongue with several liters of wine—and Tessa and I ascended the wide marble steps unaccompanied.

"I am very put out with you, *chérie*," I murmured to her, although in truth my temper was already beginning to cool, merely with the awe of being inside these grand halls once again. "However, if you conduct yourself with the breeding I know your father must have instilled within you and bite your tongue on every question that comes into your head, we may just get through it without doing any lasting harm, *n'est-ce pas?*"

I heard Tessa swallow. Her eyes were huge and busy taking in everything we passed. "If I had known I was going to meet the queen," she whispered back, "I would have worn a better gown."

The entryway was flanked by two twelve-foot-sized marble statues of wolves: on the right, Armaden, mythical mother to us all; on the left, Silos Devoncroix, who had defeated the Antonov all those centuries ago. Near them and forming a single file on either side was the palace guard, the strongest and finest of the pack, all in wolf form, and a magnificent display they made, too. I felt Tessa's fingers dig into the muscles of my arm and she shrank a bit closer to me as we passed, for she had never seen so many of us in our natural state before— actually, I did not think she had ever seen anyone but me—and they watched her with sharp suspicious eyes, as well they should. Her step did not falter, though, and she held her head high, which was all to her good fortune. If she had gone into a panic, I doubt that even I could have protected her from an attack.

Such was my confidence in her that, until the moment was past, I had not even considered the danger.

We walked through the great gallery with its forty-foot ceilings and magnificent tapestries depicting great moments from our past, its fine family portraits, its sculpture and enormous, glittering chandeliers. The gallery was illuminated by a high dome with many glass panels that refracted sparkling sunlight to even the dimmest corners of the great room, and Tessa twisted her head back, awestruck, to gaze at it as we continued.

There were others in the gallery, some in wolf form and some not. I nodded to those I knew and received their startled glances and infrequent recoils with what I hoped was cool aplomb, looking for all the world as though strolling the halls of Palais Devoncroix with a human on my arm was merely the latest fashion. Nonetheless, while on any other occasion I would have lingered to enjoy the treasures that were on display in that room and would have quite enjoyed sharing them with Tessa, I did not stop to chat or to browse. At times I moved so purposefully I think Tessa's feet actually left the ground.

At the end of the hall there was a set of double doors and two attendants, one in wolf form and one in human. It was here that the public area of the palace ended and those with business within were directed further. I was expected, and the attendant, though he did look long and hard at Tessa, told me that Mlle. Devoncroix would receive me in the garden room.

We went through the double doors. Another escort took us through the maze of winding corridors to the garden room. Tessa, with thanks to all the powers that rule, was too overawed by all she saw to so much as utter a whisper.

The attendant opened a set of stained-glass doors and stepped back. Without ceremony, we entered.

I had been in this room once before and had found it quite as breathtaking then as Tessa did now. It was a large room floored with colorful Moroccan tiles which formed a mosaic of werewolves in natural and human form tumbling in play in a garden. In the center was a raised fountain whose falling waters, I suddenly realized, would disguise the voices within this room from all but the most astute werewolf ears. On one wall was a hanging garden modeled after the famous terraces of Babylon, and on another a marvellous Fragonard of maidens at play, fully twelve meters high and ten long. The other wall was of alternating panels of clear and stained-glass, and it opened out onto an enclosed garden through a set of tall stained-glass doors precisely like the ones through which we had entered.

"Oh, monsieur," Tessa whispered, her eyes enormous and her cheeks flushed with wonder as she looked around. "I've never seen anything more beautiful!"

I was about to agree that this was one of my favorite rooms, but just then the stained-glass doors opened from the garden. Elise Devoncroix, ruler of all our kind, stood there silhouetted in a halo of bright sunlight, and I couldn't speak at all.

I had never seen anything more beautiful.

Nine

SHE WAS A TALL FEMALE, AND STRONG, WITH LUSTROUS HAIR THE COLOR and sheen of the sun which fell in satiny waves to her hips. Her figure was long and lithe, her muscles like tempered steel encased in satin, and she was wearing on that occasion a gossamer blue garment, sans shoes, which clung to every curve and sinew with a gentle allure that would have been envied by a Botticelli maiden. Her features were sharp and alert, her eyes fire blue, her bearing and her movements as graceful as a deer.

She could recite any poem or scrap of musing by whichever human or werewolf you might care to name at any given time. She could sing an aria in a voice so exquisite even humans had been known to fall to their knees weeping. She could play an étude or paint a landscape that could easily rival anything hanging in the Louvre, all while working a logarithm in her head or analyzing a complicated chemical formula as casually as someone else might read a newspaper. She could outrun any werewolf in the pack, and outhunt them, too. She was perfection personified—which was, of course, why she was now our pack leader.

She came into the room, leaving the doors open to the scented garden behind her. I dropped Tessa's arm and took a few steps forward where, with my eyes politely lowered, I awaited her pleasure.

"Alexander," she said, coming toward me. Her voice was warm and throaty, and it caused the skin along the line of my spine to prickle with pleasure. "How good to see my old dancing partner again. Now that you're here, I must give a ball and show you off!"

She grasped my head and gently drew me to her, testing the scent behind each ear—which traditionally holds the seat of truth—and allowing me to do the same with her. Then she kissed me on either cheek in the way of humans, and stepped back, smiling.

Power became her. She had acquired a poise since I last had met her, a stature that had matured the enchanting young girl I once had known into a queen deserving of the name. Her scent was of certainty and determination, passion and humor, bright air and clean, living things. It was intoxicating.

She glanced at Tessa with a slightly upraised eyebrow. "And so, monsieur, you have brought your little pet for my inspection. I have heard a great deal about her."

"I thought she might amuse you," I put forth with my best effort at nonchalance.

The laughing glance she threw me told me that Elise Devoncroix knew precisely how this human happened to be within her palace walls—through either her own ears or those of her spies—and found the entire situation vastly entertaining. I was wretched with humiliation to have been bested by a human before the eyes of my queen, but knew my only recourse was to take it in good grace.

I set my jaw, pasted a pleasant expression on my face, and extended my hand to Tessa. "Mademoiselle Devoncroix, may I present Tessa LeGuerre, daughter of my boyhood friend Stephen, and a human."

Tessa stepped forward, her fingertips barely touching mine, the other arm crossed upon her breast, and she dropped into the most graceful curtsey I have ever seen. "Your Majesty!" she said breath-lessly.

Elise clasped her hands together in delight, her eyes sparkling. "But, Alexander, she is as charming as I've heard!"

"She has her moments," I agreed somewhat dryly.

Elise reached out her hand to help Tessa up. "Tessa LeGuerre, on your feet. And you mustn't address me as 'your majesty,' for I am not your queen, am I? 'Mademoiselle' will do."

Tessa stood, blushing prettily, her eyes shining with the kind of admiration that Elise, simply by virtue of her nature, effortlessly inspired in everyone, both werewolf and human. "I'm sorry, I didn't know." Rarely had I known Tessa to be at a loss for words. "It's just that—just that you—all of this—you're so magnificent!"

Elise laughed musically, and I tried hard to keep my lips from twitching. Elise drew Tessa's hand into the crook of her arm and gave it a welcoming pat. "Alexander, she is a treasure. Come, let's sit by the fountain and be cozy. Tessa, does Alexander treat you well? Because if ever he is cruel to you, you have only to send me word and I will have him publicly stoned."

I caught Elise's teasing look, but Tessa did not. She replied sincerely, "Oh, no, mademoiselle, I wouldn't want that! Although," she added in a slightly altered tone, "if the same should apply to a certain man-servant, I'm sure I shouldn't object."

Elise laughed again and left us to the cushioned benches at the foot of the fountain while she took her own chair upon the dais a few steps above. It was a charming nook, surrounded by greenery and the splash of water, and one might have been deceived into imagining it a place conducive to nothing more than a harmless chat between friends. Yet, screened from sight, sound and scent as it was, the little garden alcove would also make a perfect interrogation room.

My admiration for her skill—smooth, gracious and utterly disarming—almost overcame my trepidation. Or perhaps it was only my guilt working imaginary anxieties. I had just spent a winter abroad in the company of outlaws, and upon my return I was summoned immediately to the Palais and taken to a soundproof, private audience with the queen; perhaps I could be forgiven my uneasiness.

Elise said, "I enjoyed a bottle of your wine last evening, Alexander. I believe this will be your very best vintage."

"You have an excellent palate, mademoiselle," I returned, pleased. "It will be at its fullest flavor this year and the early part of next."

"I have put it in my personal cellar but would like to order more, if I may, as gifts."

I told her I would have my vigneron contact her steward without delay, and we chatted for a few moments longer about other neutral subjects. Tessa was rapt upon our every word but did not once interrupt. Sometimes, I was beginning to think, I underestimated her, and on the whole it was all going much better than I had any right to hope.

And then Elise said, "How good it must be for you to be settled home again after so much travelling. I hope we provincials won't prove too dull for you now."

"Never a danger of that, mademoiselle," I assured her gallantly.

"Well, at least you can keep us entertained with tales of all your adventures. Where was it last—Siberia?"

My spirits sank. She knew.

"You flatter me to take such notice of my poor comings and goings." From now on every word would be weighed and measured for its dozens of possible meanings, our very conversation a dance of diplomatic possibilities. I hated these games. And loved them.

But she was more direct than I expected. "And how did you find matters there?" she inquired, with the politest of interest.

I smiled. "Very cold."

"Winter is perhaps not the most propitious season for such a journey."

"I shall remember that in the future."

She held my gaze gently, steadily. I tried not to blink. She said, "Now, monsieur, I may have to reconsider asking you to entertain at my next soiree if you cannot tell a tale better than that. You have travelled all the way to Siberia in the dead of winter, and all you have to say for the journey is that it was cold? Did nothing happen to you along the way worth mentioning at all?"

It took every ounce of will at my command to restrain my heartbeat, to keep my voice light. I could feel a small sweat break out upon the back of my neck and knew in another moment she would smell it. The best I could do to save myself was to tell as little of the truth as I could manage to justify myself. "Very little," I told her. "St. Petersburg was beautiful, but no one we know was there. I made a stop at the Winter Palace, but the Czar and Czarina were not in residence. I travelled north for a time and hunted elk and caribou. I'm afraid I had a minor scrap with some northern dwellers, but I came out of it with my skin and hurried home."

"Indeed? That sounds exciting."

I could no longer meet her eyes. "Not really," I hedged. "I didn't acquit myself very well and find the whole thing rather embarrassing."

She might have let it go at that. At least I convinced myself at that moment that she might have. But the instant I had finished speaking, Tessa began to fidget beside me and before I could find a way to forestall her, she burst out, "Why don't you tell her?"

I couldn't believe it. I felt my face and my fingertips grow cold, and for that one crucial instant when I might have stopped her—if anything this side of heaven or hell actually could be thought to have a chance of stopping Tessa—I could do nothing but stare at her.

Elise's eyes narrowed, although her voice held that same relaxed, mildly conversational tone as she inquired, "So, is there a story after all? Indeed, Alexander, why don't you tell me?"

I tried desperately to recoup. "Because there's nothing to tell. Really, mademoiselle, the one thing you must understand about this wretched little human is that she's hopelessly given to exaggeration—"

"I am not!" Tessa insisted, and got to her feet. "Actually, Mademoiselle, he's only being modest. Perhaps he doesn't want you to know how he fought for your honor and almost lost his life—"

"My honor, is it?" Elise's eyebrows went up and she sat back in her chair, her attention fixed upon Tessa. "My dear child, please tell."

I could do nothing but listen in helpless, desperate resignation as

Tessa told. Blithely, eagerly and barely pausing for breath between statements, she informed the queen—the woman I most wanted to impress in the world—that I was related to a traitor, involved with a covert, outlaw organization, and had conspired in a plot to overtake the throne. She didn't miss a detail: Denis's elaborate plan to insinuate himself into the palace using my connections and then to seduce the queen into accepting him as her mate; my initial admiration of his proposal and eventual refusal of it; my precipitous departure from the house; the trap Denis set for me; and the attack by his minions. Of course, Tessa made me sound quite the hero; of course, she couldn't have known any better; of course, in human culture, interfering in the affairs of another can be a perfectly acceptable, even admirable, thing to do. Had I had the strength left in my arms, after listening to her destroy my status and future word by word, I would have strangled her.

I expected guards to appear as soon as she had finished speaking; the best I hoped for was that I would be dragged from the grounds and ordered never to return. But even as I tensed myself for the on-slaught of brutal hands—or perhaps even teeth—Elise turned to me and observed with soft admiration, "What a loyal creature you have in her, Alexander! One must assume that any werewolf who can in-spire that kind of devotion is deserving of further attention, don't you think? And what a perfect little mimic she is, although . . ." And she turned to Tessa with a kind smile. "I do believe you may have left out one or two points, my dear. Like the way Denis Antonov teased his brother so mercilessly for being a human-lover and mocked him with-out words when he refused to put on the cloak of the Brotherhood." This last she said while looking straight at me. Her voice was quiet and gentle with sympathy. "And how, despite all of this, his heart was broken to be driven from his brother's house and betrayed in the night."

I got slowly to my feet. There was no disguising my heartbeat from her now, or my breath or the myriad of emotions that flooded every pore: astonishment, relief, wonder, dread—shock. "And so, mademo-iselle." My voice was oddly hoarse, and tight in my throat. "You knew my story all along." *And waited to see if I would tell it*, was the unspoken ending to that statement. This was her test of loyalty to me. Had I passed or failed?

She rebuked me mildly. "I would be a poor queen indeed not to be concerned when the movements of one who bears my name take him into the enemy camp. You're a loyal Devoncroix and an honorable werewolf," she told me, "but I knew that already. What I did not know was how trustworthy you were—or perhaps I should say, I did not know how much you trusted *me*."

She smiled, and stood. I went forward quickly, offering my hand as she descended the two steps. "Fortunately for you, your human friend has spared you the necessity of answering that question. But I would like to hear it anyway." She held my gaze, and although there was nothing more than mild curiosity in her own, it was a powerful thing. "Would you have told me, Alexander, if she had not?"

I dropped my eyes. "I didn't want to offend you," I said. And I added, because honesty was what she had asked for, and what she deserved, "And I didn't want to risk my status."

She touched my face, directing my gaze to hers. She searched my eyes. "Yet you could have stopped her from speaking."

I managed to smile. "No, mademoiselle," I said. "I could not."

Tessa looked from one to the other of us anxiously. "Did I do something wrong? Was it a secret, monsieur? You didn't tell me so."

Elise removed her fingers from my face and left a pleasant tingling where they had touched. As difficult as it had been to hold her gaze a moment ago, it was now that hard to look away. But I managed to do so, long enough to reassure Tessa. "No, *chérie*, you did nothing wrong."

And I saw from the smile on Elise's face that I had spoken the exact truth. She extended one hand to Tessa, and the other she slipped under my arm. "Come, we'll be a party for luncheon, just the three of us. Tessa, I like you very much and want you to feel free to visit me any time. Perhaps now, if you're not too occupied with other matters, you both will stay some days and help me entertain my guests. What a lovely summer we'll all have together."

And that was the beginning of the best time of my life. And the worst.

PART FOUR

Lyons, France

Spring, 1898

᧞

Cleverness, in a human, is not necessarily a desirable trait.
—AMADEUS SINGLETON, WEREWOLF 1763

Without passion man is a mere . . . possibility.
—HENRI FRÉDÉRIC AMIEL, A HUMAN 1882

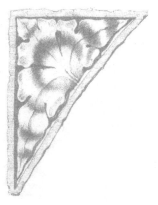

TESSA

Ten

DURING THAT LONG, LONELY AND SOMETIMES FRIGHTENING WINTER while Alexander was away, Tessa had thought more than once of simply leaving the house in Paris. No one would have stopped her. Certainly no one would have been sorry to see her go. But had she left she would have been just another human looking back on a life that might have been, and she thought nothing could be more unbearable than that. So she waited, and she watched, and she learned.

And what she learned was both useful and incidental, fascinating and tedious. She learned, for example, that Mme. Crolliere, for all her sternness, could be gotten around if asked about her family. She learned that the raising of the young was afforded the highest priority among their kind, requiring the dedicated attention of both parents for the first fragile months of life and involving the entire pack as the child grew. She learned that werewolf gestation lasted only six months, and that females were fertile well into their seventies and often mothered a dozen children or more, although rarely did pregnancies occur closer than three years apart—age three being the year that children were considered mature enough to care for themselves sufficiently that the parents could turn their attention to the raising of another. She learned that the mating bond was the one association that was impossible to break, and that it lasted, in tenderness and affection, for a lifetime. And she learned that Crolliere was mated to Poinceau.

When Tessa expressed her astonishment over that revelation, exclaiming that she never would have guessed, Mme. Crolliere tapped her head in a superior fashion and replied, "There is no need for you to know, human girl. *We* know."

She was told that they often lived to be one hundred fifty years old, although she didn't entirely believe it. When one half of a mated couple died a natural death by disease or old age, the other spouse usually followed within a few hours or days. She learned, too, that infants were born in wolf form to a mother in wolf form, and retained that form until they were six weeks old, at which time they began to change spontaneously from wolf to human and back again. It was always an exciting time for the family and friends to see which human characteristics the infant would possess, and much boasting was done about how early the child began to change, or with what frequency.

The children developed quickly, walking with confidence before age one and mastering the art of language by age two. Most of those famous personages in history designated "prodigies" by humans, Tessa was given to understand, were in fact werewolf—something else she was not entirely certain she believed.

Once they learned to control the Change at will, which happened around the age of three, they spent a little over half their time in human form. It was common, although by no means required, to sleep in wolf form. It was, however, considered the height of bad taste to display oneself in wolf form before humans, and they never, if it was at all avoidable, allowed a human to witness their Change.

She learned that they were exceptionally vain, and never lost an opportunity to point out their innate superiority. When she witnessed Marcel the stableboy snap the spine of a snake which had been bothering the horses, she demanded to know why he didn't simply find a pistol and shoot the thing. He replied disdainfully, "I have the advantage over every other creature on earth as it is. Only weakling humans need weapons."

Although the werewolves in whose care Alexander had left her took their responsibility seriously and were for the most part cooperative in answering her persistent questions, many of the details of their existence Tessa gleaned by accident, by extrapolation and by deduction. The things she wanted most to learn—the mechanics of their ability to change from one form to another, how it felt and what precipitated it and what they thought while changing and what parts of themselves transferred from one form to another and how they came to possess such a miraculous ability—these were questions that remained forever unanswered, and gradually she came to understand that the questions themselves were considered rude and intrusive. Eventually she stopped asking.

She learned that they were extremely facile with tools and mechanical devices of all kinds; even the youngest of them could glance at a device once and immediately understand how it worked, then disassemble and reconstruct it to work more efficiently in a matter of mere minutes. They were fascinated by gadgetry and were constantly seeking newer, easier and faster ways to accomplish ordinary tasks.

She learned they were gregarious, loyal, fiercely protective of their own, unexpectedly playful, possessed of a dry wit and a sharp—if ofttimes selective—memory. And Tessa learned that, despite their almost uniform contempt for her and all her kind, they found her presence among them stimulating, even challenging. They loved a challenge, and the hours they spent debating among themselves as to who should be responsible on any given day for her entertainment, education or care helped enliven a dull dark winter. Tessa learned she had little to fear from them, and much about which to wonder. Yet she knew she would never, no matter how much she learned, be completely at ease among them—or welcomed by them.

The winter spent in the tutelage of werewolves prepared her well for the spring at the Palais—if anything at all could be said to have prepared her for this, the strangest event of her life thus far. They enjoyed the hospitality of the queen for six weeks, and it was a grand mélange of the bizarre and the magnificent, during which Tessa was paraded out like a monkey on a string at every event to be petted and fawned over, scrutinized and queried. At first she resented the arched eyebrows, the ritual circling, the rude stares and critical observations— for the werewolves who visited the Palais were justifiably haughty and aristocratic in the extreme. But then she recognized the display for what it was. Elise, by presenting her at every official function and to every important guest, was making it known that she, Tessa LeGuerre, a human, was under the protection of the queen. This not only made her an exceptional human, but, because of her association with Alexander, raised his status in the eyes of others of his kind.

What she did not know—not then, at any rate—was that Elise was making another statement by displaying the human girl who had come under her favor, and that by doing so she was serving her own purposes far more than Tessa's.

The Palais was a vast and endlessly enchanting place, with every conceivable luxury and modern convenience, and Tessa never grew tired of exploring it. There were bathing rooms in which water was warmed without the aid of a flame and filled marble tubs large enough to accommodate several people at a time. There were electrically operated lamps in almost every room which responded to the touch of a hand, and when Tessa, big-eyed but trying desperately not to reveal her lack of sophistication, commented upon the ingenuity of Mr. Edison (whose name she had only incidentally read in a newspaper), Alexander and Elise exchanged a knowing look and burst into laughter. "Yes, indeed, Mr. Edison," Alexander repeated and raised his glass with twinkling eyes, giving her to believe that Mr. Thomas Edison had very little to do with electrical lights at all and that she was quite the ingenue for thinking he did.

One of the last places to be explored was the art gallery on the third floor. There were many breathtaking works of art scattered throughout the palace, for a love of color, form and the intrinsic sense of completion that make a work of art great was, Tessa had learned, something all loups-garous had in common. The most impressive pieces were, however, grouped together in the gallery that ran the length of the third floor and encompassed, by means of a set of tall spiral staircases, the whole of the fourth floor. This upper gallery was almost over-whelmingly immense, but was divided into several smaller rooms by heavy double doors. The doors to some of those rooms, farthest toward the end of the gallery, were kept closed due to the fragility of the very old paintings.

It was common to see werewolves strolling through the gallery sin-gly or with others at any time of the day or night, gazing at the paint-ings, sitting before them in profound meditation, or merely casting pleasured glances toward the canvases as they strolled, seeming to take some kind of deep comfort from merely being surrounded by art. No one ever explored those back rooms, however, and while the doors were not locked—Tessa had noticed there were no locks on any of the Palais doors—she had been told that they were opened only on special occasions or to admit technicians specifically trained in the cleaning and care of old paintings. Those were, of course, the only rooms in the gallery Tessa was interested in seeing.

There were no electric lamps in this part of the house, for which Tessa was grateful. She still found the devices intimidating. She left the gallery door open long enough to strike a match, glancing behind her to determine whether anyone would stop her. The corridor behind her was empty, but she had learned long ago that the evidence of the eyes meant nothing where these creatures were concerned. Someone might have heard her, or smelled her passage, and even now be round-ing a corner to forbid her entry. She wasn't afraid of them—after all, Alexander was most insistent that she improve her education in the arts and was constantly questioning why she did not take advantage of the opportunities afforded her here—but she didn't like to be scolded, and she didn't want to do anything that would lower Elise Devoncroix's opinion of her. So she waited, and watched, but the cor-ridor was empty. She justified that as permission to enter.

One by one she lit the gas lamps, and one by one the portraits came to life. They were all portraits, and they were all magnificent, and gradually Tessa came to understand that they all had been painted by loups-garous. Handsome men, comely women, and except for their beauty, not so different from those in the family gallery of any other aristocratic house of France. Not so different, that is, until one noticed the wolves.

In the more recent paintings, those depicting costumes from two hundred years ago or earlier, the presence of the wolves was almost innocuous—running in the background, peeking out from behind garden shrubs or wooded paths, sometimes playing as cubs amidst delicately gowned females in a glade or woodland setting. Some of the most stunning portraits featured wolves without humans at all— a single wolf resting upon a sunny hillside, posing before a rosy fire, lifting his head in a howl of triumph.

But as Tessa moved backward through history, the portraits became more disturbing. In one painting of a red-haired woman in a Renaissance costume, the storm clouds as seen through her castle window formed the faces and sharp slanted eyes of wolves. In another, a man stood upon a moonlit hillside and, arms outstretched, addressed an assemblage of wolves—wolves in the meadow, as far as the eyes could see, alert, attentive, listening to what he had to say. In another, wolves and naked children with long silky hair shared a feast of bloody meat. In yet another, a naked woman with silky blond hair cascading over her breasts and hips but with no hair at all around her private parts caressed a powerful black wolf whose commanding gaze dominated the portrait, and the look in her eyes was pure adoration.

But by far the most striking—and, in many ways, horrifying—portrait occupied the full length and breadth of a specially constructed wall in the farthermost room, a room that was empty of all else except the huge canvas. In it, a larger-than-life-sized wolf, his male member enormous and engorged, his eyes blazing yellow, prepared to mount a naked human woman. Her dark, wind-tossed hair suggested wildness; the fierce triumph in her eyes spoke of seduction well planned. The evidence of her humanity was in the dark hair beneath her arms and between her legs. In the background a cascade of history unfolded across a shadowed plain—troops of humans and bodies of wolves, bodies of humans in the jaws of wolves, wolves at rest in green paradise, humans at war in filthy cities. From the sky the ghostly shapes of creatures half wolf and half human, half human and half wolf, looked down upon it all in serene judgement. The impact of the painting was overwhelming, sickening, terrifying—but mesmerizing. Tessa could not take her eyes away even as she knew she could stare at it for decades and never see all the hidden details, never know all its encrypted messages.

"Does it disturb you?"

Tessa whirled, catching a gasp in her throat, at the voice behind her. Elise Devoncroix sat on a blue velvet viewing divan less than six feet from Tessa, and how she had arrived there unnoticed Tessa could not begin to imagine. Her hair was braided into a thick rope over one shoulder, and she wore purple bicycle trousers and a tight-waisted, full-sleeved silk shirt. Her boots were scuffed, and she carried a pair of worn leather gardening gloves in her hand. It was details such as these—the gloves, the boots—that never failed to put Tessa at her ease around the queen, and it had occurred to her to wonder once or twice whether Elise—so magical, so powerful—somehow manufactured them just to make Tessa comfortable.

Tessa turned slowly back to the painting, and answered honestly. "Yes."

"It's called 'The Conception,' and it's quite the most valuable thing in my collection. Wars have been fought for it, as a matter of fact. It's over five thousand years old."

Tessa cast an incredulous gaze on her and Elise nodded. "Oh, yes, quite true. You're only surprised because you're accustomed to measuring civilization in human terms. But our culture is much, much older, and our accomplishments, naturally, much more notable. Of course," she added, rising to stand beside Tessa, "the pigments are not as stable as we might like, and are particularly susceptible to deterioration from the chemicals produced by human breath and . . ." She looked meaningfully at the lamps Tessa had lighted. "Smoke."

Instinctively Tessa took a step back, dragging her gaze from the canvas. "I'm sorry," she said quickly. "I didn't mean . . ."

Elise smiled. "I suppose we might stand here for a few more moments. And I'm curious. What is it about the painting that disturbs you most?"

Unlike Alexander, Elise never teased Tessa by speaking in a language that was not completely her own, but always addressed her in English—as a matter of courtesy, Tessa thought. But like Alexander—and every other werewolf she had met—Elise could switch languages with uncanny ease, and never revealed the faintest trace of an accent.

Tessa returned her attention to the painting, though the answer to the question was obvious. "I was told—that is, Alexander explained to me that such a thing . . ." She made a small, shy gesture toward the canvas. "That the mating of humans and werewolves is impossible."

"That's true. The painting is meant to be symbolic." Elise's voice was patient, but Tessa thought she detected the faintest trace of condescension there.

"I understood him to say that the very notion of such a thing was . . . disgusting."

"Do you find the depiction before you disgusting?"

Tessa looked again at the powerful, aroused wolf, the fierce and sharp-eyed human woman, and she swallowed hard, nodding.

"Then you see our two peoples have something in common," replied Elise.

"But no human artist painted this," Tessa pointed out. "No human wars have been fought over it and no humans treasure it. How can you place such a great value on something that's both untrue and morally offensive to you?"

Elise laughed softly. "Well, now, a question asked is halfway to the answer, isn't it? Unfortunately, I'm not sure there's a satisfactory answer for that, at least not one I can put in human terms. It has to do with humor. With the pleasure we take from mocking ourselves and our icons. No, there's no word for it in English, or in French. Do you speak Latin? No? Well, it doesn't matter. There simply isn't a human equivalent, although 'irony' is close. We value the painting *because* it is untrue and offensive and because it causes us to question what we value. Also, of course, because it is a marvellous work of art and tells a masterful story."

Tessa shook her head helplessly, unwilling to turn away from the painting. "I don't understand," she said.

Elise slipped her arm through Tessa's, patting her hand gently. "Then," she said kindly, "today you have learned something very important."

Tessa looked away from the painting and into the eyes of Elise Devoncroix. The contrast between the grotesquerie of the depiction and the porcelain beauty of the reality was startling, disorienting.

"You will never understand us, Tessa LeGuerre," Elise said, not unkindly. "Our two species are alien to each other. We came to accept that truth long ago. And if you are ever to be content, so must you.

"Now come," she invited, drawing Tessa away, "let's put out the lamps before irreparable damage is done. I will probably have electric lamps installed here as soon as our scientists discover a way to keep the heat from drying out the canvases. I can't help but think heat will do far less damage than fumes, though."

Tessa cast one more uneasy glance over her shoulder at the painting. Elise watched her indulgently. "Final thoughts?" she suggested. "What will you tell Alexander about your sojourn into the art history of our kind?"

Tessa was thoughtful in her reply. "Why is it," she said, "that in your legends and mine—in your art and mine—the woman is always depicted as the originator of all our troubles?"

Elise laughed out loud with delight. "What a lively debate we'll have at the dinner table tonight!"

They put out the lamps and left the gallery arm in arm, and Elise never once reprimanded Tessa for going where she should not have.

Eleven

THE FAMILY OF ELISE DEVONCROIX HAD BUILT ITS CONSIDERABLE FOR-
tune on shipping—for *les loups-garous,* as Tessa discovered, though
they were not overly fond of large bodies of water and often made
poor swimmers, had an uncanny mastery of the sea. This was due in
part to their innate navigational abilities, and in part to simple skills
like hand-eye coordination and masterful shipbuilding. Moreover, in
the early thirteenth century, an enterprising Devoncroix had laid claim
to most of the coal deposits in the British Isles, for werewolves had
discovered the convenience and efficiency of coal long before the human population began to deplete the forests to such an extent that the
price of firewood became prohibitive.

Their acute sense of smell allowed them to locate deposits of oil and
gas far beneath the surface of the earth, and the coal mines gave birth
to a new fortune. The same skills were used to locate mineral deposits—gold, silver, precious stones—and the fortune grew.

They were shrewd, they were bold, and they were imaginative.

From these two solid bases—shipping and mining—the Devoncroix had built a financial empire that criss-crossed Europe and the Americas. Each generation brought a new component into the mix: railroads, in the case of Sancerre, who had been Elise's father; and, from Elise, perfumery. Tessa, who had very little interest in the complexities of industry nor knowledge of how it worked, was nonetheless overawed when she considered the vast influence of the Devoncroix, and the possibilities that were implicit. Sometimes she thought she must not have understood correctly at all; most of the time she found it more practical to simply ignore what she did not understand. One thing, however, became quickly apparent, even to her: while the position of "pack leader" might be purely symbolic and the associated responsibilities nothing more than traditional, the real power inherent in being a Devoncroix was financial.

What Elise Devoncroix had inherited in the year of 1897 was more than a fortune, less than a kingdom. Centuries of ritual and circumstance descended to her, as well as the moral responsibility for the preservation of certain values, skills and traditions. She opened the Palais for theatricals and athletic contests. She made available its pools and rivers for recreation and its vast, protected wooded areas for running. And although theoretically these areas were open to all werewolves through the dictates of noblesse oblige, Tessa learned that only the very highest ranking were invited to the Palais, and no one got past the guards without an invitation.

Many of the werewolves who visited the Palais sought Elise's advice, intervention or financial aid, which she dispensed according to the validity of the request and the deservedness of the claimant. Others came to inspect her, to determine her strength and her weaknesses and to decide whether or not it might be worth their while to challenge her in battle. Tessa was outraged to learn this and demanded why her guards ever allowed such traitors to come into her presence. Elise just laughed.

"But those are the very ones I *want* to see," she explained. "How else can I know who my enemies are?" Then she shrugged and added,

"If they do challenge me they'll be killed, and if they don't they will be rewarded for their wisdom and their bravery."

It seemed to Tessa a great foolishness and a waste of time, but she had too much respect for Elise to say so.

Elise gave her approval to marriages and officiated at births, and kept in her head the family tree of each member of the pack. This seemed to Tessa an astonishing feat, but Elise took it as a matter of course, for it was something she had learned from childhood, much in the way human children learn the alphabet and, once learned, never give it a second thought. The matter of families, of births, deaths and marriages—or matings, as they were called—was of the utmost importance in their society, ranking far above squabbles, conquests or even the acquisition of wealth. Tessa found it odd that such an ordinary thing should be elevated to almost reverential status among a people who otherwise seemed almost completely ruled by pragmatism.

"Our numbers are fewer than yours," pointed out Elise, not unkindly, "which may cause us to value such things more highly than you."

"Or perhaps," suggested Alexander with a hint of bored annoyance, "it is simply that we *are* more valuable than you. *Vraiment*, mademoiselle, I don't know why you persist in indulging this bothersome child's curiosity upon subjects that don't concern her in the least."

"Because it amuses me," replied Elise smoothly. "Do I need another reason?"

Alexander's eyes narrowed in quick recognition of his own words when he had been asked the same thing by Gault. Tessa smothered a giggle behind her hand, and Elise laughed out loud, and in a moment a reciprocal spark of appreciation shone in Alexander's own eyes.

He caught Tessa playfully around the waist and drew her to him. "Sharper than a serpent's tooth is a treacherous female," he declared. "I can see now my mistake in bringing the two of you together."

"It is always a mistake to underestimate the cunning of a woman," retorted Elise.

Tessa added, "Or a human."

They laughed together, and Alexander kept his arm around her waist as the threesome walked through the gardens. Tessa leaned against him, secure and content, and was once again struck by that sense of wonder that her life should be so perfect.

"What a foolish werewolf Denis Antonov must be," Tessa said to Elise after a moment. "You never would have married him."

Elise cast an amused glance toward Alexander and replied, "I don't know, Tessa. Perhaps I would have. I understand he's very handsome and almost as charming as his brother."

Alexander assured her, "Not nearly."

"But he never could have convinced you he'd reformed," Tessa insisted, "and he never could have made you hate humans."

Elise was thoughtful. A shaft of sunshine sparkled on her face as they came out of the dappled shadow of a canopy of trees, and she narrowed her eyes against it, adjusting the curve of her wide-brimmed straw hat. "Perhaps not," she said. "Perhaps I wouldn't have cared."

She saw Tessa's shock and she smiled. "Matings among us are not necessarily ruled by passion alone, Tessa. Denis is a strong werewolf whose vision for the pack is not entirely wrong. He can command a crowd and hold a pack together; this he has already proved. He would sire strong offspring. And there is an advantage to bringing the house of Devoncroix and Antonov together again. In fact, it would appear that the only area in which we disagree is on the subject of humans." She pursed her lips in mock consideration. "What a clever girl you are, Tessa, to bring this to my attention. I think perhaps I should give it some serious thought."

Alexander was not amused. He dropped his arm from Tessa's waist. "I don't like to hear you talk that way, even in jest."

Elise tossed him a mildly challenging look. "Because it makes your defense of me less noble?"

Alexander answered seriously, "Because it's wrong."

Elise looked at him for a moment, and then smiled. "I'm glad you think so."

But even though they were smiling at each other, and even though when Alexander offered his arm to Elise she took it, Tessa wished she had never brought the subject up. She took Alexander's other arm when he offered it, but the ambience they had shared a moment ago was not so easy to recapture.

They stopped for a time to watch a lawn tennis match across the way, and Elise and Alexander talked about the upcoming Festival of the Summer Moon, which would draw werewolves from all over Europe to the Palais. Tessa eavesdropped for a while, but then was distracted by an impertinent young male who was doing tumbling runs through the fountain in the nude. His companion was a smaller, female, caramel-colored wolf who chased him with no apparent real intention of catching him. Such sights never failed to startle Tessa, for nudity was quite common among them and considered not in the least objectionable. To appear in wolf form within sight of a human was not, of course, nearly as acceptable, and this had been the cause of tension at the Palais since Tessa's arrival. Elise's attitude toward Tessa had made it clear that the human was welcome, but it was unfair to require visitors at the Palais to avoid their natural forms for Tessa's sake. Tessa knew this was a source of resentment from the other werewolves, yet she could do nothing about it. And whenever she happened upon one of them in his natural form she was as uncomfortable as he was; she always felt for one brief disorienting moment as though she had crossed some invisible line from one world into another and must hasten to step back before she lost her balance.

The male caught scent of Tessa first and turned. Seeing her, he wrinkled up his nose at her in a challenging, mocking gesture, but then he noticed her companion the queen and his expression quickly changed to consternation. Both he and the taffy wolf sprinted away, disrupting the tennis game when they dashed across the court. One of the players tossed a racket at him.

Alexander said, scowling, "These young ones have no manners at all."

"You're right." Elise's gaze followed the scene with disapproval. "But then, who is there to teach them? The pack has fallen into disarray, Alexander; no one has any pride or sense of purpose anymore. I take full responsibility for that."

"You haven't even been inaugurated pack leader yet," Alexander objected. "I don't see how you can blame yourself for a circumstance that has taken centuries to develop."

To which Elise replied simply, "If I am to be pack leader, I must."

They walked in silence for a while. Tessa, who felt that somehow the incident was all her fault, followed quietly.

Then Alexander said, "I think it would be best if we made our departure by the end of the week, before guests start arriving for the Festival."

Elise raised her eyebrows in surprise—although it seemed to Tessa the surprise was somewhat feigned, and that Alexander knew it. "You would insult me by leaving before the Festival? Everyone will think I treat my guests so badly they can't even be bribed to stay with promises of bottomless wine barrels and acres of food. How shall I hold my head up?"

He smiled. "I will return, if you like. But if you expect a decent vintage to fill your bottomless barrels, I had best go and see to my vineyards."

Tessa knew that wasn't right. Alexander had very little at all to do with the making of wine or the tending of the vineyards, and often boasted that his employees were of such high caliber and such a refined degree of loyalty that he could disappear for years and return to find a business that had grown tenfold in his absence.

Then Elise inquired pointedly, "And Tessa? Will she return, too?" And Tessa understood.

Alexander glanced at her, and it was clear this was a subject he would have preferred not to have raised in her presence. It was equally as clear that Elise knew it.

He replied, "I think it's best that Tessa return to my estate for a while. She can visit again after the festival."

Tessa had no intention of remaining silent at that. "Why?" she demanded. "I've been to other of your parties, I've met other of the guests. Am I a secret, then? Are you ashamed of me? What is so extraordinary about this party?"

"Yes, Alexander," invited Elise, threading her hand through the crook of his arm as they left behind the tennis lawn for the formal gardens. "Please explain your logic to us."

Alexander's voice was tinged with exasperation. "A great many guests will come who have never met Elise before," he told Tessa. "It's important that she make a good impression. There will be certain— activities in which you cannot participate, at any rate. You would be bored."

Tessa just stared at him. Dimples appeared at the corners of Elise's mouth as she explained, "What he means by 'guests,' Tessa dear, is 'suitors.' I will be expected to choose a mate from the crop of this season's finest."

Tessa was so intrigued by this that she almost forgot her pique at Alexander. "Why, it's just like a fairy tale!" she exclaimed, and Elise laughed.

But Alexander's tone was brusque. "If you had applied yourself to your lessons as you've been told, you would know that the source of most of your so-called fairy tales lies within our most deeply held traditions. That, however, is not the point—"

"How will you do it?" Tessa inquired of Elise. "How will you know which one to choose?"

"Well, that's ever the question, isn't it?" replied Elise, amused. "How does one ever? Perhaps you will help me make up my mind, Tessa."

Alexander's voice was oddly stiff and subdued as he said, "I think this has gone far enough, mademoiselle."

Elise turned to him. Her expression remained pleasant, as did her voice, but there was something hard in her eyes; something which, although she barely glimpsed it, Tessa immediately recognized as a challenge.

Elise said, "What has gone far enough, Alexander?"

He hesitated. That, if nothing else, was enough to alert Tessa to the import of the moment, and she came to understand something more important was being debated here than her right to attend a private festival. She knew when to be silent and watchful.

Alexander took Elise's arm and turned a little from Tessa, lowering his voice to build an invisible wall of privacy around them. "Elise," he said, "I know what you have been trying to do and I admire you for it. But there are some among us who won't understand about Tessa, and you can't afford to make any enemies just now."

Elise's eyes flashed. "How fortunate I am to have you to advise me on what I can and cannot afford to do, monsieur."

"I meant no offense." But anger worked in the muscles of Alexander's jaw. "I brought her here. I don't want to be responsible for embarrassing you."

"Embarrassing!" gasped Tessa. Hurt and outrage prompted her to speak where wisdom dictated silence. "Am I an *embarrassment* to you?"

Elise raised a hand to soothe her, although her eyes remained, full of anger and challenge, upon Alexander. "You are not an embarrassment, Tessa LeGuerre. You are a perfect example of how charming and intelligent and perfectly worthwhile a human being can be. I am surprised your so-called guardian hasn't discovered as much for himself!"

"Curse it, Elise, you know what I mean." Alexander's voice was tight, and he did not look at Tessa.

"I do," Elise returned, "and I must say I'm disappointed. I had taken you for one who had the courage of his convictions. Perhaps you are more like your brother than I first thought."

An angry flush stained Alexander's cheeks and his eyes went dark. "That is unfair."

"Is it?" Elise's color rose as she confronted him, her chin high, her shoulders back, and her bearing, in stature and mastery, every bit as powerful as Alexander's. "Prove me wrong!"

"My only concern is your welfare! You said yourself the pack is in disarray—is this the way to unite it? And how can you hope to rule at all if you cannot attract a suitable mate?"

"You dare to question me!"

"I dare to *counsel* you, mademoiselle! There is a difference between standing firm for one's beliefs and tossing away your future on a whim!"

"And you would know that difference, I suppose? Pray, enlighten me!"

"That is what I'm trying to do!"

Tessa took an instinctive step backward. Anger when expressed between two powerful werewolves was a terrifying thing; it seemed to suck the oxygen out of the air, to cause static to crackle in the ears, to raise the temperature of the earth. Tessa found herself taking an involuntary step backward even as she cried, "No, mademoiselle, you are wrong!"

Elise whipped her head around, her blue eyes on fire, her lips set tight, her hair whirling about her body like a halo of lightning. Tessa felt her courage desert her in that moment, for even a werewolf would have quaked beneath the temper of Elise Devoncroix. Yet as small as she felt, as frightened as she was, she knew she had to finish what she had begun.

"He is nothing like his brother," Tessa insisted breathlessly. "I will leave or I will stay, whatever you wish, only—don't accuse Alexander so unfairly, and please don't be angry with him!"

Slowly, Elise's expression cleared. The faintest of smiles touched her lips as she looked from Tessa to Alexander. "And so, monsieur," she remarked, "while I'm not sure you deserve such a staunch defense, I say once more that anyone who can inspire the loyalty of such an innocent creature deserves a second chance."

Alexander managed to look at the same time embarrassed, annoyed, and proud. But the anger was completely gone from his tone, too, as he replied dryly, "Tessa is many things, mademoiselle, but I am not certain innocent is one of them."

Elise turned from him and reached for Tessa's hand, tucking it beneath her arm confidentially. "Now, Tessa, you must be the final judge. Tell me honestly, for I will know if you lie, what is your assessment of Alexander Devoncroix's character?"

The intricacies of humor wherein it applied to werewolves continued to elude Tessa, and she could never be certain when Elise was teasing her. She did understand, however, that the queen would know as easily as Alexander did if she lied, and she racked her brain to find something commendable to say about him. Considering the fact that she was quietly furious with him for trying to get rid of her, not to mention her seething hurt over his use of the word "embarrass," this was not an easy thing.

"I think he is very forthright," she ventured carefully.

Alexander groaned softly.

Tessa drew a breath and plunged on. "He is often thoughtless and self-centered. He can be arrogant and opinionated and deceitful, if it serves his purpose. He is vain and autocratic. Frankly, mademoiselle"—this gave her some pleasure to say—"I have often thought him to be something of a peacock."

The dimples that bracketed Elise's mouth appeared again as she glanced at Alexander.

"However," Tessa concluded, "he is kind to subordinates and he can always be relied upon to keep his word. I have never known him to be anything less than fair."

She could have said more, but she was afraid she had already gone too far. She didn't dare look at Alexander.

"Well, my dear," said Elise, arching one eyebrow, "you have just described the perfect loup-garou. Perhaps I should put Alexander on my list of possible challengers."

Alexander took a step forward, meeting her eyes boldly. "Perhaps you should."

Elise held his gaze for a moment, and then she murmured, "Ambitious as well. A most admirable combination. What a pity you are so outrageously fixed in your opinions."

But Alexander, instead of rising to his own defense, merely smiled. "Yes, isn't it?"

And there it was: a storm quickly risen and just as quickly gone, sublimely typical of the mercurial temperaments of their kind. Tessa, however, who understood neither the argument nor its unlikely resolution, could not forget so easily.

When they linked arms to continue their stroll, Tessa turned to go back to the house. They did not even notice she was gone.

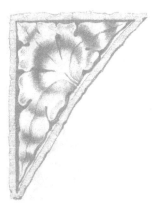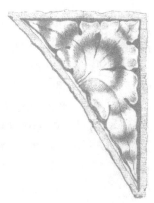

Twelve

TESSA WAS A FAMILIAR SIGHT AROUND THE GROUNDS AND WHEREVER SHE
went she met with an attitude which, while it was far from deferent
or even welcoming, was at least tolerant. Perhaps if she had been able
to appreciate how truly unusual—even outrageous—it was that she
be allowed within the gates at all, she would have been more understanding. As it was, she was constantly on her guard, and never completely comfortable unless she was with Alexander or Elise.

It was the same in Alexander's house, of course. The difference was
that there were human servants there and human tradesmen and human associates of Alexander's who visited regularly, yet they only
made Tessa feel more isolated. None of them shared her secret. None
of them would understand—or perhaps even believe her—if she
shared it with them, and she had long since realized that she would
never tell anyone else. To tell a secret, her mother used to say, diminished both the secret and the teller. Tessa understood at last what she
had meant . . . and, oddly enough, she thought she understood why

her father had kept his secret from all except a wide-eyed child who was too young to know the difference between truth and fairy tale.

The result was that Tessa was not only alone but lonely. She had no friends, no confidantes, no one with whom to explore her feelings or share her confidences or from whom she could seek advice. When she was with Alexander none of that mattered. He filled her hours with such challenge, such excitement, that she could not imagine wanting more. But when he was away she felt her isolation acutely.

If asked whether she was happy at the Palais Devoncroix, she would not have given an unqualified yes. She was awestruck, fascinated, humbled, intrigued. But she was also often uneasy, always uncertain, sometimes even frightened. She would never get used to sights such as she had seen that afternoon—the naked man and the wolf running across the tennis lawn. Nor could she grow accustomed to the guards who ceremoniously accompanied Elise everywhere she went, often in wolf form. The otherworldly beauty of the guests at the Palais, their odd behavior, their narrow-eyed gazes, their habit of speaking of her as if she weren't there . . . all of it combined to remind her she was an intruder on perilous ground.

Yet she did not want to be sent away. She did not want to be left at the Lyons house without Alexander. She did not want to be left alone again in a strange place with nothing but the company of creatures who found her alternately amusing and annoying and who remained as baffled by her as she was by them. She did not want to be dismissed in the way one would send a child to bed before the adult party started.

She spent the afternoon preparing her arguments. Alexander, she knew from experience, could be intractable when he had made up his mind, but Elise was more reasonable. Whether this was a difference between male and female or a simple quality of leadership, she did not know, but she *did* know it was in Alexander's best interests to please his queen. It remained for her, then, only to persuade Elise to speak more strongly on her behalf.

Tessa LeGuerre was twenty years old, and human. Life was very simple to her.

* * *

Only on rare occasions did Tessa dine alone, for if Elise wasn't making a point of showing her off before guests, Alexander joined her, claiming that to dine alone was an affront against the very nature of civilization. There were times, however, when the protocol that governed them, odd as it sometimes seemed to Tessa, required that both Alexander and Elise be present for a function at which Tessa was not invited. She was proud to display what she considered a very mature and forgiving attitude on those occasions.

She was bitterly disappointed that night, however, when Alexander sent late word by a very smug and deprecating Gault that Tessa was to have supper in her room. If there was an apology or an explanation accompanying the message, Gault did not share it. Nor did he deign to satisfy her repeated questions as to how Alexander was otherwise occupied, although it was clear he knew, and he upbraided her sharply for her curiosity—something he never would have dared to do in Alexander's presence.

To her credit, Tessa did not deliberately plot to be disobedient. Alexander's comment about her being an "embarrassment" to Elise still stung more than she liked to admit, and she wouldn't have intentionally done anything to prove him right. She assumed Elise had important dinner guests and Alexander was busy either entertaining them or trying to impress them—two occupations to which werewolves seemed to devote a great deal of energy. Now, when she needed all of Alexander's goodwill, was not the time to annoy him by making a fuss because he left her to dine alone.

She waited until her tray was brought up and the dishes laid out on the small table that was set in the curtained alcove of the window embrasure. She nibbled at the bread, stirred the consommé, broke the fish into pieces with her fork. She drank half a glass of wine, and tasted the chicken. She parted the curtains to look out upon the dark summer garden.

Only it wasn't entirely dark. A clear third-quarter moon was bright in the sky, reflecting shades of royal blue in high-floating clouds, dancing off the cascading fountains and shimmering statuary. The night-blooming plants were woven throughout the garden in an intricate, complex pattern which, Alexander had told her, was designed to appeal to werewolf senses and which could be fully appreciated only by them. The alabaster blossoms were lush and fragrant amidst the green satin foliage. Almost any time of the night Tessa could expect to find the garden occupied by admirers, most of them in human form but occasionally in wolf. For this reason she never ventured into the garden alone after dark.

But tonight the garden was deserted.

Tessa rose from the table and pulled the curtain back, searching the landscape. All was still. She unlatched the window and stepped outside.

She stood close to the window for a time, the light from the room spilling out to illuminate the night around her. The ground was spongy beneath her slippered feet and damp with dew. Jasmine scented the air. In the distance she heard something faintly, like the call of a bird. Nothing else stirred.

And then she heard a voice. "Elise!" It was Alexander's voice, and he was laughing, just beyond the garden but not too far away for Tessa to feel the relief of recognition. She stepped away from the window and started down the moonlit garden path.

A shape streaked past her, cutting a diagonal across her path, causing her to shrink back with a cry choked off in her throat. It was a blond wolf, sleek and powerful and fast—so fast that Tessa barely recognized the form for what it was and then it was gone, exploding into the shadows only to appear a moment later caught in the glow of moonlight as it was about to spring over a high hedge. Muscles rippled, limbs stretched, fur glistened as the wolf seemed poised for just a moment in mid-flight, caught between heaven and earth upon the wings of the moon. And then it was over the hedge.

On the other side of the hedge there were voices, muted exclamations and sounds of revelry. And then there was another sound: a howl, a cry of power and passion and absolute triumph. The voices were drowned out by the wolf call, while from the deep woods and far meadows, the hills and valleys of far-off countryside, there came an echo of answering wolf cries. Far away, farther away, closer now and closer still. The pack was coming home.

Tessa's instinct was to run, to turn back toward the light and flee frantically toward it. Yet for those few seconds when terror had her in its grip and she might actually have done so, she couldn't move. And then the thrill descended on her, the sound of that call, so close, so fierce, so powerful. Alexander was behind that hedge. Had the call been his?

As she stood there, uncertain and undecided, there was an explosion of movement and laughter, and before she could react they burst into the garden—four or five of them, naked, playful, tumbling and chasing one another like children. At the forefront was Elise.

Tessa had never before seen a naked woman. And of all the shocking, incredible things she *had* seen in the past year—that she had seen this night alone—this seemed the most appalling. Elise, the graceful, regal queen, the masterpiece of composure and dry wit, without her clothing was long-limbed, svelte and tight-muscled, her body as slim and hairless as a child's. There was no softness around her abdomen or her waist; her buttocks and thighs were firm. Her hair cascaded in wild disarray around her shoulders and down her back, catching in the sweat on her face and breasts. Naked as she was, her power was a primal thing, fiercely seductive and blatantly confident, and Tessa knew without another moment's thought that the blond wolf who had streaked by earlier had been none other than Elise Devoncroix.

It all unfolded before her in a flash of voluptuous abandon, a portrait of hedonism spun on moonlight and bare flesh. Elise outraced the others by no more than a body's length, but it was clear she could have doubled the distance had she wanted. Alexander was closest behind her and in an instant, with a mighty spring, he dove for her feet, catching her ankle, dragging her to the ground. She gave a high squeal that was more delight than alarm, a singularly human sound of girlish fakery, and they rolled over and over in the soft grass, naked limbs entwined, laughing, gasping.

Another male caught up to them and launched himself at Alexander. The three of them became a tangle then, wrestling and rolling, and the sounds that came from the mélange were only semihuman—throaty growls and grunts and half-verbal snaps of warning and victorious laughter. Alexander pushed the challenger away and he began to wrestle with another male. Elise made as though to run again, but Alexander caught her by the waist and, still on his knees, drew her to him. He pressed his face into her abdomen and she caught up handfuls of his hair, laughing like a child as she lifted them to the breeze and let them fall about his shoulders again.

And that was the tableau Tessa would carry with her for a long, long time. Alexander, naked in the moonlight, broad shoulders glistening, lustrous hair ruffled by the breeze, his hands cupping Elise's perfectly formed buttocks, lifting his face in laughter to hers. Now she wrapped one leg around his neck and now he dragged his tongue up the length of her thigh, burying his face in the apex of her legs as though to drink in the scent there. She laughed and spun away from him but circled him again and, dropping to her knees behind him, playfully sank her teeth into his shoulder. He caught her hair and turned to face her, and she framed his face with her hands and looked long into his eyes. Alexander held her gaze. She smiled and their faces came together, not kissing, merely nuzzling. Then Elise dropped her head to his lap and, her eyes glinting up at him wickedly, took his genitals into her mouth.

And then someone exclaimed, "This is precisely why we should not allow humans at the Palais!"

And after that one voice broke the spell, everything seemed to Tessa to move in slow, jerky motion, to be distorted and out of step, like silhouettes cut from the fabric of another reality. Alexander glanced at her mildly and remarked, "It's only Tessa."

Another voice said, "I suppose this means we'll have to kill her. What a pity. I was just becoming accustomed to her scent."

Laughter.

Elise said, getting gracefully to her feet, "Don't frighten the child. We shouldn't have been in the garden. And that, I think . . ." She gave a flirtatious toss of her head toward Alexander. "Was not my fault. Come, I smell mutton. Are we starving?"

There was more babbling, more voices, more movement. But Tessa did not remain. She turned and stumbled back up the garden path, through the window and into her room, then blindly into her dressing room where she collapsed on the floor and began to vomit into the basin.

Alexander came to her an hour or so later. He was sleek and well groomed, the satiny hair with its blaze of platinum brushed to a soft sheen about his shoulders, his strong lean body now covered by a ruby smoking jacket and light woolen trousers. But Tessa could see the shape of his legs through the trousers, and smell the musk of the night on his skin.

Tessa had bathed and changed into a freshly pressed flannel night-gown, and the chambermaid had been in to clean the room and re-move the supper dishes. Nonetheless, Alexander paused when he entered the room, his nose lifted to the air, and sniffed. "You've been ill," he observed. "Was the fish bad? I'll have someone speak to the chef."

Tessa turned away. Her voice was dull as she replied, "I'm not ill."

"Nonsense. You're as white as marble and just as cold." He came over to her, his voice softened with concern. "Eh, chérie—"

She jerked away and crossed the room quickly when she felt his hands rest upon her shoulders, and his murmur changed to an excla-mation of impatience. "What a bothersome girl you are! Now what are you brooding about?"

Tessa whirled on him, her eyes wild. "What *was* it?" she cried. "What was it I saw? Was it a—a mating ritual? How can you come to me and talk so innocently after—after—" She could not finish. The last word caught in her throat and choked there, and she couldn't get the image out of her mind of him embracing a naked Elise, of Elise ducking her head to his lap . . .

Alexander's expression reflected pure bafflement. "Great gods and fishes, what are you babbling about? A mating ritual? Are you mad? Celine was right—this *is* the trouble with having humans underfoot!"

Tessa's heart was swelling like a great bloody bubble in her chest, threatening to burst, choking off her breath, hoarsening her voice. But she could not remain silent. Not if it meant her life could she have remained silent. "How can you come to me after being with her?" Her fingers dug into her throat, trying to capture the pain, and her eyes went hot with the agony that spilled over. "After what you did—what she did—how *can* you?"

Alexander gazed at her, uncomprehending. "I swear before all that I know, I don't think I will ever understand you. Sometimes I wonder if it's worth the trouble to try."

The tears spilled over, scalding her cheeks, but Tessa refused to sob. Alexander noticed and his expression gentled. "Tessa, dear heart . . ." His tone was tender, but he made no move to approach her. "Why do you live among us if you are not prepared to accept what we are?"

As though in echo she heard Elise say, *You will never understand us, not really* . . . And she saw again the curve of Elise's tongue as it swept around Alexander's genitals.

Tessa raised trembling fingers to her lips, and she had to turn away. "I don't know," she whispered. "I don't know."

And though the words were barely formed, the whisper hardly spoken, Alexander heard. He came to her, standing close behind, and embraced her. "Come, *chérie*, I would not have you hurt for the world. What has made you weep? No, don't tell me, for I will weep as well. Just be still in your heart and let me make you warm."

He swept her into his arms and carried her to a large chair by the fireplace, where he held her against his chest and stroked her hair and let her spend her tears.

"You know I adore you, don't you?" he murmured at last, kissing her hair. "But you mustn't be so foolish. You try my patience."

"And you try mine," she replied thickly, wiping her face with the silk handkerchief he had pushed into her hands.

He smiled. "That's better. Now, no more tears. You've already ruined this jacket and I haven't another article of clothing I'm willing to sacrifice to your human silliness."

She looked up at him, the handkerchief clenched tight in her fist. "I can't help being human, and you must explain to me why I'm silly."

"Because you mistake an ordinary pack run for a mating ritual," he responded with only a trace of impatience. "Because you find offensive what we find pleasurable and because you allow your own ignorance to make you weep. We are different, you and I, and that's all you need to know."

She said carefully, "Then you—and Elise—are not . . . coupled?"

"Of course not." She thought a faint tinge of color hazed his face. "The notion is absurd. And it wouldn't be done in front of you even if we were."

He looked solemnly into her eyes. "Tessa, you don't belong here. It was a mistake allowing you to stay this long. What you saw tonight upset you, and I don't even understand why. I can't protect you from what I don't understand and can't foresee, so there is no solution for it but to send you back to the estate. I'll stay on at the Palais for the Festival, but then I'll be back for you and perhaps we'll go to Capri, would you like that?"

Long before he had finished speaking, Tessa was shaking her head, the handkerchief bunched in one fist and a lapel of his jacket in the other, but she was not entirely sure why she did so. To stay in the midst of such abominations as she had witnessed tonight, to face Elise again . . . to be exiled to the Lyons house, a stranger among strange creatures, to leave him here with Elise . . .

She said, "The queen . . ." She found suddenly that she couldn't speak of the creature by her first name, as a friend might. "She wants me to stay. You heard her say it. You can't send me away."

"You are my responsibility and she has no say in this," Alexander replied sternly. "You were not an invited guest. She can't keep you here."

"I don't want to be sent away."

"You're not being sent away. You're being returned to the place where you belonged from the beginning. Stop agitating yourself; your heartbeat is deafening. At least you're warmer."

All Tessa wanted to do was to snuggle into his embrace, to let his heat seep into her soul and to let his strength give her peace. Yet she made herself push away and get to her feet. She walked a few steps away, twisting his handkerchief in her hands.

"Why do you want me to go?" she asked in a voice that was as steady as she could make it.

"I told you that. This is not the time or the place for humans. There are things we enjoy that you cannot, and things we do that make you uncomfortable. You'll be much happier at home with the human servants, and perhaps you can spend time with D'Avagnon and learn something of winemaking. That would make your father proud."

She was suddenly intensely resentful of his bringing her father into the discussion. She turned to face him. "I don't have your ears to hear a lie, nor your nose to smell one," she said with simple dignity. "But I would request nonetheless that you tell me the truth. I have been humiliated once tonight already."

A small frown pierced his brow, and a moment of uneasiness crossed his eyes. "I have told you the truth of it."

"But not all the truth."

He stared at her, and a faint alteration of his features suggested he was surprised by her perception. "No," he admitted. "Not all of it."

Then he sighed, and stood as well. He went to the table by the window, poured chocolate from the pot into a floral china cup, stirred, and tasted it. Then he said, "Tessa, there are machinations at work here in the palace that I don't expect you to understand and in which you shouldn't be involved. Elise . . . she is genuinely fond of you; I wouldn't want you to be in doubt about that. But her schemes are much grander in scope than one human, or . . ." And here he paused, and dropped his eyes, and seemed briefly uncomfortable. "Or one werewolf." He regarded her intently. "She is using you, *chérie*, to make a point to others of our kind, and the game she is playing is a dangerous one. I would rest easier if you were away from here."

And that, then, was the end of it, and it had been that simple from the first. Tessa might wheedle and whine and complain and try her best to change his mind, but what Alexander requested of her, if it meant his peace of mind, she gave. Such was the nature of their relationship; hadn't she always known that?

Yet leaving him was to abandon him to a way of life she did not understand and against which she had no defense, to surrender him to those—both male and female, both kind and cruel—who might yet seduce him from her. And leaving him meant stepping out of the circle of his companionship and his protection into a world that did not welcome her and held no comfort for her; without him, in that world, she was nothing. How could he not understand what he was asking her to do?

She came over to him and laid a hand lightly upon his arm. "I will go," she said, "if you say I must. But first tell me this." She searched his eyes solemnly, earnestly, and she could not keep the touch of anxiety from her voice. "Am I still your dearest treasure and your truest friend?"

He smiled, and put aside his cup. He took her face in both his hands and looked into her eyes. The thrill that went through her with his touch, with the power of his gaze, was a mesmerizing thing. It did not occur to her to wonder whether he was aware of the force he could exercise over the human will with such innocent weapons; she simply chose to believe he was not.

"*Toujours, chérie,*" he said softly. Lightly, he kissed her lips. Then, with the tip of his tongue, he tasted the curve of her cheek, the delicate flesh at the corner of her eye, the soft skin over her temple. Tessa's eyes closed beneath a shiver of exquisite sensual pleasure, and her breath stopped in her chest.

He encircled her with his arms, he rocked her close. He rested his face upon the top of her head. "Always," he repeated.

And so it was that, less than a week later, Tessa was standing atop the hill that backed up against the woods of Alexander's Lyons estate, gazing over the endless leagues of vineyard and winding road and wildflower meadow, wondering if she had made a mistake. In the very far distance, if the wind blew just right to separate the leaves of the trees, she could see the filial tops of the great iron gates that guarded the Palais Devoncroix. She knew from memory that the decorative ornaments atop those gates were forged-iron sculptures in the shape of crouched wolves, but of course she could not see the details from here.

She could walk to the Palais in an hour or two, it was that close. And yet it was as far away as the continent of Australia, or the evening star.

And as she stood there gazing, aching, wondering, a voice spoke behind her. "Ah, what a touching picture. Tessa LeGuerre, a human, thrown from the gates of paradise."

Tessa whirled, catching a gasp in her throat, but saw nothing. Heart pounding, she started to back away.

And then from the shadowed woods a figure emerged. He was tall and fiery-haired, with eyes the color of blazing waters and a smile that could melt stone at the center of the earth. He was the most magnificent werewolf Tessa had ever seen.

He simply stood there, his expression gently mocking, his gaze compelling. "Poor dear," he said. "Whatever will become of you now?"

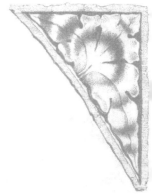

ALEXANDER

Thirteen

As my brother had so astutely pointed out all those months ago, I was quite infatuated with Elise Devoncroix, and had been for years. I knew I could rely upon my innate charm, my natural ability to entertain and my considerable wit to ensure invitations to all the important fetes and perhaps a few informal dinners, but even I for all my ambition did not expect to become one of her closest confidants in such a short period of time. That position I owed entirely to Tessa.

I can't help but reflect sometimes on the unpredictable irony of life. Had I but known how much Elise's political agenda would have been enhanced by the presence of a human in her household, I would have captured one with a net, if need be, and presented it to her. As it was, I had the secret weapon that would win her approval living under my roof the whole time and I had done my best to *keep* it secret. Coincidence, and Tessa's obstreperous nature, had conspired to put me in the queen's good graces almost against my will.

Why, then, one might justifiably ask, had I sent Tessa home? The answer is complicated.

I confess that, at that age, I was far more interested in a good wine and a shapely leg than I was in the tides and eddies of political philosophy. In fact, I had never before given much thought to whether or not the pack *had* a philosophy, and I was not the only one. That was why, at the turn of the century, with humans even then lining up the economic and industrial chess pieces that would lead them into global war, we faced more danger than we knew.

Only one person in the entire pack had the vision to understand the consequences of our apathy, and to know what must be done to end it. Fortunately, she was our leader.

If the pack could be said to be defined in any way at all during those days, it was divided along these lines: the radicals like Denis who thought the parasite humans should be exterminated from the earth, the radicals like me who found humans entertaining and charming companions, and the vast majority in between who found humans a necessary nuisance and who simply wanted to be left alone to conduct their business and their matings and their petty squabbles in peace. Never before had a ruler seen fit to make his or her opinion on the subject of humans known, if in fact he even possessed an opinion. Even I, who at first was delighted by Elise's open-mindedness on the subject, could not understand why anyone in a position of power—and with so many far more important things to concern her—would choose to make a point of it now.

But that was precisely what Elise was doing. She was using Tessa to demonstrate where she stood on the question of humans, and she was doing it in the most emphatic, revolutionary way possible— throwing down the gauntlet, as it were, to anyone who dared disagree with her stance. This was at first endearing, even admirable, for who cannot respect a werewolf who chooses the hard road over the easy? Power, after all, cannot be given, it must be won, and if Elise chose to test the loyalty of her friends and advisors through their reactions to Tessa, I was happy for Tessa to serve.

It was when she spoke of allowing Tessa to stay for the Summer Festival that I became uneasy. Such behavior was not brave. It was not defiant, powerful or rebellious. It was merely reckless.

Hundreds of werewolves from all walks of life would be converging on the secluded Palais for those two weeks surrounding the Summer Solstice, and their behavior at all hours of the day and night would make our innocent frolic in the garden outside Tessa's room seem as tame as it in fact was. To have a human present at these very private celebrations would have been an insult; it would have been beyond eccentric and far into outrageous. That was where I had to draw the line.

I told Tessa the truth: Elise was exploiting her and I didn't like it. Tessa was an outsider with no place in our intimate gatherings; I didn't want to see her hurt. But more important, I didn't want to see Elise hurt. And Elise, by planning to boldly trot Tessa out before the Summer Festival and announce her a welcome guest, was plotting political suicide—if not, in fact, a death of a more meaningful sort.

So that was the most obvious reason I had to send Tessa from the Palais. The second reason was a bit more subtle. Elise and I had become great friends and constant companions, with Tessa, like a winsome child, to bind us together. I wondered whether we would have anything in common when she was gone.

The third reason was petty and unbecoming, and I would never have confessed to it at all had not Elise, who was not a bit pleased with my summary decision to exercise my authority over Tessa without consulting her, confronted me on the issue.

"I think," she announced, bold-faced and unblinking over the wineglass half raised to her lips, "you were jealous."

We had escaped from the chaos of the Palais for a quiet luncheon in town. We found a table in the sun where a fountain splashed a few dozen steps away, and we dined on rabbit and Devoncroix red. The air was scented with lavender and redolent with the thousand lush aromas of last night's rain and spiced with the musky silk of Elise's hair, warm in the sunshine. I looked splendid in a light summer worsted and a deep blue cravat; Elise was lovely in pale lilac. She wore a straw hat covered with violets low over one eye and pearls around her wrist. We turned heads, the two of us, and we both enjoyed that. It was, in short, a perfect afternoon.

Until she brought up the subject that had lain between us like an unwashed garment ever since Tessa's departure.

I replied gallantly, because I had no choice, "Mademoiselle, I would be a fool not to be jealous of anyone or anything that deprived me of your company for even a moment."

She inclined an eyebrow. "There's that, of course. But I think you were equally as jealous of the time Tessa spent away from you." She sipped her wine. "She's quite in love with you, you know."

I replied lightly, "All humans adore me. It's a curse."

She looked at me with a steady unblinking gaze which I could not meet for long. "You are cruel, Alexander, to encourage her and then discard her."

"I haven't discarded anyone!" I was quite uncomfortable now, as I began to suspect she was serious. "What can you be talking about?"

"Tessa LeGuerre is a female," she said in mild exasperation. "A human, but a female nonetheless, and she has lived all these months with a virile, attractive male. Young humans' heads are filled with fantasies under the best of circumstances, and of course she expects more of you than you're able to give."

This was really becoming quite embarrassing. "Don't be preposterous. She's only a human! She may not often act as though she knows it, but I assure you she does. What you suggest is really quite absurd, and you insult my intelligence and hers." I glanced away, hoping to put an end to the ridiculous turn of conversation. "I've never known you to be of a puerile bent of mind, mademoiselle. It doesn't become you."

She shrugged. "And I shall tell you something else. You were bothered by the fact that she could be as fond of me as she was of you. Perhaps you were afraid that if she grew accustomed to living with us, you would eventually come to be less special in her eyes."

I didn't like that, mostly because there was more than a grain of truth in it. But I kept my expression bland and disinterested. "I would never presume to argue with you, mademoiselle."

"Oh, Alexander, don't bore me! If you don't presume today, it will certainly be the first time."

I tried not to frown. "I was merely trying to preserve the peace of the afternoon for a little while longer. Until I finish my wine at least."

"Finish it, then." Her expression was as impatient as her tone. "Why do you think I brought you here away from the others if not to talk where their ears couldn't hear?"

I lifted an eyebrow. "Secrets, mademoiselle?"

"Truths," she said shortly, facing me down with a gaze that would have brought any sensible werewolf to his knees. "I wouldn't beg them from anyone but you, Alexander."

Disturbed, I put down my glass. "You have no call to beg me for anything, mademoiselle," I assured her sincerely. "My life is yours for the asking. Surely you know that."

It was the proper reply from a subordinate to the pack leader, but I meant it as much more than that. And I was embarrassed by the sudden boyish intensity of my emotions.

The faint gentling of her features was almost a smile, and it reassured me somewhat. "If I have need of your life, Alexander, I will let you know. Right now I need something you may not be so willing to give."

"The truth," I supplied.

"Why did you send Tessa away?"

"You've guessed the most of it."

"There's more."

I knew without being told that Elise was not interested in my small personal reasons for sending Tessa home; she had named most of them already and to continue along that vein would have insulted her. I knew that by raising the subject I was endangering my favor in her eyes, but she had asked for the truth. I gave it.

"You're a strong and beautiful queen," I told her. "The pack will love you for who you are and will accept you without question once you're mated."

I saw the impatience mounting in her eyes and abandoned diplomacy for bluntness. "But you're young, and I think naive in many ways. This festival is the first time most of the pack will have a chance to form an impression of you, and from what they learn about you here, the word will go out around the world, for better or worse. With it you'll be able to attract a mate—or not. You'll command the respect of the pack—or not. You'll shepherd the pack in unity, or you'll cast it into a hopeless scission of bickering and posturing. I think you would be well advised not to do anything dramatic without considering the consequences."

She regarded me thoughtfully. I did not even try to meet her gaze for longer than was strictly polite. I had already risked enough and I had nothing to prove to her. I took up my glass again.

She said at last, "So. Your concern is for the pack."

"Of course. Isn't yours?"

She got to her feet abruptly. "Come with me."

Hastily, I swallowed the remainder of my wine and left some bills on the table for the human proprietor of the cafe, whose food I had enjoyed and whose establishment I hoped to visit again. By the time I caught up with Elise she had crossed the street.

"Tell me," she demanded when I arrived, "what do you smell?"

There was just a hint of a breeze, and the streets, walks and shops were filled with humans and the trappings of their kind. In a single half-drawn breath I smelled human sweat and horses, leather, cotton, silk, yeasty bread, dung, a dizzying plethora of wines, roast meat, fresh greens, fat sizzling on black iron; smokestacks from the factory across the Rhône, stale water, machine oil, rosemary in a clay pot, spoiled milk, turned earth, turpentine, tobacco and Elise, Elise, Elise of silk and body oils, of faint salt and sharp spice, of strong muscles and satin skin, Elise. With difficulty I tried to focus my attention on what it was specifically she expected me to smell.

"There," she said impatiently, and nodded toward a woman just coming out of a shop two doors down.

"Ah," I said appreciatively. "Lemon thyme, cassia, and the base— ambergris? One of your perfumes." I had, of course, given myself a short course in perfumery long before coming to the Palais. "It's most alluring."

She gave a short nod. "The human women can't buy enough of it. And do be good enough to tell me, if you please, the name of that very excellent wine we had at luncheon?"

I grinned. "Château Devoncroix, of course. No one in town would dare serve anything less."

She started walking down the street. "Tell me what else you smell, monsieur, when the wind is right."

I was beginning to understand her game. "The factory across the river. It makes wagon wheels, I think."

"And are you aware who owns that factory?"

"Of course. Frederick Parcon, *loup-garou*."

She said, changing the subject, "Do you have enough money, Alexander?"

A surprised chuckle escaped me. "Yes, thank you. Quite enough."

"Some might even call you wealthy."

I shrugged. The subject didn't interest me much.

"Most humans, in fact, would call you extremely wealthy. As they would M. Parcon, whose family makes carriage wheels in London, Brussels and Philadelphia. And both of you put together haven't a fraction of the fortune that I have."

I was utterly baffled as to her point, but was wise enough to stay silent.

"Look around you, Alexander." Her face and her voice were tight with frustration, and she made a short commanding gesture with her wrist. "Tell me what you see, what you hear, what you smell. They're everywhere!"

"Humans," I replied, enlightened.

"And do you detect a single loup-garou within a kilometer?"

I smiled. "Of course not. They are all at the Palais, enjoying the festival."

She gave a smothered growl of exasperation and walked away from me with steps made clipped by the narrowness of her skirt. I watched her go for a moment, then took a running step to catch up, pushing back my laughter. "Surely, ma'amselle, at some point in your education someone has pointed out to you that the human population outnumbers ours considerably in just about any city on earth."

"Precisely," she responded, and turned on me. There was no amusement at all in her eyes. Only grim truth. "And shall I tell you something else, M. Devoncroix, which perhaps has been an oversight in *your* education? Humans drink wine. They buy carriage wheels, they burn coal, they ride on trains and they purchase passage on ships. Moreover, they sit upon the councils that govern nations, they make the rules that constrain commerce, they own banks and railroads, they build cities and libraries and factories and shipyards."

She was speaking in rapid, mellifluous French now, and the sound of her voice was such a pleasure of the senses, such a stirring of the emotions, that it was difficult for me to concentrate on what she was saying. I replied soothingly, "As they have always done, Elise. None of this concerns us."

She regarded me for a long and solemn time, and I could not have looked away had I wanted to. There was in her gaze the weight of a responsibility so heavy I could not begin to guess at it, the sadness of a wisdom hard earned, and age far beyond her years. In her eyes was compassion for generations not yet born and the vision to know that their fates rested in her hands. And in her eyes was the knowledge that she, and only she, would answer for their unfulfilled dreams.

"Who, then," she inquired of me simply, "should it concern?"

Before that day I had worshipped her, adored her, fantasized about her. But it was at that moment that I began to love her.

We walked in silence to the river and stood looking out across the water. There were pleasure-seekers in painted boats making ripples in the current, pretty girls in white dresses and pale parasols, strong young men in boaters and gartered shirtsleeves. Upriver a big barge throbbed and groaned, pushing its cargo south. I confess I would not have known what to say had an answer been required of me. My heart was full and my throat was tight and I knew with every fiber of my being that everything I had ever valued in my world was about to change.

Elise began to speak with a quiet intensity. "We are standing on the edge of a new century, Alexander. The rules have changed. It isn't enough to be what we are and to raise our families and fulfill our ambitions in amused disregard for the others who share this world with us. We are too few, and they are too many."

She looked at me. "Do you know how long it's been since anyone called the pack together? Oh, we have our festivals and our gatherings and our regional celebrations, but we're scattered to the ends of the earth and we have nothing, really, in common except our species. We haven't been a real pack since the time of the Antonovs."

I answered cautiously, "We had a reason to bind together then. Food, shelter, protection . . . times were harsh and we were primitive. We had common enemies to fight—the weather, starvation, predators . . ."

"Humans," she said, when I would not. She turned her gaze back to the river. "We have not been tame so very long, Alexander."

Still guarding my voice, I said, "Surely you're not suggesting that we would do better to return to those days."

With a gentle smile she shook her head. "Our greatest pride is that we never have to return to those days. But I think, in giving up our rough past for châteaux on the river and elegant dinner parties and gas lamps on every street corner, we may also have given up our greatest strength."

I was uneasy, because for the first time in our acquaintance I did not know—at least to some vague extent—what Elise was thinking. And because I could not help but recall those who, believing that civilization was a weakness, had chosen to prove their strength by returning to live in the wilderness of Siberia . . .

She smelled it on me, the question and the anxiety, and she gave me a quick, reassuring smile. "Did you ever think," she inquired unexpectedly, "about how my illustrious ancestor really overthrew the Antonov?"

"Why, through cunning and boldness," I responded, relieved to be on a topic with which I was comfortable. "Everyone knows that."

She held up an admonishing finger. "Ah, but without one other component, no amount of cunning or ambition in the world would have made his plan a success. Shall I tell you what it was? Will you guess?"

I shook my head.

"Timing," she said. "The time was right when old Valkyn broke his neck and the cub Leo took over, it's true. But there was an even more important element at work there. It was *time* for the pack to move on. We had outgrown our hunting grounds, outsmarted the humans, begun to acquire leisure time and wider interests. We were moving into an era of enlightenment and expansion already, and had we not been, nothing the Devoncroix could have done would have led us there."

There was a low quiet fire in her eyes as she looked out over the water. And though her gaze was focused on the distant shore she saw much, much farther. "We are moving into a new era, Alexander. The time is past when all it took to conquer the earth was to be faster and stronger and smarter than anything else that lives on it, because now there are others who are just as strong and just as fast, and if they aren't as smart as we are, they are smart enough to use what we have taught them, and to build on it. We have to come together now if we are to survive in the world that waits for us."

I said, "I admire your ambitions, mademoiselle, and I share them. But I confess I fail to see how any of it can be accomplished—or what part Tessa, a simple human, can play in your plans."

Her smile was secretive and full of confidence. "Not just Tessa," she responded, "but all humans."

At my baffled expression she turned again and continued walking, her tone and her movements full of energy, her voice a symphony for the ears. "And so we have Marcionetti, the finest shoemaker in all the pack, who outshines the best of all the human shoemakers in Italy. Why? Because he is werewolf. He is faster, brighter, more inventive, with a greater eye for detail and a finer sense of perfection than any human craftsman could hope to achieve. But does it occur to him to market his product to humans? Most likely not, or if so, he does it grudgingly, and as an afterthought. And so he competes with a dozen other shoemakers—all of them fine, all of them werewolf—to supply the pack, which leaves him perhaps three months of the year that he is busy making shoes. The rest of the time he must take up another trade—bookbinding, perhaps, or sail making, and again he competes with other bookbinders and sailmakers in the pack, all of whom are dividing up ever-smaller pieces of the same pie. They feed their families, yes; they have work to keep their hands busy, yes. But do they achieve greatness?"

"But if they came together . . ." I murmured, almost understanding.

She completed my thought with controlled excitement underscoring her voice. "And if they saw the globe instead of just the pack as their marketplace—that is their strength, Alexander. That is *our* strength."

"But surely, mademoiselle, this is no great secret. We have conducted commerce with humans for centuries and always profited from it."

"The best of us have," she agreed impatiently. "Your family, mine, a dozen or so others, and we have increased our own fortunes quite nicely. But what about the pack? What about the shoemakers and the builders and the blacksmiths and the bookkeepers? What are they working for, what can they hope to achieve beyond their own short lifetimes? Do they not deserve greatness as well?"

"And so you will call the pack together," I said. My voice was soft with awe and humble with admiration. This was something that had not been done since the time of the first Devoncroix. The implications of what she planned, if it could in fact be executed, were mind-stunning.

"More than that," she replied with an impatient shake of her head. "To bring the pack together is just the first step. Oh, Alexander, don't you see?"

Now I detected the urgency in her voice, the anxiety in her scent. She gripped my arm and looked at me with eyes ablaze, the magnificence of a passionate conviction in her face. "For the first time in history humans have the potential to actually compete with us in areas in which we have always been the masters. Once before they encroached upon our territory, in the old black times, but it was easy enough to defeat them. They had crude weapons, we had teeth and claws. Their strength was no match for ours, and we were the faster and more agile. We could hear their plots and smell their approach.

"But we can't outrun them anymore, for soon trains will run even faster than we. Shall we use our teeth and our claws against bullets? We've known for centuries the absurdity of that. We are a civilized people now, and we've learned to live in peace with humans, to avoid them when we can and to pity them when we must. But we cannot ignore them. We cannot forget that they can, by the simple fact of their ambition, still pose a threat to us.

"So if we can't outrun them and we can't ignore them, we have but one choice if we are to maintain our position of dominance on the earth. We must outsmart them. We must use our senses to smell them coming, to hear their plots, to know their plans. We must do it together—and we must do it for profit."

It was so beautifully simple. The prize has always been power. In times of old, power meant territory, a piece of land where game was abundant and water flowed freely and shelter was strong and easy to secure. In this bold new century, this dawning industrial age, power meant money. This was something that I, with my lucrative vineyards and my banks, had always taken for granted. Only a true visionary would have understood the broader implications.

"Let the tradesmen and the scientists and the technicians and the engineers all come together under one name," she continued, her eyes bright and her voice rich with excitement. "The pack name. Let them pool their resources and their talents and build a power base from which to negotiate—even manipulate—the human marketplace. *That* is our destiny, Alexander, that is our calling."

She was beautiful. She was brilliant. I adored her with all my soul.

I said humbly, sincerely, "I am honored to know you."

It is one of the deepest compliments one werewolf can give to another, implying an admiration so vast that it encompasses body and soul and puts one's own personal vanity far into the shadows. It is reserved for only the rarest of occasions: victory in battle, an act of unselfish heroism, a life-changing idea or discovery or breakthrough in thought. I had never said those words before, nor could I imagine ever meaning them more.

Her eyes shone, and she held both my hands in hers in a brief, firm grip. "I knew you would understand. I knew you would see immediately."

She turned and, linking her arm with mine, began to walk back toward the village. "Of course, one of the first obstacles we must overcome is the pack's natural disinclination to do business with humans."

"And that, then, was where Tessa came in."

She nodded. "I must let them know where I stand on the issue. Let them see a human inside the very gates of the Palais and let them know that times have changed, and that the pack will change with them."

"You were wrong in your approach," I insisted firmly. "Wrong to use Tessa in such a way—who is only one human, after all, and not particularly representative of her species in any meaningful way—and wrong to force her on members of the pack who aren't ready to be dragged into this new era of yours. If you had kept Tessa at the Palais during the festival, nothing but disaster would have resulted, I can promise, and you would have gotten off to a very bad start with a pack from whom you intend to demand much over these next years. Besides," I added after a moment, "I wouldn't think that by now there's any doubt in anyone's mind as to how you stand on the subject of humans, so you have accomplished your purpose without inconveniencing or embarrassing anyone."

She was thoughtful for a time, and I saw the slow curve of a smile touch her lips. She slanted me a glance beneath the brim of her hat. "Quite clever, Alexander, and I shouldn't doubt that you're right. Perhaps I should seek out your advice more often."

"Perhaps," I returned, "you might even start listening to it now and again."

She laughed. "I'm comfortable with you, Alexander. You'd be surprised how few of my acquaintances about whom I can say that."

I replied smoothly with the question I had been aching to ask for weeks. "Is that, then, why you've had me spied upon?"

She pretended surprise. "Have I done that?"

"You have excellent ears, mademoiselle. But I doubt that even you could have overheard from here conversations that took place in Siberia."

"Hmm." Neither her manner nor her pleasant demeanor changed. "Quite right."

My humor was gone now, and I didn't try to pretend otherwise. "Or perhaps you send minions to follow all of your subjects when they leave the country."

She sensed my displeasure and her tone grew subdued. "No, not all."

"Only those you suspect of treachery."

She was silent for a time, and I thought I had overstepped my bounds. Then she answered, in a voice that was quiet and strained, "Only those I would give my honor to protect."

This was not at all what I had expected. A half-dozen pithy retorts had been swirling around in my head in case she answered my previous statement in the affirmative. But for this—so surprising, so unpredictable—my step actually faltered and all I could think to say was, in astonishment, "And where was your protection when I was fighting for my life?"

She smiled. "Guarding your flank, you fool. Didn't you notice?"

I shook my head mutely.

She gave a slight tilt of her head, perusing me with repressed amusement. "Not that it matters. You acquitted yourself quite well without them."

At some point during this remarkable conversation I had let her arm drop. Now she walked on without me, toward the carriage that waited across the street.

I moved quickly in front of her, blocking her path. "Why?" I demanded.

She looked up at me with eyes that drank my soul. I no longer felt my heart beat, or my breath move in and out of my lungs. All I felt was her gaze, living in every part of me. "Oh, Alexander," she said softly, "don't you know?"

And here, then, is the one thing all males have in common, both human and werewolf: the capacity to be rendered utterly helpless in mind and body by nothing more than a look from the woman they love. I was lost in such a look, held breathless, mindless and speechless by it.

When I made no reply she dropped her gaze, smiling gently. "Perhaps I'll answer your question with one of my own. Can you guess why I have just confided to you things I have never discussed with another soul, not even my father, the great Sancerre?"

I knew I should make some light and easy reply, to rescue myself from the doe-eyed foolishness into which I had fallen. But my throat was like parchment and my thoughts like taffy. All I could answer was, honestly, "Mademoiselle, I cannot."

"Because," she told me, "when you presented to me your reasons for going against my wishes and sending Tessa away, your only justification was the welfare of the pack. And when I remarked upon that, you replied without hesitation, 'Of course.'" She gazed at me solemnly. "That's why, Alexander."

She took my arm again and we walked to the carriage.

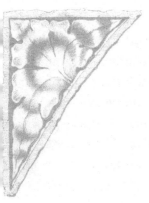

TESSA

Fourteen

IT HAD TAKEN DENIS AND HIS HAND-PICKED, CAREFULLY SCREENED AT-tendants a month to travel down from Siberia. They moved slowly to avoid detection, employing human conveyances and sheltering in human hostelries to study their customs and absorb their mannerisms. He had spent another two weeks in the heart of Paris, that sweltering, filthy, human-infested city, to make certain the smell of the north was off his skin, and he waited until the countryside was filled with werewolves travelling to Lyons for the Festival to move closer to his goal.

His time was well spent. The news was all over Paris about Alexander and his human pet, how he dressed her up and took her to the theater and wore her on his arm like a new cuff link at receptions given by important families. Denis was not surprised. Alexander was always involved in some nonsense or other, and usually his escapades concerned humans. Once, with an older brother's indulgent tolerance, Denis had believed that Alexander's reckless behavior was the natural result of youthful ignorance. Now, of course, he knew better.

Alexander was dangerously misled, a radical whose stubborn temperament and unsound ideas could easily combine to push him over the edge toward revolutionary. Considering his position of prominence in the social hierarchy, he was capable of doing a great deal of harm. Denis had always known Alexander possessed qualities of greatness. He had once even allowed himself to envision Alexander as his second lieutenant in the army of the Brothers of the Dark Moon, which he himself would captain. It wounded Denis deeply to know that would never happen; that Alexander's talent was to be twisted into uselessness, wasted on a battle he was destined to lose.

Denis, however, still had a mission, a purpose that was unmuddied by torn allegiances and false alliances. And he could not let Alexander stand in his way. He would instead use Alexander to further his own ends, just as he had planned to do from the beginning. Such, after all, was the difference between a great leader and a common dung-eater.

And so he came, and he watched and he listened. And in no time at all he knew his brother's weakness, and his own strength, and the plan began to form.

Tessa LeGuerre, the human who would be werewolf. It really was ridiculously simple.

No one recognized him in Paris, and he took pains to stay on the fringes of *la société loup-garou* and always just a step or two below Alexander's social class so that whatever gossip there might be about the new werewolf in town would not reach his ears—or if it did, he would be unlikely to take note of it. There was at that time, as there perhaps has always been, a nonconformist element in Paris: artists, philosophers, radicals and lunatics. They passed their days on the steps of the Bibliothèque or on the Left Bank; they distributed pamphlets warning of the end of the world or drew gorgeous nudes in chalk on the sidewalks just for the pleasure of watching them melt away in the morning rain; they huddled in coffeehouses to debate the wisdom of a thousand ages and they haunted university hallways. This, then, was where Denis chose to lose himself. And he had rarely felt more at home.

There were some things Denis missed about civilization. Alexander had reminded him of them when he visited. A good game of chess. The smell of newsprint, the taste of Beaujolais. The electric excitement of ideas buzzing back and forth among young minds. And gadgetry. He was fascinated by the technology and inventiveness that were in evidence everywhere he turned: the automobile, the gramophone, moving pictures. The only thing more enthralling than exploring these grand new vistas was speculating upon how much grander they could be without the interference of humans.

Everything that he saw and smelled and heard only confirmed his belief that the time was right for change. And that he was the werewolf to usher in that change.

Difficulties ensued, of course, when Alexander took his little human to the palace—although the actual fact of his doing so could not have fit better with Denis's plans had he ordered it himself, and he was immensely delighted when he heard the news. For a short time, though, the flow of information was interrupted, and Denis was left to learn patience until gossip began to filter out from the Palais gates. Everything he heard helped him to refine his intentions, until at last he was ready to set in motion the events that would change life for all his kind—indeed, for all upon the earth—forever.

This moment in history, when he walked out of the shadows and spoke aloud to Tessa LeGuerre, had been written before the dawn of time.

She recognized him almost immediately, which he found flattering. Her eyes grew big and her face lost some of its sun-washed color and she said in a small choked voice, "You—you're Denis Antonov. Alexander's brother."

And she cast a quick furtive look over her shoulder as though searching for wolves in the bushes, or judging how far she could run before being brought down like a deer. Denis was amused.

"I am indeed. And I've come to tear you limb from limb and eat you raw."

She swallowed hard and drew back her shoulders, seeming to come to a realization of her foolishness. "Alexander isn't here."

"Curse the luck."

He continued to stand there, smiling lazily at her, bareheaded in the summer sun, shirtsleeves rolled up and jacket carried carelessly by a hooked finger over his shoulder, looking nothing like Alexander had described him—and looking exactly as he had described him. Tessa fought a brief but visible battle to regain her composure.

"You knew that, of course," she said in a moment. She managed to make the tenor of her voice almost indifferent.

He inclined his head in the affirmative.

"You should come to the house anyway," Tessa said. "I'll send word to your brother—"

He said, "Thank you, but it's such a lovely afternoon I think I'll sit on the hill for a while. Can you spare some time to keep me company?"

"No," she said immediately, and he laughed.

"He has made me out quite the monster to you, hasn't he?" Denis spread his jacket on the grass and folded his long legs into a sitting position upon it. Wrapping his hands around one upraised knee, he glanced up at her, eyes twinkling in the sunlight. "Confess, Tessa LeGuerre—aren't you curious about why I've come?"

He saw the answer flicker across her eyes even as she replied stoically, "You've come to see your brother, naturally."

"Or to kill him?"

She drew in a sharp breath and he shrugged. "I know he's told you that story. He's told everyone that I'm a brother-killer, and frankly, I don't object. It makes me sound so much more fierce, and I'm always grateful for anything at all that enhances my reputation."

Now a shadow of curiosity, even hesitation, darkened her features and she said, "Would you have me believe Alexander lied? That you didn't try to have him killed?"

"I see you know very little about us after all. A well-told lie is a matter of pride with us, and why shouldn't he lie if he wishes? In fact, I'm not even sure Alexander knows the truth about what happened that night."

She said cautiously, "Which was?"

"There are factions among my followers that have always believed that those who aren't with us are against us. When Alexander fled my house under cover of night, they took matters into their own hands."

"But you did not order it?"

"Be logical. What would it benefit me to kill my own brother? Why should I risk my most valuable fighters on such a pointless mission?"

She looked at him thoughtfully. "It's true," she agreed, "that self-serving motivations are a matter of pride with your kind. But so . . ." Her eyes narrowed. ". . . is a well-told lie."

He laughed out loud, surprised. "You *are* a clever little human, Tessa LeGuerre! I can see why Alexander is enchanted with you—as is half of Paris!"

And like any human female, she responded to the flattery, whether or not she believed it was sincere. She drew a little closer. "If you didn't come to kill Alexander, why are you here?"

"To see you."

"Why? What did Alexander tell you about me?"

"Nothing, actually. He never mentioned you once the entire time he was with me."

He correctly interpreted that small stammer in the natural rhythm of her breathing—undetectable to any but werewolf ears—along with the faint tightening of the muscles between her eyebrows, to mean hurt, and he was pleased. He added, "Of course, there was no reason for him to, was there?"

She chose not to answer. Instead she demanded, somewhat sharply, "Then why have you come to see me?"

"Because I think we have a common enemy, you and I."

A crease appeared between her brows, signifying impatience, curiosity or disbelief—perhaps all three. "Who?"

"Elise Devoncroix," he replied. "The queen."

She stared at him for a moment, nonplussed. Then she made a sound which could only be described as an exclamation of laughter, and she turned away. The ruffle at the hem of her narrow skirt swirled to show kid boots and a few inches of snowy petticoat, and the brim of her straw hat bent back when she faced the breeze.

"Good day, Monsieur Antonov," she said, starting away. "I'll be sure to tell your brother you called."

"I wish you wouldn't do that."

His hand was on her arm, and she hadn't even seen him move. In a flash of outrage and fear, she tried to pull away, but his grip, though not painful, was impossible to break.

"It wouldn't be safe, you see," he said softly.

"Let me go." The eyes that she raised to him now were angry and defiant but screened uneasiness. "Safe for whom?"

"For me, of course." He smiled, and this time when she pulled on her arm he let her go. "Who else should I be concerned about?"

Tessa rubbed her fingers over the place on her arm he had gripped, searching for a bruise or merely trying to wipe the feel of him away. It wasn't easy to erase his touch once he'd made it memorable, and she continued to rub.

Yet she remained defiant as she said contemptuously, "You are a fool. Alexander would never hurt you. He is too civilized. And the queen Elise is not my enemy."

His smile only gentled with puzzlement as he tilted his head toward her. "How strange. You've been closer to us than any other human has managed in recent history, you've lived in our midst, you've made a study of us, am I right?—but you know nothing about us."

He saw the working of her throat muscles and heard her swallow her uneasiness, and though she postured angrily with a flash of her eyes and a flaring of her nostrils, he smelled confidence evaporate from her skin and knew she was vulnerable.

"Alexander would see me dead by any means necessary if he could do it without endangering himself," he said, "and he wouldn't be much of a werewolf if he missed the opportunity. As for Elise Devoncroix, what would you call someone who steals the thing you cherish most if not an enemy?"

Tessa's frown was challenging and, as he had expected, she picked up on the last part of his statement, not the first. "What has she stolen from me?"

He said kindly, "I can't believe you don't know."

She cast her eyes briefly to the side, and her fingers tightened on her arm. But when she looked back at him, her expression was resolute and her tone was angry. "You know nothing. You don't belong here. Leave now and I may not tell him you were here."

But before she could move off again, he challenged her softly. "Who will you turn to, Tessa? When you go back to the house, who will you ask for help? To whom will you make your report? There's no one in residence to protect you from me but humans—humans who wouldn't believe your story if you told it."

She said sharply, "And do I need protection from you, monsieur?"

He smiled. His smile was and had always been his most beatific feature. "What do you think?"

For a moment she looked undecided. Then she said harshly, "I think I would do well to call the guards right now."

He laughed. "If only you had guards." He surprised her by extending his hand to her, his eyes still dancing. "Tessa, come, walk with me for a while. I have no reason to hurt you, and if you know anything about us at all, you know that's true. Let me bring you my case, then tell me, when I'm done, whether I was a fool for coming here."

She looked at his outstretched hand, but she did not take it. She looked at his face, her expression skeptical and reluctant—and intrigued. "What case?" she inquired.

He picked up his jacket and gestured toward a path that led down the slope and wound through the vineyard. After a moment, she joined him.

She kept a safe distance as they walked among the vines, and when the way became narrow she held back to let him precede her. She never took her cautious, watchful gaze from him, as though she could actually outrun him or outfight him if indeed he tried to harm her. Merely knowing how she thought made Denis smile.

She couldn't stay silent for long. Most humans couldn't.

"How do you know so much about me?" she asked when they were into the Cabernet vines. She automatically moved to one side, leaving a width of shady tied vines between them. "If Alexander didn't tell you, how do you know?"

"I listen. I made it a point to listen for news of you. You interest me, Tessa LeGuerre."

She was hopelessly susceptible to such innocent flattery. "Why?"

He plucked a leaf and crushed it between his fingers, inhaling the fragrance. "Ah, a wet spring," he said, disappointed. "Still, the summer has been good. The press may be passable yet." He tossed the leaf away. "Less than a year ago you stole into my brother's house and tried to kill him in his sleep. Now you call yourself his 'secretary,' you have been introduced to some of the most important werewolves in Europe and you have entree to the very Palais itself—which I believe is a first for a human, even in the Devoncroix rule. What should not interest me about that?"

"Why don't *you* go to the Palais for the Festival?" she demanded suddenly. "Face your brother, tell him he was wrong about you. Apologize to the queen for your plot against her, ask her mercy. Instead of skulking about here like a common—"

"Criminal?" He chuckled. "That's what I am. An outlaw, a renegade, banished forever from polite society and the Devoncroix reign. And I have no intention of apologizing to the queen, since I am not at all sorry and continue to plot against her."

Her heartbeat speeded up with that, and alarm tainted her breath. "They can smell you," she said, "or hear you, the werewolves on the estate, and they'll want to know why you're here."

"Actually, no," he replied, and with a note of apology in his tone so as not to make her seem too stupid. "They have all departed for the Palais, and no one is left but humans. I shouldn't take such a chance otherwise. This is something I made certain of before I came to you."

"Why did you come to me?"

"Ah, a woman who knows how to keep to the point. Not a common trait among your species."

They had reached a division in the rows and he glanced over at her. A gust of warm wind blew the brim of Tessa's hat back again and tossed the ruffle of her skirt. She squinted in the sun and straightened her hat brim, but when she started to take a step forward her skirt was caught on a supporting timber. She bent to release it, but Denis was swifter.

She jerked her hand back when her fingers brushed his and her eyes flashed surprise and quick fear. Denis smiled, amused, and cocking his head a little as though requesting permission, he carefully lifted the little bit of lace from the splinter that had snared it.

But he did not straighten immediately. Holding the bit of petticoat between his fingers, he let the backs of his knuckles brush her cotton-stockinged ankle, then travel upward along the path of her Achilles tendon. He heard every muscle in her body contract with stiff shock, her heart lurch into motion, her breath catch with a stifled mewling sound. He let the skirt fall over his hand and encircled her calf with his fingers, stroking the trembling muscle and its flimsy cotton covering, smelling her fear and her musk. Thrill and terror were one for her, and like a rabbit in the jaws of a predator, she was paralyzed by the thrall of power.

Yet she whispered, heart pounding, blood surging, in a voice so small it barely moved her lips: "Don't."

He stretched his fingers to the back of her knee, felt the heat and the faint dampness there, and stroked slowly downward between the two tendons. He heard the sound of her teeth pressing together, suppressing a gasp or a cry. He moved his hand farther upward until he touched the bare flesh of her thigh. He smelled her sex, felt the muscles tremble. Desire and terror. It was an intoxicating mix.

He removed his hand and her skirt fluttered out one last breath of sexual sweat and fear before settling around her ankles again. He straightened to stand beside her, his face close to hers.

"Frightened, little Tessa?" he murmured. He made his breath engulf her, his gaze hold on to hers. "What did you think I might do, I wonder?"

Blood was pulsing in the vein of her throat, giving off heat in her face. Her lips were flushed but dry, and she swallowed before she spoke. "Go away from me," she said hoarsely. "Leave me alone."

He smiled. "You go away from me, Tessa LeGuerre. No one is holding you here."

But she did not move. She simply stood there, her breath light and quick, her eyes searching. "What do you want? What are you trying to do?"

"I am trying merely to prove a point," he said. He stepped away from her, releasing her from the snare of his presence, and began walking again. With a small, unconsciously imperial gesture of his hand, he indicated she should join him. Almost without hesitation she fell into step beside him.

"You see, Tessa, I will not force myself upon you in the middle of the night. I will not snap your neck the moment your back is turned or carve you up to boil in my stew. I have the power to do so if I wish and you couldn't stop me. The point is that I do not wish."

She was still trembling, her heart beating in jerky contractions and releases. He could hear it. Yet he felt a fleeting admiration—liberally mixed with amusement—for the effort she made to control her voice and pretend disdain.

"And this is supposed to put me at my ease with you?" she asked. "For this I should be persuaded to help you?"

"Have I said I needed your help?"

"Why else would you come to me?"

"I rather thought we might help each other."

"You have nothing that I want."

"You want him to be your lover, don't you?" Denis returned quietly, easily, and without breaking stride. "You want him to lie naked between your legs and put his organ inside you and spill the fluid of his magic into your womb so that you might hold him beside you forever and in that way be a part of what he is. And he's told you that's not possible, that such as we cannot consort with those of your kind." He shrugged. "Another lie, or perhaps a mere exaggeration. While it's not something to be encouraged, or even to be discussed in polite company, there are those who find quite some pleasure in carnal activities with humans—much in the same way they enjoy dining with humans and working with humans and even inviting humans into their homes."

She turned on him, her cheeks white and her eyes ablaze. "You are a beast masquerading in the form of a man. How can you know these things? How dare you speak them aloud to me?"

He ignored her, maintaining his easy stride and his conversational tone. She was forced to either keep up or be left behind, never to know what he had to say.

"Alexander has ambitions," Denis continued, "as he should. But it's the queen Elise who is the most ambitious of all, and she is the reason your own ambitions will never be fulfilled."

"Do you think I don't know why you're saying these things? You who hate humans and would like to see us all exterminated?" Her voice shook with rage and distress, but it was anxiety he smelled on her skin—anxiety that he might be speaking the truth, and a guilty acknowledgement that somewhere deep inside she had had these suspicions before. "You want to overthrow the queen and put your evil plan into practice and—"

He couldn't help laughing. "An evil plan, have I? How very high-blown and dramatic it sounds, but a bit much even for me. And if Alexander has told you I want only to exterminate humans, then I am very disappointed in him indeed. Yes, I aspire to the throne, but only because I believe it to be the best thing for our people. And despite what you've heard or think about the Dark Brothers, we do not intend to eliminate any species from the earth. We want balance, equanimity and a restoration of the proper hierarchy of power. We believe we should be allowed to indulge our true nature, not be forced to hide it. We would have a separation of our two species, a division of territory, and freedom to conduct our affairs in the way we see fit. We ask only to be acknowledged for what we are and to be left in peace. Is that, after all, such an evil plan?"

She was silent as she marched beside him, her fists clenched, her jaw set. He could hear the swish of her breath through her nostrils, the thud, thud of her heart.

"But you're still angry with me. Nothing I tell you will gain your sympathies even though you know, deep inside, my plan for our people is a sound one. I should abandon my case and leave you for now, and return when I can be more charming. But I won't do that, Tessa.

I will give you more credit than to believe you would refuse to hear the truth just because it's told to you badly."

"What truth have you to tell me?"

"Elise Devoncroix has used you for her own purpose. She has pretended to be your friend, but she is bred from centuries of royalty and you could never be more to her than a fine horse or a hunting dog is to your own queen. *She is a species apart.* You know that. She feels no loyalty to you, she has no thought for your feelings or your needs—why should she? You are of no consequence to her except as how you further her ends."

He knew his words had struck a secret truth when she said sharply, "The point."

"The point, my dear Tessa LeGuerre, human, is that Elise Devoncroix intends to use Alexander just as she has used you, as a symbol to rally the pack behind her when she puts into motion her plan to turn us all into a pack of human-lovers."

Tessa said impatiently, "I doubt Alexander would consider himself badly used, any more than I did."

Now Denis stopped, and moved before her, looking down upon her gravely. "You thought my plan was diabolical. What you failed to understand is that, where the welfare of the pack is concerned, there is no boundary a devoted leader would not cross. Elise plans to use Alexander by taking him as her mate, and once that is done he will never return to you."

He felt the change of temperature that was the blood leaving the surface of her skin, heard the scrape of nails against flesh as her hands contracted involuntarily into fists. He smelled the sickness of strong emotion that wept like a cold sweat from her pores. And he saw the dull shock and pain in her eyes.

She said hoarsely, "How do you know this?"

"Because that's what I would do," he replied simply. And when he saw the parchmentlike stiffness start to relax in her face he added, "And because it is impossible to keep secrets from those whose ears can hear whispers across the miles and who know what to listen for.

I told you, Tessa, I have done nothing but watch and listen since I came to France. My purpose is too important to do otherwise."

She never took her eyes off him as she said, "Your purpose?"

He did not answer immediately. Instead he turned away from her casually and plucked an embryonic grape from a cluster on a nearby vine. "This vineyard is over a thousand years old, did you know that? Long before the Romans came to Gaul, we were making wine here. Long after they departed, we are making wine here. We will continue to make wine from vines that are the very descendants of those among which you stroll today, long after your people have disappeared from the face of the earth, and we shall barely notice your passing. A matter upon which to ponder, wouldn't you agree?"

"I don't know what you're talking about."

Denis crushed the small grape between his fingers. "Of course you don't," he replied patiently. "And that is the point. Alexander is a species apart. The finest humans who ever made wine are hundreds of years away from approaching the wines that he creates in his spare time. They lack the capacity to even wonder *why* he is so much their superior. And that is why it is so difficult for me to make you understand what must be done now.

"But first I must ask you something. Why, when you made your plan to kill Alexander, didn't you use a gun? It's so much neater and more reliable, and seems to be the weapon of choice among humans."

She blinked, disoriented by the question. "I—I didn't have one."

He looked at her carefully. "I thought perhaps you didn't know how to use one."

"All Englishwomen know how to shoot," she replied with a brusque impatience and a touch of disdain. "Why are you asking this? What difference can it make?"

"But are you a good shot?" he persisted.

Caution leveled her voice, narrowed her eyes. "What do you mean by good?"

"At a hundred paces, are you good enough to hit, say, a wolf?"

She drew in a single breath sharply, the darks of her eyes dilating. She whispered, "What are you saying?"

"You know the answer to that, Tessa." He said it quietly, holding her gaze.

And she did. She darted her gaze away, but not before he saw understanding there, and guilt and horror and yes, in a flash quicker than a half-stammered heartbeat, affirmation.

"You want me to kill the queen." She had to say it out loud.

"I want to save my brother—and the pack."

She gaped at him, her eyes big with incredulity and denial. "You're mad!"

"To think you would do it," he pressed mildly, "or to ask it of you?"

"Both!" she cried.

And he smiled. "Perhaps neither. She must die, Tessa, you know that, for both our sakes. The only question is whether Alexander will die with her."

Her heart was beating hard, fast and furious, a frantic rabbit racing through the brush. She didn't speak; she didn't have to. Everything he needed to know he smelled on her skin, heard in her breath and her pulse and the swelling of her blood.

"Leave this place," she said hoarsely. "Don't ever bother me again."

"I shall not leave," he replied. "Not until I've accomplished my purpose. But if you wish me to leave you alone . . ." He shrugged. "I'll oblige. I thought we shared a mutual concern for Alexander, that's all."

"You just threatened to kill him!"

"Not unless I have to. The queen is in my way, Alexander is not. You can save him. You can save him—and you can keep him. All you have to do is this one little thing, this thing that comes so easily to your kind."

She said flatly, with a dull note of disbelief in her voice, "Commit a murder."

"But isn't that what you came among us to do all those months ago?"

Confusion shadowed her face as she turned away. "You're mad," she repeated. "Mad to think I would do this thing." But her voice held less conviction than it had only a moment ago.

"Perhaps." He moved closer. Lightly, his fingers fell upon her shoulder. He heard her heart thudding, the fabric of her dress sliding back and forth over her breasts with the lurch of her breath. "But it is only reasonable, Tessa LeGuerre, for you to consider it."

She jerked away from his touch and without another word left him, pushing through the vines, not looking back.

He watched her go calmly, smiling a little to himself, with long-seeing eyes until the leaves stopped stirring in her passage. "Poor little human," he murmured. "What a pity that for all your vast education no one ever warned you about conversing with the devil."

When the long gray wolf eased itself silently out of the vines and came to stand beside him, Denis dropped his hand companionably to its head. "Don't worry," he said, and smiled again. "She'll be back. Had I not been sure of that, I never would have let her go."

Fifteen

ALEXANDER'S HOUSE HAD AN ODDLY DESERTED FEELING TO IT, WITH NO one in attendance except human servants. Poinceau, Lavalier, Mme. Crolliere—all were gone, and without them to supervise, the humans were lazy and indolent. There was no one to drive Tessa to the Palais, and she had to struggle to saddle a horse for herself, losing precious minutes in the process.

Denis Antonov. The very name had the power to invoke evil, like a chant muttered over a fire. He *was* evil. He had proved that with his demented scheme to murder the queen, with his arrogant assumption that she, Tessa LeGuerre, would assist him. And when she remembered his touch and what it had done to her, she went hot with shame. The queen had said he was handsome, and he was. She had said he was charming, and he was. She had not mentioned, however, how persuasive he was, how powerful. Even Alexander had not prepared her for that. There had been times when he had almost convinced her that everything he said was the truth, when she had *wanted* to believe it. His power frightened her. Her response to it made her weak.

The horse shied and danced as she turned down the long avenue that led to the Palais, and she knew it smelled the wolves watching from the shadows. She held the horse tightly in check and directed her eyes straight ahead and pretended she didn't feel their hot gazes burning into her back.

She dismounted at the front steps before the gazes of the dozens of curious, disdainful werewolves who were strolling up and down the broad staircase or milling lazily around the front lawn. Some of them sniffed the air and moved close to her, but she dodged past them quickly and ran into the front hall.

For over a month she had called this place home, but now it frightened her. The marble floors echoed with the voices of strange werewolves in flamboyant dress—transparent, shapeless robes of bright scarlet and yellow, feather boas and tall hats fashioned after animal heads. Some were naked, others were in wolf form. They looked at her askance when she passed, or shrank back with horrified, disgusted expressions and murmured among themselves. Tessa hurried by with lowered eyes, her heart thudding hard.

At the double doors which led to the interior living areas two attendants stepped forward, blocking her way. She had not expected this.

"Please," she said, a little breathless, "I have to see the queen."

The two looked down at her, stone-faced.

"You know me!" she cried. "You've seen me here every day for the past six weeks!"

They shared a glance, and seemed to relent somewhat. "You're not on the list," one of them said in a moment. "No one else is allowed in."

She drew a breath to protest, but knew it would be a waste of time. Frantically she cast about for an idea. "Alexander," she said quickly. "Alexander Devoncroix—just send word to him. Ask him to come down. I just need to see him for a minute."

"M. Devoncroix is not in the Palais," was the reply.

She wanted to demand to know why he wasn't there, where he had gone, when he would be back, but realized such behavior would avail her nothing and would only fulfill the worst expectations of the were-wolves who were watching her. She felt a small sweat break out on the back of her neck and she knew they could smell it.

"Will you send word to the queen?" she asked, beginning to lose hope. "Will you tell her I'm here?"

"The queen isn't in, either."

She swallowed back a choking sensation in her throat. Denis's words came back to her about Elise and Alexander and she pushed them away furiously. Of course they were together. Alexander was the queen's favorite; everyone knew that.

She had to get a message to Alexander. If he knew his brother was here, if he knew what Denis had planned, he would send out an army to stop him. But if she, Tessa, told anyone but Alexander that his out-law brother was waiting for him at home—what would that do to Alexander? Couldn't he somehow be held to blame for Denis's presence, for the threat to the queen? No, she could trust this information to no one except Alexander or Elise. And if she delayed here much longer Denis might discover what she had done. There was no guarantee that he had not followed her here already.

She said abruptly, "Gault. Send for him, please. Tell him there's an urgent message from the estate."

One of the guards slid open a small grate in the door and spoke softly to someone on the other side. When he resumed his post, eyes straight ahead, Tessa could only assume the summons had been sent. She turned away, pacing.

Gault kept her waiting for almost a quarter of an hour, and by that time she was so agitated she was ready to burst out with the entire story and throw herself at his mercy. If he had been even the least hospitable she might have done so, for she knew, no matter what his attitude toward her, his loyalty to Alexander was unquestioned. But Gault stepped through the double doors, sniffed the air elaborately, and said, "Oh, it's you." He turned on his heel to go.

"Wait!" She caught his sleeve, dropping it immediately at his haughty gaze. "I need your help. I have to talk to Alexander. Where has he gone?"

Every werewolf in the building was watching them, listening to them. Gault was as aware of this as she was and it only increased his disdain. "Obviously, somewhere you can't find him. Perhaps he has left the country, or thrown himself into the sea. I couldn't blame him. What does it take to convince you you are not wanted here?"

"Say what you like," she said, refusing to back down from him. "Be as cruel as you must. But I *will* see Alexander."

"So he can toss you out again? As much pleasure as that would give me to watch, I wouldn't put him to the trouble. Go home, foolish human. This is no place for you." And he raised his voice to add, clearly enough so that even those on the far reaches of the lawn could understand, "As you have been told over and over again."

She realized that Gault was more annoyed with her for endangering Alexander's status by disobeying an order and appearing here on the day of the Festival than for any other reason. Denis was right. She didn't belong here, and she was welcome only as long as it suited the queen's political purpose. But she couldn't leave without getting word to Alexander.

She stepped close to Gault and said in a low, furious voice, "Listen to me, you pompous little toad. What I have to say to Alexander is a matter of life and death, and the queen won't thank you for keeping him from me, either! Now, you may tell me where to find him or I'll wait here until he comes back—and if I wait I'll make certain every werewolf in the Palais sees me and knows you are the reason I'm here!"

He scowled down at her fiercely. "I'll call the guards and have you ground up into pig fodder!"

"The guards won't touch me and you know it."

He looked at her for one more long contemptuous moment, and then turned a corner of his lip upward in a dismissive sneer. "Take your chances with them if you want. You've quite spoiled enough of *my* day."

He turned again to go.

"Wait!"

Tessa went to the guest book that stood on a small dais in the center of the room, snatched out a blank page and scrawled a note: "A visitor from the north has come making threats. You are in danger. I don't know what to do. Please come at once. Tessa."

She folded the note twice and then again, and she pressed it into Gault's hand. "I will go," she said, "if you promise to give that to Alexander the moment he returns. Don't delay. Something—something terrible will happen if you fail."

He regarded her with cold eyes and she feared she had just lost her last chance at persuading him. But then he lifted his head, as though sniffing the air, or hearing something. He listened for a moment, and a cruel little smile lifted the hard edges of his mouth. "Give it to him yourself, stupid human." He held out the note to her. "You'll find him in the west garden, just down the steps."

Tessa was moving almost before he had finished speaking. Gault grinned with satisfaction as he watched her go, then dropped her note into the fire as he turned to go back to his private quarters.

Tessa must have known in the back of her mind that anything which gave Gault so much pleasure could not be good for her, but she was intent only on reaching Alexander. If she could just get to Alexander, everything would be all right. She fled the room, weaving through the crossfire of cold werewolf gazes and curious werewolf sniffs and down the front steps, onto the lawn and through the hedges, where even more of the same awaited her. She turned toward the west garden, which was reached by a set of steps that descended into a sun-splashed little copse of willow trees and tall pink lupine.

And that was when she saw Alexander, and Elise.

ALEXANDER

Sixteen

WE WERE MOSTLY SILENT ON THE RIDE BACK TO THE PALAIS. I WOULD like to say it was out of consideration of the driver, and the fact that the business we had discussed was not for ordinary ears. But the truth was my head was spinning in such a marvellous ecstasy of hope and confusion, of excitement and expectation, that I could barely form a thought, much less a word.

Owing to the Festival, which by its very nature made formality of any kind seem out of place, protocol was much more relaxed at the Palais than was customary, and when the carriage pulled up before the wide front steps, our arrival was marked by nothing more than the appearance of a footman with the carriage step. There were several dozen werewolves in sight and hundreds more within hearing distance. In the lazy warmth of the late afternoon they were languid, stretched naked upon the grass or lying upon flat rocks in the sun, stroking each other, licking away the sweat, laughing throatily at some witticism or another. Cubs played in the fountains or climbed upon their elders' fur; couples strolled, in parasols and gloves, along shady garden lanes and read to one another from volumes of poetry, revelling in the meter and the sound of the words balanced against the still sunny afternoon. From deep inside the Palais I could hear the sounds of a dozen different musical instruments, from pianoforte to viola to voice, each creating its own song and together, to my ears, forming a symphony. I felt, in that moment as I stood on the steps looking down at my queen and my love, a rush of joy so intense I could barely contain it. Never had I been so glad to be a werewolf.

I took her arm and guided her down the steps toward the west garden, where fewer were gathered and some small privacy could be obtained. I was selfish with my love. I wanted to extend our time together by whatever means I could, and I wanted to keep her to myself for as long as possible.

We reached the bottom of the steps and I said, "Shall we take the waters?"

Others before us were soaking in the heated pools that were situated within a fern grotto at the back edge of the garden. I could smell the steam and the floral petals that scented the water, and it was alluring.

Elise reached up and pulled out the hatpin that held her hair bundled beneath the charming little violet-covered hat. She removed the hat and tossed her head, and her hair fell like a veil of gold over her shoulders. She combed it out with her fingers. "Perhaps later," she said. "I promised to speak with the chef about next week's menus, and the group from Scotland has arrived—can you smell them? I should make them welcome."

I nodded, concealing my disappointment. We walked a little away, taking our time, for she seemed no more anxious to part company than I was. Our fingers brushed when we moved, and we enjoyed the touch and the smell of each other.

"You have not told me," she said at last, "what you think of my plan."

"Haven't I?" I chose my words. "I think it is brilliant. I think it is bold, timely, pertinent. I think it is our salvation. And I think it is quite a challenge for one werewolf to expect to achieve in her lifetime."

"Perhaps," she agreed. She stopped then beneath the shade of a mulberry tree, and looked straight at me. "But not for two."

She never took her eyes off me. I could not have mistaken her meaning had I been blind, for the gentle power of that gaze all but made my knees buckle. My world tilted on its axis, spun wildly out of control, blossomed in color and light. I said hoarsely, "I love you, Elise."

Her eyes shimmered. "My dear, dear Alexander," she whispered, "I know."

She lifted her hand, and with her knuckles she stroked my cheek, my ear, and, releasing one finger, delicately, expertly explored that sensitive curve of the skull just behind the ear. Sun and sound and the world around me faded away.

We had played the sex games before, we knew each other's taste and feel and zones of pleasure, just as we knew the same of dozens of others with whom we ran. We were comfortable with each other, easy and compatible. But she had never touched me like this before, never held me in that fire-eating gaze, never deliberately unleashed the full power of her sexual allure.

Her scent enveloped me: the wine-sweetness of her breath, the sunshine of her hair, the salt of the skin between her breasts, the musk of sex. The tip of her finger, like heated silk, lightly teasing the center of my most erogenous zone was agony. For with her touch, with her scent, with her questing gaze, the query was implicit: Would I find her desirable? Could she arouse me?

My own sexuality responded immediately and with a ferocity that shocked even me. I moved close to her. I touched her throat, her jaw, her ear. Heat from her loins flowed into mine. Her pulse roared in my ears, captured my heartbeat, dragged it into her rhythm. With the most delicate, sliding, almost liquid motion I touched her there, just behind the ear.

My muscles cramped and beads of sweat broke out upon my forehead as I fought back the Change that she, with nothing more than that simple, erotic touch, pushed me toward. And, to my everlasting triumph, I saw her own features go waxy, felt the flash of heat that consumed her body, and knew the sorcery was mutual—whether or not she had intended it to be.

I caught her hand quickly, before we went too far, and held it tightly. "Foolish girl," I said huskily, and was in part surprised that enough of the human form remained in me to form words. "Did you have to ask?"

The image of her was burned upon my brain, the need for her burned into my soul. I couldn't take my eyes from her. Nor could she from me. She said softly, "You are the fool, Alexander Devoncroix, fretting over whether or not I would be able to attract a mate . . . when it is clear, and has been clear for weeks to everyone but you, that I have already chosen one."

How to describe my emotions then? Can anyone who has ever loved fail to know them even without being told? Doubt, disbelief, wonder, joy, the purest ecstasy it is possible to know outside the mating bond. The discovery. The promise. A future unfolding that holds not one but two hearts fast together. Ah, is there in all of creation anything more perfect? Can there be in the life of man or werewolf or beast that crawls a moment more precious than the moment in which he discovers that he is loved?

It would have been easy then to let passion sweep us away. It would have been fitting, it would have been right. But in matters of state, things are rarely so simple—no more than they are in matters of the heart.

I took her hand and brought it to my lips. I said thickly, "Elise. You are my only treasure."

And then I caught the scent that had been there all along, so familiar to both of us that neither of us registered it as unusual until suddenly there was a sound—a rustling, a step, a half-caught breath—to go with it. We turned as one, Elise and I, toward the steps.

"Tessa!" I exclaimed.

But she was already running away, and did not answer my calls.

Later, I would spend hour after despairing hour trying to piece together the events of that day from Tessa's point of view. If one could know the future, it has often been said, one would do nothing but live in the past. Perhaps. Perhaps the knowledge would paralyze us completely. I know, for my own part, it would have at the very least made me more alert.

In fact, that afternoon I spent less than ten minutes on Tessa and her mysterious—and annoying—behavior. Elise questioned the door attendants and the guards as to whether Tessa had asked for her specifically, and when they seemed anxious that they had done wrong by not holding Tessa for questioning, she replied impatiently that they must not be foolish, the human Tessa was to come and go about the palace without impediment as she had always done.

But to me she said sadly, "We've hurt her feelings, I'm afraid. Do please send for her, Alexander, and let us make amends."

You may believe I had matters of far greater import on my mind than the feelings of Tessa LeGuerre. I was torn between the desire to do anything to please my beloved enchantress and a justifiable impatience with Tessa that she should distract me from what was, after all, the most crucial moment in my life thus far.

I said, trying to keep the note of irritability from my voice, "She is a spoiled child, and I will do her no service by indulging her further."

"She is lonely and bored. Your house will be empty by now, with all of the werewolves coming for the midsummer run—"

"There are plenty of humans to keep her entertained." But at the look of reproval she gave me, I softened. "I can't bring her back here on the night of a Festival run, you know that. We've had this argument before. And Tessa knew she was being disobedient to come here, which is why she ran when we saw her. I'm sorry she's lonely, but it can't be helped. I will send a note to her tomorrow. Perhaps I'll take her to town for sweets."

Elise smiled, passing her hand over my hair in a light, caressing stroke. "That would be kind of you, Alexander."

I basked in her approval and in the gentle radiance of her smile.

Then she said, starting up the steps, "And now I think I will follow the example of the rest of the pack, and rest in the sun for the run tonight. Perhaps I'll see you," she added, with a coy glance over her shoulder, "in the forest."

And I replied gallantly, "You may be sure of it, mademoiselle."

And this, then, was the way of it between us, for even in the deepest matters of the heart it is important not to allow our passions to govern our behavior, for good or ill. Of course I did not want to part from her, even for the space of the afternoon, any more than she did from me. There were words to be said, looks to be exchanged, caresses to be shared. Yet how meaningful could those words have been had we not believed that we had the rest of our lives in which to say them? And knowing that we would never touch again in the way we had touched before only made the anticipation more sweet to savor.

Yet I confess as she left me, the emotions of a young male in love consumed me. I was awash in foolish happiness. I found her scent on a strand of my hair and I brought that strand to my nostrils, inhaling deeply, letting her aroma flow through my bloodstream like an intoxicant. Fierce possessive joy, deep and holy wonder, weak-kneed desire—these were only a few of the emotions that leapt and tumbled within me as I stood upon the steps as helpless in ecstasy as a cub with first Change. The werewolves who passed me had no trouble determining the cause of my thrall and grinned at me in companionable understanding; still, I wanted to tell someone. She had chosen me. She had touched me with the intent to arouse me, and desire had flamed in her blood as well. She wanted *me*, my Elise, my queen, the living embodiment of all that was strongest and purest and most perfect of our kind—she had chosen *me*. I wanted to shout it to the world, I wanted to howl it from the highest hill, I wanted to grab the next person who passed and dance around in circles and exclaim my wondrous secret. And the oddest thing was that the person I wanted most to tell was Tessa.

Of course I told no one, although Gault, who smelled the musk of Elise's experimental caress upon me, knew immediately and seemed smugly unsurprised. To have made a comment of any sort would have been unconscionably impolite, however, and so he began to fuss about my toilet as I stripped off my town clothes, muttering about that "wretched human girl" and her impertinence. I did inquire whether or not he had spoken with Tessa, and he replied that she had insisted she would speak with no one but me and made a great fuss when he told her I wasn't at the Palais.

"She accused me of hiding you from her," he added with a sniff. "As if I would bother myself to lie to an insect such as she. When I heard you arrive, I sent her to you. Didn't she find you?"

I paused to glance at him, suspecting mischief—which would not have been so unusual a thing coming from Gault, considering it was directed at Tessa. But his expression was bland as he carefully smoothed out a crease in my trousers.

I walked naked to the tub, and he added as an afterthought, "She did scribble a note for you, but I was so out of patience with her by then I tossed it directly into the fire."

I turned to glare at him. "What did it say?"

"I didn't read it. How important could it have been?"

On another day I might have upbraided Gault for his presumption, but there was at that moment no shred of anger anywhere within me that I could summon forth for the occasion. Besides, he was right. Everyone of importance was here, at the Palais, and nothing that happened abroad this night could be of much concern to us. Human servants could deal with any emergency that arose at the estate until my return. I would see Tessa in the morning, and whatever problems she had—if in fact she had any problem at all—could be resolved then.

I settled into the sunken bath filled with steaming water and scented herbs, and soaked there until my muscles were like taffy and my mind stripped of all but its purest, deepest instincts. Then I stretched out upon the smooth, sun-heated stones outside my chamber and, one by one, masked all sounds from my ears save one rhythm, one pulse, one life. With my lover's heartbeat as my mantra, I sank deep into the river of the soul and there the two of us floated away.

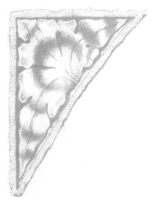

TESSA

Seventeen

TESSA DIDN'T EVEN REALIZE SHE HAD DEPARTED THE PALAIS UNTIL SHE dismounted the horse in the stableyard of Alexander's estate, stumbling a little as she released the stirrup. She left the animal standing there and started toward the house, moving like a sleepwalker while the tattered pieces of her world swam about her head.

You are my only treasure, he had said. Elise. His only treasure.

What a fool she had been. Of course he loved Elise. And of course that was why he had sent her away. That night in the garden . . . he had lied when he said it meant nothing. He had told her he and Elise were not mates, but he had lied. The noble werewolf, whose hands and lips and sweet words had loved her so well, had in the end behaved no better than any human male when he found a woman he loved better.

Tessa wanted to feel angry at him for this. All she felt was broken.

Denis had been right. All that he had said to her in the vineyard . . . he had been right.

There would be an advantage in bringing the Antonovs and the Devoncroix together again, Elise had said. And when Alexander had refused to cooperate with his brother's scheme, perhaps his motives had not been so honorable after all. He must have known even then that he wanted Elise for himself.

Ambitious, Elise had said of him.

These were the things that were swarming around in her head, darting and screeching at her and plucking her with pincerlike claws. Tessa felt small and insignificant and lost, bleeding from a thousand wounds.

And yet above it all there was a clarity, stark and unquestioned, a simple truth. She stood on the steps of Alexander Devoncroix's house and she looked at its blank faceless windows and she knew at that moment she could turn away. She could simply walk down the drive and never look back, and all of this would be behind her. But if she went forward, her life would never be the same again. Either way, all that she had known and loved and believed to be true was over.

It was over. She should walk away. But she could not.

She went up the steps as though in slow motion, leaning heavily on the rail. She went through the doors. She tugged off her coat and hung it on the carved hook in the foyer. She proceeded through the house with its wide light-swept corridors and tall cool rooms, and Denis Antonov was waiting for her in the receiving parlor. He rose when he heard her footsteps and beckoned her enter with a glass of wine in his hand. "I decided to accept your kind invitation to come to the house," he said, smiling. "Will you share a glass with me?"

A coldness settled in the pit of Tessa's stomach which was not fear but something much deeper. "Who let you in here?"

He raised a reproving eyebrow at her tone. "A human girl. Should she have refused entrance to her master's brother?" He glanced around. "A modestly fine dwelling, but I could never be comfortable here."

Somehow Tessa made her numb lips move, made her voice sound almost normal. "Why should you, when you will have the Palais?"

Confidence warmed his eyes as he sipped his wine. "I see you have given my proposal some thought."

Tessa took off her gloves and her hat with its pretty green ribbons dampened by the sweat of her distress and the dust of the road. She placed them on a gilded table that had carved cherubs for the legs, and she went to the big window that overlooked the vineyards. Alexander had told her a werewolf could smell a lie. She dared not lie to this one.

"I think you were right about"—here her voice almost broke—"the queen and Alexander."

"Of course I was."

"She means to marry him."

"I'm not surprised."

"I can't stop her."

"Of course you can."

It was another moment before she felt strong enough to turn and look at him. Her palms made damp spots where they pressed against her skirt. She kept her hands flat at her sides.

"This thing," she inquired evenly, "when must it be done?"

She saw the light of avarice in his eyes, a glint above his wineglass. "Tonight," he said. "I will show you the place to wait, where she's sure to come and no one will notice you. In the confusion of the pack run, you can easily escape."

"But for how long?" she returned sharply. "I'll be killed if they catch me."

"Silly child, they won't catch you. One human smells much like another to us, and how are they to know it was you? Come." He moved to the setee before the fireplace and lifted a long wooden box from its resting place there. "I have a gift for you."

He opened the box and held it out to her. Inside, nestled against a gray velvet lining, was a walnut-stocked, brass-trimmed rifle.

Tessa's throat went dry. A few moments passed before she could speak. "If I refuse to assist you," she managed to say, "if I find your game is not to my taste—what will you do then?"

His voice and his face grew cold. "I will send an army and kill them all in their sleep. This way will be less bloody, but it matters little to me. You should remember that if I come for the queen, Alexander will be the first to die. She will not be allowed to take a mate."

For a long time Tessa didn't move. She stood there with her eyes fixed upon the rifle in the box, then slowly she stepped forward and picked it up and held it in her hands. Denis smiled.

Alexander, she thought, *don't desert me now. Come home, please ...*

Yet she knew even then, in some small still part of her mind, that the history of this night had been written the moment she entered Alexander Devoncroix's house, and she was but a pawn in events much larger than she could even imagine. She could do her best, but that was all.

And she knew, too, in that same small still part of her mind, that her best would not be enough.

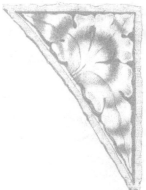

ALEXANDER

Eighteen

WE ARE A PEOPLE WHO LOVE CELEBRATIONS, GATHERINGS AND REVELRIES and will exploit any opportunity for festivity. The four major festivals of the year are celebrated on the change of seasons—Vernal Equinox, Summer Solstice, Harvest Moon and Winter Solstice—and are rooted in antiquity. Human pagans long ago appropriated our holidays and somehow began to associate them with moon worship and sorcery, perhaps because we must have seemed the masters of sorcery to them, and because of our great fondness for assembling on moonlit nights. As for the origins of the celebrations, no one remembers. We did not develop as an agricultural society, so the change of seasons cannot have meant much to us, and our only relationship with the moon is the fact that it facilitates hunting. Nonetheless, the festivals have not lost their appeal and are celebrated much in the same way today that they were eons ago.

Of all the seasonal celebrations the Summer Festival was the most well attended, for obvious reasons. June in central France is a most hospitable place, and what could be more conducive to the pack run—an essential part of any celebration—than the mild, bright nights, lush greenery and rushing streams of summer?

I think in times of old the Summer Festival had much more of a bacchanalian flavor than its modern expression. But even though we are a more civilized species in many ways, the purpose of the run has always been to indulge our baser instincts. This we do with triumphant abandon.

To run with the pack is perhaps the single most thrilling experience a werewolf can have outside the mating bond. It is the very essence of what we are, strength through unity, power through the order of hierarchy; the mastery of flesh and nature. Whether the available pack consists of a half-dozen neighbors after a dinner party or a formal gathering of candidates competing for a job or a position of power, the run is the most honest, determining event of our lives.

And the Festival runs are the quintessential definition of what it means to be a werewolf. Between moonrise and moonset on the night of a Festival run, lives may be changed: old conflicts resolved and new ones begun, mates chosen, young conceived, debts forgiven, friendships forged. This is why we would perish if forced to spend all of our time in human form and why all of us, whether we confess it or not, feel pity for humans, who are trapped in their one shape and their one life and ensnared by all the foolish stiff-boned defenses that go with it. Stripped naked, we can hide nothing from each other. Reduced to our most savage instincts and glorying in them, we are as nature intended, unafraid and unashamed. How can one help but pity a species that will never know the dignity of respect, trust and companionship granted to us each time we do something so simple as indulge ourselves in our purest natures?

Most of us rested that day, gathering our energy for the athletic demands of the night, and many of us fasted to sharpen our hunting instincts and to better appreciate the exquisite sensual pleasure of the first kill. We began to assemble at dusk, gathering in the gardens, parks and clearings that surrounded the Palais, assigning ourselves to groups according to our status and our family ties.

I myself rose naked from the stones when they began to cool, and felt the promise of what was undoubtedly to be the most significant night of my life prickle in my belly. The electric scent of others, hot with expectation, was in the air. It went through me like a sexual thrill. And, as with the best of sex, I controlled my appetite, savored the sensation, let the anticipation become part of the ecstasy.

I gave Gault permission to depart before me, and he thanked me for my indulgence by shedding his clothes and transforming before me. Ah, that was sweet. He had a dramatic flair and a visceral appeal which had rightly earned him a reputation as a heartbreaker among both males and females of our kind. It brought me to the edge of arousal. The burnt-spices scent of his Change lingered in the room and I luxuriated in it, stepping into the deepest cones of aroma with my arms upraised and letting it drip over me like fragrant dew.

Murmurs and whispers and inarticulate half-formed moans of pleasure and impatience filled my ears, a soothing background sea that rose and ebbed like the tide of my pulse. I took a glass of wine to the terrace outside my room and watched the sunset, listened to the tide of murmured voices, felt the swell of the rising moon in my blood. Only when I detected the whisper of her scent on the air did the simmering broth of sensation in which I indulged myself reach its boiling point. It became an exercise of will to restrain myself as I walked through the garden, following the lure of moon and the woman who, by doing nothing more than breathing the air I breathed, drew me helplessly, rapturously into the circle of her flame.

The night was deep and purple on the far edges of dusk, and the rising moon was a pale and shadowed silver above the curve of the hills. Hovering over all was a faint haze of mist which would dissipate as the night deepened and the temperature equalized, but which was soft on the vision and muffling to the ears. I came into the garden and paused for a moment to appreciate the beauty of the scene before me, the rulers of the earth gathering to celebrate their magnificence. Some, like myself, moved naked through the dusk, shoulders and thighs silvered in the pale light. Others draped themselves in silk robes that swirled and fluttered gracefully in the breeze. Some, mostly the gravid or those of middle and lower status, had transformed already, but even among them the mood was tense and expectant. We moved together, in wolf and human form, following the silent call of our leader.

She stood atop the ancient Calling Rock in the clearing. She wore a waistless silk robe of that rich blue which was her signature color, fastened on either shoulder to leave her arms bare. Her chin was lifted, her shoulders were high, her eyes quietly surveying and assessing her pack. Nothing moved about her at all except the aurora of her hair, which rippled and lifted around her shoulders and waist with the rise and fall of the breeze.

We assembled around her, hundreds of us, in the ritual clearing that had been designed for this purpose, arranging ourselves according to age and status. I was young, unmated and of high status; I would have taken my place at the forefront of the circle even if I had not already lost my heart to the queen. But as I stepped up beside the other strong young aristocrats who would vie for her attention tonight, with the ache in my belly and the fire in my brain, I was filled with a sense of certainty and a strength of purpose beyond anything which even I, who have never been at a lack for confidence, had ever known before. Had she merely beckoned me with her finger I could have left gravity behind and flown through the air to her side.

But she did not beckon me. Her eyes moved one by one over the assembled aristocracy, greeting them, and one by one they dropped their eyes. But when her eyes met mine I held her gaze, letting her read my heart there, my promise, the ferocity of my passion, the boldness of my spirit—bold enough to match her own, strong enough to run beside her. It was difficult, the meeting of the gazes, and she did not make it easy for me. My heart thundered and my muscles ached and darts of lightning stabbed into my brain. But just as my skin broke out with a layer of sweat and the backs of my knees began to tremble, she closed her eyes, and her expression softened into an expression of beatific serenity. A preternatural stillness fell over the assemblage.

She lifted her hands and released the shoulder clasps of her garment, which puddled about her feet like a mountain waterfall. She stood naked before us, the most beautiful female on earth, the strongest, the wisest, the fastest and the fiercest of all our kind, and we longed for her as one; we held our collective breath in simple, inexpressible adoration.

She raised her arms and tilted back her head, elongating the muscles of her torso and thrusting forward her breasts. She tightened the muscles of her buttocks and her thighs, rising up on her toes until the smooth lines of her calves were hard knots of powerful muscle. Taut pectorals sharpened the shadowed indentations beneath her arms as she flexed her hands, spreading her fingers to the sky. Our hearts pounded, pounded to watch her, to feel her. The gathering electrical stream around her body caught her hair and lifted it like a playful wind sprite away from her form, swirling and floating on unseen magnetic currents in the air. My throat closed with the beauty of it.

And then, with a cry that went through to our very souls, Elise Devoncroix sprang into the air, and gathering the particles of the night about her in a fearsome swirl of color and sound, she became herself, our queen.

Ah, for words to describe such a moment. The roar of a hundred werewolf voices responding to her call, the density of light and power and surging magic as all around me werewolves embraced the Passion; the tide of swelling, pulling, swirling, pulsing sensation. The song of werewolf. The symphony of Passion. It anchored itself in my solar plexus, deep in the womb of my soul, spreading itself outward in a series of hot rippling thrills that stole my breath and robbed my mind of all but the most basic coherence.

My penis grew stiff and hot, my testicles throbbed with engorgement. My veins filled and swelled and pulsed, flooding my skin with heat, blurring my vision, roaring in my ears. My hands were numb and heavy, my feet like clubs, my lips thick and inarticulate, incapable of passing a sound save for the cry, the song, the inescapable, inevitable fierce and savage, joyous answer to the call of my leader. *My life for you*, it said. *My soul for you*, I answered.

And, oh, the pain. The sweet savage twisting of need, the roar of desire, the sweat that burst like droplets of blood from my skin and dripped onto the ground. I trembled. I cried out, letting my voice ul-

ulate long into the clear night sky. I raised my hands to the sky and I luxuriated in every sensation, in each exquisite attenuated throb of pleasure and need, in each tightening pull of fierce desire. I immersed myself in the electric musk of a hundred Changes, I drank in the Passion of werewolves great and small and I let it torture me, let it strengthen me. I wanted to know it all. And when at last I had drained every gram of sensation from the moment, when I above all remained sweating, straining, aching, holding on to my human form by sheer force of will, I released my essence into an explosion of fever and purpose; I surrendered to the Passion.

When the convulsions of sensate pleasure subsided, when I was whole and strong and cognizant again, clearer in head and stronger in body than I had ever been before, she was there, my beautiful blond wolf, sapphire eyes fixed on mine, sparking with challenge and magnetic in their allure. I leapt for her. We ran.

If I could recount in perfect detail all the events of the night that followed, I should be the greatest historian who ever lived. I make no such claim. It was rather a blur of sight and sound and scent and taste, of emotion and sensation and passion; yes, passion. Muscles stretching, wind streaming through my fur, the smell of green, of night, of Elise.

The scent of game reached us across the night and Elise, master hunter, signalled the kill. She went into the ambush crouch and as it happened, I was among the four swiftest to attend her. In perfect harmony we circled and when the buck broke to run, I was in the position to bring him down.

As I charged, a brown wolf called Girare, anxious to prove himself my better or merely overexcited by the hunt, broke to my left and cut me off. The prey panicked, circling to bolt, and the fool Girare launched himself at the buck, catching him by the back leg and bringing him down.

Screaming with pain, his eyes rolling wildly, the buck kicked and thrashed and almost succeeded in getting to his feet again. Elise sprang forward and snapped the neck of the poor beast between her jaws, ending its misery. At the same moment I got Girare by the scruff and tossed him aside like a pup. He would never hunt with us again, nor would we be likely to do business with him on any matters of consequence in the daylight world. A werewolf who cannot discipline himself for the hunt is unlikely to be reliable in any situation where judgement, strategy and cooperation are called for. Thus are fortunes gained and lost on the night of the pack run; thus are characters truly revealed.

With the smell of blood in the air and the fire of triumph coursing through our veins, we were all on the verge of abandoning discipline. The moment Elise sank her teeth into the throat of the beast the pack surged forward, snapping and growling, each fighting for the first taste of flesh still warm from the bone. I pushed myself into the melee, skirmishing with one or two to demonstrate my determination, drawing blood when I had to. I reached the carcass and showed my teeth to an impudent youth who had ambitions to dine next to the queen. He backed off without argument or hesitation.

I dropped my head and tore open the chest cavity. The rush of steam and the taste of salty blood made me dizzy with pleasure, infusing my senses like sweet summer wine. There is no moment like that moment, no taste like that taste. I could feel the others trembling with tension and growling with hunger around me; I could feel Elise watching me with narrow, cautious eyes. I dipped my head again and tore the heart from its ligaments. Oh, the sensation of teeth sinking into firm blood-filled muscle, the slick flesh upon my tongue, the sharp wild taste of it, and how I longed to flee just then with my prize in my mouth, to hide someplace and savor the delicacy to its last shred. The craving was so intense my stomach cramped, and blood-tinged saliva dripped from my mouth.

I took the heart and laid it at Elise's feet. She inclined her head in acknowledgement, then took my offering away from the carcass to enjoy it in peace.

I feasted with the rest of the pack, and we listened to the sounds of other groups making other kills, we tasted triumph and ecstasy on the air. Afterward we rested for a time, grooming each other and playing at tumbling or wrestling matches in the glade. I must confess I acquitted myself quite well for the sake of my queen, although it's true that, after I had established my dominance at the kill, few would challenge me.

The moon was high and brilliant through the leafy foliage when Elise rose and gave the call to attention. We were barely on our feet when, with a leap and a flash of her tail, she was off into the woods, long muscles propelling her through the air so swiftly her paws barely seemed to touch the ground, blond fur streaming like moonlight. I was so struck by the beauty of her departure that I lost valuable seconds in merely admiring her, but perhaps it was just as well. The challenge in this kind of run is as much against oneself as against others in the pack, and when I began to run there was only me, and the night, and Elise.

I cannot say when I left the others behind. Compelled by her scent and the joy of my own strength, muscles stretching, wind whipping, leaping over hedges and dodging beneath branches, I caught up with her where the thick woods began to break for the course of a wide stream, just above where a waterfall splashed to quench the meadows below.

With an enormous exertion of effort I pushed myself to close the last ten meters between us, and tagged her on the shoulder. We tumbled together to the ground, mouthing each other's necks and muzzles, tasting sweet night-scented fur, burying our noses in the intoxicating scent of one another. Then, in a burst of joy and energy, we leapt together to run.

We took the Queen's Trail, a private course worn out by many generations of Devoncroix for the exclusive use of the royal family and invited guests. The trail was straight and smooth and devoid of obstacles. Here a werewolf could let his eyes glaze over and his muscles go long and simply run; run until running felt like flying and no one could swear one was not the other, run until lungs could gasp no harder and heart could pound no louder, run until the dictates of his own body declared he could run no longer.

We might have mated that night, in our own private celebration of the unity we knew was inevitable. The night unfolded long and sweet before us and we were awash in our adoration of each other. The world was made for us and us alone; upon its palette we would paint the story of our love and the mural of our mastery. And so it was, euphoric from the exercise and deeply involved with nothing outside the presence of one another, that we paused to drink at the stream. We dipped our tongues into the water that seemed purified by moonlight, we filled our nostrils with the damp warm scent of each other and our gullets with the clean cool water and could have asked for nothing more in the world. That was when the ground between us abruptly exploded.

It was a gunshot, and the bullet had missed Elise by mere centimeters.

We did not know that then, not at least with our conscious minds. By the time we recognized the sound and related it to a world we had almost forgotten—the world of daylight and humans and machines and cruelty—instinct had propelled us far from the scene. We leapt the stream, we ran for cover, we put out the warning cry to the pack.

A gunshot, from the deepest woods of an eight-thousand-acre estate that was guarded day and night by werewolves. Only humans use weapons, and no human could have gotten that close to the queen without assistance. No human should have been able to get that close at all. Yet one most undeniably had.

The events of that night are shreds and blurs of ruined memory. In moments the pack was streaming in, rallying around its leader. Guards surrounded her six thick to escort her to the Palais. The pack milled in confusion and anger. When I was sure she was safe, I broke away and ran back to the spot by the stream.

I do not claim to be a tracker, but I have a passably good nose. I found the bullet in short order, and traced it back to the tree in which the assailant had hidden in the branches high above our heads, waiting for us to drink at the stream. I think I knew, though, even before I went through this ritual of tracking, finding, scenting. I must have known.

The weapon, an ugly metal rifle, was in the weeds a few dozen feet from the site. Her scent was everywhere, sharp with fear, acid with desperation, sickeningly familiar. Tessa. My Tessa had done this thing.

I wished for the night to swallow me up and take my soul, for nothing short of that would ever ease my pain.

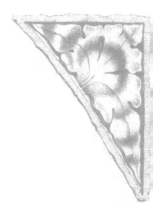

Nineteen

AH, THE BETRAYAL, THE HORROR, THE FURY. TESSA, MY TESSA, WHOM I had loved as a sister, a child, a friend. *Tessa,* who knew my secrets and my weaknesses, who had my trust and my love, whom I had taken into my home and nurtured as one of my own . . . it was worse than a knife through the heart and for a time I almost wished she had not missed the mark on that first attempt, for to live with this kind of pain was more than anyone should be required to bear.

I had brought her here. I, in my arrogance and stupid confidence, had brought her onto this sacred ground where no human had ever trod before. I had let her seduce the affection and the faith of my queen—no, I had encouraged her to do so, swelling with pride at the charmer she had become and the tricks I had taught her. I had done this thing, and for it, the woman I loved with all my soul had almost died.

Then there was the anger. And the anger, though it had the great virtue of swallowing up the black pit of hurt, was a huge and dangerous thing, far beyond my control. I stood there near the tree that was filthy with the scent I once had loved, bathed in the moonlight that only moments ago had seemed so beneficent, and I shook with rage. I roared deep in my throat with boiling, blinding fury. If I had lifted my head and given out the call, Tessa would have been torn to scraps and bone by a hundred sets of teeth before she could turn to run. I didn't call, not because I was concerned for her safety, but because I wanted to reach her first.

I followed her trail rapidly, effortlessly, for it led back toward the Palais, not away from it. If I had thought about that I might have found it odd, but at the time I was too full of rage and fear for Elise's safety to think clearly about anything at all.

I had little need to worry about Elise. The grounds of the Palais were flooded with light and surging with angry, alarmed werewolves. Some had changed into human form, some had not; all were looking to someone else to explain how this could have happened and why and what was to become of them now. In seconds the queen's hunters would discover what I had already, and all their questions would be answered.

I tore up the Palais steps past the guards, who did not challenge me—any more than they would have challenged Tessa. And why should they? Had they not been told only today that Tessa LeGuerre should be allowed to come and go unmolested just as she had always done, and hadn't that order come from the queen herself? Oh, what a clever, viperous human she was. How diabolically she had planned this.

At some point in the chaos of the inner hallway I changed into my human form. This I did instinctively and without thinking of it, perhaps because I feared what I might do to her if I confronted her now with the weapons of my natural form, which were even more powerful than her human-made ones; perhaps it was simply because I knew I would need my voice more than my teeth and claws.

I pulled on trousers and a shirt but did not know whether they were my own. Barefoot, shirt undone, my hair tangled with briars and brambles, I burst into Tessa's bedchamber. The heavy door exploded off its hinges with the force of my entry and I lifted it and flung it into a corner, where it toppled a corner cabinet and sent numerous bottles and porcelains crashing to the floor. Tessa cried out and sprang away from the impact; she backed up against a wall when she saw me.

"You!" I roared at her. "This is the way you return my love? This is the way you reward my trust? With a *gun?*"

Upon speaking these words, upon seeing her face, which held no denial, and hearing her silence in the wake of my accusations, I was for a moment inarticulate with rage. Tremors of helpless anger shook me and I clenched my fists and fought back the involuntary Change that threatened to consume me.

"You brought a weapon to this place." I had to say it out loud, enunciating every syllable, watching her face, reading her eyes. "You knew you would not be turned away. You learned of the Queen's Trail—and why shouldn't you? No secrets were ever kept from you here—and you went there where none but she would run, safe from the dangers of the pack, and you hid yourself in a tree where the wind would carry away your scent, hid there like a common filthy human huntsman." My voice was shaking. I didn't care. "You knew my wolf form, and you knew Elise's, for you had seen her in the garden that night before she changed. When we stopped, when we were directly below you and unaware so that you could have taken either of us through the head, you fired your weapon."

I wanted her to deny it. In my heart I pleaded with her to say something, anything that would convince me to disbelieve the evidence of my senses. *One more clever lie, Tessa, you who are so adept at lying, one more facile deception. Make me believe you one last time; try, I beg you . . .*

But she said nothing. She simply crouched there, quaking in terror of my rage, her big eyes filled not with remorse for her actions but with fear of the consequences. What was I to do? What was I to feel?

"Speak, curse you!" I shouted at her. "Deny it if you will! We have your scent, we have your footprints! The guards are coming for you now and they will shred you into fodder if you do not confess your crime! Talk to me, damn you!"

And when she remained silent—whether she was too frightened to speak or too stubborn or whether I simply did not give her a chance—I grabbed her arm and pulled her toward me roughly, meaning to shake some sense into her. There was a cracking sound and she screamed—a horrible sound of wretched pain—as I felt the bones of her arm snap like twigs between my fingers. She sank to her knees with the agony, her arm twisted at a bizarre angle in my grip, and it was another moment before I thought to let go. She collapsed onto the floor, whimpering and gasping and cradling her poor crushed arm to her chest. I watched her without sympathy, almost without comprehension.

"Why?" I demanded hoarsely. And again: "*Why?*"

She lifted a face to me that was white and disfigured with pain, streaked with wetness and stiff with effort. She spoke at last. "Because," she answered in a small broken voice, "I loved you."

Oh, for an explanation of this thing humans call love. It persuades them to commit the most vile offenses—to lie, cheat, steal, and murder—but cannot endure the simple trials of fidelity or child-rearing. It seeks, more often than not, to serve itself and imprison its mate; it can excuse any wrongdoing or shortcoming, it overrides justice and common sense. It does not, in fact, bear any resemblance at all to the emotion we know as love and seems to me a very dangerous thing. Yet we must allow that, for humans, it does exist. And for poor Tessa, who never understood at all what its consequences might be, love was the only explanation she required.

I stared at her for a long time, sickened and uncomprehending, all of the fight gone out of me. Then I sensed the guards behind me and, with a small gesture, signalled them to take her away.

I watched them drag her from the room, for by now she was only half conscious, and my heart swelled to bursting with sorrow. More than trust died that night, more than love. As Tessa LeGuerre, assassin, human, was pulled from that room and from the deepest, secret chambers of my affection, I watched the demise of a dream, and a future that was never meant to be.

TESSA

Twenty

THE PLACE WHERE THEY TOOK HER WAS REMINISCENT OF THE LEGENDS Tessa had heard as a child of dungeons deep and strong, yet it was infinitely worse. Worse because it was real, and worse because it was happening to her.

She was awash in a sea of throbbing, swelling pain; pain that robbed her of cognizance and logic and care for anything except that pain. She did not recall most of the journey to her cell, except that it was down several flights of stairs; this she knew only because she fell many times, sometimes tumbling down half a flight or more before the hands would jerk her to her feet again and the pain would explode so fiercely she lost consciousness.

The room was cavernous and smelled of age and earth and death. There were no gas lights and when the guards lifted their electric torches Tessa had a dim, swirling impression of metal bars half a foot thick, of chains forged from iron so heavy they could have anchored a ship, and her mind recoiled from imagining the kinds of creatures these devices were designed to restrain. But the worst was not the cages or the chains. The worst was the narrow, forged iron box into which they forced her, forced her even though she cried out and struggled, for the first time in her panic breaking her own personal vow and screaming out Alexander's name. They threw her into the box as though she were no more than a bundle of cast-off rags, and the force of the impact caused red lights of agony to burst behind her eyes. The last thing she heard before she passed out was the echoing clang of the heavy door slamming shut.

After that there was timelessness and pain, blackness and cold. So cold. It was no longer than a few moments, and it was a lifetime. When she heard the turning of a key, the creaking of a hinge, she thought she was hallucinating. She looked up through a haze of agony as the great iron door swung open, and was momentarily blinded by the light.

She turned her face away, squeezing her eyes closed against the stabbing shard of pain, and when she opened them again, Elise Devoncroix was kneeling before her. On one side of her was a huge, shaggy gray-and-brown wolf whose wild-fur scent filled the narrow space and whose sharp gold eyes were alert and merciless. On the other side stood a man of massive musculature and size, whose single hand could have snapped Tessa's neck effortlessly. He, too, watched her with eyes that would like to kill.

Elise had a small blue vial in her hand, which she uncorked and offered to Tessa. "Drink," she commanded. "It will ease the pain."

But Tessa just stared at her, breathing hard. She made no move to take the vial.

A flicker of angry impatience crossed Elise's eyes. "I won't poison you," she said. "Although it would be a mercy for you if I did, considering what lies ahead of you. We do not execute humans, Tessa," she said coldly. "We merely make them wish that we did."

In a moment Tessa took the vial with a badly trembling hand and lifted it to her lips. She drank the sweet black liquid down, and even as she swallowed felt the warmth spreading along her nerve pathways, smoothing away pain the way a hot iron smooths away wrinkles. The absence of the agony was dizzying.

Elise watched the relaxation of the muscles of her face, the clearing of her eyes, and when the potion had done its job she nodded in satisfaction. She reached for Tessa's broken arm and spent a few moments deftly probing and manipulating, rearranging mangled bones. Tessa felt nothing except the gentle pressure of Elise's fingers on her flesh, the warmth and the skill of them. When she was finished she splinted the arm between two flat pieces of wood and tied it close to Tessa's chest in a sling. "It will heal, eventually," she said disinterestedly, "although it may not be as much use to you as it was before."

She sat back on her heels and regarded Tessa with quiet blue eyes and a face that revealed nothing. Her hair was tied back at the nape, and she wore a red wool gown with a high neck and long sleeves. Tessa looked at her and stored the details in memory. She was still the most beautiful creature Tessa had ever seen.

Elise said, "My trackers picked up the scent of a strange werewolf on you. It's faint, and doubtless would not have been noticed except by one who was looking for it. Will you tell me who it is?"

For a moment Tessa didn't answer. The effort seemed entirely too great. She leaned her head back against the cold metal box and she said dully, "I never meant to harm you, mademoiselle. Please believe that."

Elise studied her gravely for a time. "You have committed a grievous crime against us, Tessa. You betrayed a trust by using the secrets we shared with you against us. You brought a weapon onto our grounds and you fired it at one of us. Whatever your intentions were, whether or not damage was done, these are heinous acts that cannot be forgiven. You will be punished, and I would not stop it if I could. But for my own sake, and for that of Alexander, who loved you, I would like to know why."

Tessa slowly turned toward her, and she had no spirit to try to hide the desolation in her eyes. "He wouldn't believe me," she said. "No answer I could give . . . would bring back what I've lost."

"I have no balm for a broken heart," Elise said gently. "And you must have resigned yourself to your loss when you set upon this course."

Tessa said softly, "Yes."

And then the fog of self-involved sorrow cleared a little from Tessa's eyes, and she met Elise's gaze. "It was Denis Antonov," she said. "He is the werewolf."

There was a slight relaxation in the queen's tight posture, a faint flicker of question across her eyes, but no other sign of her astonishment. She said thoughtfully, "Ah. That would explain a great deal." Then, not unkindly but with an authority that would not be disobeyed, she demanded, "Tell me."

Tessa began to speak. She told the whole of it: how Denis had come to her with his outrageous plan, how he had threatened to bring an army and kill both the queen and Alexander if Tessa did not cooperate. How Tessa had run to the Palais to try to warn Alexander, and how she had been refused admittance.

"And when I saw him with you, in the garden..." Here she dropped her eyes, as much from fatigue as from shame. "When I saw the two of you, and heard what you said to each other...I acted foolishly. I began to think—for a moment I thought that Denis was right in what he said, that you only pretended to be my friend and that neither you nor Alexander had ever cared for me at all. That you had tossed me aside when I got in the way of your plans, and that your plans included only each other. I ran away. It was all too much and...I ran away.

"Then I realized that it didn't matter what you thought of me, or whether you and Alexander were—well, lovers. Because Denis was going to kill you both and it would be my fault. I kept thinking, all that afternoon I kept thinking that Alexander would come, that surely he would read my note and he would come. But when I saw you at the stream, just as Denis had said you would be, I knew Alexander hadn't read my note. And it was too late to do anything else. I knew that when Denis heard the gunshot he would think I had done my part, and you would be safe for a little while. It was the only thing I could think of to warn you. So I fired over your head."

Elise looked at her with eyes that were filled with sorrow and gentleness. "My dear, dear child, what have you done?"

Tessa whispered thickly, "I never would have hurt you. Never."

Elise touched her cheek lightly. "I believe that. But I'm not sure even I can help you now. You've broken one of the strictest rules of our society by firing a weapon on Palais grounds. No one will believe it was for a noble reason, or care. You must go before our tribunal, which is something no human has done in uncounted generations. You will not be allowed to speak in your own defense. Only a werewolf can speak for you. I am allowed only to present the facts of your actions, not the reasons for them. I don't see any help for you."

"Alexander," Tessa said hoarsely. Desperately she searched Elise's face for some sign of hope there. "He will speak for me. He won't let anything bad happen to me. He'll help me."

There was kindess in Elise's gaze, but also pity—and a reluctant truth. "He feels betrayed, Tessa, and he's very angry. I am not permitted to try to persuade him in the case, for he will be called as your judge. You must understand—Alexander is a werewolf of high status and influence and you've shamed him before all the pack. I'm not sure he's thinking clearly right now."

Tessa said again, "He won't let anything bad happen to me." It sounded like a plea.

Elise inclined her head and got to her feet. When the iron door clanged shut behind her, Tessa repeated, "He won't." But her whisper was swallowed by the dark.

The dungeons of the Palais were two stories underground, designed to imprison werewolves in a less enlightened time. The walls were several meters thick, the stone floors buried beneath several hundred tons of compacted earth. There was no fresh air supply and no water; those brought there were not expected to live long enough to miss either. The chambers were completely soundproof even to werewolf ears, so that the cries of the imprisoned would not disturb the residents above.

The place was ancient, but the Devoncroix dungeons had not been so often used as one might suspect. The offenses which warranted such confinement were few; they included treason, neglect of an infant, corporeal crimes against humans which endangered the pack, and the offender was brought here only to await the judgement of death.

No one shared the dungeon tomb with Tessa. No one remembered the tunnel exit by which bodies had been removed for cremation in days of old—or at least no one who was in a position to do anything to prevent the entry of an intruder by those very tunnels. One guard was posted at the top of the stairs leading from the Palais to the dungeon; Denis never saw him. The other guard, in human form, was posted outside the iron box that held the prisoner. Denis snapped his neck with a single twist the moment the guard caught scent of him.

He plucked the bolt from the lock and pulled open the door. Tessa, lost in the world of blackness and silence, did not know he was there until he swooped down upon her. His hand came up under her chin with crushing force; he snapped her head back against the wall.

She was still in blackness; she saw nothing, not even the blacker shape of his form descending on her. But she knew his voice. She knew his touch. She knew his anger.

"Stupid human." His voice was a low growl. "How could you miss such an easy target? I led you to the place, I set you in the tree, I put the gun in your hands. I should have known better than to leave my fate to the hands of a clumsy human." His hand closed, squeezing her neck like the stem of a ripe fruit, choking off her breath. "I should kill you now. Nothing would give me better pleasure. But unfortunately, you are more valuable to me alive."

Abruptly he released the pressure on her throat. Her breath returned in a single hoarse gasp. "Come along." He pulled her roughly to her feet. "We only have minutes."

Tessa jerked away from him, clawing and kicking when he tried to grab her again. It was like fighting a demon in the dark. He got her hair and pulled out a handful. She flung herself against the far wall, hissing into the dark, "You are insane if you think I would go with you! I'll die first!"

"And die you will." She could feel him now, using his night vision to locate her, moving close. His breath brushed her cheek, and his body gave off a faint heat that seemed somehow to block the cold air that seeped out from the stones. "You'll die in a pool of your own vomit and urine, writhing in pain, screaming to die, begging to die. And this is what you prefer to me!"

She shrank from him, twisting her face away, but he moved closer. His clothes brushed her skin, his breath seared her face. "Look at me, Tessa. Can you see me? No? I can see you. I can see terror in your eyes and blood on your clothes and I can smell despair on you, Tessa LeGuerre. Do you think they'll stop at a broken arm? Do you have some fantasy that if you stay here, if you repent your crimes and beg for mercy they will forgive you, your beloved Alexander and the noble queen?"

He grabbed her shoulder then, shaking her once, hard. "You know nothing about us!" he hissed into her ear. "Nothing!"

"Why?" she muttered. Desperately she searched the dark. "Why would you rescue me?"

"For my own purposes, I assure you, and after they are served you may run back to the dungeon or fling yourself to the dogs or rot in hell for all I care. You surely didn't think I would have only one plan and trust it to a human, did you?" Out of patience, he swept her into his arms, her face pressed against his shoulder to muffle her screams, and carried her like a child.

There was nothing so remarkable about their escape. Denis knew that the queen, deep within the protective walls of the Palais, would be protected by a regiment, but who would care for the fate of one human who had neither the strength nor the wits for escape and who was destined for judgement at any rate? No personnel would be wasted on her; no one would be expecting trouble from her.

He had taken a chance on entering the grounds, but was proven right in his hope that the confusion would disguise his scent and that he would be lost in the crowd. The trackers would know him, yet he avoided them. The queen would know him, and so would Alexander, but he had no intention of getting close enough to give them the chance to identify him.

He used his nose to follow the tunnel, the smell of dampness, the smell of cold, the smell of river air. He kicked aside piles of fallen rubble and dragged Tessa over when they proved to be too much trouble to move. They came out of the earth near the river, on the far side of a patterned garden. The Palais lights were distant, but guards were not. Denis could hear them patrolling not two minutes away at a fast run. He waited until the turn of their footsteps and the direction of the wind would carry his voice away from them, and then he set Tessa on the ground, holding his hand tightly across her mouth.

"Run," he said, low and quiet into her ear.

He released her and stepped quickly away, moving toward the river as he stripped off his shirt. Tessa did not move.

"You were a fool," she said, "to trust any part of your plan to a human."

At first he barely noticed her, and her words were like the annoying buzz of insects in his ear. It didn't matter what became of her now; he was finished with her. But then something struck him as strange about the way she stood there, her bandaged arm strapped so awkwardly to her chest . . . strange and quiet and inexplicably eerie, the way she simply stood there with her heart slow and steady and her breath unhurried, watching him.

He tossed his boots far into the bushes to better mislead the trackers. His shirt he flung in the other direction. "Don't waste your breath chattering, you silly girl. You will need it to plead for more balm when the one they've given you wears off, although by then it will probably be too late."

"I am an excellent shot," Tessa LeGuerre said, quite clearly. "What makes you think I missed?"

He turned slowly to her. Her smile was oddly calm, her shoulders straight, her head high.

"What?" he said, in the slow dread way of someone who knows the truth but finds it far beyond reason to believe.

"You know nothing about us," she replied simply. "Nothing."

She lifted her head and screamed, "Here! We're—!"

Denis lunged at her, cutting off her cry in mid-echo as he flung her into the river. He followed, diving into the sluggish flow only half undressed. But it was too late. Already he heard the guards.

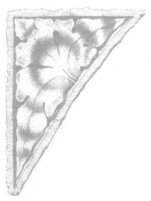

ALEXANDER

Twenty-one

AS HAPPENS SOMETIMES IN MOMENTS OF DEEP STRESS OR SORROW, I WENT into my natural form without consciously willing it, or remembering the Change at all. There is a danger in this, of course, especially for unmated persons, that the depression will grow so deep, the comfort of the wolf form so soothing, that we will never again summon the energy to transform ourselves into our human shapes and face the problems that drove us to ground in the first place. I was to know many tragedies in my life and some—though I would not have believed it then—would cause me even more sorrow than this. But Tessa's betrayal was the first, and the loss of her the most wrenching emptiness I had ever known. I took refuge in my wolf form because I could not have borne the pain otherwise.

I do not recall how I spent the remaining hours of that night, only that sometime after moonset some instinct called me home. And home was wherever I might be at my queen's side.

I moved into the house and past the guards, to the queen's inner chamber. A spiral formation of guards was in place—whereby a series of ever tightening circles of guards, half in human and half in wolf form, surround the palace, the inner chamber, the bedchamber and even the bed itself of the queen—signalling a state of heightened security that was more symbolic than practical. Tessa was imprisoned, and the threat had been eliminated.

Or so I thought.

All of the pack had volunteered to take their turn in joining the formation; it was an honor to be able to display one's loyalty in such a way, to unite again against a common enemy—in this case humans, and all they represented. I wondered if it broke Elise's heart as it did mine to see her dream of joining forces with humans perverted like this. A bullet in the night and all of history is changed. Such is the way of humans, and no surprise. But it was brutally unfair that our world should also be so rocked by their capricious violence.

I did not know whether I would be welcome, or would, in fact, be driven out by virtue of my association with Tessa, yet I was prepared to take my place in the formation. Somewhat to my surprise, the spiral parted to admit me into the royal bedchamber, and then beyond the draperies that enclosed her sleeping dais, to the bed itself.

She was curled among the pillows in her natural form, sleeping lightly, as of course she would. She opened her eyes when I approached, and there was no reproof there, no disdain, no anger. There was instead only relief, and welcome. She beckoned me.

I jumped up onto the bed beside her, and the long sigh she released said, *Now you are here. I am safe.* My Elise. She felt this. After all I had inflicted upon her, she wanted me still. That was when I knew I would survive this horror. I could endure this loss. For Elise, I could conquer anything.

We lay together back to back, and eventually fell into a more-or-less regular pattern of sleep. And here is the interesting aspect of our situation that night: in wolf form she could not tell me what she had learned from Tessa or warn me of Denis; perhaps if she had, I would have been better prepared. Yet if either of us had slept that night in human form, it is unlikely we would have survived the events that were to come.

The guards deployed around the bedchamber rotated shifts every hour from inner to outer chambers so that no guard remained so long in a single position as to become complacent or comfortable with his duty. It was virtually impossible for an enemy to slip through such lines of defense, and considering the fact that the enemy—so far as any of us knew—was at that moment languishing in a prison from which not even a werewolf could escape, I should have slept easy next to the one I loved. I did not.

With every rotation of the guard I was awake, though I concealed the fact carefully. I can't say why, except that I think even we have senses of which we are not completely aware, and that night a secret sense was whispering to me of danger. It wasn't until the fourth rotation of the guard that I understood why.

The bed where we slept was on a dais, surrounded by two sets of draperies—heavy tapestry to seal in warmth in the winter and filmy gauze to keep out insects in the summer. On this warm summer night only the gauze draperies were drawn, but there was a corner at the foot of the bed where the tapestry drapes pooled, and it provided perfect cover for the guard who slipped through them and stood next to the bed on which the queen slept.

I think he was startled to see me, but I was so still he must have believed he could finish his business before I stirred. And in fact he might have done so, for I never saw the thin wire stretched between his hands with which he intended, presumably, to garrote the queen. What I did see was the way he moved toward the center of the bed, where Elise slept, and how he bent near her. Still, he might only have been checking that she was well, which in some loose interpretation of his duties might have been within his rights. But as he bent over, his hair fell away from his face and I saw something else.

He had only one ear.

This, then, was my first inkling of what must have really been going on that night, of the conspiracy against the queen and of the mastermind behind it. I didn't reason it out then, of course. I didn't think at all. Between the time I saw him and the time I moved, there was not so much as an indrawn breath. In absolute silence, as swift as a striking snake, I lunged at him, and opened his throat with one slash of my claws.

Elise was instantly alert and on the defensive, springing at him as I did; blood sprayed the bed, the wall, my fur and Elise's as we all crashed to the floor together. The guards surrounded us instantly with much snapping and tearing and braying of alarm, but they were too late; the last of the killer's life bled out between Elise's jaws.

For me, the crisis was not over. Propelled by fury and fierce in my certainty, I left Elise to her victory and broke from the room. I could not spare the energy or the time it would take to change into human form, and I was faster and stronger as wolf. I burst through the open window and into the night, quick on the trail of my brother Denis.

But I was too late. Even that vengeance was to be denied me. I had not cleared the first garden wall when the howl of triumph reached me, signalling the capture of the enemy of the queen—and his human ally.

The tribunal assembled at dawn. Justice is swift in cases such as these and the pack would have nothing less. History records this moment in song and splendor, but I recall it as a very stark and undramatic affair.

Perhaps I am not the best judge of memory, however. I can never look back upon that night without seeing it all in the shades of gray that would color the rest of my life. My brother, and my dearest Tessa, conspiring together to overthrow the pack leader and murder the woman I loved. When I traced the smell of Tessa to the weapon, I had thought I knew despair as black as it could get. But despair had not even begun.

The huge inner courtyard with its glassed ceiling and its tall sheltering trees and plants was crowded with those who would attend the judgement; a thousand or more of the highest ranked were given viewing space, while their underlings milled about in the hallways and gardens, putting together pictures of the proceedings with their ears and noses. All were in human form, deigning not to show their natural selves to the traitor and the human, and all were clothed.

Elise, wearing the royal blue of her station, took the seat of judgement on the dais beneath the rising sun. She called me to stand beside her, thus making clear to the pack without a word what was my role in the entire affair. I stood at her right side, one step below her. My muscles were stiff, my senses alert, and my heart was filled with hate.

Denis was brought up first, shackled hand and foot and so tightly bound with heavy chains that even if he had been able to change he would never have escaped. He was still wet from the river into which he had tried to escape, his hair dark and tangled in limp strands around his shoulders, his sodden woolen trousers riding low on his waist. Yet he held himself like a king, even when the roar of the crowd shook the courtyard and echoed off the ceiling. He neither flinched nor bowed but looked straight ahead, his head high and his gaze strong, turning to show himself to the crowd proudly and deliberately. The disdain in the curve of his lips was a challenge to them all, for though they had rejected him, though they had arrested and convicted him, he had won tonight. He would never be their leader, but he had proved his way was the right way: humans were the enemy, never to be trusted, bent on the destruction of us all. The lesson he had taught us on that score would echo throughout the reign of the Devoncroix queen, tainting everything she did or hoped to accomplish.

I wanted to kill him. That was not, of course, within my purview.

When they brought Tessa up, I could barely glance at her. She was wet, too, from having been tossed into the river by Denis just before he himself had dived in—although whether it was with an intent to drown her or merely to disguise her scent from the guards, no one ever said. I do recall wondering why the guards had bothered to pull her out; it would have been easier on her to be left to drown.

Elise allowed the assembled witnesses to vent their fury on Denis with their voices for as long as they would, and he endured it with arrogant contempt. If they had been loosed to pelt him with stones or tear at him with their teeth, I am convinced his demeanor would not have altered. He was royalty. About that I have never argued.

When the roar began to die, Elise spoke in a loud clear voice. "Denis Antonov, son of Falquois and Chanson, brother of Charles, Minet, Lissom and Alexander, grandson of Simon and Leonette..." And so it was required that she name us all unto three generations, and she did, and we shared the shame and the responsibility for this, a member of our family gone bad. As she spoke, each one who was named and who was present ritually stood and turned his back on the offender, except for me. I had been called to stand in judgement, and I had to watch it all.

When the naming was finished, Elise said, "You are accused of plotting to overthrow this regime by the most devious and unworthy methods. You have conspired with the human Tessa LeGuerre, seducing her into your scheme with threats and promises, using your wit and your power over her to persuade her into actions whose consequences she was incapable of understanding, using her own innocent nature and her position in this house to further your foul ends. Is this a true statement?"

I was astonished. In that carefully couched accusation, in those brilliantly chosen words, she had not only put an end forever to any gossip that she had endangered us all by giving Tessa the human free access to this house, but she had made Tessa appear as much a victim as were any of us, therefore acquitting herself, Elise, of any accusations of bad judgement for trusting Tessa in the first place. Could her dream be saved? Could any part of her plan to one day unite the pack in commerce with humans be salvaged? This I did not know. But in one masterful stroke, in a single, carefully chosen sentence, she had snatched Denis's victory from him and returned the confidence of the pack to herself, where it belonged. And she had done it in such a way that Denis could not argue with her.

Nor did he try. I saw in his eyes that he recognized her ploy and his own limited options and—I will say this—he was noble in defeat. With the faintest of inclinations of his head to acknowledge she had bested him, he replied, "Mademoiselle, it is a true statement."

She continued. "You are further accused of buying a weapon for this human and of placing it in her hands, of inciting her emotions, of aiding her to penetrate the grounds during the run and instructing her as to how best to lie in wait for the pack leader so as to assassinate her with that weapon. Is any of this true?"

He answered, "All of it is true, mademoiselle."

You must imagine how this sounded to the pack. These were heinous crimes, cowardly, shameful. Rather than march boldly to the Palais to confront his adversary and claim his rights, rather than challenge the queen in lawful battle as others before him had done, he had used a human. He had purchased a weapon. He had helped the human penetrate the security of the pack by instructing her on how to reach the Queen's Trail. And he had used the power of the strong over the weak—his own manipulative abilities over human emotions—to bring about the murder of one of his own kind. This was an offense to us all. This was beneath contempt. It sickened me to hear, for this was the first time I knew the details of the plot.

And I could not bear to think about how easily my Tessa, in whom I had put so much faith, had been turned against me . . . if indeed she had ever been true to me at all. That was a pain that would gnaw at my gut for months to come.

Elise went on. "And when your plan failed and your human operative was captured, did you not then persuade one of your own lieutenants to infiltrate the guard in my sleeping chamber for the sole purpose of strangling me while I slept with a piece of wire you had given him?"

By this time the room practically crackled with the outrage and repressed fury of a thousand werewolves, for though it would be against protocol to indicate by voice or manner an opinion on the charges while they were being read, what was done to their queen was done to them. And Elise gave Denis no chance to respond; she continued without a breath, "And did you at the same time murder one of my guards and free the captured human Tessa LeGuerre so that *she* might be blamed for your perfidies? You may answer."

Denis answered, quite calmly, "I did."

It was too much. The anger in the inner courtyard was so intense it made my spine prickle, tugging at the pheromone deep in the center of my brain which always responds to the smell of werewolf fury with the need to change and do battle. I was hardly the only one to fight that instinct. If we had lived a thousand years ago, Denis would have been bloody meat between our teeth by this point.

How ironic that the thing he sought most to defeat—our civilized nature—was the one thing to which he owed his life then. But somehow, watching him, I got the impression that he was not grateful for it. He would have preferred, I think, to have died in violence, having obtained in death the savagery he had never been able to completely claim in life.

Elise said, "Denis Antonov, what have you to say to the pack?"

Ah, she took a chance there. But the right of the condemned to speak his last is an ancient and honorable one, and what could he say that would undo the damage his actions had already done?

He turned then and faced the pack. A stillness fell as he commanded them with his gaze, and a chill went through me as I was reminded of what a powerful leader he would have made. His voice was loud and clear and reverberated like a percussive instrument through the room.

He said, "I deny nothing. You may find my crimes abominable and my methods abhorrent, but nothing that I've done was without purpose. I have used a human for my own ends. Does that not merely prove how easily they can be used? I've manipulated her emotions and persuaded her to abandon her principles. I did so effortlessly and with pride, for the principles of humans are quickly abandoned. I have used the power of my wit because I *have* the power, just as does each one of you. Should I be ashamed of this? Should you?"

He paused to let the echo of his words die down, to let the force of them settle into the solar plexus of each and every werewolf present. He swept them with his gaze, measuring them, challenging them. For now, he had his pack. He savored it.

"I put the weapon in her hands, it's true," he said. "But she fired it at your queen. I put the suggestion in her head, but she thought of murder. In one afternoon this human whom you have received into your parlors, told your secrets to, pampered and preened like a pet for show, was turned from adoring sycophant into assassin. It was not difficult. After all, the first one of us she ever met she tried to murder in his sleep with a kitchen knife, and it is this person who now stands as my severest judge."

Silence. Many had not known this. But to my surprise, Denis did not press his advantage. He was an orator, a master of drama, and he knew when to stop. He had achieved his purpose.

"These are the true statements." His voice rang out, solemnly, clearly. "This is the lesson I would leave with you. Do with me what you will, judge me as you must. But know that, tonight, I have given my life for you."

Ah, what a spellbinder he was. What a presence. Even I, who knew him so well, was moved to aching by that speech, and why should I not be? He meant every word of it. He knew he had no chance of escaping justice. He knew nothing he could say would change his fate. But he had used his last words to make his life count for something, to turn his loss into victory. What a leader he would have made.

For the truth is, his sacrifice was not in vain. Even today there are those who remember his speech and abide by the lessons he imparted that night.

Elise rose to her feet. "Denis Antonov, of the crimes of cowardice and treason you are found guilty. For your judgement, I turn to the one you have most grievously injured, your brother Alexander Devoncroix."

She did not have to do this. It was a gesture of extraordinary generosity on her part. She was the one whose life and regime had been threatened; she was the one who had almost lost everything to his treachery. Yet she knew my pain and my sense of betrayal; she offered me the final revenge.

She said to me, "For these crimes, you may order death, exile or mercy. What say you?"

I stepped down from the dais. My footsteps made loud clicking sounds on the stone floor which echoed throughout the deathly still

DONNA BOYD

enclosure. I stepped before my brother. I looked into his eyes for the last time.

Mercy was not an option. He knew this. He expected death. He was prepared for it.

But for a werewolf, there are some things much worse than an honorable death. To be cut off from the pack, to live out one's days alone without a mate, without companionship, without protection or hunting partners or the simple sound of a voice lifted in song . . . life is always short in cases such as these, yet it seems to last forever.

Hardening my countenance and my heart against him, I said loudly, "Exile."

I turned my back on him, but not before I had the satisfaction of seeing the surprise in his eyes. He hadn't thought I would do it. Even then he hadn't believed I had the courage.

The pack roared its approval.

When the sound died, Elise turned to Tessa. I had just condemned my brother to a slow and torturous death, but my courage failed me at this. To face what lay ahead was more than any werewolf should be asked to bear.

But face it I must.

Elise said, "Tessa LeGuerre, human, you are accused of crimes most grievous against a people not your own. You have harmed no one. You have acted as best you knew how when confronted with choices beyond your understanding. Yet you have betrayed a trust. You have brought a weapon onto these grounds and you have fired it. You have conspired with one who is our enemy. These things cannot be denied, nor can they be accepted."

She paused for a moment to let the truth of her words settle in. As a human, Tessa would not be granted the same right to speak as Denis had been, and no werewolf present would speak for her. Only later did it occur to me that she might not have understood this, and that, if given a chance, she might have mounted some kind of defense for herself. But it had been generations since a human had come up before a werewolf tribunal, and none of us were fully prepared for all that

270

had taken place that night. Perhaps we can be forgiven our mistakes and oversights for this reason.

Perhaps there are some mistakes for which forgiveness is not possible.

"I turn for judgement to the one you have most grievously wronged, the one who once loved you, and brought you into our midst."

Elise spoke to me from her dais. "Alexander, this tribunal holds no power over human life. Your choices are exile, rehabilitation or mercy."

It seemed to take a lifetime before I could turn to face her. It was perhaps a few seconds.

And there she was, my Tessa, with her father's nose and generous mouth, with her huge brown eyes that had beguiled me so often . . . there she stood shivering in her wet clothes with her thin crushed arm strapped to her chest and her face paper white and her eyes so big, looking at me. How could I turn my face from her? How could I harden my heart?

I stepped forward and stood there looking down at her. The huge room crowded with faces, the thousand heartbeats and breaths faded away. The brother who had betrayed me, the woman I loved, the anger and the passion, these too were gone. There remained only Tessa and me, the memories, and a great empty mourning for what might have been.

I lifted my hand and touched her cold cheek. I caught a strand of her hair and curled it around my finger for the last time. How innocent she looked, even then. How trusting.

"Ah, *chérie*," I said softly, "how well I have educated you, *n'est-ce pas*? I taught you the secrets of our nature. I taught you art, and music and philosophy. I taught you to stand your ground and voice your opinions and yes, you have argued well with the best of us." Here I almost smiled, remembering how she had amused me, how proud I had been of her. But the impulse to smile faded, if ever it had been there. "And now . . ." Involuntarily, my voice went husky. "I have taught you how to break my heart."

She had harmed no one. She had done nothing but be true to her own helpless human nature. Her cries, it was true, had brought the guards who captured Denis, and for that reason alone the pack would have forgiven me for ordering rehabilitation. It would have been easy to do. Looking into those big anxious eyes, I knew it would have been so easy.

I dropped my hand, I raised my head. I said in a loud clear voice, "Exile."

I saw the shock and the horror of protest fill her eyes; I heard her cry out. She had expected mercy from me. I think even Elise was surprised, for hadn't she done everything in her power to pave the way for my sentiment?

But Tessa had betrayed me, and worse, she had threatened the one I loved. I could never trust her again. I turned my back.

Beneath the approving thunder of the crowd I heard Elise whisper in concern, "Alexander . . ." And Tessa was screaming, struggling against the guards who held her, crying out to me, "No, you can't do that, you don't understand, you can't send me away! You don't understand, Alexander, I love you, I will always love you, don't send me away!"

I remembered then that being sent away had always been the thing she feared the most. The memory twisted in my chest like the blade of a knife, just for a moment; then I flung up a hand to block the sound of her voice, and I walked away.

Elise began to speak. "The prisoners will be taken aboard a Devoncroix freighter to the place called Alaska, where none of us abide. There they will be set free one day's walk from any human population. The human will be supplied with two days' worth of food and water, matches, and garments suitable for the climate. The other will be given a cloak in which to hide himself. They will be transported from this place tonight and set sail . . ."

I didn't hear any more. I pushed my way through the crowd, shoulders straight and eyes stern ahead. I left the courtyard, the Palais, the grounds. I didn't change, I didn't run. I just walked and walked until I couldn't hear the sound of Tessa's sobs in my head anymore.

PART FIVE

Alaska

1898–1899

❧

In wildness is the survival of the soul.
—GRIGORI ANTONOV, WEREWOLF   1237

There is only one passion, the passion for happiness.
—DENIS DIDEROT, A HUMAN   1782

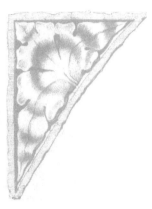

DENIS
AND TESSA

Twenty-two

DENIS'S FIRST REACTION UPON AWAKENING TO FIND HIMSELF IMPRISONED in the cargo hold of a ship deep in the North Atlantic was absolute astonishment. They had injected him with a tranquilizing substance soon after the verdict was pronounced; this he had known they would do. They had apparently kept him drugged until all ports of call were well behind them, for the safety of both the crew on board and the humans in port. They were wise to do so. He would have escaped had he been able; failing that, he would have done as much damage as possible in the attempt.

Astonishment. It was the last thing he remembered before being dragged from the judgement hall as well. His plan should not have failed. It was brilliantly conceived, simple to execute; it should have been flawless. Yet, thanks to the wretched, treacherous human, it had failed. That was astonishing.

And then to be captured. To have his second plan fail, to be delivered into the hand of his enemies by the very human he had saved from prison . . . And she had done it so calmly, so easily. He should have been outraged, but all he felt was . . . astonishment.

No, none of this had been in his plans, but no great endeavor was undertaken without risk. To have failed was very bad; to be captured was worse. But he had been prepared to die for his Cause from the beginning and the only challenge remaining to him was to die well. No one could take that from him. And yet, somehow, his brother had done just that. His own brother.

He was astonished.

Then he was furious. Furious in the way a caged wild animal is lost in a wave of savage, instinctual fury; fury that came from the depth of his soul and blotted out his brain, hot white fury that flashes hard and consumes everything in its path; fury unto death. It was the kind of roaring, unreasoning rage that only a creature who lives very close to his nature can fully experience, demanding no explanation or justification other than that it *is*; it was magnificent in its power, cleansing and liberating. It pushed him to the very edge of the Change, and, if not for the lingering effects of the drug in his system, would have no doubt pushed him over.

He grabbed the iron bars of the cage which held him and twisted them until he actually thought he could hear the metal bend. He gritted his teeth against the howl that was building inside him, he set his muscles, he tore at the bars until rivulets of sweat ran down his face and soaked his hair and blurred his vision. He flung himself away and collapsed into a corner of the cage, spent.

In the haze that followed he became aware of other things. The thrum of engines and shifting of metal plates which was the movement of the ship. The sway caused by cresting waves and the smell of fuel. The smell of many, many things, none of them pleasant: the werewolf crew, whose blood was made of brine and whose skin was leather-tough; how he despised them. The wooden freight boxes, the cargo of wool and porcelain and kerosene and wine, crated glass packed in newsprint, and brass clockworks. Salt and dead fish, sun-bleached timbers, wood mold. Cold sea. Stale bread and rat droppings. His own unwashed body and damp, rotting clothes. Human offal, human sweat, human blood, human sickness. The human Tessa was lying upon the floor of a cage much like his which was bolted to the wall a wolf's length away, watching him through swollen, slitted eyes that might have been those of a corpse.

It was dark and dusty in the hold, the only light being that which seeped through the cracks in the decking overhead. The ship was well built, and such cracks were few and far between. Denis had little difficulty seeing what he would with his night vision, but knew the human could see little more than shape and movement. What must that be like, he wondered dispassionately, to not even see the rats until they were nibbling away at your toes and fingers? Had it driven her insane? He hoped not. She didn't deserve so easy an escape.

He listened to the sea rushing by and the voices and movements of the werewolves who operated the ship. He learned nothing useful from them. Like many of his kind, Denis had an instinctive dislike of large bodies of water that was rooted in both superstition and practicality; he was innately suspicious of those who not only endured but thrived upon the sea. Constant winds confused scents and the salt water destroyed them altogether. The cacophony of currents and surges, splashes and roars, was a never-ceasing distraction, disguising heartbeats and hiding whispers. What could one believe of one's senses under such circumstances? The mighty queen could have devised no crueler punishment for him than to cast him adrift in this liquid hell for the weeks or months it would take to reach exile. He wondered if *he* might grow mad.

In a moment he remembered the human, and he turned his gaze sharply back to her. She had not moved, the slits of her swollen eyes fixed upon the place where he was.

"How long?" he demanded.

She didn't answer.

"How many days have we been under way, human girl?" he repeated curtly, but still there was no response.

She was sick, he knew that, and very weak, but she was still breathing. It gave him some grim pleasure to imagine the pain she must have endured once the anesthetic she had been given for her injured arm wore off, once she was tossed into this close dark place with the rats. How she must have fought it, screaming and screaming in the dark until her voice was gone, and screaming still until she was too weak to do anything but let herself be tossed back and forth against the bars of the cage at the whim of the sea . . . Weeping, begging for surcease from the excruciating pain, finally falling into a semiconsciousness tormented by whatever black dreams humans dreamed from the depths of their despair. He could smell the fever on her still, and he wondered if she would die. Again he hoped not.

Then she whispered, "I don't know. I don't know how long."

She closed her eyes, and did not speak again for many days.

The mariners came once a day to feed them, water them, and take away their waste pots, which was how Denis learned to measure the passage of time. He did not try to engage them in conversation or elicit their support; to do so would have been a waste of energy. Similarly, he made no attempt to escape, for even if he were able to overpower every crewman on board and single-handedly commandeer the entire ship, there was no place for him to go on the high seas, no port where he would be any less an exile from the pack than he would be in Alaska. This was a simple truth; to deny it or try to change it would have been another foolish waste of energy.

The life he had known and planned to live was now maddeningly, inexplicably gone. Perhaps one day he would find a way to get it back, but he would not do so aboard this ship.

It would have been impractical to carry enough food to sustain an entire crew of werewolves for weeks at a time, so the diet aboard ship was supplemented with protein packs—little squares of kelp and desiccated animal parts compressed into tasteless, compact loaves. Denis received one of these loaves a day, which was enough to sustain life but no more. Tessa was fed an even more disagreeable diet of bread soaked in whatever leftover gruel, broth or grease the galley had to spare. But as disgusting as her fare was, Denis found himself hungering for the bowls of slop she left untouched as the days went by.

For weeks he had forced himself to retain his human form, and the stress of the conditions under which he lived made it seem even longer. His muscles cramped; he couldn't sleep. There were times when he had to physically restrain himself from simply letting go and sinking into the Change he needed so badly, and the effort to do so was so great it left him weak and shaking, gasping and wet. But his captors knew very well how to keep him subdued; they fed him just enough to keep him alive in human form. Should he revert to wolf form, caged and helpless as he was, he would starve to death in a matter of hours.

This, then, by definition, was torture: to be trapped in this dark airless space with the smell of human and filth, to be surrounded by water and deafening winds, to watch one's muscles wither from disuse in an iron cage too small to even stretch out full-length in sleep; to hover on the edge of starvation, forced to use energy he could not afford to maintain a shape that was not his own long past the time that nature allotted. Werewolves had gone mad from lesser trials.

But not one of those things, nor all of them in combination, were the source of his real torment. In his fevered dreams he tore flesh from bone and consumed it raw and steaming. He raced the wind and splashed through mountain streams and stood poised and still with a thousand textured scents floating on the air to him, caressing his brain, lingering in his fur. He saw sunshine, he tasted green. And when he awoke the ache of longing was so intense that it cramped in his gut. But that was not what made him cry out, or toss and moan in his sleep from nightmares he could not escape. The real torment consumed him night and day, became an obsession from which there was no surcease, and it dwarfed all other anguish. It was the question to which he would never know the answer: Why had this happened? How had he failed?

Denis Antonov was born for greatness. This he had always known. It wasn't until his late boyhood, when he began studying the life of his illustrious ancestor Mikal Antonov and comparing it with the shallow, inconsequential contributions of his present-day family, that he knew in which direction his greatness would lie. But in truth it would have made little difference what the banner, what the cause. Denis was born to lead. That the Brotherhood of the Dark Moon suited his own philosophy was a happy coincidence for the built-in followers it supplied. A leader was nothing without a pack. But no leader, regardless of the strength of his character or the dedication of his pack, could hold his position through desire alone. He had to have cunning, imagination, foresight, wisdom, power, determination, a sense of justice, a grasp of the inevitable, a vision for the future; he had to be *right*.

Denis had never been wrong before. He had never, once he set his hand to a carefully plotted, well-conceived course, met with failure. The consequences of failure, as he well knew, were severe; he did not take reckless chances, he did not burn his bridges, he did not plunge ill-informed into a plan from which there was no escape.

He did not dispute his punishment now. He had failed. He had been bested by the Devoncroix queen and a human female; he had left his pack to be scattered to the wind or hunted down like herd beasts when the Devoncroix took it into her head to do so. Families would be torn apart because of him. Children would starve through the winter because of him. Noble young werewolves with strong hearts and minds would have no more songs to sing because of him. Because of him, the future would die.

There was no punishment too severe for a failure such as that.

But never to know *why* . . . to be unable to look back and point with clarity to one's mistake, never to know precisely what misjudgement or false information or flaw in logic led to one's downfall . . . that was torment. That was almost beyond bearing.

In his self-involved agonies he all but forgot about Tessa. She never spoke, either to him or to the mariners who attended her. Occasionally she ate some of the gruel they brought her and drank the water, and the smell of the fever left her skin, so that it appeared she would not die after all. But she rarely stirred. She was easy to forget.

And then one day when the pain of shrivelling muscles was very bad and he was startled out of the depths of a black nightmare by the sound of his own hoarse cry and gasping breaths, she spoke.

"What's wrong with you? Are you sick?"

Denis drew himself up against a chill, wrapping his arms around his knees, pressing his shoulders into a corner of the cage nearest the wall where, it seemed, there was a little warmth. He was wearing the same clothes in which he had been condemned—trousers only and cotton stockings, shirt and shoes having been left on the riverbank a lifetime ago. As his metabolism dropped, it became more and more difficult to maintain his normal body temperature, and frequent chills were a symptom of the deterioration.

He said roughly into his knees, "Don't pity me, human."

She replied with a sudden ferocity that surprised him. "I have no pity for you. If I had the means I'd open your veins and lap up your blood from the floor while it drained out of you."

He was interested enough to lift his head. "I'm sorry I can't oblige you."

He could smell the leftovers in her bowl, almost three days' worth. His mouth filled with saliva. "I'm hungry," he said.

"I'm glad."

"Push your bowl across to me."

"No."

"You would have me starve when you have food to spare?"

She said nothing. He took that as a sign she was weakening.

He shifted across the cage to the side nearest her. "Push your bowl through the opening," he urged her persuasively. "Then slide it across the floor as far as you can. I can reach it from there."

He heard her rustling movement in the dark, saw her turn to look at him. She said distinctly, "I would see you rot in hell first."

"My dear, we will both have that pleasure soon enough," he replied patiently. "In the meantime, have you none of that compassion for which humans are so—unjustifiably in my opinion—renowned?"

"No."

For the first time since being caged here, he was distracted enough from his own misery to be almost amused. He settled his back against the bars again, abandoning the quest for the moment.

He said, "You hate the wrong man, you know. It is your beloved

Alexander's fault that you're here, not mine. I only acted true to my nature. He's the one who betrayed you."

She was silent for a moment. Then she said, "You are the betrayer, and you turned against your own brother. He loved you. He was in awe of you. And you returned his affection with a plot for murder."

"I am the traitor? I am the betrayer? I don't see my brother chained in an iron cage in the middle of a cold sea!" He was abruptly angry with himself for allowing her to provoke him, and he deliberately brought his tone to neutral. "You're a fool for defending him after what he's done to you."

She said nothing. She knew it was true.

But he could not bear the silence filled with lies; it angered him almost as much as her words had done. "I loved Alexander, in a way you could never understand. Everything I did, I did for love of him. That's why his betrayal hurt so much."

Tessa said, "You wanted the queen. She loved him instead. That's why you hate him."

He made a sound that was an inarticulate expression of contempt. "Things are so simple in your narrow human world! I care nothing for that snivelling female and would have killed her if I could. More important matters were at stake than the love of a girl-queen."

She stirred in her cage, interested and alert. He took pleasure in having said the words, for the truth tasted all the more sweet in its power to hurt her. "You were right about me the first time. I *do* want to see all humans exterminated, or at the very least to cull their population by nine-tenths, for I suppose we would need some of them to serve us. If I had succeeded in taking over the pack that would have been my only agenda, and it will be again when I escape from this place."

"When you told Alexander you meant to present yourself as the queen's mate—"

"A lie, to test his loyalty."

"You intended all along to kill her."

"Of course."

"And Alexander?"

"He made his choice. He knew the chances he took when he set himself against me, and I would have shown no more mercy to him than he has done to me."

She said in a low quiet voice, "Then you are as evil as I thought."

His eyes narrowed in the dark to better make out her face. "I am werewolf," he said. "No more, no less. You would do well to remember that."

He added, "And I think you will also now agree I was right. Your kind and mine deal best when we deal apart. If you hadn't crossed that boundary between our world and yours, this entire tragedy could have been avoided."

In a voice that was muffled and less energetic than it had been a moment ago, she replied, "Tragedy *was* avoided."

This was unexpected. "What?"

"You wanted me to kill my friend and your queen. You wanted me to betray Alexander, whom I loved. If I had done so, it would have been a tragedy. But I didn't."

"Don't ennoble yourself! You were mad with jealousy. You all but begged me to help you plot your revenge. Your only failing was poor marksmanship. That was the tragedy!"

But he remembered her standing on the riverbank with that odd, proud tilt to her chin, saying, *What makes you think I missed?* He felt the coldness gather in his belly. Could it be that simple? Could *that* have been his mistake?

You know nothing about us . . .

He said, "I'm curious. Why did you call the guards? Amuse me by telling me. Were you so foolish as to think they would spare you for helping them to capture me?"

She moved in the dark, lying down in her cage and cradling her head on her elbow. He thought she wouldn't answer. He found himself straining in the silence, waiting for her reply.

Then she said softly, "No. That's not why I did it."

"Why, then?"

"Because I knew you wouldn't let Alexander live. It wasn't in your plan. If you escaped, Alexander would die. So I couldn't let you escape."

"You say whatever eases your conscience now. But when you took the weapon in your hands, your passions were in control and you meant to kill."

Tessa's voice was growing tired, weakening with effort. "I went to the palace to warn them. Your spies should have told you that. I pretended to go along with your mad scheme because I couldn't think of another way to keep you from killing them. I knew if I fired the gun the whole pack would be alerted and you would be stopped."

He stared at her incredulously through the darkness. "You did this? You did this for a man who broke your arm into a hundred little bones and then set you adrift in the middle of an ocean?"

She began to shiver, drawing herself up tight in the cage, and her voice was muffled with fear and repressed tears. "He didn't understand. He didn't know. Elise will tell him and he will come for me."

Denis found her blind, unquestioning loyalty outrageous and infuriating. "No one is coming for you, stupid girl!" he shouted at her. "You are on a ship a thousand miles from home and no one is coming for you! The queen was glad to be rid of you, don't you know that? You have sacrificed your life for nothing!" She did not reply, and the misery he could smell on her gave him no comfort at all.

He had his answer, and he hated it. To lose a battle was bad. But to be defeated by one's own ignorance of the enemy . . . that was unconscionable. He had been wrong about the human girl. He had misjudged her. *That* was the flaw in his plan.

He found the whole issue more disturbing than he could consider, and he did not engage her in conversation again, lest he learn even more that he did not want to know. She never relented on the food issue, and in fact seemed to force herself to eat more as he grew weaker, almost as though to defy him. Thus was the myth of human compassion once again disproved.

On that, at least, he had not misjudged her.

*   *   *

They made port in Alaska where Norton Sound formed a smooth arm of the Bering Sea, near a place called Anvil City. The city was little more than a mining camp which consisted mostly of mud paths, canvas tents and eager miners who were sifting out enough gold from the beaches and the streambeds to keep them searching for more. Word spread quickly of the ship's arrival. Anticipating this, the mariners had stocked up on essentials and within hours a lively negotiation was in progress for flour, beans and coffee, all of which happily sold for ten to twenty times their purchase price. In the midst of the furor the two prisoners were quietly taken off the ship and into the wilderness.

This is not to say no one noticed their passage. The fierce-eyed man with his long, tangled red hair, naked shoulders hunched and covered with sores, his gait pained and lurching and every rib of his torso individually prominent, would have been cause for gossip even if his hands had not been chained behind his back. The woman, except for her torn and soiled skirt, could hardly be identified as a female. Her hair was matted, her eyes sunken, her mouth drawn tight about her teeth like that of a corpse. She held one splinted arm at an odd angle, and stumbled when she walked.

The miners heard many stories about the couple: that he had started a mutiny and she, his lover, was the captain's wife. That they were murderers in exile from the States. That they were simple stowaways. The talk was lively for a couple of days after the pair was loaded onto mules and led toward the mountains by four thick-necked, long-haired sailors. Campfire speculation became even more intense the next day when the mules and the sailors returned, but the couple did not. Within an hour the ship left port.

Most of the men figured the two had been taken out and shot, or—if their executioners were feeling less merciful—simply abandoned. Some noted they hadn't taken any supplies worth mentioning with them. Others expressed regret over the loss of the woman. No one suggested intervention of any kind, nor did they question the sailors in anything more than a perfunctory way. This was Alaska, the farthermost end of the world, and not a place where men came to answer questions. Besides, no one wanted to spend any more time than was strictly necessary in the company of that crew. There was something distinctly disturbing about them all.

A mining camp by its very nature was not a close-knit community, and within days the excitement of the ship's call was forgotten with the rumor of a new strike. So, then, were the two prisoners.

The terms of exile had stipulated that they be taken a day's walk from any human population, and that was precisely how far they were taken—the distance a werewolf in human form could walk, leading a mule, between sunup and sundown on a late-summer day in north-western Alaska. With every breath of clean, green-scented air that Denis took, he felt himself growing stronger, clearer in head and straighter in body. Could he have survived another day caged on board the ship? He didn't know. But he knew without a doubt he was going to survive now.

He used the muscles of his legs to steady himself astride the mule as he looked around, drinking in the sweeping vista that surrounded him as if it were life-giving broth. The blue of the sky dizzied him, the sharp bristling green of towering firs hurt his eyes. He could smell water, pools and rivers and tumbling falls of it, and the hot blood of moose and elk and deer. Rabbits burrowed in their holes like ants in a nest, his for the plucking, and ducks and geese waited to be swept from their clumsy lairs. He was so hungry he could have flung himself to the ground, filled his belly with grass and loved it like nectar. But he had discipline, he could wait. For the promise he could smell on the air with every breath he took, he could endure whatever was re-quired. The torment was at an end. This was not exile. This was Par-adise.

When he happened to glance over at Tessa, clinging to the back of the plodding little mule, he saw the terror in her eyes and the dread that pinched her face as she gazed at the hugeness of the sky, the wildness of the spaces, the emptiness of nature in its newborn state. Denis wanted to laugh out loud at the irony of it, at the exquisite joke fate had played upon his brother and the Devoncroix queen. Alexander had thought exile to be a fate worse than death for Denis, but for Tessa he no doubt thought it a mercy to spare her life. Truth had proved him wrong. The human girl would be lucky to survive a night in this wilderness, while a werewolf could live forever on the bounty of the land. Yes, it was amusing. It was delightful. Denis grinned full-toothed at the girl who would not give him her gruel, and he thought she understood why. She quickly slid her glance away.

When the sky took on a purple tone the sailors consulted with one another briefly and, with evident relief, stopped walking. They pulled Tessa off her mule. Denis sprang down lightly and, despite his weakened state and bound hands, kept his balance perfectly.

One of the sailors unlocked his chains. Denis flexed his arms and gently rubbed the bruises on his wrists. The sailors showed no fear of him, and why should they? He was too weak to do much harm against the four of them, and too smart to expend energy trying.

One of the sailors took a thick wool cloak lined with sheepskin from the saddlebag of his mule. "The werewolf is to be given a cloak to cover himself," he recited, and handed Denis the garment.

Denis took it politely. He held the other werewolf's gaze. "You might have worshipped me," he said. And then he smiled. "You may one day still."

The sailor broke his gaze with difficulty, then turned quickly and unpacked the remaining items from the bag. "The human is to be given two days' supply of food and water, matches, and clothing suitable to the climate, which she is wearing."

They dropped two canteens and an oilcloth-wrapped package of protein squares on the ground at Tessa's feet. Taking the reins of the mules in hand, they started back the way they had come.

"Wait!" Tessa cried. She ran after them. "Don't leave me here! Take me back to the coast, a ship will come, don't leave me! I can't find my way back by myself! Wait!"

One of the sailors turned and pushed her hard, throwing her off her feet and flat onto the ground. Whether she lost consciousness or merely her breath, she was silent, and the sailors began to laugh and talk as they resumed their trail back.

All of this Denis noticed with only the smallest part of his mind, and cared about not at all. It had taken all his self-restraint to keep from disgracing himself in the presence of the sailors, from sinking into his natural form helplessly and fully clothed. The moment their backs were turned he let the cloak drop to the ground and he ran a few steps away, tearing at the fastenings of his trousers.

He peeled off his stockings; his trousers fell away in shreds. He stretched naked in the dusk, weak and scrawny, trembling and tight, aching like a newborn cub. He lifted his fists to the orange-streaked sky, he threw back his head. With a cry, he surrendered himself to the Passion.

Drunk with freedom, mad with hunger, he descended onto all fours and began to run.

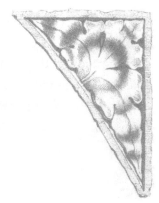

Twenty-three

TESSA WATCHED HIM. SHE HADN'T MEANT TO, BUT AS SHE LAY ON THE ground gasping through lungs that no longer seemed willing to draw in air, as she fought the roaring in her ears and the graying of her vision, she managed to get herself up onto one arm and then she saw him.

He stood naked perhaps two dozen steps away from her, his body starkly white against the darkening sky, the skin marred with bruises and red sores. There was little musculature left in the arms that he raised to the sky, only the shape of bones. His belly was sunken, his ribs and hipbones sharp beneath their frail covering of flesh. The straining tendons of his neck, the tight indentations in the muscles of his buttocks, the whipcord lashings of veins and tendons in his calves—these were the signs of a man near death from starvation, and Tessa was shocked.

But she had forgotten he was not a man.

He threw back his head and raised his fists, and his body began to tremble; she could see the twisting anguish on his face, and then she realized it was not anguish at all, but triumph. She felt it in the air, the tightening, the thinning; she saw it in the light, the shimmer and the pulse. She felt it in the seat of her soul as, with a cry that stabbed her ears and reverberated through the twilight, he drew the magic to him.

Tessa fell back, throwing up a hand to shield her eyes, for she did not want to see this thing, not here, not now; she could not bear to witness it. But it was too late; she could not look away. She watched helplessly as Denis Antonov, killer, deceiver, mad powermonger, reached to the heavens and covered himself in a glory he did not deserve, returning to earth as the most magnificent creature which had ever walked upon it.

The wolf was fiery red against the sunset, rough and rangy with ice blue eyes. Tessa should have been in fear of her life, but at that moment all she could do was stare at him, consumed by wonder and by the bitter, bitter unfairness of it all. He barely seemed to notice her. He stretched his limbs and ran, defiant in his freedom, mocking her with his escape.

That was the moment when loneliness descended upon Tessa like a poison arrow that had been long in finding its mark; it pierced her heart and spread its icy agony inch by inch throughout her body. Not because Denis was gone. Not even because, when she struggled to her feet and looked around in slow, dread desperation, there remained no sign of the sailors or the mules that had brought her here or any indication of the direction in which they had gone. Nor was it the vast towering wilderness that surrounded her, the strangeness of it, the isolation. It was because for an instant, just an instant as she watched Denis transform, she was taken back to the first time, and Alexander. She tasted again the magic; she was dizzied by the awe, humbled by her own awakening reverence. She had seen the miracle; she had believed anything was possible. And she had been wrong.

That was what Denis had brought back to her. There was no miracle. There was no great pattern of divine sorcery that fashioned these creatures, there was no form or reason. They were neither greater nor lesser than she, merely different. And she did not know them at all.

Yet for them, for the sake of the miracle and the love of one who possessed it, she would die a slow and horrible death here, alone. Until that moment she had not fully comprehended the truth of it. It was over. No one was coming to save her. Alexander would not see his mistake or change his mind, for he wasn't, after all, a magician, and he could not undo what had been done. He was gone. She was alone. And she was afraid to die.

She started to weep then. She sank to her knees and turned her face to the sky and let the sobs come, crying out loud deep into the night where there was no one to hear.

The first night she spent on the ground, wrapped in the cloak Denis had left behind, too exhausted and numb from emotion to feel the cold or the discomfort. When she awoke, the grasses were brittle and there was a light dusting of snow on the cloak and in her hair. She had a cough. She tried not to think about the kinds of creatures that might have come upon her in the night, and she did not linger to make a fire. She did not even think about doing so. She tied the two bags of supplies across her shoulders and started moving into the sun, moving to stay warm and for no other reason.

The walk was hard and she was weak. She discarded the awkward splint, only to discover that the bones of her arm had knitted badly on the journey. Foreshortened ligaments had caused her wrist to twist awkwardly, drawing her thumb and fingers downward so that her hand was almost useless. Her arm ached all the time, and occasionally, when she carelessly moved it, a blinding sharp pain reminded her that some of the breaks were not entirely healed. It took her a long time to gather wood for a fire with only one hand, and when darkness came she had to shelter where she could, close to the pile of sticks and broken branches that would keep her warm.

She huddled near the fire throughout the night, shivering at the shadows it made and biting back cries with every new and terrifying sound that issued from the forest. These were sounds like none she had ever heard before: grunts and growls, the screams of cats, and when she heard the howl of a wolf she leapt to her feet, whirling around wildly and staring through the dark first in this direction and then in that, not certain whether she feared or hoped for what she would find. But no blue eyes glowed back at her from the dark, no shape was silhouetted in the moonlight, and if Denis had seen her fire, his cry had been a warning—or a mocking, triumphant greeting—not a threat.

If indeed it had been Denis's voice she had heard.

With that thought, a new terror lurched in her chest and she turned another twenty degrees, straining through the dark—and then she saw the most wonderful thing. Lamplights. Two, three, and, when the wind moved the branches of the trees below, perhaps even more. Lamplight, or firelight, or perhaps just the glow of candles by which the miners measured out their take at the end of the day; it made no difference. The tented encampment lay in the valley below her, and now she knew in which direction she must travel.

It did not occur to Tessa to question what she would do when she got there, what allies she could expect to find in those rough men or how, in her present circumstances, she could hope to bargain her way on board a ship in the unlikely event that one should make harbor there. Her spirit was battered and her body was weak and reason had no place in this savage land. Like all lost creatures, she had no plan or purpose except to seek her own kind.

She spent the night tending the fire to ward away the beasts, and at sunrise she forced herself to consume some of the tasteless squares of protein the sailors had left in her pack. She noted that it was to her advantage that they seemed to have no idea how much a human would eat in two days; they had left her with much, much more than was required.

Though the morning was damp and bitter cold, there was no snow, and her cough was a little better. She put out the fire and started down the slope in the direction from which she had seen the lights.

It did not take her long to realize she was following a streambed toward the camp and, beyond, the sea. Later, she would understand that was the reason her path had brought her so close to Denis's, for even though he had the ability to hunt a far range, the water source would keep him close. Tessa thought little about water other than to consider leaving behind the heavy pouches that made her shoulders ache and slowed down her progress. Surely she would be at the camp by sunset. Surely. But because she was no longer certain of anything, least of all her own judgement, she continued to carry the water.

She had been walking perhaps an hour, for the mist was barely above the stream, when she heard the cry. It stopped her steps dead; it went through to her bones, and for one moment—one heart-stopping, incredible moment, she thought the scream was human.

She turned toward the sound, heart pounding, skin cold, and then it came again—only this time more clear, more piercing, easily identifiable as the cry of an animal in pain. It was close, close enough to raise gooseflesh on her skin; it chilled her blood.

She resumed her pace, even quickened it, and then the cry came again, more helpless now, more desperate. It was so close. Just beyond the stand of spruce to her left. If she walked on straight she would pass it. If she veered to her left . . .

There was just enough that was human inside her, just enough curiosity, to make her plow through the high grass to her left, past the shadowed spruce with the low mist rising, cautiously parting the undergrowth near the stream.

He was there, the big red wolf, sleeker and more well fed than when she had last seen him, but in obvious agony. His chest was heaving with rapid harsh breaths. His fierce blue eyes showed their whites when he rolled them toward her. His back right leg was caught in a steel trap.

There was a great deal of blood. The sounds that came from him were high and sharp. She stood and looked at him for a long time.

"And so, mighty loup-garou," she said softly at last, "the grandest of all your kind, brought down in the end by a bit of steel and spring fashioned by a human."

She felt she should have smiled; Alexander would have smiled. So would Denis. But she could not quite manage it. She looked at him for a moment longer, and then she turned and walked away.

The sun had almost cleared the trees when she found her way back. He was weaker. The blood had clotted around the wound and soaked into the ground. His breathing was quicker, shallower, and his eyes were closed. Tessa moved close, and closer still. When he made no move, nor even a sign of noticing her presence, she felt safe in kneeling beside him. She stayed there, with her hands clenched on her knees, until his eyes opened a slit and he looked at her.

"You'll want to know why I'm doing this," she said. She made her voice clear and distinct. "The answer is because you would *not* do it for me."

That was not the whole truth. The rest of it she was not ready to admit even to herself. She took hold of the top jaw of the trap with her good hand and used her foot to steady the bottom. Slowly, laboriously, she began to pull the trap apart.

A low growl emanated from his throat and he showed his teeth. Beads of sweat popped out on Tessa's brow and her thigh muscle quivered from the awkward position. When the sharp teeth of the trap left his flesh, the wound reopened and he made a vicious snarling, snapping sound; she almost lost her grip. Finally she managed to lift the top hinge of the trap a few inches above the leg and she gasped, "Do it! You have to free yourself—I can't hold this much longer!"

He gave a mighty lurch and scrambled away, dragging his broken leg behind him. Tessa was barely able to get her foot out of the way before the muscles in her arm collapsed and the jaws of the trap snapped shut. She fell to the ground on top of it, exhausted, and when she looked up again, Denis had disappeared into the undergrowth.

She scanned the brush for him, but made no further effort to find him. After she had regained her breath she wiped the perspiration from her face with an aching, unsteady hand and said, "You're welcome."

She picked up her packs and resumed her course.

She didn't make very good progress. She kept looking over her shoulder uneasily, and she was no longer certain she was going in the right direction. The grass was high and sometimes the undergrowth was impassable; then she had to backtrack and go around. Once she heard the predatory cry of a wild animal and it sent chills down her spine.

She did not know how long she had been walking when she saw the big-winged carrion-eaters circling overhead. She knew she had not gone far. She stood and watched them, shivering in the sun, for some time.

It took her most of the day to retrace her steps and to find where Denis had hidden himself. Still in wolf form, he had crawled beneath the low-hanging branches of a thick, prickly-leafed bush where, presumably, he would be safe from predators. His breathing was hard and fast and his eyes, though slitted open, were glazed. Flies buzzed around the clotted blood on his leg. If he noticed Tessa he gave no indication, and she backed away quietly.

She brought him water in a piece of curved bark and set it near, with some of the protein squares the sailors had left her beside it. When the shadows lengthened and she could see his breath steaming on the air and his body shivering convulsively, she crawled as close as she dared and tossed his cloak over him.

She spent hours gathering broken branches and dead limbs and by nightfall had the fuel to build a fire big enough to keep the wild things away and warm enough to allow her to sleep, now and then in snatches, even without the warmth of his cloak.

When she awoke he was crouched across from her, feeding sticks into the dying fire. She caught a cry in her throat and scrambled away from him on all fours until she tripped on her skirt and sat down hard, gasping. He didn't glance up.

The orange-and-blue lights of the fire planed his face grotesquely, but did not exaggerate his sunken cheeks and dark-circled eyes. He held the cloak tight around his shoulders with one hand, and the hand that thrust sticks into the fire was not quite steady. His injured leg, which was stretched out to the side of his body, was swollen to easily twice its size from calf to ankle and its color, beneath the streaks of caked blood, was dark and mottled. But the wounds made by the sharp teeth of the trap were now merely bruised indentations, and the bones were straight.

He stirred the fire until sparks flew and flames caught and surged, and then he tossed the last stick onto the fire. He lowered himself heavily to one arm and was still for a time, breathing slowly through flared nostrils.

Then he said very lowly, as though the effort were almost more than it was worth, "Why did you come back?"

Tessa inched slowly back to the fire, watching him cautiously. She stretched out her hands to the flames. She answered at length, "I saw the birds. I wondered . . . if you would be strong enough to protect yourself from the things that come at night." And then she added slowly, softly, and almost to herself, "Because if you died, it really would be over. There would be nothing at all to remind me of what happened to me in France, nothing to prove it was real. There would be nothing to explain why I am here."

Denis said nothing, but she could see his eyes watching her from the shadows. The fire crackled and the flames danced, and eventually his eyes closed, and he slept.

When the sky turned indigo with the prelude to dawn, Tessa walked out until she could see the valley, and the faint flicker of light as some early riser stirred his fire for coffee.

She left the sack containing the protein squares for Denis and refilled her own canteen at the stream. She planned to be back among her own kind before nightfall, and she would not need anything else.

She started following the stream again, and this time she was not distracted. The sun was bright, and though the air was cold there was no wind, and she was warm enough even without Denis's cloak. She drank all the water from her canteen.

As dusk began to fall a small knot of fear started to form in her belly. What if she was going in the wrong direction after all? What if the camp was farther away than she had thought? She had left the matches with Denis, inside the pocket of his cloak. What if darkness came and she was alone in this wild forest with no fire?

And then she smelled the woodsmoke and went weak with relief. She was going in the right direction. The camp was near.

She quickened her step, pushing through the undergrowth toward the clearing she could see faintly ahead. She splashed through the shallow stream, and slipped on the bank going up the other side, landing hard on her hands and knees.

Heavy hands fell on her shoulders, hauling her to her feet. She caught a cry in her throat, but what began as relief turned to cold fear as she looked into the bearded, tobacco-stained face of the man who held her.

He grinned at her, showing yellow, broken teeth. "Well, now," he said, "what have we here?"

Tessa struggled then, and tried to break away. He held her firm. She cried out, "Let me go!" and kicked at him, but he just laughed.

Another man came out of the shadows, and another.

Tessa began to scream.

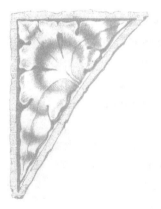

Twenty-four

IT WAS HUNGER, IN THE END, THAT DROVE DENIS DOWN THE HILL. Hunger, which in his former life had been a condition he was barely familiar with, now was the axis upon which his world revolved. Avoiding hunger, obeying hunger, following hunger carved the paths that determined what course his life would take. He was a slave to the need to survive.

When he had first surveyed this wild paradise he had been overwhelmed by its splendor. Here was bounty enough for a hundred werewolves, a boundless pack, and he could not understand why none of his kind had settled here before. Here it would be possible to live one's entire life in wolf form and never worry about going hungry; here one could run without fences, hunt without inhibition, drink endlessly from clear running streams. Here, where humankind had barely touched, a single werewolf could be a king. An entire pack could rule the world.

That was when he had first begun to realize that his life was not over. It had, in fact, just begun, and the future was unfolding with a magnificence he had never dared to dream before.

He had feasted that first day after the sailors released him on fresh-killed deer; he gorged himself right down to the bone, and when his desperate body metabolized that, he killed again, swiftly, easily, and ate until he could hold no more. Living on instinct, half drunk with gluttony, his wolf-form mind thought no further than the next kill, the next long drink of cold rushing water, the run that would strengthen his muscles and make his spirit soar. He could have lived like that forever.

It was therefore a bitter irony that, in this place so far from human habitation, he, a master of the wilderness, should fall victim to one of humankind's simplest devices for taming nature. And that, because of it, he was once again on the brink of starvation in the midst of plenty.

The protective instinct that caused him to automatically revert to human form once the basic healing was done had saved his life, for the energy reserves he had stored with two days' gorging had been almost depleted by the injury itself. But in human form he couldn't hunt; he couldn't even travel far enough or fast enough to help himself to the kills made by other predators.

In human form the healing of his leg was decelerated significantly. The bones were tender and the newly rejoined ligaments as thin as membranes; almost a week had passed before he was able to support his own weight. Whatever energy he had to spare after fighting off fever and getting himself back and forth to the stream to drink was spent in foraging for firewood to keep his human form warm. And after the protein packs that Tessa had left were gone, he was reduced to scratching for grubs beneath the rapidly freezing ground or trying to snatch fish from the stream with his hands. Sometimes he was successful at this, sometimes not. As the nights got colder and he grew weaker, he was consumed with frustration, hating his human form and the restrictions that kept him bound to it; hating humans and all their murderous devices; hating, in particular, Tessa LeGuerre because he could not stop thinking about her.

Over and over he kept coming back to a single truth: he had misjudged her. He had counted upon those natural human characteristics of jealousy, greed and revenge to serve him effortlessly with the queen, but somehow Tessa had overcome her nature and instead acted in a manner that was disturbingly close to honorable. Her loyalty could not be swayed or destroyed. She had refused to do harm to one she loved. She had, perhaps, lived among werewolves for so long that she had begun to adopt some of their traits.

You know nothing about us, she had said. It infuriated Denis to think she was right.

She had saved his life. He understood why she had done it, but that she had done it at all was a puzzle. She had come back, she had built a fire, she had left him food. All of his life Denis had lived according to a certain set of truths about humans. To suspect now that he had been mistaken about those truths, however slightly, was deeply disturbing.

In wolf form no such uneasiness would plague him. In wolf form nothing required analysis, motivations did not matter, and what he did not understand he could ignore. It angered him to be plagued with uncertainties now. And he resented the fact that it was Tessa who had left him condemned to live or die in human form, and that questions about Tessa consumed far more energy than he could afford.

Still, if he had not smelled the roasting meat from the miners' camp, it was unlikely their paths would have ever crossed again.

For several mornings as the cold wind rose and hard dry snowflakes brought the taste of a crisp northern winter before evaporating in the air, Denis had been forced to listen helplessly to the sound of herds on the move. He wasn't afraid of the coming winter; he was a winter hunter who thrived in rough terrain. But if he lost the herds, his chances of survival in the kind of weather he knew was coming were diminished by half. And he couldn't hunt—not even well enough to pick off the sick and the old who straggled behind—until his leg healed.

He knew if he changed one more time the hormonal surge would complete the healing of his leg. But unless he was near an immediate food source, the energy expended would leave him too depleted to hunt. And that was when the winds shifted, bringing the smell of an approaching storm—and of roasting meat. He remembered the human camp.

He drew his cloak around him and, using a sturdy branch to aid his weakened leg, started down the hill. The "day's walk" turned out to be slightly less than that, and he reached the outskirts of the human habitation shortly before sunset.

The smell of their dying campfires and of their stored-away food made his stomach cramp and his mouth wet, yet his sense of caution caused him to linger in the shadows, sweeping the clearing with slitted eyes, testing the air, listening. He had been listening to their conversations for miles, filthy, unlettered savages whose only concerns seemed to be how much gold they could carry out before the snow flew and how best to ease the swelling between their legs. Many of them had already left ahead of the storm; perhaps a half dozen remained to winter over in the stick-and-clay lodge they had built in a shelter of evergreens. It was from there that the smell of cooked meat emanated.

Tessa was there; he had caught her scent earlier, and it was of sickness and pain. There were other smells, too, in addition to the filth of human waste and sweat, of unwashed wool and rotting shoe leather; there was the smell of hard new whiskey and sex, and he came to understand that the men, loud and drunk, were having sex with Tessa. This interested him less than it should have, less than it might have under other circumstances. Human males, weakened with drink and distracted by sex, were unlikely to reach for guns. That was all he needed to know.

He let the cloak drop, and knowing that it might well be for the last time, he called the Passion to him.

For years afterward, stories would be told of what happened that night, and with each new telling the legend would grow until it bore no resemblance at all to the actual events. In fact, it happened so quickly and was over so fast it's doubtful any of the drunken men who witnessed it would, singly or together, ever be able to give an accurate account.

Denis ripped open the canvas covering that served as a door with one mighty swipe of his paw and charged inside the room. There he paused for no more than a split second to get his bearings, head lowered and teeth bared in a bone-rattling growl. This is what he saw in that half moment before they were able to react to him: One man with a filthy, tobacco-stained beard was squatting by the fire, rubbing his crotch and grinning while he turned a fatty rump of boar over a spit. Another was asleep in his chair with a jug in his hands that contained nothing more than harsh-smelling fumes. There was a table made of a stump of barked tree, and it was piled with tools and cast-off scraps of clothing and some metal plates crusted with food; there was a bench and another chair, and some nests of rags on the floor that smelled as though they were used for beds. The guns were by the door, where Denis now stood.

Tessa was on the floor, half in the shadows of the fire. The front of her dress had been torn open, and her breasts were black with bruises. Her face was discolored and lumpy with blows, her lips cracked and bloody; one eye was swollen shut. Her skirt was pushed up over her naked legs and a man was between them, his flabby buttocks rising and falling with repeated grunts as he thrust into her, while another man, giggling in a high weird way, held her head and tried to force his penis into her mouth.

Those men were between him and the meat on the fire.

Denis leapt upon the back of the man who was between Tessa's legs, sank his teeth into his neck, and flung him against the wall. The man at Tessa's head stopped giggling and started screaming like a woman, his member withering as he backed away. Furniture overturned. Someone was running. Denis whirled and launched himself at the man who was stumbling for the guns. He brought him down a few steps from the door. Someone was screaming curses in Russian, another in English. Someone else was just screaming. The smell of blood was strong. Tessa was on her knees now, pressed into a corner, and the small whimpering sounds of terror she made were not directed toward him, but at the men who ran from him.

He whirled again and struck out blindly; this time he caught an arm and ripped out a section of flesh. More blood sprayed. They started to run for the door, all of them, tripping over each other, grabbing for their guns, dropping them. Someone fired a round into the wall. The explosion shook dirt from the roof in a fine shower and overturned a lamp. Fire and kerosene smelled strong.

Denis grabbed the meat from the fire and sailed past them through the door, and when bullets peppered the snow at his feet he barely noticed. He gulped down the hot meat in the shadows of the burning building and felt it flooding through muscles, fueling him for the hunt.

It was while he paused there, tearing off chunks of the life-giving meat, that he noticed a set of small light footprints in the snow leading away from the cabin. He noticed them and knew that they were significant, and that they pleased him on some level. But already he was too much inside himself to question why, and already the hunger was driving him again. He left behind reason and worry and everything else that connected him to the world of men, and he ran for the wilderness.

The temperature dropped and the snow fell, but the storm that was promised in the wind was still a sunrise away. This was good, because it meant he could hunt and feed more easily; it was bad, because while he hunted, men with guns hunted him.

They were poor hunters and they never came near him; nonetheless, he kept a cautious distance between the sound of their voices, the smell of their filth and greed, and himself. Eventually that meant he had to double back, closer to their camp than he liked. That was when his trail started to cross Tessa's, and dim memory stirred.

In the stand of evergreens surrounding the charred, smokey ruins of the lodge he found his cloak, and again a memory tugged. It smelled of her. It smelled of smoke and earth and his own pain, too, of his skin and his fur and of the leaves in which he had made his bed, but it also smelled of her.

The edge of the hunger was gone, though the urge to hunt was not, and for a moment he stood over the cloak, irresolute, sniffing the wind. Somewhat to his surprise, curiosity won the battle. He raised his head and shook himself and leapt into his human form.

He found her not five hundred yards from the ruined lodge, nestled beneath a sapling tree where the weeds grew high and had not yet begun to bend with snow, curled into a ball on the ground. He dropped down beside her.

"What's wrong with you?" he demanded. "Why are you lying here? Your bones aren't broken and you don't have a fever. Why are you lying here on the ground?"

She didn't move and didn't speak; she just held herself in that tight little ball with her arms around her knees and her eyes open and staring at the dark, and she said nothing.

"Do you want to go back to them, is that it? Are you already missing your filthy human society? Well, perhaps you should go back at that. You'd have a longer life than if you stay here to be eaten by bears."

But at his first words a sound, choked and desperate, came from her throat, and her eyes closed and her arms tightened around her knees and she began to rock herself, moaning so softly that even he could barely hear the sound. It was as though the cry, and the pain that caused it, were locked so deeply inside her soul that her voice could not express them.

Denis felt an anger he could not explain, and an astonishment. The concept of rape was foreign to him, though he knew it existed. He knew the men had used her and hurt her and exhausted her with their lust, that they had beaten and subdued her, but he found none of that surprising in the least. It was the kind of behavior one expected from humans and he assumed Tessa had expected it as well. But that she now lay, whimpering and unseeing, exposed to the elements and seemingly oblivious to the fact, that she had run this far and yet no further—this he could not explain or understand and it angered him. This human female had survived the love of one werewolf and the manipulations of another, had endured a voyage across the North Atlantic and exile in the wilderness, had twice saved his life and shown nothing but courage before him and his kind. Yet it had taken humans to defeat her. That astonished him.

He said roughly, "They will find you here, don't you know that? They'll find you and drag you back and use you for their whore again, and if that's what you want you have only to stay here and do nothing."

She hunched her shoulders and pressed her face deeper into her knees. Her thin shoulder blades looked ready to pierce the worn fabric of her gown, and she trembled convulsively. She would never survive the night.

Denis set his teeth. "I can't stay here. There's no food here. They're hunting me already. They're hunting you, too."

She made no response, nor gave any sign that she heard him.

Denis stood up. He looked down at her for a while, angry and undecided, waiting for he knew not what. She didn't move.

"I owe you nothing, Tessa LeGuerre," he said angrily.

He swept his cloak off his shoulders and dropped it over her. He strode off into the night, and waited until he was well out of her sight to resume his natural form.

He set his face for the wilderness and did not look back again.

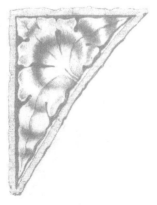

ALEXANDER

Twenty-five

OUR MATING CEREMONY WAS PLANNED FOR THE TRADITIONAL HARVEST Moon. There was some trepidation on my part as to how I would be received by the pack as Elise's potential mate because of my relationship to Denis and Tessa. But I had dealt from strength with both of them and acted with honor throughout it all, and among the pack pragmatism prevailed as always. I was strong, I was of noble status, and the queen wanted me. It was enough for most. There were whispers, of course, about my unfortunate association with the human and about my renegade brother, but there always are in these cases. As long as the whisperers made no attempt to denigrate my queen, I let them pass unnoticed.

Within a week of the judgement on Denis I took a battalion of our strongest fighters to the far northeast with news of Denis's defeat. Though it was heartbreaking for me to close up Palace Antonov, there was some comfort in the fact that the pack itself did not resist me. They all dispersed peacefully enough, for though they carried in their hearts their dark philosophies and always would, without unity they were nothing. Some drifted back to the cities, some went wild, some returned to Europe with me. Such is the power of a single werewolf among us. Without Denis, they were nothing, and they accepted the only protection that was offered—mine.

Elise and I did not talk about Tessa. It was not that I forbade her to broach the subject with me, but she knew my heart well enough to understand how the topic hurt me still. In fact, during the entire summer the name of the human I had so loved was spoken only once in my presence, and that was by the most unlikely person.

Gault came to me shortly after I returned from Siberia. I was in the midst of inventorying the Lyons château and packing my personal belongings because, although I planned to keep the house in Paris and a smaller cottage near Bordeaux, there would be no point in maintaining the Lyons residence once I moved permanently to the Palais. Chaos had reigned for days, with five or six housemaids in every room dusting and washing and placing things into barrels, while I tried to make lists of my books and my collections and my favorite furnishings. More than once I had caught myself lifting my head to call out impatiently for Tessa, for this was just the kind of task she would have set to with enthusiasm. Every time I did I felt a stab of loneliness in my belly that all but cut off my breath. I missed her, and the knowledge shamed me.

Gault stood before my desk and without preamble said, "I will be leaving your service at the end of the week, monsieur, if it pleases you."

For a moment I just stared at him. Then I threw down my pen and snapped, "It does not please me! What is your complaint, Gault? Are your accommodations not luxurious enough? Do you desire more wages? Have you no taste for living at the Palais? Speak up, confound you, for I have no patience with this nonsense!"

Gault replied, stiff-faced, "I have wronged you. It's my job to serve your best interests at all times, and I've failed to do that. I can't stay with you under those circumstances."

"When have you failed me? What have you done?"

He said, "I'm the cause of your unhappiness now. I deliberately sent the human girl to find you when I heard you with the queen. I knew she would be upset. But if I had shown you her note, or read it at least, we might have been able to prevent her foolish treachery. She was not a malicious girl, I think. Just . . . ignorant."

I hardly knew what to say, or how to feel, nor in fact which emotion to address first. I was surprised, because I hadn't realized my unhappiness was evident. After all, what reason did I, bridegroom of the queen, soon to be the most powerful male in the pack, wedded to the most exquisite creature who had ever drawn breath and the woman I had adored for years—on what grounds could I possibly claim unhappiness? And there was guilt, because I *was* unhappy, and could not hide it. And there was a deeper surprise, mixed with gentle gratitude, to hear Gault defend Tessa, however weakly, at last. And there was pain, raw unmitigated pain, to hear her name spoken out loud, to have her face brought into my mind's eye, to feel the regret and the sorrow and the helplessness all over again which Gault's words, though kindly and sincerely meant, had raised.

I knew I could keep none of this from my eyes, and I didn't try. But after a moment I took up my pen again and turned my attention back to my lists. Or I pretended to. "Nothing you could have done would have made a difference," I said flatly. "Our course was set the moment she came into my house."

Gault said quietly, "Yet you still grieve for her."

My pen stopped its meaningless movement and I stared unseeing at the page for a moment. "No," I said slowly. "I grieve . . . for innocence. My own, and hers."

In a moment Gault nodded, and I thought he genuinely understood. He turned to go, then hesitated. "Monsieur."

I looked up, pulled from my gray thoughts.

He said, "I want it understood that—what I mean to say is that I see how it will be under the new queen's rule, and with your opinions being much the same, I hope you won't let any careless remarks I may have made in the past stand in the way of . . ."

As my expression grew more and more bemused, he broke off with a brief intake of breath. "You know, don't you," he said plainly, "that the things I've said about humans in the past were meant in jest? With so much talk about the Dark Brothers and what they intended to do—I simply wouldn't want there to be any confusion about my position on the issue."

I raised an eyebrow. "You surely don't think you would still be here if there was? The queen has a very effective intelligence force, I'm told."

He seemed relieved. "Yes, I suppose that's true." Then he hesitated before adding, "I can deal with humans, if I have to. I don't like them much, any more than I like felines or spiders in my milk, but I can tolerate them fairly when it's called for."

I had to smile. "Gault, you've sniffed the wind and set your sail to catch it. You are a sterling opportunist."

He smiled and bowed deeply to me, touched by the compliment. "Thank you, monsieur."

It was to our good fortune that most of the pack reflected Gault's attitude, and I began to suspect that even more would come around when it became to their advantage to do so. As for myself, I had only one interest in humans: to make as much money off them as possible.

It was therefore more than a happy coincidence that provided me that summer with the opportunity to nourish my relationship with Alphonse Rothschild, who had long had an interest in buying my Paris bank. The details of the transaction into which we eventually entered are for the textbooks; suffice it to say that there was a great deal more maneuvering going on behind the scenes than human economists will ever discover, and that I found the manipulations sufficiently distracting to help me put the memory of Tessa and the pain she had caused me out of my mind, at least for the time being. And yes, ironically enough, what started out for me as a bitter mockery of humans and all their vanities ended up the most monumentally profitable venture in which I had ever engaged, and became a model for the way the pack would do business in the future.

Needless to say, Monsieur Rothschild did not acquire my bank.

*　　*　　*

Perhaps my recounting of events has caused marriages of state to seem passionless, regulated affairs. I assure you, nothing could be farther from the truth. As the date of our mating approached, I was as terrified as any human bridegroom—not of my ability to perform, for I was supremely confident of my own virility and Elise had more than once proved her ability to arouse, but of the truth of it, the permanence and responsibility, the overwhelming commitment.

From childhood we are taught the sanctity of the mating bond. We know that it is a marvel, a miracle, an all-consuming surrender of will and individuality to a single, transcendental purpose: to conceive and raise young. But we are never told how, exactly, this awe-inspiring thing occurs, or how it will affect us or how we may prepare for it. The reason, of course, is that there is no way to explain it to one who has not experienced it, and certainly there is no way to prepare for the one single moment that will change one's life forever. This is terrifying.

But there was a broader perspective, and to ignore it would be a disservice both to Elise and to me. This was a marriage of state; we both knew that. Yet I had never aspired to be consort to a queen; I wanted only to love a woman. Elise, who had spent her life preparing to rule, would have abandoned it all for me. Of this I am certain. In matters of the heart, werewolves do not deceive each other. And because we had this foundation of simple unquestioned certainty, it was possible for us to extend our attention to the pack, and what our mating would mean to it.

Tragedy had touched us personally, but for the purposes of the pack events could not have conspired to present a more perfect opportunity for change. Once, Elise had wondered out loud to me whether anyone would respond if, in this modern age, she put out the call to the pack. But she had no need to call the pack: within the space of a year we had been brought together by a funeral, a festival disrupted by an assassination attempt, and now a mating ceremony and coronation. Even one of those events would have been remarkable in a single generation; the confluence of all of them presented such a unique sense of unity and, yes, patriotism within the pack that we would have been irresponsible in the extreme not to take advantage.

And so, while I was occupied with the House of Rothschild, Elise was putting into action her own gentle plan for guiding the pack into the future. There was a diamond mine in Australia, she informed her jeweller, which was owned by humans yet reported to be in possession of a fine blue diamond which she very much desired for her coronation jewels. And when she was last in Vienna she had dined at a charming coffeehouse where the human chef had prepared a confection of dark chocolate and black cherries which she would like to serve at the mating celebration; would her staff be good enough to acquire the recipe? And there was a human clockmaker in Switzerland whom she had employed to make a gift for her betrothed, but only if he could work in partnership with the wood-carvers she had chosen. Of such small beginnings, such simple things, are great ideas made manifest.

Not once, in private or public, was the subject of Tessa LeGuerre or the murderous Denis Antonov raised to cast a pall over our union. Elise was already a powerful ruler.

Guests began arriving weeks in advance from Europe, Asia and America. During this time a festival atmosphere prevailed throughout the Palais, with athletic competitions and symphony orchestras and productions of the finest ballets and operas every night. The most renowned chefs in the world prepared our feasts, and yes, some of them were human—as were, for the first time in our history, some of the performers, musicians and service personnel. Was it a political occasion? Of course it was. But it was also the finest mating celebration that has ever been staged.

Three days before the Harvest Moon all the guests were in place, and the Palais was sealed off. Humans were, of course, sent away. Then came the best of the music, the best of the food, the best of the passion. There was dancing; there were serenades deep into the night, there was copulation and courtship and promises made under the moon. The air was sweet with musk and the sound of werewolf voices; Elise and I were feted and pampered, massaged with exotic oils, tenderly fed the most delicate cuts of meat and the most potent wines. It was really quite marvellous.

On the night of the Harvest Moon the pack assembled in the

meadow surrounding the Calling Rock. Elise and I were led out in our ceremonial robes while a thousand voices lifted in song surrounded us. I thought no moment could surpass that one: the music, so rich and so complex that it seemed to have a life of its own, practically lifting us off our feet; the yellow moon huge in the background, taking up half the sky; and my bride . . . ah, my bride. *That* was the moment, when I looked into her eyes, when I was caught up in her gaze and transported by it, when I realized that this magnificent creature had chosen me, that I soon would belong to her and she to me for the rest of our lives—that was a moment so humbling, so transcendental, that I thought I would weep from the beauty of it. My nervousness vanished, my uncertainty was caught by the wind. I was filled with the power of absolute adoration.

We cast aside our robes. We stood naked before each other, with the wind in our hair and the song in our ears and we touched, fingertips to fingertips, and the touch was electric. We released our Passion.

Ah, this is a terrifying thing, to give over to the Change in perfect synchronization with another werewolf; terrifying and erotic and wholly transporting. It strips the mind, it takes the senses. It was unlike anything I have ever experienced before, and it is indescribable unless one has already experienced it for oneself. I dare not even try.

Humans have struggled for centuries to find the words to describe the pale emotion they call love, and have succeeded only in demeaning and cheapening it. We, who are privileged to know in truth what humans can only dimly yearn for, also know the value of silence. This union of souls, this seamless blending into one what once was two, is beyond the frailty of human comprehension and well it should be. It awaits each werewolf to discover for himself as though it were for the first time in the history of the world.

And yet there is a part of it I must find a way to tell, an essential truth I must share. There was the chase, the capture, the moment of penetration wherein I, the male, commanded her body and she, the female, commanded my soul . . . and wherein we both lost ourselves in the wholeness of one another.

When two werewolves come together as mates such a flood of information is exchanged, such an influx of thought and emotions and experiences, that the whole becomes greater than its parts, if a great deal more amorphous. It is often days, even weeks, before the newly mated couple can sort out their individuality again, thus the traditional "honeymoon." But I specifically recall certain peaks in the wave of life's essence that poured from me into her, from her into me: Elise, two years old, proudly bringing home her first rabbit, only to be laughed at by her brothers who had killed a deer; my heart ached for her. Myself, age five, winning the Long Race, failing in my first symphonic composition; her love encompassed me. Denis, seducing me into the dark rite of the Brotherhood; Elise, who once seduced a human male into having sex with her. Ah, yes. There were no secrets between us. This is the glory of it. And the pain.

And then there was Tessa. This is how it came to me, in a flood and a jumble of all the other intense emotions and demanding memories of two lifetimes: Tessa, and what I believed to be the truth, and Tessa, and what Elise knew to be the truth. The shock, the pain. Elise: *My love, you did not know!* And I: *Tessa, no! Why didn't you tell me?*

But you must understand this was only a millisecond, a flash of lightning, as our lives, our whole and entire lives, passed for review and were absorbed one unto the other. And then there was the carnal urge, the sheer pleasure, the power and the dominion and the magnificent, singular, driving lust that consumed us, commanded us, controlled us until at last my seed exploded into her and her womb opened to embrace it, and our son quickened, and was given life. This, then, was the purpose. This was all that mattered.

It would be weeks before the full drugging effect of our merging began to dissipate, before we completely understood all that we had captured inside our heads one from the other. This was a private time during which we were intensely protected by the pack while we explored the depth of our emotions and gradually began to sort out our individuality again. We lay in the sun, we made love, we listened for hours on end to the sound of our infant's growing heartbeat. We marvelled at each other. And, eventually, we talked about Tessa.

Tessa, who had fought off Denis's wiles the best she could with her small human weapons and her wit, and who had, in fact, never betrayed me at all. She had run to the palace that day to ask for my help and to warn me about Denis; that was what had been in the note that she gave to Gault. And when I had not responded, she had done the best she could.

She was afraid if she defied Denis outright that he would do me harm, or find another, quicker way to eliminate the queen. By pretending to go along with him, by firing the warning shot, she hoped to buy time. This is what she had told Elise. And it is what she would have told me, if I had given her a chance.

For this is the great tragedy of it, the one lesson in my life worth repeating now. The facts were all there for me to know. The opportunities were there for me to uncover those facts. But in my rage I did not allow Tessa to answer the questions which might have cleared her; instead I broke her arm. In my hurt and, yes, embarrassment, I did not give her the chance to defend herself before the tribunal. In my arrogance I assumed the worst about her—I, who had always prided myself on a lack of prejudice about humans, was just as quick as any other to leap to the worst possible conclusion.

I allowed my passions to overrule my judgement. This is the most dangerous mistake a werewolf can make. And this time it had resulted in a disaster whose repercussions would be greater than even I could imagine.

Elise had never intended to conceal anything from me. How could she have? She assumed that since I had interrogated Tessa first—and had done so with enough intensity to break her arm—I had gotten the truth. If I had asked Elise she would have told me about her conversation with Tessa in the dungeon, but why should I ask? If *only* I had asked. But I was young and angry and so deeply hurt. Throughout that horrible night of treachery and trauma, was there any point when I might have struggled through my shame and my pain and talked to Elise in words about it? I don't know. I only know that, once again, I was wrong. And we all paid a horrible price.

Elise had been surprised at the harshness of my punishment for Tessa on that night, but would never think to question my judgement—and assumed I was judging with all the facts. Her sorrow was almost as intense as mine that she had not at some point broached the subject with me, questioned me, made certain that I knew what she knew about why Tessa had acted as she had. Regrets. They are useful only if one learns from them.

The irony was bitter. That we, masters of the earth, imbued with all our superlative senses and so proud of our ability to uncover even the most elaborate deception, had been undone by a simple miscommun-ication. Anger, pride, intolerance and arrogance; these are the demons that stalk us from the shadows, taunting us with their power, robbing us of our destiny. I had fallen victim to them, and I was ashamed, and sick at heart.

Long before the honeymoon was over, and without a word ever being exchanged between us, Elise and I knew we had to go after Tessa and bring her home.

But even we, the most powerful creatures on the earth, could not control the climate that closed the ports of northwestern Alaska for all but a few weeks every summer. It would be months before we could undertake the journey. By then I was very much afraid it would be too late.

TESSA
AND DENIS

Twenty-six

THEY WILL FIND YOU HERE. TESSA KEPT HEARING THOSE WORDS OVER AND over again in her head. Every time she closed her eyes, every time she thought she was too tired to go on, the voice would come again: *They will find you and drag you back with them,* and then she couldn't lie down, she had to keep moving. The snow blew and her feet grew numb, then burned with icy pain, but she huddled deeper inside the cloak and plodded on. The wind was like shards of ice stabbing through to her bones. It ripped at her skirt and tore at her naked legs and all she wanted was to lie down in the snow, curl up tight with her back to the wind and close her eyes. But she kept hearing that voice, and she kept moving. Perhaps if she had not, she would have died that night.

There was no part of Tessa's mind that remembered the details of what had happened to her in any coherent form. Being seized by rough hands at the stream, being forced to the ground while a big hand clamped down over her mouth and nose, smothering her, and other hands tore at her clothing—that was an ugly story she had heard long ago. Of the blows they rained on her face when she screamed, of the mouths that smelled of rotted teeth and whiskey, of the laughter, of the ways they hurt her she remembered nothing except as glimpses of waking nightmares. The part of her that could reason and question and link together events to make a cohesive whole was buried with memories she refused to unearth.

She walked through the night, and when the morning came and the wind stopped, she found a snow cave formed by the low-hanging, snow-covered branches of a fir tree. There she burrowed like a ground-dwelling creature and slept and dreamed no dreams.

And thus was the pattern of her days, light unto dark. She walked until she could walk no more; then she would sleep, burying herself beneath an insulating blanket of snow. When she found berries on the bush she ate them, and sometimes they made her retch. She ate for the same reason she moved: not because she wanted to or even understood the reason for it, but because it was instinct. And instinct was all she had left now.

Of the woman who once had read Molière and danced with a werewolf there was no trace. The young girl who had dreamed of miracles and been touched by magic was gone. And whatever she once had known of humanity had been extinguished by the brutality of humans.

Sometimes she would see tracks in the snow made by a large animal and vague memory would stir, but it sifted through her grasp like chaff in the wind. Nothing that moved in the forest or cried from the mountaintop could frighten her now. Neither the splendor of the sunset nor the fury of the storm impressed her. Her body kept moving, but her soul had retreated into a dark place deep inside, like a small hard seed waiting for the spring to be reborn.

And yet there must have been a part of her that knew she would not see another spring, and even would be glad to die. There were matches in the inner pocket of the cloak, yet she did not build a fire. When the second snow came she couldn't find any more berries. Sometimes she was feverish and coughed up bloody phlegm. She grew weaker every day.

And then one day she awoke to find a big red wolf standing over her. He had in his jaws a haunch of meat, which he dropped at her feet. He walked a little away and sat down, watching her. She closed her eyes again and drifted into a feverish sleep, but when she woke again he was still there. She felt neither fear nor wonder, nor did it occur to her to try to run away. She was too weak to do anything at all, and the cough was worse.

And so it was as the hours passed. Once she awoke and he wasn't there. Instead, there was a pile of sticks on a patch of bare earth that he had dug in the snow. The next time she opened her eyes he had returned, and the pile of sticks had grown. And when night came and the wind began to rise she realized that she was no longer shivering; for the first time in memory she felt warm. The wolf was curled up beside her, his body heat radiating like a coal furnace. She fell asleep to the sound of his rhythmic breathing, and in the morning her fever had lessened.

At some point, she was never quite sure how or when, she began to understand the purpose of the sticks that were piled up in the circle of earth, and she remembered the matches. She roasted meat on a stick and, in a sudden frenzy of greed, pulled off the hot flesh with her fingers, eating until she could hold no more. He watched her fixedly, and when she was finished he carried off the remainder to consume in private.

A series of days and nights passed in this fashion; she ate the meat he brought and consumed snow for water, and at night he kept her warm. The cough lessened; she grew stronger.

And then came the morning when she awoke and he was not there. For many hours she did nothing. But what she felt was an odd and strangely disturbing sensation: loneliness.

She followed the tracks in the snow.

At the end of the day she arrived at the entrance to a rock cave whose solid walls kept out the wind and whose temperature inside was a good twenty degrees higher than that outside. At the entrance of the cave was a pile of dry wood and two rabbits.

And so became the pattern of their days. Denis hunted and scouted for shelter, and Tessa followed mindlessly, gathering firewood when she thought of it, minding the matches. At night he waited for the bones she discarded, the cooked fat and charred flesh, with narrowed eyes and wet tongue. And when the wind howled and the snow fell, he moved into the circle of the fire, sleepy-eyed, and stretched out beside her. She slept with her fingers entwined in his fur.

And then came the morning when she awoke to find a human male, fully naked, sitting beside her, looking down at her gravely.

"Tessa LeGuerre," he said, "talk to me."

When called upon to explain to his reasoning mind why he had returned to her, Denis had a simple answer: A leader without a pack was nothing. It was instinct to care for the helpless in the midst of bounty, to conquer the enemy when challenged, to demonstrate superior hunting skills under harsh conditions; those were the rules of the pack.

And yet there was another, older and even more powerful instinct at work; painful to contemplate, incomprehensible, but undeniably there. He had built his life on the firm belief that a werewolf was meant to live as close to his nature as possible; that the only paradise worth having was one that was devoid of humans, in which a werewolf could live on the bounty of the land in wolf form for all of his days. This was a basic tenet of the Brotherhood, an ideal they all worked for and never hoped to attain . . . yet suddenly Denis *had* attained it. He had a continent to himself. The nearest tribe of humans was so far away that even the strongest wind brought only a faint trace of the memory of where they once had been. And even with the snow piling up and the herds moving south there was more than enough game to fuel a single werewolf to his sleekest, strongest best throughout the winter.

Yet he sought out the company of the human. The smell of the fire, the taste of cooked meat—they lured him with the tantalizing memory of something long gone yet never forgotten. Even when he was not hungry, the smell of fat sizzling in the flame filled him with yearning. Even when he was not cold, the beauty of the fire enticed him. He brought the meat; she made the fire. Could the relationship between his kind and hers that had begun so long ago be summed up so easily?

And now he had resumed his human form. There was no reason to, he did not need to, but he *wanted* to. This was something else he could not have predicted, and did not entirely understand. That it was directly related to the human who shared this snowy plain with him was undeniable, and in many ways disturbing.

She did not answer him when he spoke, and though he had not expected her to, he was nonetheless disappointed not to hear the sound of her voice. Perhaps that was all that he needed, all that he missed: the sound of another voice. Werewolves were not meant to live alone, and that was why exile was such a harsh punishment. Under such cruel conditions, even a human was better than no companionship at all.

Perhaps it was that simple.

He said, "You are a filthy human and your stench is making me ill. I can tolerate your dullness and your weakness, but I will not share my sleeping quarters with someone so foul."

He lifted her in his arms like a bundle of rags and carried her out of the cave. His bare feet were as surefooted as a goat's on the slippery rocks, his naked skin barely prickling in the cold air. He approached the steaming springs, where greenery still grew between the rocks and no snow clung and the temperature was as mild as spring. There he set Tessa on her feet and began to strip off her grimy clothes.

"Shall I tell you what killed most of your kind during the Black Death? A simple lack of soap. It is unfortunate for all concerned that that remedy was discovered before it was too late."

She gave no reaction, either to his words or to his actions. Her limbs were so pliable as to be almost boneless when he rearranged them to undress her, and her expression did not change. He looked into her eyes and saw absolutely nothing.

He led her to the pool with its misty covering of foggy steam and stepped down into the water, expecting her to follow him. When she did not, he caught her by the waist and lifted her in like a child. Her skin prickled with the change of temperature, but she showed no other reaction. He led her deeper, until the water swirled over the jagged sharp point of her hipbones, over her sunken belly, up to her ribs.

Such spontaneous pools of volcanically heated water in the midst of subarctic regions were a phenomenon with which Denis was familiar from his homeland, and of which he had learned to take advantage whenever he could. There were few sensations more exquisite than gliding into a pool of heated water when the snow lay all around, breathing the thick steam, lying back and letting the heat seep into the muscles and the heavy minerals restore the soul. He had been following the scent of these springs for days.

He had spent some time brewing a simple soap from an emulsion of fish oil, bark and ashes, and packed it into a pouch made of deer hide. He scooped out some of the soap with his fingers now, and worked it into a lather between his hands. Briskly he spread the suds over her shoulders and her breasts and her arms, over her hips and her thighs and between her legs. She stood with her eyes lowered and her arms loose at her sides, neither resisting nor assisting him.

He grew impatient with her and turned to attend to his own toilette, scrubbing his body with the soap, lathering his hair, ducking under and letting the gentle eddy and currents of the spring carry the bubbles away. He sank down onto his knees, lost in the fog, and let the steam warm him to his very marrow. He all but forgot about Tessa.

But when he rose to leave the pool, her outstretched hand stopped him. Puzzled, he looked at her, and then he realized she was reaching for the pouch of soap.

He took the pouch from the ledge and gave it to her, and stood there as she waded deeper into the water then sank down, dipping her hair back to wet it. She began to work the soap through her hair. It was absurd, how much pleasure it gave him to watch her perform such a simple task as washing her hair. He actually smiled.

"And so, little human," he murmured, "the taste of cooked meat, the smell of soap . . . perhaps this is all that separates us from the beasts after all, and what lures us back to ourselves when we stray too far."

She stayed in the pool for hours, washing herself over and over again. Denis built a large fire and washed her clothes and his robe, then spread them out to dry. Then he went to hunt.

He brought down a boar and skinned it with his teeth, restraining his appetite in memory of the fire and the way fat tasted when crisped near the bone. He left the head and the entrails for the scavengers and severed the thick shoulders for the night's meal, burying the remainder deep in snow close enough to the entrance of the springs so that he could guard it, yet not so close as to deliberately attract danger.

He returned to Tessa in human form, for reasons he could not entirely explain. She had dressed and kept the fire going. Her hair was clean and dry around her shoulders, though it was thinner than it had once been and had lost the gloss of health. The human smell of her, only faintly redolent of sickness and pain, was not so annoying now. It was, in an odd way, almost comforting.

Without a word she took the meat from him and arranged it on heavy sticks over the fire. She worked awkwardly with one arm, using the twisted hand of the weaker one to balance and steady her work, but she was efficient. He soaked in the hot pool, and his robe was warm and dry when he emerged. They ate together, plucking meat off the bone with their fingers while the color of the fire danced across their faces.

Denis said, tossing his bone into the fire when he was done, "How I would dearly love a bottle of Devoncroix Cabernet, for which my brother is so justifiably renowned." He watched her carefully for a reaction. There was none. "And salt. I miss salt. Perhaps I'll find a deposit before long. What about you, human? Is there anything you miss?"

She continued to push small pieces of meat into her mouth, her eyes on her work.

"Nothing from the world you left behind?" he prompted. "Pretty gowns, glittering stones, handsome human men in white gloves bowing over your hand? No? Ah, well, perhaps you're right. It's all so boring, isn't it? I don't blame you for being glad to leave it behind."

She didn't even glance at him. He smiled dryly. "That's what I've always disliked so about humans. You all talk too much."

He left her not long afterward to hunt again, and slept beside her that night in wolf form near the embers of the dying fire.

*   *   *

And so they developed a new rhythm to their days. Tessa returned obsessively to the pool, washing herself, washing her hair, again and again. Denis did not try to restrain her, knowing that eventually whatever it was of which she was trying to cleanse herself would be washed away—and wondering idly whether it was the memory of civilization or the ravages of the wilderness she was trying to erase.

In the warmth of the springs she grew stronger, and the cough lessened, and a faint color returned to her cheeks. Sometimes while he slept during the day she would go out and search for green things beneath the snow, digging up roots and savories which she would simmer over the fire with water and chunks of meat in a section of rotted log that she had hollowed out to make a bowl. Denis cleaned rabbit skins and cured them over the fire, then showed her how to line her boots with them to keep out the cold, and to wrap her hands in the fur when the wind blew.

More and more Denis would join her in the evenings in human form, wrapped in the cloak that smelled like her, and sometimes he would talk. He talked about *Otello*, the Verdi opera he had seen while he was in Paris, and the scene in *Giselle* that always took his breath away. He talked about brandies he had tasted and wines he loved and books he had read. He talked mostly for the sound of his voice and the comfort of his thoughts and he began to think, after a time, that she was actually listening. But there was always a certain disappointment to hear nothing but silence in response.

Sometimes he slept beside her in wolf form, though most of the time he hunted at night, scouting the territory, sniffing the wind. He knew they would have to move soon, yet he delayed telling her as long as he could.

And then one night as they finished off the last of the Arctic hares he had cached, Tessa suddenly went still, staring beyond his shoulder at the break in the rocks that shielded the springs. And she spoke.

"Who is it?" she whispered.

Denis was so surprised that it was a moment before he related any significance to the words; before he thought to turn around and look at what she was staring at. A shaggy Arctic wolf sat silhouetted in the moonlight not fifty feet away, watching them. He had known the wolf was near, of course, but he had not realized she could see it. He almost smiled when he determined what she thought, and what had shocked her out of her long silence.

"And you, the human who could always recognize a werewolf when she saw one," he mocked gently. "No, my dear, there is no magic in this place save what you see before you. That's just an ordinary Arctic wolf, come to see what we're having for dinner."

Her eyes were big and fixed upon the shape beyond his shoulder.

Denis said impatiently, "He won't hurt you. He's just curious about me. He has a pack nearby and I share my kill with him sometimes."

Now she looked at Denis "Does he—know you?"

So, her mind was not gone after all. Until that moment he had not been sure. His relief at knowing that was surely disproportionate to the question, yet he kept his manner deliberately casual as he replied, "Alas, no. He is my brother, but he smells the strangeness on me. He won't hunt with me, and he runs when I approach."

Tessa gathered up what was left of her rabbit and put the meat in his hands, staring still beyond his shoulder toward the wolf. In a moment Denis understood that she meant him to take the meat to the animal. With a shrug, he left her to do so.

It was a long time later when he returned, and she was lying beside the fire, her head pillowed on her crooked arm, not asleep but almost. He sat beside her, sweeping a fold of the cloak over her while the remainder covered his shoulders. The cloak was cold and smelled of the night.

He said, "We have to leave here soon. These past few weeks, the snow and the wind, they have been what passes for an Alaska autumn. Winter is coming, and the game has gone to ground. We'll be trapped here if we stay much longer, and we'll starve to death."

He saw her eyes open in the dim shadows of the firelight.

"There are caves in the rocks to the east. If we go there we can find shelter. The wolves manage to feed themselves through the winter. We can, too."

She didn't answer.

"We should leave tomorrow. A storm is coming, but if we go east we'll outrun it."

Still no answer. He thought he had lost her, and that whatever spark of sentience had flared so brightly earlier was now extinguished by the prospect of leaving this place which had brought her such comfort. His heart sank.

He dropped his cloak over her, tucking it warmly about her shoulders, and stood to go.

She said softly, "I like Verdi, too."

Denis stopped in mid-step, and looked back at her. Then he went out into the night to hunt.

ALEXANDER

Twenty-seven

IT WAS AN EVENTFUL WINTER FOR US, FULL OF PLANS AND PROMISES. WE travelled across Europe, making ourselves known to members of the pack who had not been able to attend the mating ceremony, making ourselves visible to those who doubted our ability to rule. We were received by human royalty and heads of state, who knew me only as a wealthy businessman and Elise as a French aristocrat and who, in their own ingratiating way, wanted to fete us on our marriage. Now that I was looking for them I was amazed by the number of business opportunities that were presented to me through such contacts.

We bought property in Amsterdam and London, and began negotiations with Lipenstraum, the werewolf jeweller who had designed our coronation jewels, whereby we would purchase two diamond mines and he would administer them—a venture which was to have very fine and far-reaching results for all of us. Elise heard about a factory in New York she wanted to purchase and we made plans to visit there in the spring. It was a good time.

Elise took to her lying-in in late February, and would remain in wolf form until the cub was weaned some six weeks hence. I would, of course, retain my human form throughout this time in order to provide her and the new cub with those things for which human form is necessary, and to give our family unit the traditional advantage which comes of having one adult in each of our forms. This is always a difficult period for the male. But it was also a time filled with anticipation and the thrill of discovery, and the bond between Elise and me deepened day by day.

It is important to have reliable assistants in key positions of authority at such a time, for as a birthing approaches, neither of the parents is able to summon much interest in anything else. Elise and I had taken care to surround ourselves with our most trusted advisors, and we were shielded by the loyalty and the protective instincts of the entire pack. There had not been a royal birth in almost thirty years, and this one would hold a new century in his hands. It was exciting for everyone.

Elise's labor began an hour before dawn while a light silent snow drifted down outside the windows. Her sisters and mine were in attendance, but they kept to the corners of the room, whispering excitedly to each other and sending young runners to announce the news, leaving Elise and me alone to bring our child into the world as it should be.

I lay with her and stroked her fur and by my presence, strong and alert in human form, let her know in the traditional way that I would protect her while she concentrated on the physical expenditure of energy required to bring our child into the world. Unlike human women, who seem to suffer so with the travails of birth, our females, in their natural wolf form, enjoy a relatively short labor and a painless delivery. I eased our firstborn cub into the world with my own hands a few minutes after sunrise.

I knew immediately something was wrong, and the room went deathly still. A child, poised at the doorway to run throughout the Palais with the joyful news at the moment of delivery, was stopped still by the hard grip of his mother's hand on his shoulder. No one moved. No one breathed.

And this was how it was in that second that seemed to last a lifetime, the moment that would live frozen in my memory forever: the soft glow of the gas lamps, turned down low to welcome the little one; the fire dancing gently in the background as a pale lemon sun filtered through the high clerestory windows of our bedchamber. The rumpled satin bedcovering stained with birth fluids, Elise bending forward to snip the cord with her teeth while I held in my hand this fragile, mewling scrap of life . . . so small, so helpless. He barely filled my two cupped hands, his blind eyes closed and his little mouth open as he instinctively sought the teat that would ease his hunger, his fur slick and dark with the wetness of his mother's body. My heart filled with love for him . . . and with horror.

For in that moment I could see what the others could only sense. His left paw, curled under his face, was not a paw at all but a human-formed hand. His right leg was a human leg. I could hear his human-formed lungs fill with fluid as they struggled to draw in enough air for his wolf-formed body, and his undersized heart double its rhythm in a desperate effort to pump blood through wolf-formed veins.

I should have taken the child from her then. I should never have allowed it to nurse. But, oh, the agony that gripped me, the helplessness and the shock that flooded through my body like slow-acting poison. I couldn't think, I couldn't reason, I couldn't feel anything except the pain. The pain.

I dropped the child beside her on the bed and backed away, stumbling, my stained hands held out before me. I saw the stunned eyes of the women, dark with sympathy, and one of them reached for me, I think. I saw Elise, calmly beginning to clean the child. I saw the child. My child.

I threw back my head and let out a howl of sheerest agony. It was an anguish torn from my soul that reverberated throughout the Palais, across the grounds, through the whole of the countryside, and was eventually heard around the world. I turned and fled the room.

*   *   *

We refer to it as the Scourge, this curse that snatches our young from their mothers' wombs and condemns them to a slow and horrible death. Centuries of research by our most dedicated scientists have failed to produce a cure, a prevention or even an explanation. Depending upon the severity of the malformation, the infants might live as long as a month in torturous agony while their systems shut down, one by one. We would never permit such cruelty, of course. The mother will usually quietly enfold her infant in a smothering embrace, so that the last thing it knows—if indeed the poor creature can know anything at all—is the smell of its mother's fur, the warmth of its mother's love.

Occasionally a mother cannot bring herself to do this. There is no shame in this, for the hormones run strong at this time, and in the face of tragedy the power of reason is often diminished. In such cases the task falls to the pack leader, who, wherever he or she might be, will instantly come to the side of the grieving mother to ease the suffering child out of the world. We are responsible for all of the pack, and each child born into it is our own.

But when the mother of the child is the leader of the pack, there are no alternatives. I should have realized that.

But the grief was crippling, not only my own but Elise's as well, which we shared though the mating bond. For months I had loved this child, this miracle merging of my seed and Elise's, this grand creation that was the reflection of our love. I had listened to his heartbeat and to the soft sweet sounds he made as he swam and turned and stretched in the viscous fluid of his mother's womb. He was our hope, our future, and I loved him with all my heart. Now my heart had been ripped from my chest, and all I could do was bury my head in my knees and sob out loud with the agony of loss, the sorrow, the cruel, cruel unfairness of it all.

A cold winter darkness fell over the house on the edge of spring. The werewolves who had gathered to celebrate a birth now mourned a death. The pack which had come together in joy and hope to command the brave new century now huddled among themselves in superstitious whispers, wondering what evil was boded by the tragedy that had struck their royal couple. The seed was contaminated, they worried. There would never be a viable offspring. It was the Antonov blood, they said. No, it was Devoncroix. It was the mixing of the two. The union had been cursed from the beginning.

I heard them all, but nothing could anger me, nothing could hurt me, nothing could torment me more than I was tormented already. I could not even change, so engulfed in the paralysis of grief was I. I could do nothing but sit with the curtains drawn in the deep velvet room I used as a study, and I wept until I could weep no more. Gault attended me quietly, but did not intrude. When I commanded him hoarsely not to light the lamps, he let the room fall into darkness. And when he would have stirred up the fire I once again stopped him with a sharp gesture of my hand. The fire died out. I let the cold and the darkness seep into my bones until they matched what was already in my soul.

It was full night when Evelyn, Elise's oldest sister, stole quietly into the room. Her distress was evident in the salty smell of tears, the jerkiness of her movements. "Oh, please, monsieur," she whispered, "you must come!"

I roused myself like a man from the depths of drink, reluctantly, blearily and with great effort. She dropped down onto her knees beside me, her dark skirts billowing with the whisper of satin and the scent of bitter mourning perfume. She grasped my hand. Her fingers were cold, like mine. I barely recognized her.

"It's Elise," she said. "You must help her."

Nothing but that name could have brought me back, could have generated in me even the slightest wish to ever leave this room again. I lifted my head, and Gault took a concerned step forward. "What?" I demanded. My voice was strained and hoarse, and it seemed to reach my ears from far away.

Her eyes were suffused with pain and a terrible anxiety. "Alexander, you must come. Elise cannot—she won't do what must be done. You have to take the child from her."

It took me a long time to understand what she meant. Somehow I made the words come out. "It still lives?"

Gault put a comforting hand on my shoulder. "It's been hours," he said.

"She won't let anyone near her." Tears wet Evelyn's cheeks again, and the hollows of her eyes. "The first child—the grief—she hasn't the strength. Alexander, you have to do this."

I came out of the chair, stabbed through by horror and fear. "Only the pack leader can take the place of the mother!"

Gripping my arm tightly, Gault said, "Then you must be the pack leader."

I looked from Gault to Evelyn in desperate denial, and saw no escape in either pair of eyes.

"The pack is waiting," Evelyn said. "Elise needs you to do what she cannot do for herself. You cannot desert her now, Alexander."

In my mind was the memory of my cowardly flight from her side at the moment of her deepest need. When I should have stood strong to take the child from her, I had failed. I had deserted her once already. I had deserted my son.

I tried to turn away from Evelyn, lost in shame. Gault held my arm firm. "For the love of the pack," he said with low intensity, "you can't let the child suffer."

Evelyn said, "For the love of Elise . . . and your son."

I looked at her then, but it was not her face I saw. It was my mate's. My love, who needed me. My son, to whom I could give only one gift.

And the pack, who needed us both.

I walked down the corridor to the bedchamber. The assembled pack parted for me, lowering their eyes, lining up against the wall. I walked straight, my head high, my movements stiff. I became aware of the shuffling and murmuring of other werewolves gathered in the courtyard, on the hillside, in the snowy garden, waiting for word, waiting to mourn with us. For the love of the pack. I kept hearing those words.

I went into the bedchamber, I closed the door. The smell of pain and suffering was as thick as wax; it almost smothered me. Elise was there as I had left her in the tangled satin covers. Her fur showed the ravages of childbirth and her sides heaved with short rapid breaths. Her eyes, when she looked at me, were dull with confusion and pain. A low constant keening came from her throat. I had never loved her more than I did at that moment. Nor hated myself.

The infant squirmed and writhed in the curve of her belly, clawing at her fur. I could smell its pain, hear its little heart strain to bursting, hear the silent cries that emanated from its gasping, open mouth. Elise bent her head and tried to lick away its pain, then fell back, exhausted. She looked at me. Such helplessness in her eyes, such stark, hopeless agony. I felt it all in every pore of my being; I felt it all and more.

I bent over her, reaching for the child. She showed her teeth to me, warning me away with a soft low growl. But there was more defeat than threat in the sound. I caressed her head, I dropped my face to the soft fur of her neck and let my tears fall there. And then I quietly, gently, took the cub from her.

I left the room without looking back. I carried my son through the corridors and onto the balcony that overlooked the courtyard. I waited until the pack had gathered, silent and unsure, and all eyes were upon me. I lifted the child high into the air, an offering to the heaven from whence he had come. And then I snapped his neck.

It is true that no leader ever rules alone, and that as mates we are more one than two. Yet there must be a final authority, a single leader, if for the sake of ritual and nothing else. Until that night the role of pack leader had been Elise's inherited right. But by stepping in to do what she could not, I assumed her authority. The transition was effortless. I had the strength, I had the power. I killed my son, and I became leader of the pack.

I rent my clothes and sank into the agony from which the Passion was not an escape, but an expression. I ran into the night, across the hills, deep into the woods, and I howled and I howled until I had no voice left.

TESSA
AND DENIS

Twenty-eight

THE SOUND BROUGHT A CHILL TO TESSA'S SOUL THAT EVEN THE ARCTIC cold could not match. A single wolf crying to the night air, over and over again, with no one to answer him.

She knew his voice, for it was like no other. And she knew if she went to the mouth of the cave and searched the sky on a clear moonlit night she might see him profiled there, his head back, howling. *Is anyone there?* the sound seemed to say. And the echo of silence was his only reply.

Often she would hear the wolf pack calling to each other and she had learned to know the sounds—triumph, play, excitement, question, and simple song. Never did a call go unanswered . . . except Denis's. She had come to believe that the sound of a lone wolf howling was the loneliest, emptiest sound in the world.

He returned to the cave in human form, wrapping himself in the skin of a bear he had killed when he had found it, winter-sluggish, in a cave he wished to occupy. He bore the scar of that fight on his left thigh, from knee to hip, but they had feasted for weeks on the meat, and so had the wolf pack. And the thick fur provided an insulating layer between themselves and the ground when they lay down at night.

A fur skin upon which to lie, cold rock walls that were shared with burrowing creatures, a stick fire that didn't make too much smoke . . . Once, Tessa could not have envisioned the day when she would be grateful for such things. Now she could not imagine wanting more.

Denis set a slab of frozen, snow-rimmed meat to thaw upon the circle of rocks that guarded the fire. "That's the last of the cache," he said. "The game is gone here. Tomorrow we move on, ahead of the big snow."

Tessa swallowed hard, but nodded. They had moved three times since the subarctic winter had come, always just ahead of a snow that would have trapped them into starvation. Each time the journey grew more difficult. Each time she became less and less sure she would survive to reach the next shelter.

She was silent for a long time, feeding the fire, turning the meat to thaw more evenly. Words still came hard to her, the energy that was required to form them often too demanding. Denis always talked to her as though he expected her to answer and never upbraided her when she didn't, and she grew to like the sound of his voice. But to actually engage in conversation with him called for an effort that came from a place so deeply buried inside her she had almost forgotten its existence. Sometimes, though, something needed to be said, and the saying was worth the struggle. She worried about the wolves.

"We should leave meat for the pack," she said.

"No," he said sharply, and Tessa flinched a little at his tone.

"I'm not feeding them any more," he said. "It makes them too dependent on me. They would have moved on long ago if I hadn't shared my kills with them."

Tessa was silent for a time. Then she said hesitantly, "You're . . . angry with them. Because they won't answer your call."

The ferocity of his frown startled her. He looked more wild than tame himself, squatting before the fire, naked except for the bearskin, with his dark red hair tangled with the fur and the narrow angles of his face sharpened by the leaping shadows of the fire. When he spoke, his voice was harsh.

"How can I be angry with a dumb beast?" he demanded. "It would be as pointless as being angry with you." Then he added, in a slightly less abrupt tone, "They don't answer my call because, unlike humans, who are too stupid to know the difference, they realize I am a superior creature and they're afraid of me. I can't blame them for that."

He stretched out his hands before the fire and stared into the flames for a long time. Tessa thought about how desperately she had struggled to keep this small fire going all the time they had been here, digging beneath the snow for fallen twigs and branches, drying them for days before they would burn, tearing off green limbs from scraggly trees with her hands, carrying rocks one by one to the mouth of the cave to protect the flame from wind. The supply of matches was growing dangerously low. What would happen when it was gone? What if, in the next place they stopped, there was no tinder for a fire? The region was becoming more and more mountainous and trees were sparser. What if they came to a place where there was no wood at all?

Denis said softly, almost to himself, "It makes no sense that others of my kind should not have found this place. There *must* be others. Sometimes I almost think I can smell them . . ." He paused and shook his head in the way of one coming out of a reverie. "But then I realize I am only smelling my memory."

Tessa said in a small uncertain voice, "If you could . . . you would go back. Wouldn't you?"

He looked at her in surprise, and answered gruffly, "You foolish human. To live alone is no life at all for a werewolf. Did you imagine for one moment that my brother was being kind when he sent me into exile? That was the cruelest death he could impose. To live forever without the sound of another voice, without the warmth of another body, without a mate—"

He broke off, fixing his gaze intensely on the fire. Then he finished with a low harsh huskiness to his voice he could not control, "It is the cruelest kind of death."

He took the hard-charred branch that she used to hold the meat for roasting and stabbed it through the thick, still frozen slab. "Of course I would go back," he said roughly. "Wouldn't you?"

"No!" It was little more than a smothered breath, and she recoiled somewhat, as though the thought itself could threaten her. "No, I'll never go back where humans are. No. Not ever." She was breathing fast by the time those last words were spoken, her fists clenching the cloak high on her throat.

He could see the muscles of her injured arm tremble as they always did when she tried to maintain a closed fist, and eventually one corner of the robe fell open again. Denis regarded her curiously for a moment, then said, "You are a peculiar little human." He thrust the branch with its heavy meat into her hands. "Hold this." He went to the mouth of the cave.

He returned in a few moments with more wood for the fire, from which he separated several sticks of carefully measured length. Tessa watched him fashion them into a spit that spanned the fire, and upon which he placed the meat so that she did not have to hold it on the branch.

"Thus have we been making life easier for humans since the beginning of time," he remarked, and sat back from his work.

They watched the flames for a time, listening to the moisture that sizzled from the meat. And then Tessa said in a small tight voice, "Will it be very far, do you think, to the next shelter?"

He cocked an eyebrow and murmured, "My, you are practically garrulous tonight." Then he said, "Yes, it's far. But I caught the scent of big game today, maybe part of a herd trapped in a valley."

She said nothing.

His tone sharpened. "You'll die if you stay here."

Denis was surprised at the tension that crept into his shoulders and tightened his chest as her silence lengthened. And then she looked up. Her expression was weary and the hollows under her eyes looked more pronounced than they had been even a moment ago. Regretfully, she touched the hollowed-out stone she used as a cooking bowl, remnant of a long-gone band of humans, and Denis remembered how pleased she had been when he had brought it to her.

He allowed himself a small smile. Sometimes the foibles of humans were quite endearing. "I will make you a pack. You can take your bowl and your cooking stick with you, your little symbols of civilization, for of such small things were great nations formed. In a century or so, when the humans come to this wild place with their trains and their axes and their great belching stacks of smoke, we will all have Tessa LeGuerre to thank for it."

She shivered and inched closer to the fire, but the anxiety eased a little from her shoulders.

He extended an arm to her. "Come here, human, and keep me warm. The wind is bitter tonight and my back is to it."

She looked up, but didn't move. There was fear in her eyes, and that intrigued him enough to make him insistent. "You will lie with me at night but not sit with me by the fire? What a foolish girl you are. Don't you know the only reason I keep you alive is for your warmth? And your conversation, of course. Come."

He closed his hand over her wrist and tugged her toward him. In a moment she moved forward reluctantly, eyes downcast, shivering. He pulled her into the circle of his arms and knees, enclosing her in his nakedness with her back against his chest and the bearskin drawn close over them both. "Curse the need to stay in this body," he said. "I am never warm enough."

He took her stiff cold fingers between his hands, massaging them absently. A shudder went through her.

"Unfortunately," he continued, "human form uses less energy than wolf form, and the less energy I use the less food I need. Of course, I can only hunt for food in wolf form. The everlasting conundrum, without which my kind should have long ago taken over the planet."

His body temperature was measurably higher than hers, and in moments their combined heat radiated within the enclosed tent of the bearskin to produce a pleasant warmth. Yet still she trembled, muscles tight and straining, her heartbeat fluttering, her breaths shaky. The smell of fear on her skin was acrid.

Denis said impatiently, "What are you afraid of, you silly girl? Do you think I will hurt you?"

And then he realized that it was not his nearness that frightened her, but his nakedness. This amused him until it came to him that she was, after all, only an ignorant human, and she might have interpreted his embrace as a sexual thing. This interested him.

"Ah," he said, remembering the humans at the stick lodge. "You think I will use you as they did. A peculiar notion to develop at this stage. I should have thought Alexander would have taught you better."

He turned her in his arms so that she was in profile to him, and though her muscles were stiff she did not resist. She turned her head and refused to look at him.

"Come. See." Impatiently, he took her hand and pushed it between his legs, against his organ, which was flaccid and unresponsive against his thigh. "I have no desire for you. I am not a human male and I have no weapon between my legs."

An involuntary little moan was torn from her and she tried to pull her hand away, but he held it there. "Do you see? Touch me all you want. I won't grow hard for you unless I will myself to do so. I am not a mad beast out of control. I am no threat to you or any other creature on earth unless I choose to be."

She began to weep with small, choked trembling sounds. He released her hand and was about to thrust her from him impatiently when she turned her face to his shoulder and her hands to his chest. Her tears wet his skin, and the smell of salt and pain drew a surprising tenderness from him.

In a moment he touched her hair, and her hot, wet cheek. He let her lie against his shoulder and he wrapped her in his arms, stroking her head. "Poor ruined little human," he murmured. "I wonder whether I shall ever be able to make you tame again."

He bent his head over hers and the aroma of her hair and her skull filled his nostrils. Thickly human, redolent of smoke and snow and earth and bearskin and a thousand other scents now gone stale, the chronicle of their journey together. He smelled himself on her, and it seemed a natural mixture, her scent and his, a comforting one. He pushed her tangled hair away from her face; with his fingertips he smoothed the tears from the corners of her eyes. Eventually her shuddering sobs lessened, and stopped altogether, and she lay quiescent in his arms, her warm breath light upon his skin and interrupted only by the occasional hitch; her hands, which had once been closed into tight fearful fists, now open and relaxed upon his chest. There was a feeling of power in this, the frightened girl who now lay comforted in his arms, and also a great unexpected pleasure.

He understood, for the very first time, what it was that had drawn his brother—and others like him—to human companions. The knowledge came to him so subtly, so naturally, that there was no shock in it, and he did not recoil from it as perhaps he should have done. It was the feel of skin like your own, warm in the cold, a face that could smile like yours, eyes that could weep like yours, the sound of a voice like yours in the darkness. That was all. It was the feel of this small helpless creature nestled in his arms, quiet now and trusting. He made her safe. She made him strong.

That was what he felt as he held her, drinking in her warmth, listening to her heartbeat: a surcease to the loneliness, a pause in the battle. A moment's contentment . . . and more. A subtle curiosity, a tingling thread of promise that caused him to move his fingers to her throat, stroking gently there until she lifted her eyes to his, deep dark eyes that held no fear, only waiting, only question. Her breathing quickened and her heartbeat changed rhythm as he looked at her, and he remembered the day in the orchard, how he had touched her and how she had melted with his touch, been captured in his thrall. That he had done deliberately, because he knew his own power and because he could. But now as he bent his face close to hers and drank in the scent of her skin, tasted her breath in his mouth, other memories came to him unbidden; memories of werewolves who played the sex games with humans, who took them like lovers, and he thought, *I could do that for her. I could show her such pleasure she would forget the pain those humans caused her. Tessa, sweet broken human, I could do that for you . . .*

He spread his fingers along the side of her face, stroking the corner of her eye, the fragile fluttering feathers of her eyelash. Her scent was drugging, her heartbeat thickened his blood. He moved his face closer to her and closer, drinking her in by inches, by millimeters, until his mouth was a whisper from hers and her breath flowed between his parted lips. He tasted her with his tongue, her salt, her sweetness, and the taste of her made his heart pound, pound so hard that it shook the breath in his lungs, pound with dread and anticipation and a dark forbidden need. Her eyes held him like the gaze of a mother holding a cub and he was just as helpless in it, just as commanded by it. She spread her fingers then lightly over his shoulder, caressing his throat, and the gentleness of her touch, the shy sweet tenderness of it, brought a thrill of pleasure to his skin that spread with slow delicious warmth to the base of his spine, to the center of his soul.

And it was that, his own willing response to her touch, that shocked him at last out of his self-induced thrall, that filled him with horror and helplessness and the dawning truth of something changing that could not be recalled. He pushed her away roughly, so that she fell back, gasping, on the ground, and he got to his feet. He stood over her for a moment, fists clenched, breath tight and controlled. Then he strode away from the fire, out of the cave, into the darkness.

Late in the night he returned to her in wolf form and slept beside her to keep her warm. In the morning they left the cave; he leading, Tessa following the footprints in the snow.

Twenty-nine

AND SO IT WAS FOR DAYS. HE DID NOT RESUME HIS HUMAN FORM, AND sometimes he didn't come to her at all. He moved north and west, following a scent he could not define, outrunning the storms. Instinctively he sought shelters in the rock and, when he smelled the smoke, knew she had found them, too. And it was instinct that compelled him to leave a portion of his kill near the shelter each night.

But the kills were smaller and harder to share. Skinny hares, an arctic fox, sometimes rodents unearthed from the frozen ground... yet he pressed on, burning fuel he could ill afford in wolf form, refusing to return to his human form.

And then came the day when he could no longer outrun the storm.

The snow blew and piled up high, caking in his fur and stinging his ears. His paws sank deep into drifts and he climbed higher, seeking purchase on slick rocks, searching for the scent of some unwary game which had been caught in the open when the blanket of snow moved in. Automatically his body had increased its production of heat to ward off the knife blades of wind, and he could survive the cold. But his hunger was a fierce demand he could no longer ignore.

And then he became aware of something that caused him to forget even his hunger. It was the lack of something, something so familiar that it had become almost second nature, something whose absence was so disorienting that he could not even determine what was wrong for a long time. And then he knew.

The human. Her scent was gone.

He turned full circle, testing the wind slowly. He scrambled to a higher precipice and peered through the blowing snow, but all he saw were shapes in white, twilight sky, curtains of snow. An anxiety built within him that he could not entirely understand. He lifted his head and howled.

Nothing replied except the wind.

He descended the precipice, sliding on the icy surface, and began to retrace his own tracks in the snow.

A strange kind of desperation seized him after an hour or so of tracking, a coldness deep in his belly that had nothing to do with hunger. The snow was blowing so hard that his own tracks were mere icy indentations beneath a half a foot of snow, but his nose had no trouble picking up the scent of them—and no other. Always before, her footsteps had been close behind, her scent close enough to mix with his. How long had it been since he had last noticed her? Had it been a day, or only a few hours? With his eyes, his ears, his nose he tried to reconstruct a sequence of events since the onset of the worst of the storm. There was nothing. The weight of failure lodged in his throat like a lump of ice. Failure to his pack, failure to the future, now failure to her.

Darkness came, and with it a cold so fierce that there were times when he had to stop and plant his feet, head lowered to the ground, to keep from being swept away by the wind. His progress was slow and as the hours passed, the journey almost became an end unto itself, while any real hope of finding anything at its end receded into a distant memory.

And then he caught a familiar scent. He tracked it along the ground beneath the layers of snow and ice until the concentration of scent was at its strongest. He began to dig, flinging back sprays of snow until he unearthed the object with its warm memories of meat and fire. The charred cooking stick.

His heart was fast, his senses keen. He tracked in ever-widening circles, his nose to the ground, until the particles of her scent coalesced into the shape of a whole, and he started to dig again.

Her body beneath the snow was as cold as earth, her heartbeat faint and slow, so slow. The heat of her breath had formed a small pocket near her mouth where snow had not collected, and the bearskin had protected her face and head. Exhausted and nearly frozen, her frail human body had simply collapsed into the snow and refused to rise again.

He uncovered her face and cleared a tunnel for her breath, then turned and surveyed his surroundings. Spotting a snowbank that had drifted against a rock, he began burrowing into it. He used the heat of his body to flatten the walls and his claws to widen them, repeating the process over and over until the cave was wide enough for two, and strong enough to support the weight of the snow that had piled up on top of it. All the while he listened for her heartbeat, tensing against the smell of the frozen death that was creeping upon her with every minute that passed.

By the time he had freed her body from the snow and dragged her inside the cave, his muscles were trembling with exhaustion and great shivers shook him and he struggled to maintain his body temperature. With the last of his strength he pulled away the frozen layers of her outer clothing and stretched out on top of her, warming her, guarding her throughout the night.

In the morning she was still alive. The snow had fallen to obscure the entrance to the cave and he had to dig his way out. He dug open a rabbit burrow and consumed the three skinny, stringy creatures in-side without stopping for breath, and he began to prowl. The snow was still falling, but the prey was as hungry as the predators, and more than one creature was moving about. He found enough to save himself from starvation and returned to the ice cave, where he once again stretched himself over her to keep her warm.

And so it was, day after day. He hunted to keep himself alive, and he returned to keep her alive. She shivered and moaned in her sleep, and he licked her cold face and lips and fingertips until the danger of frostbite was gone. Sometimes she mumbled words to him, but he, in wolf form, didn't care what they were. And over those days he gradually came to realize a truth that surprised him: this fragile human would never survive the winter in this place, and that distressed him. It distressed him very much. He had considered many ways in which they both might die since coming here: predators, starvation, thirst, falling trees, cracking ice, earth that gave way on a mountaintop, disease, injury—but simple cold had never been one of them. She was going to freeze to death, if not now, then inevitably. He had simply not considered it before.

When the snow stopped he went in search of fuel.

It took hours, digging beneath the snow for broken branches, dragging them back to the cave to dry, hunting enough to keep himself going, searching for branches again. He dug up some ground rodents and snapped their necks, then carried them back to the cave. While still in wolf form he plucked out tufts of his own fur to use as kindling for the fire. And then, with a greater exertion of energy than he would have thought he possessed and against every instinct in his body, he transformed himself into human shape.

He built the fire with the matches she had guarded so zealously, and roasted meat in the coals. The warmth of the fire softened the walls of the snow cave, but the cold froze them again immediately, harder and stronger than before. He captured some of the dripping water in the stone bowl from her pack and made her drink it, and when she would sink again into her cold dark dreams, he forced small pieces of cooked meat between her lips. She couldn't swallow, so he chewed the meat himself and transferred it from his mouth to hers, muttering, "Eat, you stupid human; do you want to die in this wretched place?"

The hours turned into days. He hunted for fuel and whatever small game he could find, he tended the fire, he forced water and chewed food into her mouth, and sometimes she gagged on it and sometimes she swallowed. Occasionally she would open her eyes and make the effort to mutter a few words to him through broken lips. Once he understood her to say Alexander's name, and his heart clenched with an odd bitter hurt. Another time she opened her eyes and whispered to him, "It's not your fault, you know. It's not your fault I couldn't keep up."

It made him angry to hear her say that, and it also made him want to weep. He left the cave abruptly to hunt, and he never knew when he returned whether she would have taken her last breath in his absence.

His days, his nights, his thoughts and his instincts were consumed with her. He hated himself for it, yet he couldn't help it. There was no logic to it. She was a drain on his energy and his resources. She was only a human and he had dedicated his life to the belief that the world would be a better place if all humans were dead. This he knew. This he told himself over and over again, but no power on earth could keep him from returning to her. She was only a human, but she was *his* human, and he cared what became of her.

Yet he was frightened by the fact that nothing he could do would restore her failing strength, and was infuriated by his impotence. "Fight, you weakling girl," he told her angrily. He lifted her head and made her drink a tea infused from a strong smelling bark that he knew had restorative powers. She coughed and tried to swallow, but most of it spilled onto her neck and her gown. "You didn't give up in a cage on a ship with a high fever, and you didn't give up in the human lodge where they tortured you. Why do you turn your back on the battle now?"

She looked up at him, her eyes big with pain and confusion. "Leave me, please," she whispered. "Let me die. It will be less cruel in the end."

His hand clenched convulsively and he turned away from her, setting the bowl of tea aside. "I shall never leave you, little human," he said roughly, and once the words were spoken he knew them to be true. The admission went through him like a cathartic, sharply painful but oddly liberating—and somehow inevitable.

He turned back to her and laid his hand against her face, stroking her cheek. Her face softened as his touch seemed to take away some of the pain, and in her eyes he saw understanding.

"Without you," he said simply, "I would be alone."

He lay down beside her, curling his body around hers for the warmth. He drew her head onto his shoulder and stroked her hair, and she nestled into his embrace. He stayed like that until she fell asleep.

After that she seemed to strengthen a little, or perhaps she merely gave the appearance of doing so for his sake. She ate more and kept more of it down. And after so many months of hoarding her words as though they were precious jewels, now, when she could least afford the energy it took to part with them, she always made an effort to talk to him. This was her gift to him, and he would not be so poor-spirited as to refuse it.

"Do you remember the day you came to me in the vineyard?" she asked once.

"I do."

"You were so charming."

"I have been told I can be."

"You took my breath away."

"I thought I frightened you."

"You did." Her voice was but a whisper, and her eyes moved over his face. "And ... enraptured me."

He dropped his eyes. "I did it on purpose."

"I think I knew that."

"I told you many lies that day."

"I think I knew that, too."

"And many truths."

She was silent.

"I'm a different werewolf now."

"Is that good or bad?"

He looked at her. The honesty of the reply hoarsened his voice. "I'm not sure."

She took his fingers and wrapped them in hers, lightly, tenderly. He did not pull away.

The day came when he could delay no longer. "I have to hunt farther afield," he told her abruptly. "Everything is gone here, even the squirrels. I don't know how long I'll be away."

He had counted the moons since they had come to this place and knew that for most of the world it was summer. But here in the high plains the last snow was still weeks away, the return of the herds even longer than that. They could not stay here without game. But it had never been so hard to leave her.

Tessa nodded, unsurprised. "Which way will you go?"

He hesitated. "North, as we've been going."

She seemed alarmed. "There are nothing but mountains to the north. Why?"

He shook his head curtly, unwilling—or unable—to explain further. "I think there may be game there," was all he offered.

She was silent for a time. She lay wrapped inside the bearskin, her face turned to the fire, cradling her head on her arm. She said softly, almost as though she were thinking out loud, "I wonder sometimes ... If the wolves had accepted you, would you have ever come back to me?"

He thought about it for a moment. "No."

She tried to smile, but the effort seemed too great. It left her eyes exhausted. "Then I suppose I owe them a debt."

Neither of them could have guessed how deep that debt would be until Denis set off that night on the hunting trip that might well take days to complete. The night was clear and the ground hard-frozen; he set his nose to the north and kept his pace easy and ten miles or so out he caught the scent of the pack—and with it, a fresh kill.

He would have fought them for it if he had to, and he let out a ferocious howl to let them know that. But he did not have to. They had abandoned the carcass of a caribou cow fresh and steaming, ready for him.

Denis gorged himself until he was dizzy, then tore off chunks of meat to carry back to Tessa. The remainder he buried, because he knew he would need it when he returned.

"They should never have left the kill," he told Tessa, keeping his excitement carefully under control. "If we're hungry, they're hungrier. They should have fought me for it."

"Maybe they meant it as a gift for you," suggested Tessa. The scent of meat—real roasting meat as opposed to the bony rabbits and weasels he had been bringing home—seemed to have renewed her energy. "After all the kills you shared with them—maybe they remembered."

"Only a human would be so sentimental." He shook his head thoughtfully, turning the meat. "No, they would never have been so generous unless they could afford to be. And where did the big herd beast come from? They all should have fled south, and I haven't had scent of anything like this creature since the first big storm."

"What are you saying?" She sounded anxious.

He looked at her. "The wolves went north. I think it means I was right—there is game there. It's far away, Tessa, too far for me to tell now. But I have to go."

She was silent for a time. Then she said simply, "I'll tend the fire."

He found it two days later, following the scent of the wolf pack and his own driving, inexplicable instinct. He looked down upon a high mountain valley, so deep it was sheltered from the searing winds and all but the worst of the snow, fed by a rushing stream that ran freely even in these temperatures. And it supported not one but several herds of large, contentedly grazing beasts who had only to scrape away a few inches of ground snow to munch their fill of the dried vegetation beneath.

By this time Denis was half crazed with hunger and for a moment wondered if his senses could be trusted. There was no logic in this, that a herd should grow fat and tame in a valley above the clouds throughout the winter. Every instinct should have told them to travel south with the remainder of the game . . . just as it should have told the wolf pack to do the same. That the pack hunted here was undeniable; their scent was thick and their den was nearby. Sweeping his eyes carefully over the vast valley, he realized that it was virtually inaccessible from three sides, and that the narrow pass on the fourth side had been blocked off by a rock slide. Anything larger than a wolf would have a great deal of difficulty getting in and out. The herds had not migrated here. They lived here, summer and winter, possibly for generations.

His instincts had been right. He had found Paradise.

He descended soundlessly, efficiently separated a straggler from the herd, and filled his belly. The wolf pack did not interfere, nor did he expect it to. There was more than enough for all, and they would not risk their lives for one calf. For the first time Denis was glad he inspired fear in his brothers, even if it meant he would be forever separate from them.

There were no bones or scraps to leave for scavengers. Replete, Denis washed in the stream and drank his fill, then searched out a place to sleep.

He followed his nose to a narrow opening in the earth and was amazed to find, after he had gone a few dozen yards, that the tunnel widened enough to allow him to stand up on all fours, and that it seemed to go on for an incalculable distance. Curiosity overcame his fatigue, and he followed the tunnel for some time, noticing that it gave way at intermittent intervals to chambers on either side—and noticing something else, something so incredible, so utterly astonishing, that it was a long time before he dared to believe the evidence of his senses. And when finally he came to understand that it was, in fact, so, the excitement was so intense that it almost stopped his heart.

The smell of the place was ancient and moldy, layered with rock dust and rodent excrement, tiny dried skeletons and dark, damp earth. Yet woven into it all, so deep and so old it seemed to be emanating from the very rock core itself, so deeply buried that not even the sensitive noses of the wolf pack would have recognized it, was the faint but unmistakable smell of werewolf.

Thirty

DENIS LOST NO TIME IN RETURNING TO TESSA, BARELY PAUSING TO REST or feed, and completed the journey in half the time. As he had feared, her condition had worsened in his absence, and he had been able to carry none of the rich red meat from the herd beasts with him to fortify her. Instead, he roasted a rabbit and made her eat it while he told her what he had found.

"We have to go there," he said. "It's a hard journey, but there's shelter, and water and more game than we can possibly eat. It's not so cold there, either, and I suspect hot springs. There's even green stuff beneath the snow, and salt in the high rocks. And trees—so many trees we need never search for firewood again."

She listened to him with big eyes. "Werewolves," she whispered, "in this wild place. But I thought there were none of your kind here, and that's why you were sent here."

He shook his head impatiently. "They're gone now, and whenever they were here was long, long ago. But the tunnels and caves they left will serve us well, and the game, Tessa. No more hunting. No more cold."

She looked at the flames for a long time, and at the ice walls of the only thing that stood between her and death by exposure. Denis thought she would refuse to come. He wouldn't have blamed her if she had.

She said, "How far?"

He was not certain whether to feel relief or dread. "Far," he said.

After a moment she nodded, and squared her shoulders bravely. Still, he thought she never would have attempted the journey had it not been for the promise of the caves built by werewolves at the end of it. And he knew, as she surely did, that the chances of her surviving the trip to see those caves were very slim indeed. But it was the only chance she had.

The journey that had taken Denis hours to complete at top speed in wolf form took days with Tessa. He was forced to remain in human form for most of the journey, both to conserve energy and to assist Tessa. The weather, for once, did not plague them; the cold was not too bitter, and for one entire day the snow did not fall. Denis followed the trail he had marked with caches of meat, and at night they slept in tunnels carved out of snow. When Tessa became too weak to walk, he carried her.

Determination, and nothing more, took them across that mountain. Denis, in his bare human feet, negotiated slick passes that even native goats found challenging, holding Tessa in his arms like an infant or carrying her on his back. When the trails became too steep Tessa crawled, using her clothing to pad her arms and knees. They had no energy to waste on conversation, and soon had none to waste on rational thought. Denis followed his instinct. Tessa followed Denis.

And when at last they reached the valley floor, there was no exultation, no relief. Denis led her to a cave entrance that was large enough to accommodate their human forms, and they crawled inside a little way out of the wind. There they collapsed from exhaustion and slept, fully sheltered from the elements for the first time in weeks.

It was days before they were recovered enough from the trauma of the journey to appreciate the destination—days in which the energy required to build a fire or make their way to the stream to drink was almost more than the results were worth; days in which Denis, now reverted to wolf form, slept tightly with fast shallow breaths and rose only to kill and eat and in which Tessa, fighting chills and stiffening limbs, forced morsels of half-raw meat into her mouth for the sake of some dim memory about something she wanted very much to see. And gradually she grew strong enough to remember what it was.

If she hadn't found the piece of knotted wood near the entrance of the cave, however, it might have been weeks, even months, before she thought to explore her surroundings on her own. When she used the wood knot to stir up the embers of the dying fire, it caught immediately with a high bright flame, and when she lifted it from the fire the flame burned evenly, casting light toward the darkest corners of the cave. She was surprised to realize the room was bigger than she had at first thought, and when she moved toward those dark corners they seemed to give way to other tunnels. She glanced at Denis, who slept in wolf form close to the fire, but he did not stir. She moved cautiously forward.

There was an archway in the far rock wall that did not look as though it had been carved by nature, and it was tall enough for her to pass through without stooping. She swept the torch carefully before her and illuminated another chamber—a chamber which, she realized as her eyes adjusted, had a light source of its own.

The light was a dim, diffuse circle as it trickled down from a network of chimney holes through the rock overhead, and beneath it was a large circle of stones where a cooking fire might once have been laid. There was enough rubble on the floor to provide weeks' and weeks' worth of dried firewood, and there were elevated stone shelves for sleeping. Scattered throughout the debris were stone bowls and tools with sharp ends, hammered metal pots for cooking and curved spoons carved from hard polished wood. Tessa's eyes went hot with tears as she surveyed these simple implements of civilization, as she thought of what they would mean. She picked up one of the metal pots and held it to her chest, feeling weak with wonder and strong with anticipation. A place to sleep that was away from the cold ground, a cooking fire with a chimney to draw smoke, and pots to make stews and bark teas . . . these were the building blocks of hope, the possibility of the future.

She had not intended to go far from the fire, but she could not turn back when other discoveries, equally as marvellous, might await her in any of the rooms that branched off from that one. And so they did. As she moved through the labyrinth of chambers, some large, some small, each opening off the other in a random pattern, it was like travelling through time, tracing the culture of a people throughout history. The cooking stones gave way to fireplaces with elevated hearths, huge and round so as to heat the entire room. There were carved niches on the walls to hold torches and these soon gave way to candleholders, caked with wax from candles long since burned down and forgotten. There was primitive wooden furniture, most of which had long ago collapsed into piles of sticks and hewn logs, but she recognized a tabletop there, a bed frame here. And as the centuries passed she discovered tools for skinning, for digging, for carving; cooking implements forged of iron, bowls and dishes of fired clay. Civilization.

But most amazing of all were the paintings. The walls were covered with them, in brilliant colors which time had not faded, primitive at first but growing ever more recognizable until Tessa could even read the stories painted there: werewolves at hunt, bringing down the boar, werewolves at play in human and wolf form, werewolves with their cubs, werewolves in ceremony, werewolves in the Passion. The colors were brilliant blue and crimson red and rich ocher, and they seemed to glow with the phosphorescence of crushed stone, but stones unlike any Tessa had ever seen before. The murals themselves were so incredibly detailed, so beautifully worked, that they took her breath away as no museum masterpieces ever had done—not even those in the queen's art gallery. She could see the clouds in the sky and the high mountain peaks, the froth on the stream and werewolves at rest in their peaceful valley. She could not help but be transported by it all, and she brought trembling fingers to her lips. "My God," she whispered.

Denis said quietly behind her, "Yes."

She turned and the torch flared wildly. He took it from her, his expression somber and full of awe, and together they continued their exploration.

"Who were they?" Tessa asked wonderingly at one point. "Where did they come from . . . what became of them?"

And Denis replied in a subdued, questioning tone, "We have no legends of such creatures. None."

And Tessa understood that he now had reason to question everything he had ever known about his own history.

He added softly, touching one of the smooth stone walls, "This place is old . . . older than your race of people, Tessa. Older than I thought even was mine. And they have been dead for thousands of years."

Tessa thought of all she had endured to get to this place, to know this wondrous mystery, but already the ordeal was fading into distant memory. She had strong stone walls and materials with which to fashion a bed and an endless supply of firewood and real dishes to cook and eat with. She felt as though she were rediscovering the world.

But a miracle that made all the rest pale awaited them behind the stone door. It was hung upon a simple swivel post and when Denis pushed at the upper corner experimentally, it swung open with barely a scrape of protest. They crossed the threshold from prehistory to civilization.

They were at the bottom of a steep set of dusty stone stairs, and light filtered down on them from the area above. They shared a wondering look and began to ascend the stairs. At the top they stopped, their breath caught in their throats, and looked around.

The room was vast, huge, larger even than the gathering room at the Palais Devoncroix, with a high domed ceiling made of hundreds upon hundreds of thousands of tiny blue tiles, and all around the perimeter were alternating rows of transparent tiles from which the light poured down in soft dusty beams. The floor beneath their feet was pink marble, grimy with disuse, but as smooth as silk beneath the layers of dust. There were carved stone benches and a central basin with a sculpture of wolves at play which had apparently been part of a fountain. Rotted fabrics hung in tatters from the walls, suggesting the rich draperies they once had been, their glittering threads still visible after all this time. There were enormous sconces on the walls which held glass candles, and canvases celebrating the majesty of the surrounding landscape which made even nature seem humble in comparison.

Denis let the torch drop into the empty fountain. Neither of them spoke as they moved around the room, gazing at first one wonder and then the other, slowly circling the room and then moving quickly from it into the adjacent chamber, and then, swept away by wonder, helpless to do anything but exclaim in disbelief and delight, they ran from room to room, to marvel after marvel.

Here was a castle on a par with anything they had left behind, with vast, endless rooms and fireplaces big enough to burn whole trees, bathing chambers and toilet facilities and floors inset with polished tiles and semiprecious stones. There were grand chandeliers and panels of stained glass through which patterns of rainbow light flowed. Denis examined a mechanism by which a spark was designed to travel through a small metal tube and instantaneously ignite a gaseous substance inside every lamp in the room, flooding the room with light. Marvel after marvel was uncovered as they brushed away the film of age and lifted rotting fabrics to reveal basins molded of gold, bed frames carved of marble, jewelled mirrors and goblets and stunningly beautiful painted porcelains.

"There was water in these pipes," Denis said, amazed, as he placed his hand against a wall, "and I think it can be made to flow again. Have you noticed how much warmer it is in here? I think . . ." Suddenly his face was transformed into an expression of purest joy; he laughed out loud with it and, catching her hand, began to run. "Tessa, yes!"

He pulled her down a set of steps and through a corridor and she, gasping and stumbling to keep up, could do nothing but follow as they burst into another chamber. There she stood, her hand pressed to her throat, and looked out over what he had found. The room was not as ornate as some of the others. The floor was polished stone, the illumination was from a skylight far overhead, and the murals on the walls were playful, hedonistic, even erotic. There was a sound—musical, tinkling, inviting, and yet so foreign that for a moment Tessa did not even recognize it. And then she saw a shimmer, and realized that water was cascading from high above one of the walls. It splashed onto the sloped floor and drained away toward a enormous pool of foggy water.

Again Denis laughed out loud. "I knew it! Hot springs! What sensible werewolf would build a palace in such a place without access to hot springs?"

He moved toward the water that poured from the wall and reached out his hand experimentally. The exclamation he gave was of absolute, unadulterated pleasure as the water splashed through his fingers. "It's warm! Warmer than a summer rain!" He dropped his tattered cloak and stood full beneath the splashing water, his face upturned to catch the spray, arms upraised to indulge it. "Tessa, you have to feel this!"

She came forward a little uncertainly and extended her hand. A half-caught laugh escaped her as the warm water splashed off her hand and wet her sleeve. She started to withdraw, but Denis clasped her hand and pulled her toward him and then she was sputtering and gasping as sheets of water poured through her hair and ran off her face and soaked her clothes. Denis caught her to him as she stumbled, pushing her wet hair from her face, and then he held up a hand for attention, an alert expression coming into his eyes. "Wait. What is that sound?"

Tessa held her breath, listening. She heard only the splash of the water, the rhythm of the stream.

And then he smiled. "It was your laugh," he said. "I don't think I've ever heard it before."

That made her smile, too, and then laugh, shyly at first and then more genuinely as Denis wiped his hands over her face, clearing streams of water.

His eyes held a deep rich light that was so powerful it seemed to generate heat; it went through to Tessa's bones and filled her with energy from the inside out. Abruptly he threw back his head and opened his mouth to the water, letting it cascade over his face and his shoulders, shaking his hair in a glorious spray that made Tessa squeal out loud in sheer childlike delight.

"Ah, Tessa, do you know what this means?" he exclaimed, seizing her arms. "This is ours, all of it, to do with what we will." He moved his hands up over her shoulders, beneath her sodden hair, strong against the back of her neck. His eyes were alive with the intensity of hope, of relief, of promise. "I can take care of you here. I can keep you warm. I can feed us both for years, for centuries . . . you will *live*, little human." With a short, indrawn breath he tightened his fingers upon her neck, and the fire in his eyes deepened. "You will live."

She lifted her hands to his face and, on tiptoe, she sought his mouth with her parted lips. She kissed him sweetly, lingeringly, and it was a gesture that astonished him, for he had never known a kiss like that before, a human kiss upon the lips, warm and gentle and filled with affection; it took his breath away.

He heard her pulse, quick in her throat, and the soft expansion and contraction of her lungs. He heard his own heartbeat, low and heavy. The fog of scent that rose from her body was a plethora of sensation and it penetrated his every pore, all of it familiar, all of it good. With his thumb he eased a drop of water from the corner of her eye— perhaps a tear, perhaps a spray from the fountain overhead.

He dropped his hands to her shoulders, and then to the top buttons of her dress. He watched her eyes, but she did not object. He undid the buttons and pushed the sodden garments aside, over her arms, down her waist, over her buttocks, lifting her free of the pool of tattered skirts and stained petticoats, pressing her close to him, turning beneath the waterfall, holding her. Her body was weightless, molding itself to him, and they turned round and round in the cleansing fountain, lost in surrender, clinging to one another.

He licked the droplets from her shoulder, tasted the flesh of her throat. She pushed her fingers into his wet hair and touched his face and the corners of his eyes and her breath was slow and deep and reverent; his was fast and hot. Such joy filled him, such wonder.

He held her face gently, looking into her eyes, memorizing her, devouring her. Ecstasy took shape within him; a knot of fire that burned in his soul, a fist of longing that spread its fingers through every cell and fiber of his being, reaching for her. The rhythm of her breath was in his chest, the flow of her blood was his pulse. He felt the Passion begin to swirl about him, filling his veins, engorging his loins. His flesh stung, ached, tightened to bursting; he wanted to move away but he was captured in her eyes, her scent, the singing surge of her stuttering, leaping heartbeat. He felt her small hot breasts against his chest, her thighs pressed to his. He felt himself growing hard and strong against her belly and she did not flinch away, there was no fear in her eyes.

He wished her to be werewolf, almost as much as she herself wished it. But he knew she was not. He couldn't let her go, but he knew he had to.

His breath trembled as he moved his face closer to her, drinking in her fragrance, wet and hot and human, fragile and sweet. "Tessa," he whispered, "I must . . ." But he couldn't finish. Already his voice was thick and hoarse, the words hard to form. The Passion called to him, and his soul was inside her eyes. How could he let her go? How could he let her go?

She clung to him, she pressed her mouth against his chest and his throat. Her hunger consumed him; it was his own. She lifted her face to his, and it was flushed and breathless and desperate with pleading, and she whispered, "Don't leave me . . ."

And there it was, a moment unplanned and unexpected, outrageous beyond imagining and yet somehow inevitable. A moment when he looked into her eyes and was consumed by fire, wrapped in possibilities, transported by rapture. There was no logic to it, for either of them, no dread and no anticipation, no demons or angels whispering in their ears. They acted in the moment. They felt the passion, they surrendered to it; they gave themselves in joy and absolute innocence, as guilelessly as the first lovers who had ever walked the earth.

He opened his mouth over hers and tasted deeply of her; he let the taste of her, the soft sweet sound she made as she pressed herself into him, drive him to the edge of tremors. He lifted her off the floor and her legs went around his waist and he saw the triumph in her eyes, the glory and the exultation, and life filled him, swelled and throbbed and burst inside him; her life, and his own.

His engorged flesh was poised against her and she was soft and yielding and it seemed such an easy thing, such a simple and *necessary* thing, to obey the instinct that compelled them both. A simple movement, a surrender of will, and all the mystery of that dark secret would unfold before them, all the magic would be theirs. The roar of need filled his ears, his need and hers. The hot sweet scent of human musk, the dread and the promise, the fear and the expectation. There was no choice for either of them, really. None at all.

She gave a wild, high, fierce cry as he pushed inside her and he knew he should not but then thrust deeper, and he saw triumph and wonder in her eyes and then he was being swallowed up by her, melting and blending and merging into her, cell and fiber and corpuscle and neuron, being consumed by her. It was too late. He couldn't stop it. The glory in her eyes turned to terror and he felt the terror rising inside him, too; terror and power and grand helpless savagery, and he wanted to push her away but could not. It was too late, too late. It was wrong and it was inevitable and no power in heaven or on earth could have prevented it. He heard her screams and his own as the Passion swept down and consumed them both.

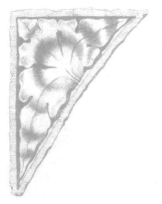

ALEXANDER

Summer 1 9 0 0

Thirty-one

WHEN I LOOK BACK UPON THOSE DARK DAYS AFTER THE DEATH OF OUR firstborn my mind recoils instinctively, and there is very little of it that I can recall. Despair, loss, bleakness. The year 1899 is lost to me, except that I went into it a brave-hearted youth who thought he knew all there was to know about life, and I emerged from it ancient, and knowing nothing.

Elise's recovery, like my own, was long and slow. I think sometimes this is a danger in the mating bond, for every pain is not only shared but doubled and we can become so absorbed in it as to almost cripple each other with grief. If only the healing of our hearts could be as swift and as efficient as the healing of our bodies, but this is the price we pay for feeling deeply. We never truly recover from a loss.

Though our tenderness toward each other was only deepened by the crisis and our lovemaking remained as intense as ever, we did not have the courage to try to conceive again. The great and glorious passion that is necessary for true mating eluded us, smothered by guilt, dampened by fear. Yes, we worried it might never come again, and perhaps that worry contributed to its loss. We had years, we knew, before the pack would lose faith in our ability to produce offspring— and thus lose faith in us—but the fear hung over our household and our mating grounds like a dusky sun that wouldn't rise.

If there was one thing that saved us from complete despair it was the pack: our responsibility for it, our duty to it, our vision for it. The daily routine of demands and decisions both great and small drew us out of the dark imprisonment of our minds and gradually captured our interest. In January of the century year we sailed to New York, which was pretty with snow and shop lights and smelled of the sweat and greed of American industry, and quite fell in love with all we saw. Elise purchased her factory and immediately set about bringing in werewolf engineers to upgrade the clumsy, inefficient equipment with which the humans worked. I purchased several tracts of property around Central Park and commissioned a house on Fifth Avenue where I thought we might like to live part-time.

In the spring we boarded our private rail car and began travelling west, meeting with members of the pack along the way, and beginning in many small ways to form the skeleton structure of what would one day coalesce into our grand vision for the pack. We kept moving, sometimes it seemed for the sake of movement alone, and then one day we looked at each other and we knew where we were going. I think perhaps we had always known.

I do not wish to make it seem as though, during this time of intense personal grief, I had forgotten about Tessa. On the contrary, the tragedy of her loss had become so entwined with the tragedy that took our son that I would sometimes awake cold and sweating from a nightmare in which I felt again the fragile, squirrellike bones of my son's neck between my fingers, snapping and twisting beneath my touch, and the face upon his tiny writhing body would be Tessa's. I am not superstitious by nature, but more than once it occurred to me that the death of my son might be my punishment for what I had done to Tessa.

We boarded a ship in Seattle and sailed for Alaska in June—Elise,

I, and an entourage of a dozen or so of our most trusted personal servants, trackers and guards. It had been almost two years, and I'm not sure what we expected to find. If Tessa had survived she would have done so by seeking the protection of her own people, and that was my hope—to find her living whatever rough existence she might have been able to carve for herself on this wild frontier, and to find her not so hardened against me as to be unable to forgive, and to bring her home.

There was a part of me that grew to believe, more and more desperately as we neared the coast of Alaska, that if I could only find Tessa and bring her back, I could somehow undo the past and all the tragedy that had now become a part of history; that my days would once again be as gay and carefree as when she had plagued my life with her constant chatter and her incessant questions; that Elise would smile again as she had smiled the summer Tessa lived at the Palais; that lights would glitter in the garden again and music would be sweet again and joy would at last come home.

We had heard, of course, about the gold strikes in Alaska but were interested only in a vague way as concerned our own mining ventures. We could not have guessed that in the time since our prison ship had docked in the rough-hewn port of northwest Alaska, a sprawling tent city reeking with thousands of violent, greedy, unwashed humans would have sprung up around that port they now called Nome. When we saw it, our hearts sank, and so did our hopes of ever finding out what had become of one lone human girl two seasons past.

We sent our two best trackers in to try to pick up a scent, and—although somewhat against our better judgement—Gault, who had never forgiven himself for the role he had played in Tessa's loss and who insisted upon being allowed to participate in her rescue. Elise made him leave behind his velveteen jacket and yellow silk cravat, and I think he rather enjoyed pinning up his hair beneath a floppy-brimmed miner's hat, but I had my doubts he would ever manage to make himself inconspicuous enough to blend into this particular human society—especially since he had to protect his sensitive nose from the stench with a scented handkerchief even from as far away as a mile out at sea.

He received a hero's farewell, however, and rowed ashore with the trackers at dusk. There was nothing for Elise and me to do but remain on board and await word from our scouts.

We spoke for the first time of Denis, and of our best and worst expectations of what we might find.

"All those humans." Elise sounded worried, looking out over the rail at the twinkling lights of the tent city, listening to their boisterous music and harsh drunken voices. "How far have they spread, do you think?"

"He would have gone as far away from humans as he could," I assured her. "He would have gone savage at the first opportunity, and there are hundreds of thousands of acres of empty wilderness to the north."

She said gently, "He had every reason to wish Tessa harm, you know. He might have killed her the moment they were alone."

I nodded slowly. This I had also always known, and this is what I had come here to find out. "But she may have been clever enough to escape him."

"She was awfully clever," agreed Elise with a hopeful affection in her voice, and she leaned her head on my shoulder, and we waited.

Gault returned at dawn, full of himself and his resourcefulness, bearing the information we needed and never expected. Indeed, he agreed smugly as we sat him down to a breakfast of tea and salmon steaks, one might expect that the task of finding out what had become of one human female among so many would be very nearly impossible— unless, of course, one was a particularly clever werewolf, and unless the human female in question was already legendary.

"This is the story they tell when they gather to pass their foul-smelling bottles around the fire," he told us, wrinkling his nose a little with the memory, "and they're happy to tell it over and over again to any newcomer, though I suspect it grows somewhat with each new telling. There are some who claim they were here when it happened, the year the ship docked and brought coffee and beans, and let off two half-starved prisoners who were taken by mule into the wilderness."

Elise and I glanced at each other but said nothing. We knew precisely, down to the fraction of a longitudinal minute, where the mariners had left Tessa and Denis, for it was to that spot that our trackers had gone to try to re-create subsequent events through their noses. Whatever Gault could tell us would be supplemental—or so we thought.

"Apparently the male was never seen again," Gault went on, "but the story they tell is how some of the miners captured the female and brought her back here to serve them—they boast about it, they're such filthy creatures—and how one snowy night a big red wolf..." He looked at us meaningfully for the time it took for him to neatly dispose of a forkful of salmon. "Broke into the lodge where they kept her, knocked down one of the walls, so they say, and went on a rampage of bloody slaughter. He killed ten, some say twenty, men before..." Once again the dramatic pause. "Carrying off the woman in his jaws and disappearing into the mountains."

The horror I had begun to feel dissolved into relieved amusement— which was in itself followed in a moment by disappointment. I sat back, reaching for Elise's hand. "And how much if any of that tale do you suppose is true?"

Gault shrugged. "All human legends have a basis in truth. I talked to a man who said he lost his arm to the wolf that night. There's no doubt it was Denis. The animal they described, even in legend, couldn't have been anything else. It seems to me twenty humans with guns would be a great many for a werewolf of even Denis's stature to subdue, but he may have killed one or two. There seems to have been some kind of fire, and the female escaped in the confusion. But here is the interesting part."

He put down his fork and touched his napkin to his lips, his expression triumphant. "I talked to a trapper who works the streams and riverbeds farther to the north—another filthy, disgusting creature whose presence I could not escape soon enough—and he tells a peculiar story about tracks in the snow and smoke from cooking fires far

into the winter. As he tells it, there are few humans ever to wander
that far afield, and he was interested in these tracks in particular because they were small and light, like a female's, and because they
seemed at times to be joined by the tracks of a wolf. One might have
dismissed the story as simply another embellishment on the carried-
off-in-the-jaws-of-a-wolf legend, except that he adds a most curious
detail. Around the campsites and cooking fires the tracks of the woman
were sometimes joined by the tracks of a bare-footed man."

I was not aware that I had been holding my breath until I heard
Elise release hers. "Denis," she said softly. "She escaped the humans
only to be recaptured by him."

"But for what purpose?" I wondered out loud, then shook my head
impatiently. "A foolish question. I never have been able to fathom my
brother's motives on any question and I shan't begin now. The important thing is that she was alive, even after she left this place, and
if she was making cooking fires she had learned to take care of herself."

Elise said cautiously, "The winters are very harsh here, Alexander.
It may not be wise to raise our hopes."

"Humans have been surviving winter for a great many years now,
my love," I replied, for I could see hope in her eyes, too. I turned to
Gault. "What became of the woman of the tracks? Did the trapper
say?"

Gault shook his head. "A blizzard came, and he lost the trail."

"Do you know where he last spotted a campsite?"

Gault smiled. "Of course. I can draw you a map."

I let him see my intense approval of him in my eyes, and then I
turned to my bride. "Then that is where we start."

Our caravan set out the next morning, complete with pack animals
purchased from the humans and every comfort technology could provide. Even as we strode along in human form I could not help but be
impressed by the magnificence of the scenery that surrounded us, the
sparkling clarity of the air, the tumbling streams and soaring, snow-
capped mountains. As soon as we were away from human habitation

Elise and I shed our clothing and transformed to wolf form, giving ourselves over to the sheer beauty of the place and the pleasure of the run.

There was no doubt in my mind that Denis would have done the same. What I could not understand was why, with all this splendor around him, he would have come back for Tessa.

Travelling in luxury, with tents to sleep in at night and wine to drink with our finely cooked meals, with candlelight and fine china and eiderdown for our beds, we reached the spot of the last campfire in a matter of days. I could not begin to guess how long it must have taken Tessa, fighting the snow and the bitter cold, gathering firewood as she went and eating only what she could catch with her bare hands, to traverse the same distance.

Our trackers confirmed the scent of werewolf which, though it was two seasons old, had been so well preserved by cold that even I could identify it as my brother's. And yes, equally as distinctive and equally as clear in this far place where no other human had since trod, was the scent of Tessa.

The trackers began a circular search grid while the rest of our party continued in the general north-northeasterly direction in which we had begun. Each night the trackers would join us at our new campsite to report on what they had found. And each day they led us deeper and deeper into those high treacherous mountains until I truly began to lose hope. In the heart of winter, in the midst of this brutal terrain, there was no chance at all that a human could have survived.

Yet over and over the trackers reported finding the scent of werewolf intermingled with hers.

"He kept her alive earlier," Elise pointed out, "for some reason of his own. Perhaps he is doing it still."

Perhaps.

Eventually the way became so treacherous that we had to set up a base camp at which we left all but the most portable of our supplies. The search had narrowed into a predictable but almost unbelievable course—straight into the heart of those mountains which, even in the middle of summer, were still deep with snow. And then, abruptly, overlaid upon the old scent of Tessa was the fresher scent of Denis. He had passed this way more than once.

We were by then in a mountain wilderness that was almost impassable, and as we progressed, the scent became so strong the trackers were no longer necessary. I could smell herds on the wind and I thought Denis must hunt here. The fewer our numbers the lesser the danger was of alerting him to our presence, so I sent back all but two of the guards, which are the minimum required by law to accompany the pack ruler at all times. They, Elise and I assumed wolf form to continue the rest of the journey.

I would not have been so reckless as to approach him in his den except for one reason: intermingled with Denis's scent was, ever so faintly and only occasionally, the scent of a human. Tessa. It was a secondary scent, overlaid upon his own, suggesting that, while she had not been here, he had been with her and carried her scent on his fur or his paw pads, or even in the glands of his sweat. Although I did not understand how Tessa could have possibly gotten this far—for we were finding the last leg of the journey difficult, and we were werewolves—Elise agreed with me; the scent was there. I was heartened to go on.

None of us expected what awaited us on the second day of our solitary journey at the end of the narrow ice trail we followed.

We rounded a hairpin turn that ended abruptly at a promontory overlooking a vast meadow. At first I thought we had walked into a trap and I was alarmed, and then I saw that the trail did in fact continue, so steep and narrow it could hardly be called a trail at all, into a rich green valley. The scent of herd animals was so strong it made my mouth water and I soon saw why—the valley was virtually replete with them. There was a wide glittering stream and many wild-berry bushes, and the thought flashed across my mind that we would feast tonight.

Just as I was relaxing in my relief I caught a whiff of what my companions had noticed long ago, and my fur bristled as my eyes were drawn to the wooded edge of the valley. Smoke. Woodsmoke was coming from a chimney in a valley that smelled of werewolves, and that chimney belonged to a structure that was so well blended into its surroundings as to be almost invisible. But when one saw it, and recognized it for what it was, the sight was astonishing. It was a vast, rambling lodge constructed of rough-hewn stone and heavy timber, designed in massive blocks and jutting abutments that made it look like nothing more than a small mountain, uprooted and transported to this place.

Instinctively I crouched down, signalling the others to do so as well. This was strange beyond description, an artificially constructed mountain in this isolated, virtually inaccessible place; a valley stocked with herd animals so fat and content they hardly seemed to have known the deprivations of winter, and the strong, fresh scent of my brother crisscrossing every hunting trail below. That he should hunt in wolf form yet return to cook his catch could only mean that Tessa was still with him.

I did not know why he had kept her, but I knew that I meant to have her back. And I also knew that for Denis, the ultimate revenge would be to kill Tessa before my eyes when I was within moments of reclaiming her. My heart all but seized in my chest with the conflicting need for action—to rush down into that valley and snatch Tessa from danger—and the equally demanding need to stay still, to conceal our scents and our sounds from him, to wait and watch.

And so we did watch for what seemed an eternity but was in fact only long enough to make sure he was not patrolling the valley or guarding the entrance to the building. Perhaps I should have waited longer, but even as we crouched there, sniffing the wind and straining our ears, he could have been laying a trap for us. I dared not delay.

I gave the signal and we proceeded cautiously down into the valley, making no effort to keep our approach a secret. To approach by stealth was to invite attack, and we had no way of knowing whether or not Denis watched us from within the safety of those thick stone walls.

The walls were thick enough to muffle sound and scent, and except for the smoke we would have had no hint whatever that anything was within. The absolute sensory deprivation was unnerving, and our heads and tails were low as we crept across that green valley floor.

Nothing stirred, not bird or rodent or werewolf breath except our own. The sky, I recall, was crisp clear blue and the shadows deep on the dark meadow grass—deep enough to hurt the eyes, deep enough to hide anything that might wish to spring forth in attack.

By unspoken agreement, Elise and the guards approached the building while I remained outside to secure the perimeter. Elise was the better fighter, and if Denis was inside she would have the advantage. There was no choice, really, and I intended to be absent from her for only a matter of minutes, for only as long as it took to make certain Denis was not lying in ambush some place we had not been able to see from the top.

As they passed through the door not a dozen yards away from me, I caught a whiff of something—pain, distress, fear, both werewolf and human—and I heard a muffled moan. My hackles rose and I swung toward the building, for there was no mistake about it: the sound I heard had been human. Tessa's.

But as I rushed toward the door the way was suddenly blocked by a huge red wolf. From whence he sprang I do not know, and how he came upon me without scent or sound to betray him is nothing other than a testament to his mastery of the art of stealth, and a confirmation of my estimate as to just how dangerous he was. He stood there before me with feet braced and teeth bared, emitting a low guttural growl of warning. There was blood on his jaws and fire in his eyes.

I did not hesitate, I did not think. I heard only that muffled moan of pain in the back of my head, I saw the blood on my brother's jowls, and my mind exploded with fury and fear for the human I once had cast out but now would have given my life to redeem. I charged.

We met in midair with a horrible clash of teeth and muscle, and I knew even then, I must have known, that it would be a fight to the death. It is possible that it might have been so even if I had not charged first, even if I had backed off when I tasted the blood on his fur and realized it was not human blood, not my Tessa's blood, but fresh meat from the hunt. But Denis was lost deep within his own protective instincts and half crazed with the desperate terror that seizes any werewolf when his mate is in pain.

Yes, I knew all this in a rush of information without understanding, too late, too late. It wasn't Tessa's blood, it *wasn't*—and then his teeth sank into my shoulder. I roared in pain and twisted, crunching his forearm, crippling him. It was self-defense, it was instinct. Instinct, and nothing more.

He came at me like a fury, like a mad thing escaped from the bowels of hell. I thought at first it was his hatred of me, the anger he had nursed for these two years until it had grown into this malignant, murderous force; I imagined how he had dreamed of this moment, plotted for it and used it to survive the harshness of the winter and the loneliness of exile. I thought it was personal, and I fought back in equal force.

Denis was the larger of the two of us, the more powerful, the more skilled in battle. Even when we were pups I had never won a play-fight against him, or a combat game. He was toughened by his ordeal, stronger than I had ever known him to be. Mere moments into the battle I was fighting for my life, and both of us were too far lost in instinct to back away.

Instinct. It is the risk we all take in our natural form, our savior and our condemnation. It opens worlds for us we never knew existed, but it blinds us to truths that are glaring in our eyes. I smelled on Denis the fury that can only overcome a werewolf in defense of his mate, yet I thought stupidly, blindly, *Mate? He has no mate!*

I felt his teeth pierce my side and the pain travelled on hot electric currents to my brain. I snapped back, tearing at the flesh of his back and securing nothing but fur. He pushed me back, flipping me over in the grass, and I desperately scrambled for purchase as he lunged at me again. He was the stronger, the faster, the more agile. It should have been easy, even to the most unschooled observer, to predict a victor. I think that as I fought desperately for my life, I knew I didn't have a chance.

A fight to the death between werewolves never lasts long; a lifetime, is all. My lifetime, and my brother's. He would kill me before the guards could reach me; this I knew. Yet with a sudden twist, a leap, a clash of teeth I had the edge. He could have easily displaced me, but he missed his chance and I pressed my advantage, knowing that I couldn't hold on much longer and had to make the most of every moment I had. Desperation. Instinct.

Yet it wasn't until I had him down with my teeth on his throat, expecting the powerful twisting move that would in a split second reverse our positions and trying to defend against it, that I realized something was wrong. I knew it, but before I could comprehend it Denis slashed at me with his sharp claws and reflexively, the way one would blink or flinch away or fling up a hand in self-defense, I tore into his throat.

It shouldn't have happened that way. He was stronger, he was more skillful. He could easily have escaped me. But he chose instead to provoke me, to lash out at me in my most vulnerable moment and to invoke an instinct I could not recall or control. And I understood too late, far too late, that he did it intentionally.

This is what happens when one werewolf kills another: the life force—thoughts, needs, sorrows, memories and dreams—of the dying werewolf flows into the mind of the other in a moment of stark and painful unity. There is a beauty to this in the wide scheme of the universe, an awful symmetry, and it is only right. Yet it is a bitter, bitter thing. It was done before I could stop it, the artery opened beneath my teeth, the death throes convulsed through his body; an instant and no more.

As my brother's blood gushed onto the ground and my brother's life force flowed into my mind, I knew the truth of it all, swift and clear and immutable, a lifetime lived as though it were my own. I saw our childhood; I tasted his love for me, his impatience and his pride. I saw his youth, his battles, his triumphs, his defeats. I felt his Passions, his infatuations, his strength and his determination and I was, for that briefest of eternities, I *was* him. I knew his ambition, his great loving plan for the pack, his deep hurt at my betrayal. I knew he acted as he had because, being Denis, he had no choice.

And I knew about Tessa. I knew the emptiness that had drawn him to her, the devotion that had bound him to her. I knew the moment when he betrayed all that he was, all he believed in and all he ever hoped to be, for passion. And I knew the toll that passion had exacted from him, and from Tessa.

I had thought I was protecting Tessa from him, but in fact he had attacked me in defense of his mate, and there is no greater, more immutable force within the soul of a werewolf. I knew my error, I knew my misjudgement; I knew he need not have died . . . and I knew that he wanted to die.

And this, then, was the hardest truth to know. This great werewolf, with all his vision and all his power, this splendid, flawed, improbable creature who, but for a twist of fate, might have led us all into the twentieth century, had hated so purely and loved so completely and was at last destroyed by both. It was possible to establish a mating bond with a human. He, who had devoted his life to despising humans, had proven this. And such a bond, so deep, so commanding, had as much power to destroy as to nurture.

Tessa had known the glory that is werewolf in that one brief, moment when she joined Denis in Passion and became his mate. She had grasped her dream at last, she had touched the magic. And for it she had paid a horrible price.

There can be no union between human and werewolf; we have always known that. No human could survive it. The act of mating itself, in all its violence and beauty, was traumatic enough to snap her mind. But the bond, the becoming, the rush of information and emotion and sensation that for us is the very essence of mating—humans are not equipped to deal with that. The power of it was more than the fragile human psyche could bear; mind and body had begun to collapse with it. Tessa was dying.

And Denis, who thought he was savage and who yearned for civilization, had paid the ultimate penalty for his sins. His love had destroyed the only thing he had ever wanted, just at the time it all might have been within his reach. The grief of losing her, of being bound in mind and spirit to a soul that was slowly slipping away, had day by day, in bits and pieces, robbed him of his own will and sanity.

The bitterness of it, the horror and the tragedy of all they had endured for this cold dark reward, was so intense that I could have died of it; the sorrow flowed into me like a black tide and filled my veins. It was too much, too much, the pain was more than I could bear and I wanted to cry out with the agony. No crime deserved such punishment as this, no love was worth the sacrifice they had given for it.

But then it came to me, a memory from Tessa, a memory from Denis, a flood of memories they had shared together. The gift of a cooking pot, a shy smile in the glow of a fire. The voice of a lone wolf raised in the night. The smell of a human, the warmth of her breath. Words spoken in the wilderness that kept the savage at bay. It had been worth it. For them, it had been worth it.

I looked into my brother's eyes and I saw it there: release, peace at last. This tortured soul who had dreamed so high and fallen so low, who had found joy in the one thing most forbidden to him . . . now he could rest. Now they both could rest.

But knowing this did not make my pain any easier to subdue. Even as his pulse slowed in my ear, as his breath stopped and his blood pooled, my mind was screaming, my body recoiling, a thousand blinding blows descending on my skull—*No, damn you, no, you can't do this, my brother, don't die!* And it was too late. I collapsed upon his lifeless body with my bloody muzzle buried in his fur and I begged some sign of life to welcome me. There was none.

In my soul, I wept.

I felt at last the nudge of a guard, calling me back to the present, and to those who needed me. I pushed myself away, I staggered back. I sat down and lifted my head and howled my grief to the sky.

It was a long time before I could make myself change into human form and enter the building. Through Denis's eyes I had seen already the wonders they had uncovered: the artistry and magnificence of a mysterious race of werewolves now long gone. None of it surprised me; all of it awed me.

I knew as well where I would find Tessa, and my wife. Naked, I ascended a staircase carved of heavy dark wood, its banisters and rails formed in the shape of hundreds of individual wolves. I crossed a smooth stone floor and entered an upper chamber made warm by a roaring fire, and I knew already what I would see: my Tessa, shrunken and worn from the rigors of a summer childbirth, her life all but wrung out of her. Elise stood beside her bed in human form, wrapped in a cloak of brushed and softened animal skins. Her cheeks were wet with tears and her eyes were aglow with wonder and her mother's arms, so long empty, now held the infant daughter born of my brother and of the human he had loved.

My eyes met Elise's, and a moment of understanding passed between us. She took the infant, the small, cooing, perfectly healthy infant, to the sunny window, rocking it in her arms. I sat upon the bed beside Tessa, and I fumbled for her hand.

"*Chérie*," I said, but my voice broke; I could say no more. I could smell the death on her. Her face was like wax and her eyes were deeply sunken and rimmed with black. Her small chest barely rose and fell with each breath. Her hand was limp and icy in my own. Perhaps, had Denis lived, she would have held on a few more weeks for the sake of the child. Without him she didn't have a chance.

With the last of her strength she turned her head and opened her eyes. Yet it seemed to take forever for those eyes to focus and recognize me. I saw the need to smile in them, but her dry, cracked lips could not form the expression. "Alexander," she whispered.

Desperately, hopelessly, I brought her hand to my lips. "I am here, *chérie*, come to take you home."

Her silence forgave me.

After a time a shadow fluttered in her eyes, and anxiety cracked her voice as awareness fought its way through confusion. "My child . . ."

"Is mine," I assured her swiftly. I extended my arm and Elise was beside us, placing the swathed bundle on the pillow near Tessa's cheek, yet never removing her protective embrace from it. "From this moment on, every advantage, every comfort, all the best this world can offer. This I promise you . . ." My voice thickened, and I stroked her brow. "My dearest treasure, and my truest friend."

Her features relaxed, and her eyes drifted closed. "It was good," she whispered, "what we did . . ." *It was good.*

As it so often happens among us, death took the mated couple within moments of each other. She died quietly, and in peace, and when she was gone Elise lifted that small, warm bundle that smelled of werewolf and looked so human and placed it in my arms. I gazed into the sweet sleeping face, and I fell in love.

It was good.

PART SIX

Central Park, New York

The Present

Thirty-two

THE SHADOWS WERE LIGHTENING BY THE TIME ALEXANDER FINISHED speaking, the fog thinning to pale, wind-stirred wisps. The clatter and rattle of awakening civilization reached them on muffled waves of sound: automobile tires and car alarms; coffeepots and horses' hooves; the thunder of subway trains and the metallic bounce of manhole covers. Voices live, and voices broadcast. Music. The city stirred and stretched and rustled sleepily. Soon the day would begin.

It was a moment before Alexander resumed. He sounded tired, defeated, as though the telling had aged him centuries instead of hours. "In another six months, our own child was born. We called him Matise."

Nicholas looked at him sharply, but Alexander did not respond. He went on. "As you know, Elise's vision for the pack was realized over the next two decades, all of us coming together with our various talents and strengths to form what is now the Devoncroix Corporation. It was with the advent of the European wars that we moved the pack headquarters to the compound in Alaska, so you see even that—the very symbol of our heritage and our power—we owe to a werewolf and a human whose story can never be known.

"We called the child Brianna. Elise would have nothing but that she be adopted into the pack and raised as one of our own. Her scent was werewolf, and the pack never guessed. Only her blood smelled of the human mix. She inherited her father's bright red hair and her mother's big eyes, her father's intellect and her mother's charm . . . She was in fact a most extraordinary female." A smile of reminiscence softened his features and the tension left his bearing as he let himself drift into kinder times. "She was, of course, remarkably bright for the child of a human, and she demonstrated excellent auditory and olfactory abilities—was in many ways as accomplished as any werewolf in the pack. But she never experienced the Passion, never learned to change form. As you know, anthropomorphs—who are in every other way werewolf, but lack the ability to change—occasionally occur in nature, and no one knows why. We let the pack think this was the case with Brianna, and no hint ever escaped about her heritage."

He drew a breath, and with it seemed to let the memories of Brianna drift away. "Other children were born to us, twelve in all, and each one a greater joy than the last. This, too, you will understand when you find your own mate."

Nicholas said, very carefully, "I have never known a brother by the name of Matise, nor a sister Brianna."

"They would be some sixty years your senior." Alexander's tone was even, but his face was like stone, his gaze fixed straight ahead on some point unseen. "They both left the pack before you were born."

"Left the pack? Why?"

Alexander hesitated. "Brianna was—unsettled. Not surprising, considering her background. To live among werewolves, but never to *be* a werewolf—you and I can never imagine how it must have been for her. Eventually she sought her own path, living a life of scandal and notoriety by both human and werewolf standards. Matise and she, being so close in age, were great friends from infancy, and when she struck out on her own—well, he had always been her staunchest defender to the pack. He continued to be so in the world of humans as well. He died some years ago."

The way he said that last, so flatly, so unemotionally, assured Nicholas that there was more to that story than had been spoken—and that now was not the time to ask for details. His head was spinning with the impact of what he had already learned, and that in itself was more than enough for him to try to absorb.

"Brianna." Nicholas said the word softly, and mostly to himself. *Only her blood smelled of the human mix.* So the blood scent in the laboratory belonged to Brianna. The hybrid spawn of his father's brother and a human woman. His cousin.

Once again the horror of the night washed over him, and with it the even greater, more powerful horror of the truth. It was a moment before he could speak again. When he did, his voice was harsh, forceful, made so mostly through his own effort to keep it from shaking. "She is more than just a monstrous abomination, a mutant hybrid that should never have taken hold in her mother's womb. She is a member of our ruling family. *Your niece.* And she is part human."

"Perhaps more importantly, she was the direct descendant of a fallen martyr of the Brotherhood." Alexander's voice was low, heavy with fatigue now, or just simple resignation. "The human offspring of perhaps the most famous human-hater of the century. Simple knowledge of her existence could breathe new life into a sect within our population that should have died out long ago. She could become the spark that ignites both sides of a battle that's at the flashpoint already."

Nicholas drew in a sharp breath. "The killer, the werewolf who attacked the lab was after the hybrid?"

Alexander took a long deep breath. The scent that came from him now was something Nicholas barely recognized in his father. It was very close to fear.

"I recognized him—not the person, but the form, from years ago in Siberia. The old pack that I dispersed . . . not all of them were accounted for. There have been tales over the years that some of them went wild, followed us to Alaska when we left Europe, and have been living like savages off the land in the far north. There was little harm in this as long as they bothered no one and brought no attention to themselves, but now it appears . . . they may have begun to organize. This one, at least, found out about the hybrid, and with such a weapon at his disposal there is no limit to the damage they could do."

Nicholas nodded, his own throat dry. "A human-werewolf hybrid would be the living proof of exactly the kinds of disasters the Dark Brothers have been warning about for centuries. It would be all they need to launch a campaign to annihilate the human race. And once it was known that this—this creature was spawned by a member of our own family, we would be powerless, everything we've achieved destroyed."

"When Denis was captured," Alexander said soberly, "the Dark Brothers lost their power. For all of this century they've been little more than a philosophy, distasteful ramblings of discontent here and there in small pockets around the world. But if these wild werewolves have taken up the Cause, and if they know about the hybrid . . ."

Alexander looked at his son steadily. "When I said you would condemn us all to war, I didn't mean war with humans. I meant war within ourselves."

Nicholas met the gaze of his elder for a long and solemn moment. The weight of the future was heavy on his shoulders. "You've kept the secret all these years. How many more must die for it?"

Alexander replied, "That depends on you."

"Why did she come back, after all these years? Where is she now? This hybrid, this—Brianna?" His cousin. His flesh. A horror, yes. But his *family*.

Alexander said, "Dead."

Nicholas stared at him. The jolt he felt was inexplicable. Over the past few hours he had been drawn into the world of Tessa the human and his uncle Denis; he had come to accept the existence of their hybrid child with horror and fascination . . . the cousin of his flesh, the sister he might have known. Miracle or monster? Now she was dead, and he would never have the opportunity to decide for himself.

"Where is her body?" he demanded. "There was no hybrid corpse in that building. Did you dispose of it?"

Alexander directed his gaze to the shadow-line of tall trees silhouetted against the graying sky. How old he seemed. Old, and . . . small, somehow. "She did not die in that room," he said, "but she is dead nonetheless. I closed her eyes with my own hands, just as I did her mother's."

Of course. Having escaped the attack on the lab, where would she have gone except to her parents—or those she believed to be her parents—Alexander and Elise Devoncroix? Their apartment was only a few blocks away, and naturally they would have taken her in . . . to die.

The disappointment Nicholas felt was acute and inexplicable.

Dead. The hybrid, the aberration of nature, the monstrous mistake that could destroy them all was dead, the threat was gone. But so was the cousin he had never known, the adopted sister who bore his family name. Whether she lived or died was not to be determined by outlaws. She was dead, and so were three others. No one had the right to do that.

If the intent of the feral werewolf had been to goad Nicholas into turning the pack against all humankind, he had failed. If his mission had been the simple destruction of the hybrid, he had succeeded. But there were others out there, if Alexander was right, and if they had achieved a sufficient level of sophistication to wreak the havoc that had been done this night, only a fool would ignore them now. Disaster had been averted tonight, but only by inches. There were no guarantees for the future.

"If there are others out there," he said lowly, "whether living in the wild or on the streets of New York . . . if they knew about this plot, and participated in it, they will be held accountable. I will track them down, and make certain of it."

"The Dark Brothers, in one form or another, will be with us always," Alexander said. His voice was very tired now. "It's vanity to believe otherwise."

"But they have failed." Cautiously Nicholas allowed himself to accept this. This time, they had failed. "The hybrid they sought is dead, and there is no proof she ever existed. There will be no war. It's over."

Alexander looked at Nicholas, and Nicholas saw hesitancy in his eyes, a kind of confusion and a debate he did not understand. "You're wrong," he said.

Alexander glanced away, toward the stand of trees again. "I'm old and I'm tired," he said, "and I've carried the burden of this secret too long. It wasn't Brianna they wanted."

Nicholas looked at him sharply. "What do you mean? What have you not told me?"

Alexander reached inside his coat and withdrew a small fat volume with a battered red leather cover. He studied it for a long time, measuring the import of what he was about to do. And then he held the book out to Nicholas. "It's in here. The evidence of all our crimes. What I have told you, and what I have not."

Nicholas stared at the small volume in horror. "You *wrote it down*?"

The faintest of smiles touched Alexander's lips. "I did not. But it has been written nonetheless."

Nicholas took the little book carefully, as though it were an explosive that could detonate with the slightest mishandling—which, in a way, was precisely what it was.

"This should be destroyed." His voice was hoarse.

"Perhaps it should. But you will read it first. All your answers are there, my son. And when you have them—you will have some decisions to make."

Nicholas looked at the book in his hands, and then at his father. "I'll read it," he said.

They sat in silence for a time, father and son, ruler and heir. There was more that needed to be said, much more. But Alexander could speak no more, and Nicholas could not listen.

In their enclosures at the zoo the animals began to stir and chatter. On Fifth Avenue, far away, came the sounds of taxicabs and the smell of baking bread sweetened with sugar, a woman's perfume, sharp tangy soap, stale cigarette smoke. And deeper still, faint and fading, werewolf blood and cold decay.

Nicholas tucked the book inside his coat, then braced his hands on his knees and got to his feet. He was not the same werewolf who had entered this park only hours ago. He hoped he was wiser. He knew he was older.

He stood for a moment, gazing down at his father. He said, though it cost him some effort, "She should not have died. Even though she was half human, even though all our lives may now be easier for it— she shouldn't have died. It was wrong. We are not killers."

Alexander closed his eyes and inclined his head, slowly and slightly in assent.

"But it's over," Nicholas said. He added quietly in a moment, "I am sorry for your loss."

Alexander replied heavily, "As I am for yours."

Nicholas walked away, the sound of his footsteps echoing flatly on the cold damp pavement. Alexander listened to the fading sound until his werewolf ears could not follow it anymore, but he made no move to rise. He thought of home, of soft yellow lamplight and time-faded carpets, of burnished leather and down bedding; he thought of Elise, who waited for him there, her anxiety and need calling him even now, her strength ready to enfold him. He thought of the responsibilities that awaited him outside this place, of the complexity of the day that was poised to unfold, and he did not move. He kept hearing his son's voice saying, "It's over."

It's over.

And now he answered in a voice so low Nicholas could not have heard it even if he had not already left the park, whispering the words in a voice that was old and broken and weighed down by grief: "No, my son. It has only begun."

Epilogue

AND SO THERE IT IS: THE STORY OF HOW WE CAME TO BE AT THE POINT we are today, or at least that story's latest chapter. What do you think, human? Are you amazed, incredulous, outraged or afraid? I don't blame you a bit. Perhaps you are simply angered, disgusted or repulsed. That is fine, too. Some among you will naturally refuse to believe any of it, or even admit that we exist, and this perhaps is the safest course. For will it surprise you, human, to learn that in the far reaches of Antarctica or the deep mountain caves of Mongolia there are those of my kind who do not believe in *you?*

So greet my tale with skepticism, denial, derision or amusement; it matters little to me. But it should matter a great deal to you.

And why, O fine human, should you care about any of it? What difference in your small, mean lives could my legends of werewolf lovers and human heroes possibly make? What do you care for secrets and superstitions, myths and miracles? Oh, I could give you answers. I could read you sermons. I could tell you parables of synergy and life circles, of species great and small who have come and gone before us because they failed to heed the lessons encompassed therein. I could tell you tales of civilizations won and Civilization lost and punctuate those tales with pleas that we all look always to the nobler side of our natures, for the consequences if we do not are dire indeed.

But let me, instead, put the matter in terms you can more easily understand. We may be few upon this earth, but our resources are great. At this moment, for example, we possess the technology to rid the earth of its human parasite in at least seven different ways. A virus here, a species-specific toxin there . . . Oh, it could be done. Easily. There are those, as you've seen, who argue that it should have been done long ago. But there are even more of us who maintain that only by working together, human and werewolf—only by looking to the past for our commonalities—can we hope to share a future, and thus we keep the chaos at bay. So we restrain ourselves, in the name of Civilization.

You are the best of us. We are the best of you. What becomes of us will, inevitably, become of you. That is why you should care. That is why I write.

I end this chapter, then, with broken silence, broken vows, broken trust. Our secrets are yours now; I pray you use them well.

I will write again, if I am able. In the meantime, look for me on the city streets, in the first-class section of your next transcontinental flight, at opening night of the newest Broadway musical. Think about what I've said, and watch for me.

You may be sure I'll be watching you.